T0188320

"Hawley delights in her humorous and romantic paranormal debut. . . . Hawley ably navigates life and love among toxic family members, fantastical chaos, and small-town politics—with some steamy scenes and plenty of dad jokes along the way. This is a treat."
—*Publishers Weekly*

"Hawley's delightful debut is a welcome addition to the witchy rom-com genre with its ecological flavor, fresh take on the demon realm with a fascinating cosmology, and enticing secondary characters who deserve their own stories." —*Booklist* (starred review)

"A delightful, smile-inducing romantic comedy between a witch and the demon she fake dates to save face in front of her demanding family, *A Witch's Guide to Fake Dating a Demon* is perfect for all fans of unlikely soulmates, banter galore, hilarious family dynamics, and April Asher's *Not the Witch You Wed*."
—The Nerd Daily

A DEMON'S GUIDE TO WOOING A WITCH

"Full of witty dialogue and steamy sexual tension, the novel unfolds at a steady pace and draws the reader in. Though this is only her sophomore effort, Hawley is bound to become a staple for readers of paranormal romances. Recommend to fans of Katie MacAlister, Lana Harper, and Molly Harper."
—*Library Journal* (starred review)

"I devoured this story! Each book in this series gets better, too. It's fun and rompy and full of fantastical shenanigans. . . . Sarah Hawley's stories feel like she's taken Kresley Cole's expansive world-building and plopped it into a small town. You get the cozy vibes mixed with the fun of the different magical races clashing. Can't wait to read the next one!"

—*USA Today* bestselling author Ruby Dixon

"A deliriously sexy romp, featuring my own personal brand of fiction kryptonite: a kick-ass heroine who puts the bad boy in his place, only to have him fall in love with her for it. Hawley has a unique talent for comedic writing. . . . I hope this series never ends!"

—Jenna Levine, *USA Today* bestselling author of
My Roommate Is a Vampire

"The tension between Calladia and Astaroth is pulled so tight that it's practically vibrating."   —*Kirkus Reviews*

"Sizzlingly sexy, endlessly imaginative, and laugh-out-loud funny, this is one of the most enjoyable paranormal romances of the year."   —*Booklist* (starred review)

BERKLEY ROMANCE TITLES BY SARAH HAWLEY

◆ ◆ ◆

A Witch's Guide to Fake Dating a Demon
A Demon's Guide to Wooing a Witch
A Werewolf's Guide to Seducing a Vampire

A WEREWOLF'S GUIDE TO SEDUCING A VAMPIRE

SARAH HAWLEY

BERKLEY ROMANCE

NEW YORK

BERKLEY ROMANCE
Published by Berkley
An imprint of Penguin Random House LLC
penguinrandomhouse.com

Copyright © 2024 by Sarah Hawley
Excerpt from *Servant of Earth* copyright © 2024 by Sarah Hawley

Library of Congress Cataloging-in-Publication Data

Names: Hawley, Sarah, author.
Title: A werewolf's guide to seducing a vampire / Sarah Hawley.
Description: First edition. | New York: Berkley Romance, 2024. |
Identifiers: LCCN 2024004727 (print) | LCCN 2024004728 (ebook) |
ISBN 9780593547960 (trade paperback) | ISBN 9780593547977 (ebook)
Subjects: LCSH: Werewolves—Fiction. | Vampires—Fiction. | LCGFT:
Paranormal fiction. | Romance fiction. | Novels.
Classification: LCC PS3608.A8937 W47 2024 (print) |
LCC PS3608.A8937 (ebook) | DDC 813/.6—dc23/eng/20240206
LC record available at https://lccn.loc.gov/2024004727
LC ebook record available at https://lccn.loc.gov/2024004728

First Edition: August 2024

Printed in the United States of America
1st Printing

Book design by Daniel Brount

*To Sarah Tarkoff—thank you for believing
in Glimmer Falls as much as I do.*

A
WEREWOLF'S
GUIDE
TO SEDUCING
A VAMPIRE

ONE

ON WEREWOLF BEN ROSEWOOD'S LIST OF THINGS TO AVOID If At All Possible, weddings were near the top.

It wasn't that he hated seeing other people happy or that he disliked cake or an open bar or dancing—well, all right, dancing was mortifying unless one was very drunk, which the open bar took care of—it was that he felt like a terrible person every time he went to one.

He raised his champagne, swaying slightly. The postceremony dinner was wrapping up and it was speech-making time. Another mortifying activity best practiced by drunk people or those who didn't have an anxiety disorder.

In vino confidence, he thought.

Mariel and Ozroth Spark, the newlyweds in question, looked at him expectantly from the sweetheart table. One witch, one demon: both people Ben cared about and didn't want to disappoint with a terrible speech.

"Mariel," he said, addressing his longtime friend and employee at his garden shop, Ben's Plant Emporium, "it has been a privilege to work alongside you and watch you thrive like the plants you care for. You've always given your time, love, and support to everyone around you, and you deserve to receive that love back a thousandfold."

Ben was sweating. He nudged his gold-framed glasses up his nose with his free hand, then peered down at the note card on the table that held his talking points.

"Now that you have Oz by your side," he continued, "you shine more brightly than ever, and I'm happy to see it."

It was a clumsy speech, but Mariel didn't seem to mind. The brunette witch was beaming, looking radiant in a white dress with lacy cap sleeves and a full skirt embroidered with vines and flowers. Next to her and wearing a black suit that matched his usual stark aesthetic was Oz—or as he had once been termed, Ozroth the Ruthless. The soul bargainer had been on Ben's shit list for a long time before he'd realized the demon was actually considerate, thoughtful, and utterly besotted with Mariel under that gruff exterior.

The normally surly Oz was now grinning widely, with lines of joy stamped beside his eyes. Those marks deepened with every year on Earth now that Oz was mortal, and Ben felt a surge of longing laced with envy. Not because Oz was marrying Mariel in particular—*marrying Mariel*, Ben's tipsy brain repeated, delighting in the alliteration—but because they were happy and in love.

This was why Ben didn't like weddings. He should be unconditionally delighted for his friends rather than sad about his own single status. He shoved down the shameful envy and glanced at the card again.

"Oz," he continued, addressing the black-haired, black-horned demon, "as you know, I wasn't sure about you at first. It isn't every day a demon comes portaling to Earth demanding your friend's soul." The crowd chuckled at that, and Ben felt a surge of relief. Thank Lycaon, progenitor of werewolves, he wasn't messing this up too badly. "But I saw how hard you fought to protect Mariel, and since then your love has grown and deepened. You prove that love with actions, not just words, which is the measure of a good man. It's an honor to know both of you and to be invited to give this speech."

He wasn't sure why they'd asked him to give a speech, but the reception had been speech-heavy so far, with family and friends of the bride and groom spouting impassioned, brilliant toasts that were all far better than Ben's.

"My skills are in gardening, not public speaking," he said, wrapping things up, "so I'm going to sit down before I embarrass myself." Another few chuckles at that. "In lieu of the brilliant oratory you deserve, I present you with a plant." He nodded toward the side of the room where another of his employees, a naiad named Rani, stood holding an orchid. She strode forward, grinning confidently in the way of well-adjusted people who didn't want to shrivel up and disappear in front of a crowd, and presented the plant to Mariel.

Mariel gasped and clapped her hands to her mouth. "Ben, are you serious? You found a Winter Sunrise?"

The Winter Sunrise orchid was rare, found only near the top of a magic-laced mountain in France where the ley lines allowed flowers to bloom through the snow. Its petals were snowy white blending into soft pink, the edges lined with orange, and the golden stamen glittered with magic.

"A rare flower for a rare friend," Ben said. He'd had to trade away a substantial selection of aphrodisiacal plants from his shop's inventory to get it, but he didn't regret the transaction.

"It's perfect," Mariel said, beaming at him. The orchid leaned forward in its pot, brushing its petals against her cheek. Mariel wrinkled her freckled nose. "Hi, baby," she whispered to the flower. "You're going to love my greenhouse."

Plants always behaved that way around Mariel. She was brimming with so much nature magic, the world came alive around her and plants acted downright enamored. Ben was a bit jealous, since werewolves didn't have any magic other than the truly unfortunate monthly transformation into a feral creature, but he couldn't deny it made her a heck of an employee at the garden shop.

Oz looked at Ben with obvious gratitude. *Thank you*, the demon mouthed.

Ben nodded in acknowledgment. Then, glad to have the speech over with, he plopped back into his seat.

His sister, Gigi, nudged him with her fork. A fork that unfortunately had residual sauce on it, leaving a greasy smudge on his navy coat sleeve. "Good speech, bro."

He blew out a heavy breath. "I'm just glad it's over."

"You're a great public speaker. I don't know why you hate it so much." Gigi shrugged and tucked back into her pasta.

His sister was thirty-three years old to Ben's thirty-eight, though he claimed she acted ten years younger and she claimed he acted eighty years older. They were both taller and more broad-shouldered than average and had the same thick brown hair and brown eyes, but personality-wise, they couldn't have been more different. Gigi was an extrovert who loved parties and public speaking, while Ben preferred time alone with his plants, books, and knitting.

Tonight Gigi was wearing a gold dress with her favorite pink Converse, and glittering piercings marched up her ears. "Thank Lycaon you're not wearing a sweater vest," she'd said when she'd spotted his navy suit earlier that day. "Someday you'll let me take you shopping."

That was an "absolutely not," and what was so wrong with sweater vests? They were sophisticated yet cozy, wrapping around his torso like a hug.

Or maybe like one of those ThunderShirts worn by quivering dogs, his judgmental inner voice said.

Ben drained his champagne.

Thankfully, the speeches wrapped up soon after. They'd gone well, all things considered. He'd had a brief moment of worry when Mariel's mother had spoken, but Diantha had spent the last two years repairing her relationship with Mariel and attending therapy. She wasn't perfect, but she was vastly improved from the pre-Oz days.

With speeches and eating done, it was time for dancing—and an open bar, thank the neurosis gods. The event space had a ceremony room decorated with stained glass, a large dining room, and an open-air courtyard where the rest of the festivities would take place. Magical light orbs drifted over the stone courtyard, and the trees enclosing the yard had been draped with rainbow fairy lights and gauzy swaths of fabric in bright colors. The night sky was thankfully clear—never a guarantee in the small town of Glimmer Falls or western Washington State in general—and the mid-August temperature was ideal. If the temperature or weather had been bad, though, one of the attending witches or warlocks would have taken care of it with a microclimate spell.

Ben smiled as Oz tromped his way through the choreographed steps of the couple's first dance with the grim concentration of a general approaching battle. Mariel didn't seem to mind the demon's straightforward but less-than-graceful ballroom style—she laughed and spun in his arms, dress flaring like a blooming lily. After Oz dipped her low and delivered a decidedly PG-13 kiss, the assembled guests cheered.

Then it was time for the father-daughter and mother-son dance. This had been an object of concern during the year leading up to the wedding. Mariel's relationship with her father was still strained from his years supporting Diantha's absurdities, though they'd made progress in family therapy. The more difficult issue was that Oz had been taken away from his demoness mother at a young age in order to be trained as a soul bargainer and hadn't seen her in hundreds of years—hadn't even known her name or if she was alive or dead. But Oz's childhood mentor, Astaroth, had made it his mission to atone for his part in that tragedy by finding her, and now Elwenna the demoness stood at the edge of the dance floor, hands clasped to her mouth. When the music started up again and Oz held out a hand, eyes glistening, she took it, and more than a few guests started weeping outright.

Ben had always been a crier, and now he wiped away a tear, sniffling. He couldn't imagine being separated from his family for that long.

He also couldn't imagine the day coming when he could spin his wife around the dance floor in front of their families . . . though he could easily conjure a memory of the last time he'd talked with his mother on the phone and she'd hesitantly asked, "So, I know you're busy, but have you given any thought to dating?"

Yes, Mom. Arguably too much thought. And the moment "anxious, workaholic werewolf" appeared on someone's vision board, she'd be first to know.

But tonight wasn't about him, so Ben gave his full attention to the two pairs spinning (or aggressively marching, as the case may be) across the dance floor, applauding and cheering them on.

Once the formal dances ended, Mariel grabbed a flute of champagne and raised it high. "Let's party!"

Music started blasting from the speakers as people of a variety of species rushed to the dance floor to begin gyrating with an enviable amount of confidence. Ben sidled up to the bar. It was manned by a centaur named Hylo he recognized as the bartender at a dive bar, Le Chapeau Magique. They had buzzed hair and a labret piercing, and their roan coat had been shaved with heart designs to commemorate the occasion.

"What's your poison?" Hylo asked.

"Whiskey," Ben said. He normally wasn't much of a drinker, but if he was going to dance—and Gigi would certainly drag him onto the floor if Mariel didn't first—he needed to drown his self-consciousness.

"How about an old fashioned?" At Ben's nod, Hylo started mixing ingredients, tapping their hooves rhythmically. The nonbinary centaur was a member of an Irish step dance troupe as well as a popular ClipClop influencer (as Gigi had informed him, being far more social media savvy than he was). Hylo presented the drink with a flourish, and Ben thanked them, slipping money into the tip jar.

He downed the old fashioned in under a minute, then held the empty glass out.

Hylo raised their eyebrows. "Dang, are you trying to get wasted?"

Ben gestured to the dance floor. "Social anxiety," he said succinctly.

"Ah." Hylo nodded knowingly. "Well, don't party too hard, all right? I'll have to cut you off if you get rowdy."

Ben wanted to laugh at the idea. The rest of his extended family was noisy, chaotic, and prone to brawling, as most werewolves were, but the number of times he'd done something that might be classified as "rowdy" could be numbered on one hand. "Don't worry, I'm a sad drunk," he said.

Hylo rattled the cocktail shaker before pouring him a second drink. "Weddings can be tough," they said. "Especially for single people."

Was he that transparent? Ben grimaced. "They shouldn't be. I just need to be a better person." He slipped another tip into Hylo's jar.

"It's nothing to do with being good or bad. Being sad or lonely or even jealous is normal—the thing that matters is how you treat people, and as far as I've seen, you've been very kind." Hylo patted his hand. "And who knows? Maybe you'll meet your soul mate here."

Ben doubted it. His life was consumed by running a small business, and what kind of woman wanted to be saddled with a werewolf who didn't even like howling at the moon?

But Hylo was being patient and understanding in that bartender/therapist way that involved emotional labor they didn't need to be doing, so Ben mustered up a smile. "Thank you," he said. "Maybe tonight's the night I find her at last."

◆   ◆   ◆

DID BEN HATE DANCING?

He didn't remember. All he knew was that the world was tilting, the glow-orbs overhead had doubled, and he was flailing his arms to a pop song he didn't know the name of. Around him, other guests wiggled or stomped or flapped their wings in similarly chaotic fashion.

"I love this song!" shouted the pixie hovering a few inches off the ground. Themmie—short for Themmaline—Tibayan was a Pixtagram influencer and a good friend. Her naturally black hair was bespelled purple and pink, and her iridescent wings shimmered. Along with Gigi, she'd been one of the instigators of the Get Ben on the Dance Floor campaign.

"Me, too!" shouted a British demon with pale blond hair and black horns who was gyrating on the opposite side of the small circle they'd formed. That was Astaroth, Oz's former mentor, who had been kind of evil before a bout of amnesia had improved him immensely. The improvement was also due to his partner, Calladia Cunnington, who had reformed the demon during a road trip nearly two years ago. Astaroth's memories had returned, including the knowledge that he was half human, but he'd remained on

Team Good and now lived with Calladia on Earth, visiting the demon plane on occasion to help implement progressive societal reforms.

Astaroth was an *incredible* dancer. He'd spun Calladia around the floor in a waltz earlier—only wincing a few times when she stepped on his toes or headbutted him while trying to take the lead—and now he was doing an enviable John Travolta impression. He was also ridiculously handsome and an expert swordsman, and Ben had reflected more than once that the universe needed to spread out its gifts a bit more evenly.

Thankfully, being surrounded by good dancers and internet-famous pixies meant fewer people were looking at Ben. Thus, he was free to flail.

"When are you going to get hitched?" Themmie asked Astaroth, slurring her words. There were little hearts painted on the apples of her brown cheeks.

Astaroth looked toward the bar where Calladia was ordering drinks, and his face softened into an utterly infatuated expression. "Neither of us particularly believe in the institution of human marriage, and we don't need a ceremony to be bound together forever."

"Aww," Themmie said. "But what about the tax benefits?"

Astaroth grimaced. "Right. Sometimes I forget humans are determined to suck the money and joy out of everything." He shrugged. "Maybe someday, then, but I'll let her lead the way. I'm just fortunate to be able to love her for as long as I can."

A sharp ache took up residence in Ben's chest. What he would give to be able to love someone with all his neurotic heart . . . but who could possibly love him back?

Drunk flailing took a sharp turn into drunk moroseness.

Themmie turned to face Ben. "And you? Got your eye on anyone special?"

Ben's eyes were not fixed on anyone special, but they did abruptly grow watery. The ache spread and deepened, and he stopped waving his arms. "No," he said sadly.

Themmie looked alarmed at his sudden shift in mood. She returned to the ground, then wrapped a small hand around his arm. "Come on," she said. "I need a breather."

She didn't even come up to his shoulder, but pixies were stronger than they looked, and Themmie had no problem manhandling him off the dance floor. The world spun, and Ben staggered before face-planting into a tree.

Themmie winced. "Let's sit you down." She guided him to a bench. "Head between your knees."

Ben obeyed, bracing his elbows on his knees. He closed his eyes, trying to suppress the urge to vomit. Damn the whiskey. If he were a normal person, he wouldn't need to get drunk to dance at his friend's wedding.

He'd said that last bit aloud, unfortunately.

Themmie patted his back. "Normal is overrated," she said. "But want to talk about it?"

Ben didn't. He really, really didn't, especially not to an internet-cool pixie some fifteen years younger than him who generally had at least two or three significant others. That was why he opened his mouth and spilled the entire story to her.

"I'm thirty-eight and single and haven't dated in nearly a decade. My business takes up all my time, and I like to knit, and I'm not even a properly rowdy werewolf, and who could ever love someone who feels this anxious most of the time? I should like all the howling and biting things, but I just feel out of control, and no one else likes sweater vests even though they're *wrong* about that, and what if nothing about me is attractive and I die alone in a ditch?"

He sat back up in time to see Themmie blink rapidly. "Wow,"

she said. "That was a lot. Uh, let's back up. For starters, what's wrong with knitting?"

"People think it's boring," he said forlornly. "I should have a manly hobby like . . . like woodworking or sword fighting or hunting elk with my bare hands." The best he'd managed in wolf form was a particularly ornery rabbit, and he'd felt guilty afterward.

"Hobbies don't have genders," Themmie said. "And you don't have to be some stereotypical macho woodsman to be attractive. Also, you're not going to die in a ditch, knitting isn't boring, and sweater vests . . . uh, I'm sure they have many merits."

"Many," he said fervently. "Argyle is wonderful." Such a pleasing pattern.

"I'm sure it is," she said soothingly. "So you're lonely and want to date, but you're also anxious and not sure someone will like you just the way you are?"

"That's precisely it." How quickly she cut to the emotional core of the matter, like Hylo had. "Have you thought about being a bartender?"

Themmie cocked her head, looking confused. "Uh, not really."

"You'd be great at it," he said vehemently. "Not the drink bits—or maybe the drink bits, I don't know—but all the listening and shit. Stuff," he clarified. "Shouldn't swear in front of a lady." His mother had drilled that into him growing up, but it was hard to remember sometimes, like when drunk or hanging out with his creatively vulgar cousins and friends.

Themmie laughed. "I fucking encourage swearing. And thanks, but let's go back to you. I think you have many lovely qualities and just need to find the right person who will appreciate them."

That was precisely the problem. "Don't know how."

"Well, you could go to some singles mixers around town—"

He shook his head, instantly regretting it when his brain sloshed in his skull. "People. Bad."

"You interact with people all the time at the Emporium."

"That's different. I know what to say and do there." There were specific rules about interaction in a place of business, and he knew the entire shop top to bottom, down to the well-being of individual leaves. In his sphere, he was the expert and authority. If challenged, he could be brave for the sake of his employees and his business, and if he ever felt uncomfortable, his reputation for being serious and levelheaded meant he could hide his inner turmoil with stoic silence.

At a random public event, much less one designed to spark romance, he'd be a disaster.

"Dating apps, then," Themmie said, pulling her phone from a pocket in her yellow dress. "You don't have to meet anyone in person until you've chatted online."

"Don't know what to write." Also, having never downloaded more than a few basic apps on his smartphone, he had a feeling he was too out of touch for that. He even kept handwritten ledgers at the office, preferring to practice his calligraphy rather than attempt Excel. Spreadsheets were undoubtedly helpful but lacked a certain artistry, and whenever he heard the words *pivot table* or *conditional formatting* he wanted to flee.

"Just give some details about who you are and what you're looking for. Like *I'm a werewolf, six foot four* or whatever, *I like knitting and own my own business. In search of someone who enjoys gardening*, blah blah blah. Then upload a nice picture of you. I'll even take it for you!" She raised her phone and snapped a picture of him, then winced as she eyed the screen. "Okay, maybe when you aren't quite so drunk."

"Cake!" someone screeched from across the dance floor. "Time for cake!"

The music cut off and people started moving toward an enormous four-tiered cake being wheeled out—half pumpkin spice for Oz and half chocolate for Mariel.

"Let's put a pin in this," Themmie said, standing up. "But promise you'll at least try to set up an online dating profile." She reached a hand down to help him up.

"I promise," Ben said, staggering to his feet. "Thanks, Themmie."

He watched from the back of the crowd as Mariel and Oz fed each other slices of cake, taking frequent breaks to kiss each other. They were so in love, and Ben teared up again with a mix of sincere joy and longing. He clapped and hollered as loudly as everyone else and accepted a slice of cake from Mariel with a grin.

She slid an arm around him in a side hug. "Thanks for being here," she said. "You're the best."

Ben certainly wasn't the best, but he would never do anything to dim her blissful glow, so he smiled and laughed and congratulated her again. Later, as the newlyweds exited the venue beneath an archway of sparklers and magic fireworks, he cheered until his throat was hoarse.

Then he took a rideshare car home and threw up in a bush in his front yard. Feeling marginally better after vomiting, he grabbed a glass of water, changed into pajamas, and collapsed on his brown faux-leather couch. Bleary-eyed, he grabbed his phone and started searching for dating sites.

Bumbelina, OkEros, PaganMingle, FarmersMarketOnly, Howly Ever After . . . none of them felt right. He sighed and switched to browsing something more practical.

The Emporium had done extremely well in recent years thanks to the quality of the plants, Mariel's magic touch, and the rare varieties he was able to get his hands on from international connections. He'd purchased the empty space next door and would soon be opening an adjoining coffee shop and bar, with a goal of eventually adding a small stage for lectures, music, and stand-up comedy. He wanted Ben's Plant Emporium to become a real community destination.

Most of the construction work on the Annex—as he was calling the café space—was done, and he was now sourcing decorations. The current project was a rock-and-crystal terrarium to display succulents next to the muffins.

He'd had some luck finding bulk quantities of unusual stones on eBay, so he switched to the site, squinting through the alcohol haze. *Blue sexy rock* he typed in, having briefly forgotten the word *crystal*.

The first listing was for an old rock-blues album on vinyl, which was not helpful. The next was for an outrageously expensive sapphire that would supposedly give the wielder an erotic aura. He briefly considered it, wondering if he would have an easier time meeting women if he had an erotic aura, then decided it would be disingenuous to lure a woman in that way even if he could afford it.

The third entry gave him pause . . . and then he started to laugh.

Dark Arts Sexy Succubus She-Vampire TALISMAN
PARANORMAL POSSESSED BLUE CRYSTAL DARK ARTS
SEXY CONJURE ROCK

The image was of a small, faceted blue stone that looked suspiciously like plastic, and the starting bid price was $0.99. No one had bid thus far, and the listing was closing in a few hours.

Ben read the description, growing more entertained with every word. Questionable capitalization aside, the poster didn't even know how to spell *succubus*, and they were trying to position this as a rare, possessed artifact.

This is a dark Vampire Succbus named Eleonore. She is 5'8"
tall with flaming red hair and emerald eyes. Very sexy,
comes with her own Knives. Hisses. French.

". . . Knives?" Ben muttered, eyeing the photo of the tacky blue "crystal." "Hissing?"

She is very Angry in nature but at least some threats are Jokes! Good friend, maybe good girlfriend I do not know, will do Anything for you—bite vengeance murder Jenga etc, Eleonore does All

"*Murder?*"

Dark Vampire Succbus Eleonore angry sexy French BUY NOW but BEWARE you must be firm, she has Attitude but very worth it if you want Assassin, TV watcher, best Friend, maybe-girlfriend, you will not regret it, please pay at least One Million gold doubloons, DARK VAMPIRE SUCCBUS ELEONORE

"Dark Vampire Succbus Eleonore," Ben intoned to himself in a dramatic voice. Then he laughed, feeling better than he had since before he'd started crying on the dance floor. What a hilarious scam. He was too cowardly to set up a dating profile, but by Lycaon, he was just drunk and easily amused enough to buy a vampire succubus—or succbus—assassin girlfriend in the shape of a plastic rock for the low, low price of $0.99.

He put in his bid, then promptly passed out on the couch, still smiling.

◆   ◆   ◆

TWO WEEKS AFTER THE WEDDING AND THIRTEEN DAYS AFTER the worst hangover he'd had in a decade, Ben looked down at the knitting project in his lap and groaned. He'd dropped a stitch a few rows back.

This project was a scarf for his mother, who had mentioned needing some new warm clothes for the winter. Next he'd make a matching one for his father and a hat for Gigi, and that took care of the first part of his holiday gifts.

He was close with his parents, as he was with his extended family in general. Werewolves were inherently pack creatures, and though Ben had long been the introvert of the family, he still had dinner with his parents and sister whenever he could get away from work—rare these days—and he was a frequent visitor at his aunt's Shabbat dinner. His uncle had married into a Jewish family, and as a result, the extended Rosewood-Levine clan was rarely without good food to eat or something to celebrate.

Knitting for the entire array of grandparents, aunts, uncles, cousins, second cousins, and friends so close they'd become honorary Rosewood-Levines was too daunting a task for a man with only two hands, so for the most part he only knitted for his immediate family. But his second cousin had just announced her pregnancy, so he had roughly six months to make his traditional "welcome to the family" baby blanket.

Lots of knitting, which normally wouldn't be a problem . . . if he wasn't currently preparing to expand the Emporium. His business took up the majority of his time, and arranging the permits, construction, decorating, supplies, and staffing for the expansion had resulted in a lot of lost sleep over the preceding months. But failing to produce gifts for his family was unthinkable, so if he had to cut back on sleep even more, he would.

Ben was reaching for a crochet hook to fix the mistake when the doorbell rang. He set the knitting aside and stood, brushing sandwich crumbs off his T-shirt and plaid pajama pants. It was a Saturday, and though normally he'd be at work, the builders had requested "no hovering" as they finished installing appliances. So here he was, catching up on projects at home while fretting about everything that could possibly be going wrong at the office.

He padded to the front door on bare feet and opened it to see a griffin with a palm-sized package in her beak and a clipboard held between two claws. A brown company vest announced the griffin's employment at a prominent shipping chain.

The griffin spat the box into Ben's hand before holding out the clipboard. "SIIIIIGN," she shrieked.

Griffins were highly intelligent but struggled to speak non-avian languages intelligibly, considering their beaks. They also smelled downright terrible to sensitive werewolf noses. Ben smiled politely and took the clipboard, ignoring the stench. He might smell equally bad to the griffin, after all.

"I didn't order anything," he said, looking between the box and the paper. The sender was listed as *THE WITCH IN THE WOODS*, with no return address, and the signature line on the receipt sat beneath text that read, *I assume full responsibility for the hellion, no take backs*, which struck him as nonstandard language.

"SIIIIIIIIIIIIGN."

Maybe he'd bought something online for the store and forgotten about it. It was definitely his name and address. Ben didn't want to make a fuss, so he nodded and signed. "Thanks," he said, waving awkwardly at the griffin before she launched into the air to continue her route.

Back in his living room, he sat on the couch and opened the box. Beneath layers of glittery tissue paper was a small plastic bag with a blue faceted stone inside, no bigger than his thumbnail. His brow furrowed. This was vaguely familiar, but why?

The stone proved to be plastic when he pulled it out. He studied the overhead light through it. Why had he ordered a fake plastic jewel? He sniffed it a few times, and *whoa*, it smelled great. Sweet in a luscious, spicy, complicated way even his rarest lilies couldn't match.

A piece of paper was nestled in the bottom of the box. The paper was fragile and browned with age. On it was written: ELEONORE.

A vague memory surfaced—something about eBay? He grabbed his phone and scrolled through his email. Sure enough, there it was—a receipt from two weeks ago informing him he had won the auction for *Dark Arts Sexy Succubus She-Vampire TALISMAN PARANORMAL POSSESSED BLUE CRYSTAL DARK ARTS SEXY CONJURE ROCK*.

He laughed, surprised all over again by the bonkers listing. No one else had bid, and now for the low price of $0.99—well, $4.28, once shipping was included—he owned a plastic rock that supposedly housed the murderous, red-haired lover of his dreams. He could only imagine how the seller must have cackled realizing some poor sap had fallen for the scam.

"Well, Eleonore," he said, "it's a pleasure to meet you."

The plastic jewel, predictably, did not respond.

Feeling silly and rather sleep-deprived, he dramatically lowered his voice. "Show yourself, succubus."

A sudden wind whipped around the room, rustling the papers on his desk and making the curtains flutter. To Ben's shock, the crystal began glowing electric blue. The wind and light swirled into a tiny cyclone in his palm that grew and grew before spinning to the middle of the room. Then the blue light flared white-hot, making him shield his eyes.

When he lowered his hand, there was a woman in his living room.

And not just any woman.

The most beautiful woman Ben had ever seen.

She had wavy, waist-length red hair, green eyes, and an hourglass figure that defined the term *bombshell*. Her lips were full, her cheekbones high, and her skin a smooth porcelain he felt the urge to brush his knuckles over to see if it was as soft as it looked. Her formfitting blue shirt was the same shade as the jewel, and she wore black leather pants and thigh holsters containing knives that took Ben back to his formative crush on Lara Croft.

She smelled *incredible*.

She was also glaring at Ben like she wanted to disembowel him.

"Uh . . ." he said, confused, awed, and deeply alarmed.

In response, she opened her mouth to reveal sharp fangs and *hissed*.

TWO

ELEONORE BETTENCOURT-DEVEREUX WAS A RARE CREA-
ture in many ways.

The first: She had been born to an immortal vampire sire and
a mortal succubus mother and was thus a hybrid with unique
traits from both species.

The second: She'd seen many centuries pass, despite inheriting
her mother's mortality.

The third: She'd been chained to a crystal, magically compelled to obey a witch's every command.

Those commands had largely involved murder.

Eleonore glared at the man who had ordered her out of the
crystal. The binding spell allowed the crystal's owner to turn her
insubstantial and shove her into a rock whenever they pleased, so
the fact he had been able to force her to manifest a physical form
meant he had assumed control of the stone, and thus her.

Which meant the Witch in the Woods had set her free at last . . .
only to present her to a new jailer.

On the one hand, that meant Eleonore could finally shred that

evil witch into bloody spaghetti with her fangs, now that the binding spell had been transferred to someone else.

On the other, she now had a new villain to worry about and
fantasize about killing, and who knew if he would be worse than
the last? People always disappointed, and centuries of bitter experience had taught Eleonore there was no limit to how low humanity could stoop.

The man was gaping at her. Somewhat like a fish, or perhaps a
Star Trek redshirt about to meet his demise. She took his measure,
wondering what fresh misery he would deliver. He was tall—about
half a foot in excess of her own height—with the broad shoulders,
shaggy hair, and animalistic energy of a werewolf. He had a neatly
trimmed beard and wore gold-rimmed spectacles, a stained
T-shirt, and soft, plaid-patterned pants. Attire chosen to make a
person underestimate him . . . if it weren't for the silver weapons
gleaming from the couch beside him. The spikes were long and
sharp, and though they were currently tangled in thick, colorful
thread, she had no doubt they would be effective when jabbed into
an enemy's neck.

Eleonore entertained a fantasy of shoving one into his jugular
and watching the blood spurt before she lapped it up. Her fangs
throbbed, and her stomach was so hollow it hurt. It had been a
long time since she'd fed . . . in any way.

"I, uh . . ." the werewolf said, nudging his glasses up.
"This . . . Huh."

Eleonore bared her fangs and hissed at him again. "If you mis-
treat me, wolf, be assured that someday—be it today or tomorrow
or fifty years hence—I will find a way to break this enchantment
and torture you in a thousand horrible ways before cutting out
your liver and eating it in front of you."

"Oh," he said, blinking rapidly. "Wow. That's . . . descriptive."
He swallowed, Adam's apple bobbing. "Sorry, who are you?"

She scoffed. "Don't play the fool. I'm sure my prior mistress told you everything." A former mistress whose name Eleonore didn't even know, as the foul woman had never shared anything beyond the moniker "the Witch in the Woods." Whenever Eleonore had been summoned, whether to murder an enemy or to acquire a human for the witch to drain of life, or sometimes just to read the newspaper out loud or watch *Star Trek*, her captor had worn a hooded cloak, so she didn't know what the witch looked like either. The witch's hands were pale, with a slashing scar across her right palm from the spell that had imprisoned Eleonore, and she'd glimpsed long black hair once, but that was hardly enough information to go on.

God's bones, how was she going to find the witch in order to kill her?

The werewolf shifted from foot to foot. His eyes darted to her face, then away, as if her presence made him nervous. Ha! As if he couldn't control her every action. He could tell her to slit her own throat and she'd grab one of those weapons on the couch without hesitating, mystically compelled to obey.

Rage burned in her breast. Hunger gnawed at her stomach and her mouth was dry with thirst. Her ravenous succubus need fixated on the bulge pressing against his soft pants.

Maybe she could intimidate him into masturbating, bite him, and *then* revisit how she would like to torture him.

"Are you . . . Eleonore?" the werewolf asked.

"Obviously," she spat.

He blew out a shaky breath. "Wow. I thought the eBay listing was a joke."

He sounded American, but she wasn't attuned to his slang, since she hadn't physically left the witch's cabin or spoken to any other beings since her last official mission in 1969. She'd been summoned a few times since then for *Star Trek* marathons, of course—she'd seen all of *The Original Series* and most of *The Next Generation*, *Voyager*, and *Deep Space Nine*, since the witch grew bored without company—but she wasn't sure when exactly those summonings had been. "Eeebay listing?" she asked, confusion joining her fury. "What is this eeebay you speak of?"

He reached toward the couch, and Eleonore tensed as his hand passed the silver spikes before retrieving a small rectangular object. "I'm Ben. Ben Rosewood," he said, holding the object up. "Please don't eat my liver. I just want to show you something."

Saying *please* moved a command into the category of a request, but this "Ben" had no need to order her not to harm him. The binding spell ensured she would never be able to hurt him.

She eyed his large, capable-looking hands, then the object. It didn't look deadly, but neither did a lot of terrible things, Eleonore herself included. Ben tapped the black rectangle, and a screen flared to life like the television in the witch's forest home, emitting an unnatural light.

Ah. Eleonore's shoulders relaxed infinitesimally. She'd seen this on *Star Trek*. It was a Personal Access Display Device, like the one Captain Picard used to seek information, although this was a compact version, easy to hold in one hand. The witch had told her *Star Trek* was fiction, not a documentary, but apparently there were commonalities with today's world.

Had humanity conquered the stars yet? The last time Eleonore had left the cabin to acquire a human for the witch, the American government had been about to send a man to the moon. An unimaginable feat . . . especially to a woman who had spent her youth wrapped in furs and leather, sharpening her sword with a whetstone while gazing up at the cosmos and wondering if the stars were the silver thrones of the gods.

Now she knew there were no gods. Or if there were, none deserving of worship.

The werewolf stepped toward her gingerly. "Don't hurt me," he said, holding out the PADD.

Eleonore bared her teeth. His second order after demanding

she show herself. What would the third be? "I wish I could," she replied bitterly.

Ben's eyes darted again. He was approaching her at a sideways angle, as a swordsman might to limit the size of the target for his opponent, and her eyes were drawn to his pectorals. "eBay is an online retailer," he said. "You can buy things from other people around the world. Your, uh, rock was listed. I thought it was a joke."

Eleonore snatched the PADD from him, peering at the glowing screen. During her last summoning for an evening of watching *Star Trek* reruns, the witch had told her of the so-called "internet," a place where people could communicate, shop, and learn anything they wished by visiting "web pages." Eleonore had had difficulty envisioning it, but she'd assumed it was a plane tangential to the physical one, perhaps inhabited by scholarly spider creatures with access to the multiverse, and that Picard's PADD could access this realm through witchcraft.

Her first look at the internet was underwhelming. Black writing filled a white page, and there was a picture of a tacky blue crystal, nothing like the quartz she'd first inhabited or the polished malachite the witch had forced her into after the quartz had been damaged in the 1700s. The last time Eleonore had been embodied, the witch had said she'd found a more modern and durable vessel, but Eleonore hadn't seen what her new prison looked like before being banished inside it.

Dark Arts Sexy Succbus She-Vampire TALISMAN PARANORMAL POSSESSED BLUE CRYSTAL DARK ARTS SEXY CONJURE ROCK, said the PADD.

Eleonore's brow furrowed. "This is a nonsensical string of words."

"Right?" Ben ran a hand through his thick brown hair, which would be just long enough for Eleonore to sink her fingers into and grip in preparation for beheading him. The movement sent a waft of his natural scent her way, and her lower belly clenched at the sweet yet masculine aroma. Just her luck that her new jailer should smell good. "And it was only ninety-nine cents and plastic, so I assumed it wouldn't actually be possessed."

Eleonore's head snapped up, and the werewolf flinched. "Did you say *plastic*?" She'd learned of said unnatural substance during her 1969 mission.

He grabbed something from the couch and held it out. Sure enough, the blue jewel in his fingers looked as cheap in person as it did in the picture.

The indignity! Eleonore bared her fangs at the plastic stone. She couldn't touch it herself—some stipulation of the spell—but she would love to smash the thing to pieces with a mace. Alas, even if she had a mace, that wouldn't free her from the curse—the witch had informed her she would inhabit some nearby object instead.

Wait a moment. "Did you say *ninety-nine cents*?" Eleonore asked. As she recalled from 1969, a dollar could buy a gallon of milk, three gallons of gas, or a six-pack. "My service costs the same as six beers?"

"Ah." Ben shifted again, looking embarrassed. "Less than that these days, I'm afraid."

"How much do six beers cost now?" The gall of that witch! And while Eleonore was asking questions . . . "When is now, anyway?"

Ben had the PADD. Was it possible she'd reached Captain Picard's twenty-fourth century? It seemed impossible, but perhaps her recent summonings to watch TV with the bored, foul, utterly disembowelable, soon-to-be-spaghetti witch had taken place over a longer timeline than she'd imagined.

"When is now?" Ben's eyes widened. "Wait, are you immortal?"

Eleonore gave a short, dismissive hiss, baring only her right fang. "No, but time doesn't pass for me when I'm trapped in the crystal." No aging or eating or drinking, just an eternal, hazy, hungry despair—half blurry dreams and memories, half darkness.

"How long have you been trapped?" Ben asked.

Dull, regrettably attractive man. "I can't tell you unless you let me know what year it is."

Ben winced. "Right."

When he told her a date in the twenty-first century, Eleonore's eyes widened. She looked around, assessing his house in detail for the first time. The walls of this room were forest green, the couch was brown, and the only art in sight were photographs of smiling people propped on various surfaces. Hard to find details that might anchor her in this new reality.

What was the nature of this time? Ben had the PADD, and who knew how else technology had accelerated while Eleonore had been dreaming cold, empty dreams? It wasn't the twenty-fourth century, but it was alarmingly close.

"I have been bound by that curse for almost six centuries," Eleonore said, the weight of it heavy on her tongue.

Ben inhaled sharply, then started coughing. "Breathed in my spit," he wheezed as he hammered his chest with a massive fist.

Eleonore eyed him. Perhaps she wouldn't need to break the spell to kill him. He might manage to do it himself.

Ben finally stopped coughing. "Sorry. I'm just—*six centuries*?"

"Yes, six centuries," Eleonore said, a scorpion's sting in her voice. If Ben had a shred of empathy—unlikely, based on past experience—maybe he would reconsider treating her the same way the witch had.

That witch had brought Eleonore out with varying frequency over the centuries, and it had rarely been enjoyable. Sometimes once a year, sometimes once every twenty—it depended on what was needed. Humans had to be sourced every fifty years so the witch could drain their energy to extend her own life span, but assassinations or spy missions could be ordered at any time.

"A six-pack costs more like ten dollars today," Ben said. At Eleonore's outraged exclamation, he cringed. "That's why I thought the post was fake. I had no idea you were actually, uh, in there."

Eleonore stared at him, trying to determine his level of truthfulness. He looked nervous. Although he was massive, he was hunching his shoulders as if trying to make himself smaller. His eyes—a warm brown a few shades lighter than his hair—met hers and danced away, and he rubbed the back of his neck while shifting from foot to foot.

The liars Eleonore had known were far more confident in their deceptions. And was the werewolf . . . bashful?

The curse meant Eleonore could easily become this man's prey, but now she considered him with the eye of a predator.

Bashful was good. *Bashful* had few defenses against her succubus half. Maybe she could entice this werewolf, then manipulate him into, first, not ordering her about and, second, helping her find a way to break the binding spell. And then perhaps she could feed from him, sinking her fangs into his neck and absorbing both his blood and the inevitable erotic response that accompanied it.

She licked one throbbing fang.

Perhaps it had been hasty to threaten his liver. It was her vampire father's legacy—during times of stress, it was fangs first, critical thinking later.

Eleonore tried to remember the rules of being enticing. She'd been very much formed from her father's mold, and though she'd loved her mother dearly, she'd never been . . . talented . . . at channeling the skills of that succubus half. No matter how often her mother had tried to train her in sensual walking and fluttering lashes and the language of coy glances, Eleonore had preferred being blunt about her appetites and opinions. A negotiation was just a sword fight that hadn't started yet.

Still, even Eleonore recognized when a change in strategy was required. She shifted tactics, popping out a hip, then dipping her chin to look up at him from beneath her lashes.

Ben gulped. She sensed a spike of carnal interest, lush and rich.

A promising start. Eleonore fluttered her lashes, feeling absurd even as she soaked in his fear-laced arousal. "So," she said, lowering her voice to a purr despite the anger still roiling in her chest, "if you didn't know I was in the crystal, why did you buy it? And . . ." She licked her lips. "What do you plan to do with me?"

THREE

INTERNAL SCREAMING WAS PREFERABLE TO OUT-LOUD SCREAM-ing, which was about all the silver lining Ben could find in this situation.

The sexiest woman he'd ever seen was standing in his living room. The sexiest *vampire succubus* he'd ever seen, who was also the *only* vampire succubus he'd ever seen. A stressful situation to begin with, but she was also apparently over six hundred years old and had threatened to torture him and eat his liver.

Cue freak-out.

How had that eBay listing been real? And what was he supposed to do now?

Despite her threats, Eleonore was now looking at him in a sultry way. Well, mostly sultry—she'd started blinking aggressively like something was in her eye, and he was tempted to ask if she needed eye drops—but then she licked her lips and lowered her voice, and that throaty murmur sent an electric tingle from the top of his head to the tips of his toes.

Still, the shift from hostility to seduction on her part was both abrupt and suspicious. People rarely tried to seduce Ben—that he was aware of, anyway—and when they did, they certainly didn't open with threatening to eat his organs. Which meant she had another reason for the abrupt change in demeanor.

When in doubt, the standard assumption was that everyone secretly hated him. Or in this case, overtly hated him, sultry looks aside. "I'm so sorry," he said, deciding to ignore the lip-licking and the way she was sticking a hip out like she'd dislocated something. "I bought the crystal when I was drunk. I saw the listing and thought it was funny, and I'd just come from a wedding, and—" He bit off the rest of that confession. She didn't need to know how pathetically lonely he was.

She blinked, a sweep of long auburn lashes. "A wedding?" she asked in her French accent.

He winced. Well, he supposed he owed her this much. She probably hadn't anticipated manifesting in his living room either. "Friends were telling me to try online dating. I . . . well, this is going to sound stupid, but the listing said you'd be a good girlfriend, and I thought it would be funny—" He broke off as she whipped his phone up again. Lycaon, she moved quickly.

She frowned and poked the black screen. "It's broken."

"It went to sleep and I have to put in my passcode." He held out a trembling hand. "May I?"

Eleonore clutched the phone, looking suspiciously between it and his hand. Then she snapped her teeth in a clear warning before giving him the phone. "I wish to inspect the pad more once you're finished."

So long as she didn't rip out his jugular, she could inspect whatever she wanted. The way she spoke, it was clear she hadn't been around modern technology. He'd have to look up the last time a six-pack cost a dollar. "It's a smartphone," he said, keying in his passcode. "A phone that also works as an internet browser and . . . other stuff. Apps and things."

Her eyebrows rose. "A phone?" she asked, sounding scandalized. "How can that be? Where is the cord?" When he held it out again, she snatched it fast enough to make him flinch. She touched the screen, then yelped when the page scrolled. "Incredible. And this will make telephone calls?"

"It will." Though he wasn't sure he wanted to introduce her to that functionality yet.

Eleonore dragged her finger over the screen, scrolling down the rest of the listing. Her nails were slightly pointed, and Ben shuddered as he imagined the tips of them sinking into his bare chest as she pinned him down for the evisceration.

Her expression darkened once more. "The rest of this advertisement is just as appalling as the title."

"It's very poorly written," he agreed.

"She was never particularly good at writing. She used to dictate letters to me, and even her thoughts required substantial editing. Though I suspect vodka played a role in this, too."

"She?"

Eleonore glared at him again, and it was incredible how those gorgeous, long-lashed green eyes could stab through him like icicles. "The witch you purchased this from." Her gaze shifted over his shoulder and went distant. "Who I will strangle with her own intestines as soon as I find her."

Apparently the brief interlude into flirtatious behavior was over, but this was far more effective anyway. Ben restrained a whimper as his heart rate spiked. Her bloodthirstiness shouldn't be sexy. It really shouldn't. But she was wearing *thigh holsters*, for goodness' sake, and his fight-or-flight impulse was expressing itself in weird ways.

What was he supposed to do in this bizarre situation?

Her bared fangs triggered a realization. If she was a vampire and had been summoned for the first time in who knew how long . . . Well, he knew what his parents would say about a host's duties. "I apologize if this is an indelicate question," Ben said, "but . . . are you hungry?"

Her head snapped up in another whip-fast movement. He'd never met a full-blooded vampire either, but he'd heard a bit about them, and they were supposed to be preternaturally quick. "Yes," she said, pupils widening until they nearly swallowed the green of her irises. Her gaze fixed on his neck. "Very hungry."

Perhaps he shouldn't have asked, because he'd now opened a can of worms. Antagonistic, hungry worms. Maybe those ones from *Dune*, bursting out of the sand to bare rows of razor-sharp teeth. And yet his body was responding, that naked hunger in her gaze scrambling his brain and making his pulse pound.

What was the etiquette for this? When he was a child, his mother had given him lessons about how to set a table or hypothetically introduce himself to the Queen, but she hadn't covered the situation of accidentally purchasing a vampire succubus online. Was he supposed to offer his neck?

Eleonore was unbelievably sexy, but Ben was smart enough to recognize that might not be the best idea, considering her hostility. Then again, she was only half vampire. Unlike vampires or demons, succubi were a mortal species like werewolves, humans, or pixies—they might have a supernatural brand of magnetism, but they didn't live forever. And although succubi were rare enough that Ben didn't personally know any, he thought he remembered that they ate like humans did. "Do you need food or blood?" he asked.

"Both." She stood perfectly still, though an electric energy poured off her and her scent had deepened and grown more intoxicating. Ben found himself swaying toward her. Her lips parted . . .

The sight of her sharp white fangs—which seemed longer now than they had a moment before—was enough to break the spell. Ben shook his head and stepped back, heart racing. "I'll make you a sandwich to start." He hurried to the kitchen, then rifled through his fridge for turkey, lettuce, and cheese. When he turned toward the counter to grab the bread, he nearly had a heart attack seeing her standing mere feet away, having arrived with no noise whatsoever. "Jesus, do you have to jump out like that?"

A crinkle formed between her brows. "I did not jump."

"Semantics." He hurriedly assembled the sandwich and handed it to her.

She snatched it like a cobra striking and stuffed half of it in her mouth at once. Then she moaned, a sound of such pure, filthy delight that Ben couldn't help but react. He laced his fingers in front of his crotch, praying the situation didn't escalate. It was embarrassing to be in the kind of dry spell that made a man get hard over a sandwich.

Well, not the sandwich precisely, although if the bread had been suggestively shaped he wouldn't put it past himself, pathetic as his love life had been the last few years. Then again, his heart was working overtime to get oxygen to his muscles in case he needed to flee; it made sense some of his blood had gotten misdirected.

The sandwich was gone in a few bites. Ben filled a glass of water and handed it over, and Eleonore drained it before sighing and sagging against the counter. "I'm always so hungry when I get summoned," she said.

Her pupils were still huge, though, and her eyes were back on his neck, so clearly she hadn't been fully sated. Ben swallowed. "I'll get you some blood." When she stepped forward, he held up a hand. "From a store. *Not* my neck."

Her face fell. Her eyes fell, too, fixing somewhere in the vicinity of his groin. "There are other arteries," she said hopefully.

Oh no. First the sandwich had gotten him going; now it was his femoral artery. He faced the cabinet, willing his body to behave reasonably. "How about I give you a tiny bit of blood to top you off while you wait for me to get back from the store?"

"Yes," she hissed. Unlike her initial hisses, which had sounded like an angry cat, this one was more snakelike and oozed satisfaction.

It was like having a feral animal in his kitchen. He had no idea what she would do at any given moment or whether or not he would come out uninjured. He fumbled for a shot glass—unused for at least ten years—and a knife, then took a deep breath. He wasn't fond of blood, but it was his fault they were in this situation, so he might as well gather his courage and feed his new vampire guest.

He cut the pad of one finger and held it over the shot glass.

There was a red-haired blur. The next thing he knew, he was pinned against the fridge with Eleonore's lips wrapped around his finger. She sucked, and a bolt of pleasure arrowed through Ben's veins straight to his groin. They moaned simultaneously, and Eleonore clawed him closer with a hand at his neck and a leg wrapped around his thigh as if to keep her prey from escaping. The tips of her nails dug into his skin, and *fuck*.

Ben's head spun in a delirium of panic and pleasure. There must be some magical aphrodisiac in her saliva, because he was instantly fully erect. He ground against her lower belly, helpless to resist, and she met his movements, rocking her hips urgently.

This was madness. But her mouth, good heavens, her *mouth* . . .

He needed to put an end to this. The situation had spiraled wildly out of control, and no matter how good it felt, he couldn't mindlessly hump his new houseguest like an animal. "Stop," he choked out.

She instantly released him and was across the kitchen in the blink of an eye, back pressed to the wall as she panted. A trickle of blood escaped the corner of her mouth, and her nipples were erect beneath her shirt. "Sorry," she said, tongue darting to collect the blood. "I lost control." She squeezed her thighs together, and Ben groaned as he realized she had also been affected by the contact.

"It's not just the blood," she blurted when he didn't reply.

"What?" he asked, having lost most of his cognitive ability.

"Losing control," she said in that throaty succubus voice. "I could sense your arousal and . . . well, I feed on that, too."

He nearly choked on his own spit for the second time in ten minutes. She could *sense his boner*? Alarm bled into horror. "I'm so sorry," he babbled, panic rising as he realized he'd inadvertently sexually harassed her. "I didn't mean to make you feel disrespected or—or fetishized or anything else. It's just—I haven't been with anyone in a long time, and you're very beautiful and terrifying, and I'm so sorry, I promise I'll never have an erection again."

Unrealistic, perhaps, but he was freaking out. He felt the urge to jump out of the nearest window. His house might only be one story, but there was a thorny bush he could head-plant into . . .

To his surprise, she smiled. "Oh, Ben," she purred, easing closer again. "I'm half succubus. I like it when you have erections."

He closed his eyes, willing himself not to do anything mortifying like whimper or come in his pants. Being near her was like riding a roller coaster of emotion. She switched between sultry and terrifying so quickly, he couldn't find solid ground to anchor himself on.

"How does succubus feeding work?" he asked. "You drink blood and eat food, but you clearly also need . . . something else." Maybe the technical details would take his mind off the image of her sucking sustenance straight from his dick.

"I need to experience sexual contact or be near sexual energy," she said. "Fucking is the most efficient way to feed, of course, but I can also feed by watching people fornicate or being near someone pleasuring themselves."

Ben whimpered, but at least he didn't come in his pants. Technical details had betrayed him. "How . . ." He cleared his throat. "How often?"

"About once a week, similar to drinking blood."

Well. This was a new logistical concern to iron out, ideally when he was far away from Eleonore and her dizzying scent. "Restaurant," he croaked. "I'll get you blood." Before he could embarrass himself further, he turned and fled the house.

FOUR

THE WEREWOLF TASTED GOOD.

Eleonore licked her lips, catching the residual drops of his delectable blood. Ben Rosewood tasted of chocolate, earth, cinnamon, and a tumult of restrained passion. There was a sharp note of fear to the blood, yes, but it didn't diminish the full flavor. The werewolf might come across as bashful, but blood didn't lie. There was a carnal beast inside him, eager to be freed.

That beast had briefly risen to grind against her, hard and hot. His sexual energy felt like the psychic equivalent of his blood—wild, rich, rare. Was he actually shy, or was it an act to distract others from perceiving the predator within? Eleonore despised lying, but she'd been forced to play many parts over the years in order to feed and kill, from knowing temptress to virginal ingenue. She knew well that what a person appeared to be on the surface rarely matched their true self, and that those true selves were almost always grim, disappointing, or disgusting.

Whatever Ben's truth, ugly as it likely was . . . *gods*, she would commit crimes to taste his orgasm. She shuddered at the thought, head falling back against the kitchen wall. She despised him for holding the crystal and thereby controlling her, but liking or trusting someone wasn't a requirement for fucking them, and it had been forever since her succubus half had fed. Her lower belly was heavy with want, and though she couldn't feed on her own orgasms, she was considering sliding a hand into her pants when the front door opened again.

Eleonore was back in the living room in a flash, in time to see Ben poke his head in. He looked mortified. "Forgot my keys." He scooped them up from a bowl on a low bookshelf. "And my wallet. And my phone." He grabbed both from the table, then looked down. "And my shoes."

Eleonore folded her arms and gave him an unflinching stare.

His cheeks grew redder above the edge of his beard, and he gave her a half wave before running out of the room again.

Strange werewolf. Wanting to understand the truth of the man who held her fate in his palm, Eleonore decided to follow him. She watched through the front window as he got into a green, boxy-shaped car. So long as he didn't drive too quickly, she ought to be able to keep up with him.

It was a common misconception that vampires teleported when they wished to move quickly. In reality, they ran—their movements just happened to have a preternaturally fast top gear. She could sprint down a block in the blink of an eye.

She waited until he was a block away before beginning her pursuit. He drove carefully, halting completely at each cherry-red stop sign in a way other drivers seemed disinclined to do. Easy prey, but the thrill of the hunt coursed through her anyway. Both vampires and succubi were predators and loved a chase. Adrenaline gave blood a sharp, intoxicating edge, much like a consensual taste of fear or pain could intensify sexual pleasure.

As she pursued Ben one sprint at a time, concealing herself behind bushes or other cars, Eleonore took measure of her surroundings. It was a warm day, with sunlight cascading over green trees and quaint houses. The neighborhood sprawled in the neatly planned way she remembered from the American suburbs of 1969, but it was saved from uniformity by the individual touches on homes. The structures were painted in a rainbow of colors, and it was evident a variety of creatures inhabited this place. One house bore the massive door and entrance ramp common to centaur abodes; another had a pond in the front yard in which a naiad reclined nude, scales shining at the border between her forehead and hair; and ribbons fluttered from a tree in a third yard, marking wishes or spells.

A supernatural-friendly district. Most cities had areas like this where magical creatures congregated. She expected the town to grow more boring and ordinary outside of Ben's neighborhood, but the opposite happened. Asphalt turned to red brick where branches interlaced over the street, and the houses grew more eccentric, with peaked gables, unusual expansions, and all manner of oddities in the windows. A pixie fluttered by overhead, books tucked under one arm, while a warlock cast illusions before an admiring semicircle of children.

When Eleonore stopped beside a parked red truck, waiting to see which direction Ben would turn, she was intrigued to see a blond woman straddling what looked like a demon in the passenger seat. The two were kissing passionately, which gave her a brief burst of energy before they broke apart, looking startled at her appearance. Eleonore had no desire to explain herself, so she merely bared her teeth and ran on.

At least that hit of arousal combined with Ben's animalistic response to her drinking had managed to take the sharp edge off her succubus half's hunger. Get too desperate for sexual energy and she might end up pinning her new captor down and grinding them both to completion, and she was feeling too spiteful to gift him with an orgasm.

She reached what looked like the downtown area, where shops and restaurants clustered around a village green. Ben pulled to a stop next to a black-painted storefront whose dramatically lettered sign proclaimed it to be NecroNomNomNoms. Eleonore crouched behind a newspaper box that held copies of the *Glimmer Falls Gazette*, ignoring a gnome who squeaked and scurried away at the sight of her.

When Ben got out of his vehicle, he was greeted by a group of people walking down the sidewalk. "Ben!" one proclaimed. "I'm surprised you aren't at the Emporium."

He grunted and shrugged one shoulder. "Construction."

"I can't wait to see the new space," someone else said. "Are you still thinking about adding a stage?"

Eleonore's brows furrowed. What space were they speaking of?

"Yeah," Ben said. "I want to get the coffee shop established first, though."

Ben was a business proprietor? Eleonore filed that away in the mental encyclopedia entry she was building. *Ben Rosewood: Werewolf, possesses stabbing implements, owns a coffee shop, either bashful or using a façade of shyness to cover up his dark nature, tastes good.*

Know thy enemy, someone had once said. Eleonore was hit or miss on that advice—sometimes you just needed to shout *Surprise*, rip out a throat, and be done with it—but this wasn't an assassination. This was psychological warfare with the highest of stakes. On one side, a werewolf with ultimate power over Eleonore's entire existence. On the other, Eleonore herself, who had learned early in life how to be a weapon. She hadn't managed to break the enchantment yet, but she refused to give up.

After a few more vague pleasantries, Ben made his excuses and disappeared into the building.

The opened door let a waft of blood-scented air out, and

Eleonore's mouth watered. At least now she knew one place to go if Ben stopped providing her with blood.

"What are we looking at?"

Eleonore spun, baring her fangs and hissing. Somehow, a woman had crept up on her and was now crouched in an identical position behind the newspaper box, peering at the shop. She had red hair a lighter and more coppery shade than Eleonore's, and black horns ran along the sides of her head, pointing straight back. A demoness.

Two demons in one morning seemed odd for the human realm, since they lived in their own plane and rarely emerged except when hunting for souls, but Eleonore didn't know what had occurred while she'd been dreaming this last time. Perhaps there was an infestation.

"Nice teeth," the demoness said, eyeing Eleonore's mouth with eyes of a pale crystalline blue. "It isn't Halloween, but I haven't seen a daywalking vampire in over a thousand years." Her forehead furrowed. "Unless it is Halloween?"

Many immortals were time-maddened, the Witch in the Woods included. The older they got, the less connected to reality they were. "Who are you?" Eleonore asked.

"I would ask you the same thing," the woman said, smiling in a vague sort of way, "but I'd just forget."

Eleonore took in other details. The demoness was dressed in a frilled white shirt, black pants and boots, and a piratical red sash, and her fingernails were filed to a point and painted black.

"It's impolite, you know," the demoness said.

Eleonore blinked. "What, staring?"

"Oh, no, staring at me is always allowed. I *am* extremely attractive." She gestured at nothing in particular. "But there should only be one hot, ominously crouching redhead allowed in Glimmer Falls at a time." Her mouth turned down in a pout. "I have to warn you—if you try to supplant me, I'll be forced to dismember you and feed you to my hellhound."

"I'm not trying to supplant you," Eleonore said, feeling like this conversation was the metaphorical equivalent of quicksand. She had stumbled into it inadvertently and couldn't get her footing. "I don't even know who you are. I'm spying on a werewolf."

"Oh, fun!" The woman clapped her hands. "My current boy toy is a werewolf. I spy on him for fun, too."

Boy toy? Eleonore filed that away to look up on the PADD later. "Is your werewolf named Ben Rosewood?"

The door to NecroNomNomNoms swung open and Ben walked out, a paper bag in one hand and the PADD pressed to his ear with the other. The coppery scent wafting from the bag made her stomach growl, and Eleonore ran a tongue over her fangs.

The demoness followed her gaze, then made a face. "Oh, not him. He's boring."

Remembering the wild taste of his blood and the silver stakes on his couch, Eleonore wasn't sure she agreed. "On a scale of one to ten, how nefarious is he?"

"Negative five," the woman said, sounding disappointed by the fact. Her gaze moved beyond Ben toward the park, and her face lit up. "Almost time for my carnal ambush of Kai." She giggled. "He's been tied up in my den for three hours."

With that, the strange woman stood, then sauntered toward the park. A red clock marked the entrance, its face covered with various runes and numbers, and Eleonore wasn't sure why it had approximately two dozen hands moving at various speeds. She watched, perplexed, as the demoness traced a fiery oval in the air, then stepped through, disappearing into nothing.

"How odd," she said. This whole town was odd. Multiple demons, strange clocks, and a hodgepodge of architecture that spoke of poorly organized city planning. Glimmer Falls . . . the name wasn't familiar, but Eleonore hadn't socialized much in the human world of the past few centuries. The majority of her time had been spent with the Witch in the Woods.

The thought of the witch made her bare her teeth. Speaking of insane. The last conversation they'd had before Eleonore had apparently been sold like cattle had jumped from the relative attractiveness of Starfleet captains—much as Eleonore regretted agreeing with the witch on anything, Janeway's carnal appeal could not be denied—to creative uses for menstrual blood to an exhaustive list of every enemy the witch had ever made, most of whom were now dead at Eleonore's hand. At the end of her rambling speech, the witch had turned her hooded face toward Eleonore, a lock of long black hair slinking out from the shadows. "I'm so glad we're friends," the witch had said solemnly.

Friends. Putain de bordel de merde. Eleonore hadn't seen her expression, of course, but the witch had actually sounded like she meant it.

Oh, she was going to enjoy turning that bitch inside out.

She looked toward the store again, then realized she'd missed Ben driving away. She whipped her head around and spotted the green vehicle turning a corner.

The Witch in the Woods was still her greatest enemy . . . for now. It remained to be seen how terrible this Ben Rosewood would be.

Eleonore shot to her feet and resumed the hunt.

FIVE

I'M RUNNING ERRANDS, GIGI," BEN SAID, PHONE CRADLED BE-tween his cheek and shoulder as he fumbled with the car keys. "Can I call you back?"

The take-out bags of blood wouldn't stay hot for long, and he wanted to make sure Eleonore fed well. His nose crinkled at the rich, coppery smell, which should have bothered him far more than it did. Unfortunately, the wolf in him liked that sort of thing. There was an itch in his gums where fangs would drop at the full moon.

His sister made a rude noise. "This is important. Or does buying decorations for your coffee shop matter more than your little sister?"

Ben was very familiar with this manipulation tactic, which was employed mercilessly in his family. That didn't mean it wasn't effective. "All right," he said, feeling a surge of guilt. "What's up?"

He put the phone on speaker and tossed it on the passenger seat before pulling out of the parking spot. The SUV was more car than he needed, but his height required accommodations. He checked his rearview mirror, then stiffened at the sight of a red-haired woman crossing the street. Had Eleonore gotten out? Then he recognized the piratical figure of Lilith, the so-called Mother of All Demons, and relaxed.

It might not be the usual response when someone encountered one of the oldest living demons, especially not one who was cheerfully, self-admittedly insane and had a reputation for violence. In fact, it wasn't even Ben's usual response, but he'd rather see Lilith than Eleonore at the moment. Lilith had been a regular sight in Glimmer Falls since her son, Astaroth, had started dating Calladia. The worst behavior she'd engaged in on the mortal plane these past two years—that Ben knew of, anyway—had been a few acts of vandalism, some mild arson, and a regrettable amount of public indecency with Kai, one of Ben's friends and a member of the nearby Fable Farms werewolf pack.

Lilith didn't seem to pose a threat to Glimmer Falls so long as her son was happy—there were plenty of other cities, countries, and astral planes to wreak havoc in, after all. Eleonore, though . . . he had no idea what sort of threat she might pose.

"—so I was thinking you'd be great at helping organize events," Gigi was saying, and Ben realized he hadn't been paying attention.

"Sorry," he said, forcing thoughts of vivid emerald eyes and sharp fangs out of his mind. "What was that?"

"Did you hear anything I just said?" Gigi's tone was annoyed.

"I'm driving," he pointed out. "And I thought I saw someone I knew."

She muttered to herself—something involving Jesus Christ, Thor, and an expletive. Despite their mother's civilizing attempts, Gigi was an equal-opportunity curser, name-dropping whatever deity, historical figure, or swear word felt natural at the time. Most werewolves were the same, though for his mother's sake Ben tried to stick to mild exclamations like "Lycaon" or "God."

Gigi cleared her throat and started again. "You know I've talked about public service before, right?"

"Yeah," Ben said, wondering where this was going. Gigi had always been interested in politics and activism, especially on the local stage.

"Well, I've decided to run for mayor."

Ben nearly steered his SUV off the road. "What?" he asked, startled by the magnitude of the announcement.

"Cynthia Cunnington is running unopposed, probably because she's blackmailed, threatened, or bribed any possible opponents. I'll be the dark horse she never sees coming." She chuckled. "Or the dark wolf, I guess."

Ben pinched the bridge of his nose with the hand not on the wheel. "Gigi, do you really want to get on her radar?" He didn't doubt his sister would make a decent mayor—as much as he teased her for being an outgoing party girl, he knew she was whip-smart, well-informed on politics, and genuinely invested in bettering the world—but Cynthia Cunnington was . . .

Well, Cynthia Cunnington.

Glimmer Falls had been founded by the patriarchs of two families: the Cunningtons and the Sparks. They'd engaged in a fierce rivalry over the generations, though the latest heirs—Mariel Spark and Calladia Cunnington—were best friends and genuinely nice people.

But Mayor Cynthia Cunnington was cut from the cloth of the older, more ruthless generations. She was all ice and ambition, as calculating as she could be vindictive. Her thirst for power was so all-consuming, she'd abused and belittled her own daughter for being "bad for optics." And while Mariel's mother had taken steps to grow closer to her daughter, Cynthia had chosen politics over family. Calladia had, tragically, been forced to cut off contact with her mother for her own mental health.

As someone with a large, loving family, Ben couldn't imagine what it would feel like to be rejected by the person who was supposed to love you above all else. But Calladia had a fighter's spirit, and she'd decided to form her own family out of their friend group, bloodlines be damned.

If Cynthia Cunnington could treat her own child like that—what would she do to Gigi?

"Everyone is so afraid of her," Gigi was saying, "and this is only her first mayoral term. Are we going to reelect her two more times, letting her taint the office for eight more years? She almost got half the forest chopped down for that resort she fabricated paperwork for. What else will she do in the name of bringing big business to Glimmer Falls?"

Ben tried a different tack. "Isn't it a bit late to be running? The election's in two and a half months."

Gigi clicked her tongue. "The window to apply closes in a few days. It's a small town—it's not like running for president or something, and Glimmer Falls always does things a bit weirdly. I just needed to pass a scrying test to ensure there isn't secret evil in my soul—nailed that, by the way—and then collect enough signatures to get on the ballot by the sixty-ninth day before Election Day."

"Shame they didn't ask me about the secret evil," he said. "I could have told them you're a menace and not to let you anywhere near public office."

"Rude!"

Ben stopped to allow an elderly centaur to carefully pick her way across the street. He smiled tightly and raised a hand in greeting when the gray-coated woman nodded in his direction. "Do you have a platform you're running on?" he asked more seriously as he turned right. "Increasing affordable housing or something?"

A movement in his peripheral vision caught his eye, making him tap the brakes, but when he looked there was nothing but a row of scraggly trees with the trademark ballooning shape created when deer and perytons nibbled away the leaves near the bottom.

"No," Gigi said. "I have given my political campaign zero thought and don't have a single idea or conviction. The only platform I know is ClipClop, so I'm going to bat my eyes and ask everyone to please give the little lady some power, as a treat."

The sarcasm was hard to miss. "Point taken." Ben sighed. "I just worry about you."

Her voice softened. "I know. But I'm not a kid anymore, and you can't plant yourself in the way of anything that might hurt me like you used to. I'm more than ready to take on Cynthia."

What Gigi wanted, Gigi generally got through hard work and sheer bloody-mindedness. Ben breathed out his instinctive urge to argue and reframed his thoughts. Gigi was running for mayor. All right. "How can I help?" he asked.

"I knew you'd come around." He could hear the smile in her voice. "I was thinking that with your business savvy and community connections, you'd be great at helping me arrange campaign events. What do you say?"

Ben considered the demands of running the Emporium, the upcoming opening of the adjacent café, the unfinished hat and scarves and baby blanket, the vampire succubus in his house, his current state of chronic exhaustion, and the limited number of hours in the day. Then he considered Gigi and how far he would go to make sure the people he loved were happy and fulfilled.

Ben sighed. "Count me in."

◆ ◆ ◆

"I'M BACK," BEN CALLED OUT AS HE OPENED THE FRONT DOOR. He didn't want to startle Eleonore if she was resting. She clearly had no issue with daylight, since she'd stood in a fall of sunshine in his kitchen after sucking his finger—and no, that was *not* a memory he needed to revisit—but he didn't know if her sleeping schedule was affected by her vampiric half.

A gust of wind whipped past him, ruffling his hair. He looked over his shoulder, but the trees in his front yard were still. Odd, but Washington weather could turn on a dime, so he shrugged and turned back around to head inside.

Eleonore was standing directly in front of him.

Ben yelped and staggered back, clipping his shoulder on the doorframe. "Do you have to do that?" he asked, clutching his chest with his free hand.

Eleonore ignored the question, eyes fixed on the take-out bag. Her hair was tangled, and her skin was sheened with a light layer of sweat that made her look like she was glowing. "A positive," she said, nostrils flaring. "And O negative. And . . ." Her nose wrinkled. "Something else."

"A medley of blood types." Ben hefted the paper bag, which contained three plastic packets of blood. "I wasn't sure what you'd like."

NecroNomNomNoms ethically sourced their blood from paid donors, and their meat menu had a roadkill section for guilty eaters. Ben rarely ate there, but he appreciated the thoughtfulness.

Eleonore's hand darted out, though she stopped an inch away from the paper bag. Her eyes raised to his, silently asking a question.

Ben nodded. "Go ahead," he said. "It's all for you."

The bag was instantly ripped out of his hand, and in the space of a blink, Eleonore was seated with her fangs plugged into a plastic bag of O negative. Ben cringed at the thought of blood spattering over his couch, but she was a tidy eater, and soon the bag was drained.

Eleonore dabbed at her lips, which were a shade of red only marginally lighter than the blood. "Who did this come from?" she asked, looking surprised.

Ben eased closer, settling onto the opposite end of the couch.

He still wasn't sure if the wrong word or movement would set her off, resulting in the abrupt removal of his jugular. "I don't know specifically," he said. "The restaurant uses a pool of donors."

"Hmmm." Her tongue darted out, lapping up the sole drop of blood that had escaped to bead at the corner of her lips. "This donor was happy."

It was Ben's turn to be surprised. "You can tell that?"

Eleonore nodded, raising the bag of A positive to her nose to sniff. "Emotion affects the flavor of blood. Anger gives a bitter spice, and grief makes my tongue tingle in a way I don't like. Happy or aroused blood is best. For me, at least. Other vampires might disagree."

He thought of how she'd sucked on his finger in the kitchen and repressed a shiver. "What did mine taste like?" he dared to ask.

Her eyes fixed on him, deep wells he thought it would be easy to fall into. "You were afraid," she said, "but you were also aroused." She shrugged one shoulder. "Though I could sense that without the blood, of course."

Ben's cheeks heated. She was so blunt about things most people would be too polite to mention. "Sorry," he said.

She cocked her head, and a lock of red hair slid over her shoulder. "Why?"

"I—" What was he supposed to say? *Sorry for being aroused and scared? Sorry you could taste it?* "I'm just generally sorry, all right?"

That seemed to flummox her. She hadn't looked away from him during the conversation, but her brow furrowed, and her stare had gained the intensity of a scientist inspecting something under a microscope. "You apologize a lot," she said.

He let out a strained laugh. "Do I?"

"No one apologizes to me," she said matter-of-factly. Then she bit into the bag of A positive and started sucking.

Ben watched, fascinated. Her throat rippled with each swallow, and a flush gradually washed over her alabaster skin. He felt the bizarre urge to follow that blush with his fingers, feel her skin heat as she took sustenance. When she was done, she no longer looked like a marble statue but a living, breathing woman with pinkened cheeks and an aura of healthy vitality. Just as beautiful, but realer. More touchable.

Not that he was going to touch her, of course, no matter what his addled instincts were telling him. It would be like sticking his hand in a lion's cage and hoping the lion was feeling friendly.

Eleonore sighed and sank back against the couch cushion, eyes growing heavy-lidded. "I normally wouldn't need to feed so much," she said. "It's been a while."

Because she'd been trapped inside a plastic rock for Lycaon knew how many years. "What's it like?" Ben asked hesitantly. "Being inside the fake crystal."

Tension stole over her face as her lips turned down, and Ben instantly regretted the question. He had a werewolf's curiosity— the *sniffing* he did at the full moon, good Lord—but she was clearly dealing with some trauma.

"You don't have to tell me," he said. "I was just curious."

Her head lolled on the couch, and she looked at him directly again. "It is misery," she said. "Not because there is much pain, but because it is . . ." She trailed off, gaze growing distant. "Hazy," she finally said. "Like being in a fog, and you do not know how long it has been or where the fog ends. The hunger is there always, like a dull ache that never gets better or worse. There's no time, no beginning or end, only what dreams and memories choose to visit." There was another pause. "And the hate, of course. Like the hunger, that never goes away."

Ben swallowed. It sounded like a horrifying existence. "Hate for what?" he asked.

"You," Eleonore said bluntly, and Ben flinched. "Or what you represent. *Her*, I suppose it would be better to say. The one who imprisoned me six centuries past."

Ben shifted on the couch, drawing a leg up to face her more fully. "Who was she?"

Eleonore laughed bitterly. "I do not know. She never gave me any name but the Witch in the Woods. I never saw her face, not even during *Star Trek*."

Ben blinked. "Did you say *Star Trek*?"

"The only good thing she did for me," Eleonore said. "The witch liked to be entertained sometimes, and your technology brought a welcome reprieve from having to read her poetry or hunt her enemies for sport."

This was enough to make his head spin. "I can't imagine."

"You should try," Eleonore said with sudden venom. "Perhaps then you would reconsider my eternal servitude."

Ben's heart rate kicked up to a higher pace at the murder in her eyes. "I don't want your eternal servitude," he said. "How do I set you free?"

"She did not tell you?" Eleonore asked. "When she sold me?"

"I've never even met her. I don't know who she is or where she is or anything. I just got a package on my doorstep."

Eleonore spat out a harsh word that was definitely some sort of curse. "Useless."

"Hey," Ben protested. "I brought you blood."

Eleonore paused. "True," she finally said.

Considering the circumstances, that was likely as close to a peace offering as he'd get. He lifted his chin toward the remaining pouch of blood on the table. "Do you want to drink that one?"

Eleonore yawned. "Later," she said, eyes drifting closed. "You can put it in the root cellar."

Moments later she was asleep, chest rising and falling evenly.

Ben dithered internally for a few moments. He had a napping vampire succubus on his couch and a bag of blood he didn't want to go stale. He also didn't have a root cellar, but he suspected a refrigerator might be the better option anyway.

After putting the bag in the fridge he returned to the living room, where Eleonore was still curled up in a corner of the couch. Ben hesitated, then grabbed a blanket from the armchair and draped it over her sleeping form.

Then he headed to his office to start researching mayoral campaigns.

SIX

ELEONORE WOKE ALL AT ONCE, AS WAS USUAL FOR HER. Whether the practice was due to years of paranoia or her vampire heritage—full-bred vampires didn't wake so much as turn on, like plugging in an electric lamp—she couldn't say. She was on her feet in an instant, scanning the room for threats.

Green walls, brown furniture, a window with drawn curtains that let a sliver of daylight through. The light was the golden hue of late afternoon where it slanted across the floor.

No annoyingly attractive werewolf in sight.

She frowned at the blanket that had slid from her shoulders to pool on the floor. Where had that come from? She remembered drinking blood, then a sudden, overwhelming wave of tiredness, but no blanket. Warily, she picked it up, then brought it to her nose to sniff.

Hot chocolate, campfire smoke, a hint of wildflowers. A comforting, warm sort of smell, almost as if it had been designed to put the smeller at ease—although since she'd tasted the echo of it in the werewolf's aroused blood, that wasn't the only thing Eleonore felt sniffing it. Her lower belly tightened, and she breathed more deeply. This was Ben's natural scent, condensed in the fabric as if he had curled up under this blanket many times before.

Why had Ben placed the blanket on her? It wasn't as if she had been cold. Drinking blood always left a pleasant flush across her skin, and his house was cool but comfortable.

Perhaps he had wrapped her in the blanket to inhibit her movements in case of an attack. It was a reasonable strategy—she'd employed it with lovers in the past. There was nothing quite like an early morning beheading attempt to put a damper on an assignation.

But the werewolf wasn't her lover, and she couldn't hurt him anyway, due to the parameters of the curse. So had he just wanted to make sure she was . . . comfortable?

Eleonore rubbed her chest over where her heart beat, troubled by the thought. It was a mortal heart, a succubus's heart. It tapped her time on Earth away beat by beat—or at least it would have, had she not been kept in suspended animation for the vast majority of her long, long life. She'd been chained by the Witch in the Woods at the age of thirty. She hadn't kept track of how much she'd aged during the times she'd been allowed out of her prison, but it couldn't have been more than five years, cumulatively.

A noise caught her attention, and she turned to see Ben poking his head around the corner. "Oh, you're awake," he said, running a hand through his thick brown hair.

Feeling oddly flustered, Eleonore gestured at herself. "Obviously."

He winced, and Eleonore felt a prick of guilt at having snapped at him for the crime of nothing more heinous than putting a blanket on her while she was asleep.

"It is a nice blanket," she said in an effort at atonement, holding it out to show him.

"I'm glad you think so," he said. "It's my favorite."

They eyed each other, two wary creatures calculating potential danger.

"Do you want dinner?" Ben asked, shoving his hands into the pockets of his jeans. "Not blood—or I guess blood if you need more—but . . . food?"

Eleonore consulted her body. She'd eaten the sandwich for lunch and then a few bags of blood, so she wasn't starving, but yes, there was a slight hollowness in her stomach that indicated a meal would be welcome in the future. "I could eat in an hour or two," she said cautiously.

"I was thinking . . ." Ben gestured at the door. "Outside somewhere? Assuming you don't mind that it's still bright."

Outside was promising. Outside meant getting to examine her surroundings again, this time in the werewolf's company so she could examine his response to the environment as well. The more information she collected about her circumstances, the better she'd be able to hopefully shape the future to her will—as much as she was able to while bound by the curse.

"I don't mind sun," she said. The perks of being only half vampire. "Outside would be nice."

Ben smiled then, and it was nearly as startling as—well, everything else that had happened that day. He looked pleased and shy as he scratched his cheek, fingernails rasping lightly over his beard. Her not-fully-sated succubus hunger whispered that it would be nice to run her own fingernails through that beard before getting her mouth on his smile, but she ignored it. "I need a few minutes to get ready," he said, "but then let's go introduce you to Glimmer Falls."

◆　◆　◆

BEN TOOK HER TO A RESTAURANT IN THE DOWNTOWN AREA, A few blocks away from where she'd tailed him earlier. He told her the history of the town as he drove, and Eleonore absorbed the information eagerly.

Glimmer Falls had been founded in 1842 by Casper Cunning-ton and Galahad Spark, two wizards from prominent families who had been drawn to the area for the magic woven into the soil. There was a vast grid of ley lines beneath the town and extending into the forest and hills beyond, and as a result, supernatural crea-tures of all kinds congregated here.

Eleonore couldn't sense the magic, but she did see a wide variety of people walking, flying, or cantering around. Centaurs, griffins, naiads, witches, dryads . . . Add to that a collection of nonmagical humans and an array of animals both mystical and not, and the town thrummed with life.

The restaurant, Brittany's, had a large outdoor terrace, and when Ben asked if she'd prefer to sit inside or outside, Eleonore tipped her face up to the sunshine and decided on a resolute *outside*. It was late enough in the day that hopefully her pale skin wouldn't sunburn. And even if it did, who cared? She'd been stuck in that plastic insult of a crystal for far too long, and even on occa-sions when the witch had let her out over the fifty or so years since her mission in 1969, they'd spent the time watching television or engaged in other indoor activities like bridge, poetry reading, or an odd game called Jenga.

She shifted in her wrought iron chair, looking around curi-ously. The restaurant was decorated in shades of blue with wooden floorboards, and gauzy white draperies fluttered overhead, creat-ing a makeshift roof. The theme appeared to be oceanic, with art depicting mermaids and sirens and pieces of beach glass embed-ded in the walls. Lights were strung overhead amid the fabric, twinkling like golden stars.

The clientele leaned toward the younger side, although Ele-onore being over six hundred years old in the body of a roughly thirty-five-year-old meant she couldn't make such assumptions. They chattered and laughed, drinking glasses of wine or strangely colored liquids that gleamed in the late afternoon light.

A serving wench stopped at the table to deliver menus and take drink orders. Ben ordered the house red wine, and Eleonore requested a tankard of ale.

She could not have guessed the complications that would come from such a simple request. What sort of ale? Light or dark? Malty? Hoppy? There was a fresh-hopped brew from the next town over as well as a hazy IPA, a cold IPA, a wheat beer, a stout, an ESB, a sour . . .

It was enough to make a vampire succubus want to flip over the table and launch into a rant about the "good old days" when things weren't so complicated and there was only one ale on tap, but the good old days had also involved more body odor and a distressing lack of indoor plumbing, so she bit down her protests and chose a beer at random.

"You like IPAs?" Ben asked as the wench hurried away.

"We'll find out," Eleonore muttered.

She hadn't dined in a large venue like this since long ago, when she'd taken her suppers in the great hall with her parents and her father's vassals. The scene was easy to imagine: torchlight flickering against stone, the scent of roasting meat for the mortals and blood for the vampires, smoke heavy on the air, voices raised in raucous celebration of their latest triumph in battle. If Eleonore had called for ale, her mother would have grimaced and suggested she choose wine instead, and her father would have complained that he didn't see the point of drinking anything that didn't have a heartbeat. Her parents would have gotten into a playful argument over it, the vampire lord with his beloved succubus bride, and Eleonore would have watched as she had many times before, a smile on her lips as she took advantage of their distraction to feed morsels of her dinner to the hounds pacing the rush-strewn floor.

It was vivid enough to bring up an old, familiar ache in her breast, though the sting had grown less acute with time. Eleonore had raged and grieved in those early centuries, which had been lived in bursts of brief violence between long sleeps, but her grief had gradually been worn down like a rock beneath a waterfall, its contours no longer sharp enough to cut.

Her hatred for the witch who had snatched her from her family, though, would never fade.

The ale arrived in a cold glass, looking paler than she'd expected. Eleonore raised it to her lips and took a sip—then promptly spat it back out.

"Mon Dieu," she said, staring at the drink in horror. "That's disgusting."

"What's wrong?" Ben asked, head popping up from where he'd been studying the menu. His spectacles were slightly crooked, and he nudged them back into place.

"It tastes like shit."

His thick eyebrows rose. "May I?" he asked, gesturing at the pint.

"If you wish to suffer, don't let me stop you."

He sipped, then set it down, looking confused. "It tastes fine to me."

Was the werewolf a masochist? Filing the possibility away in her mental encyclopedia entry, Eleonore mustered her courage and sipped again, this time managing to swallow despite her urge to spew the horrid brew all over the table. It was bitter, with an aftertaste that made her think of evergreen forests. "This cannot be ale," she said. "It's like being punched in the teeth by a pine tree."

Ben chuckled, a pleasing rumble rising from that broad chest. "Those are the hops."

He proceeded to explain IPAs and the craft beer scene to her, as well as some particulars of the brewing process. Eleonore listened, intrigued by his casual expertise. He'd changed into dress pants and a blue shirt, as well as a knitted one-piece vest that strained to contain his barrel chest. Quite restrained-looking, except he'd rolled up the sleeves of his shirt to reveal muscled forearms covered with hair.

"Very informative," Eleonore said, pulling her gaze away from those impressive forearms. It was important to assess the physical capabilities of one's enemies but equally important to stay on the correct side of the assessing/leering line. "Though I fail to see why modern people want to drink such a foul concoction."

He laughed again. "It grows on you." He raised his glass. "Though I still prefer wine."

Eleonore stared at the IPA, her newest enemy, calculating how many sips she'd need to finish it. Too many, but she was no coward and refused to admit defeat to a pint glass, so she raised the beer again. "Santé," she said, then drank deeply, repressing a shudder.

He echoed the toast and sipped his red wine. "Is that French?"

"Yes." "Santé" was the informal version of "À votre santé"—to your health. She'd said it out of habit, not because she actually wished him good health, but oh well.

"How many languages do you speak?"

Eleonore squinted, considering. "Six. Though French and English are my best."

He raised his brows, looking impressed. "Wow."

"Languages are a vampire strength," she said. "We learn them quickly and easily adapt to new accents and terminology." The only reason she didn't know more than six was because she'd been spending most of her conscious time with the English-speaking witch. The witch hadn't been the most modern of speakers, being effectively immortal so long as she stole mortal lives, but if Eleonore spent sustained time around this century's people, she'd begin to sound like them instead.

"Interesting," Ben said. "Why?"

"Because we're a predator species," Eleonore explained. "It's the same reason our bites feel good. I'm not immortal—technically, anyway—but purebred vampires are, so they need to constantly blend into new times and places. Knowing the local language makes potential prey more comfortable."

His eye twitched. "You think about other people as potential prey?"

"Only our enemies or the ones who smell nice." Like him. She nodded toward his glass. "How is your wine?"

He sipped, then made a rueful face. "I would say it's excellent, but that would be a lie."

"And you don't wish to lie?"

"I try not to as a general principle, though we all have our moments of weakness."

"Interesting," she said, parroting him. She sipped the devil IPA again, eyeing him. The werewolf was a puzzle she hadn't yet figured out the technique of solving.

He focused his attention on redoing the crisp fold of one of his rolled-up cuffs. Her vision narrowed in on his exposed forearm and the brown hair topping those eye-catching muscles. A vein flickered under the skin, and she licked one fang, imagining how his muscles would flex as she pierced him. Wondering what his noises of pleasure would sound like.

"Why is that interesting?" Ben asked, seemingly oblivious to her hungry regard.

She dragged her attention away from his muscles again. If someone on this patio would just masturbate to completion, that would be most helpful—surely then she would be sated enough to ignore his carnal appeal. "It's rare to hear lying described as a weakness," she said. "Most people I've known considered it a skill. Or a good strategy to disconcert your enemies."

"Do you think it's a skill?" he asked, gaze flicking up to hers.

The blunt question took her aback. She considered briefly, then gave an honest answer. "Yes, though I'd rather tell someone when I'm planning on ripping their throat out and deal with the issue directly than lure them in with falsehoods."

His chuckle was strained. "You sure talk a lot about ripping out throats and eating livers."

Eleonore leaned back in her chair, holding the beer close. Each sip was easier than the last, and now that she'd gotten over the shock of the flavor, she could appreciate that it tasted significantly more alcoholic than the ale of her youth. "It's been my main occupation for centuries," she said. "Murder, that is. I can't say I've actually eaten anyone's liver."

"Well that's a comfort," Ben said. "At least one of my organs is safe from danger."

She cocked a brow and glanced meaningfully toward his lap, thinking about which organ was in most danger at the moment.

Apparently realizing what he'd said, Ben looked mortified. "Internal organs, I mean." He grimaced. "You know what? Never mind."

Eleonore smiled despite herself. "So if the wine is bad, why don't you order a nicer one?" she asked, taking mercy on him.

Ben seemed relieved to abandon the topic of his manly organ. "Habit, I suppose." He raised the glass to the light, turning the stem to study the shifting liquid. "I started my own business a decade ago, and it was rough going for years. Even though we're in the black now, it's hard to break the habit of buying the cheapest thing on the menu. It took me ages to even be willing to buy alcohol with dinner."

"In the black?" she asked, unfamiliar with the phrase.

"Profitable. In the red would be the opposite."

Eleonore filed that away. "What is your business?"

His shoulders went back with obvious pride. "I own a plant nursery and garden shop."

That was unexpected. She considered the possibility he was joking, but his face had lit up while saying the words, and he had an aura of sincerity. A bundle of contradictions, this werewolf. His body nearly burst the seams of his clothing, but he put on a great show of harmlessness.

"Tell me about it," she said.

Ben told her about his lifelong love of gardening, his first job in a plant nursery as a teenager, and how he'd decided to open a shop in his hometown. He described the plants he grew, his favorite customers, and his employees—a naiad and a witch, both equally passionate about nature. He was currently expanding the store into the neighboring space and opening a coffee shop with the goal of eventually turning Ben's Plant Emporium into a neighborhood landmark and gathering space.

Eleonore listened, gathering facts and impressions to add to her mental picture of Ben. He was passionate about his business; any reticence or bashfulness melted away while he was describing it. His large hands danced lightly in the air, illustrating the layout, and his eyes were bright with excitement.

He loved the shop, that much was clear, which meant he absolutely should not have told Eleonore about it. The problem with loving things was how easily love could be turned into a weapon. Did he have no sense of self-preservation?

It was potential ammunition, though, so she collected every detail uttered in his rumbling voice. She couldn't harm him physically so long as the binding spell was in place, but part of his heart was in that building, and she could do severe damage to it should he earn her vengeance.

Which he would, most likely. No matter how earnest he seemed now, he had total control over Eleonore's existence. It would be a rare person to resist using that sort of power.

Gods, she was tired. Not just physically, but mentally and emotionally. As she looked at Ben's smile, his strong hands, she felt an ache in her chest. What would it take to find the one person whose expressions she could trust? The one person who would never harm her? Her parents' bond should have been impossible—a mortal and an immortal, falling in love across species lines—but it hadn't been. They had treated each other's hearts gently.

Eleonore had no trouble acquiring sex, but love was a rarer beast. Would she ever be able to look at a person and think: *I am safe with you?*

Not in this life, at least not as she'd known it thus far.

Ben's tale concluded when the serving wench arrived again to take their food orders. Ben apologized and asked her to return once they'd had a chance to study the menu. "I got too excited talking," he said with a self-deprecating smile, and the wench laughed and twirled a lock of hair around her finger.

Eleonore narrowed her eyes at the woman's blatant act of flirtation. She might take more after her father, but she was her mother's child as well, and she recognized an adversary.

Not that she wanted to genuinely flirt with Ben, of course. One didn't drool over one's jailer, no matter how handsome or nice-smelling—at least not unless one was hungry. But she wanted his attention for strategic purposes. Thankfully, Eleonore's narrow-eyed glare was enough to make the wench gulp and scurry away, no baring of fangs required.

Pleased with that victory, Eleonore studied the menu. She didn't recognize half the things on it, but she did understand the concept of a steak and how to eat one, although the price was alarming. She really needed to educate herself about modern currency values. She looked around and saw other patrons using their PADDs—or phones, if Ben was to be believed—at the table, fingers darting over the screens. Perhaps she could steal one and inquire about the cost of beef.

"This is a pretty place," she said, facing Ben again.

Had his gaze been on her mouth? "It's new," he said, eyes flitting back to hers. "I came here with my sister a month ago for the grand opening."

"You have a sister?" Another piece of information to file away.

He nodded. "Gigi. She's a menace."

He said it fondly, though, so Eleonore suspected he had a different idea of what constituted a menace than she did. "Older or younger?"

"Younger. She's thirty-three, and I'm—" He paused, forehead wrinkling. "Thirty-eight."

"You had to think about it?"

He tugged at his collar, looking embarrassed. "Somewhere in my early thirties it all started running together."

Eleonore laughed before she thought better of it. It was a harsh laugh, propelled by bitterness. "I wonder when my years started running together."

Ben winced, but to his credit, he laced his fingers on the table and leaned in, fixing her with a direct look rather than retreating from the lash of her tongue. "Do you want to talk about it?"

Did she? She wasn't sure. But no one had ever asked before either. And something in his brown eyes made her want to share.

"The Witch in the Woods found me when I was thirty years of age," she said. She remembered the night clearly—cold and brutal, with the stars laid out like a shining belt across the sky. Blood flushing her skin, the thrill of battle filling her heart as she sprinted through the woods in pursuit of her prey. "We were battling the vampire clan that assassinated my father."

He made a soft noise. "I'm so sorry to hear that."

Eleonore shrugged one shoulder, ill at ease. Then she remembered the ale near her hand and took a gulp instead. The pine tree burn fit well with the memory of that snow-clad forest. "It was a long time ago. The vampire clans were always at war then. Maybe they still are today; I don't know."

"I don't think so, but we don't hear a lot about vampires these days," Ben said. "They keep their affairs private."

Nothing new in that. "Vampires are very territorial. When I was young, there was a lot of conflict over access to mines or trade routes. It wasn't unusual to have a parent or friend die." Her father had even prepared her for it, telling her bedtime stories of vampires who had died fighting and instructing her in the best ways to sever an enemy's head—for that was the only way to kill an immortal. When her father had been killed, his entire clan—including her succubus mother, who normally stayed safe in the keep during wartime—had honored him by taking up arms. "We retaliated, of course. That night, my steel sang in the winter air. I took head after head in my father's name. I just didn't know a witch was watching."

The witch had approached during a lull in battle, looking like a death goddess in her dark cloak. She'd complimented Eleonore's ferocity, then offered her what she wanted most: vengeance. All Eleonore had to do was cut her palm to mirror the witch's self-induced injury, clasp hands while the witch chanted, and wait for the power the spell would give her.

Eleonore had been young and foolish then, influenced by tales of bloodthirsty goddesses and warriors raised to places of honor after falling in glorious battle. Impulsive at the best of times, she became even more reckless while drunk on bloodlust and adrenaline, and she hadn't questioned what the witch would gain in exchange. She'd also failed to ask *whose* vengeance the spell would facilitate.

Vengeance had indeed been delivered at the tip of Eleonore's sword—but it was the witch's enemies who had died. Eleonore had become naught but an instrument to be used.

The serving wench appeared abruptly, making Eleonore flinch and reach for the knife concealed in her boot, since Ben had indicated earlier that thigh holsters might not be welcome in public. She stopped herself just before drawing the blade.

"Are you ready to order?" the wench chirped cheerfully. "Or can I get you started with some appetizers?"

"We're ready to order, but an appetizer might be nice, too.

Maybe some garlic bread?" Then Ben looked at Eleonore with a grimace. "Shoot, can you eat that? I should have asked first."

It took her a moment to realize his concern, and she let out a soft breath of amusement. "Yes, I can eat garlic. Just as werewolves aren't actually allergic to silver."

The myth that garlic repelled vampires was a funny one. Purebred or turned vampires drank only blood, so they wouldn't be able to eat garlic anyway. The worst it could do was deliver an unpleasant stench in a vampire's general vicinity or a spice to the blood, and even that depended on personal preference. Some vampires liked the taste of mortals who ate garlic.

They placed their food orders, and Eleonore realized that somehow over the course of their discussion she'd drained the entire glass of IPA. Her mouth tingled and there was a bitter aftertaste resting on her tongue, but Ben was right—the flavor had grown on her, and it imparted a pleasant haze to her surroundings.

"Wait," Eleonore said as the server started to back away. She raised the empty glass, then dashed it against the floor. "Another ale, wench!"

The girl jumped and nearly fell into a neighboring table. Conversation on the terrace stopped at the sound of breaking glass, and the other customers stared at her with jaws agape. Ben's hand was pressed to his mouth, and he was cringing with what seemed to be his entire body.

Apparently she had done something out of the ordinary. Eleonore leaned across the table, lowering her voice. "Is that no longer the custom?" She had not dined outside of private assignations since being taken from her father's keep.

"Ah, no," Ben said. "I was unaware it ever was." He knelt to scoop up shattered glass. "I'm so sorry," he told the shocked-looking server. "She'll have another IPA, please. Sorry. Thank you. I'm so, so sorry."

The girl nodded and fled as another worker hurried over with a broom and badgered Ben back into his chair. Eleonore's cheeks felt hot as the man cleaned up the mess she'd made, and she squirmed, disliking the feeling of being gawked at as much as she disliked the feeling of being apologized for. Ben was averaging one *sorry* every five seconds.

Thankfully, he stopped apologizing after the worker left with his bucketful of glass. Ben laced his fingers together in front of him on the table, adopting a professorial look. The Ben Explains Things expression, which she already recognized after only a few hours, due to the fact he'd had to explain rather a lot.

"So rule number one of modern dining is not to deliberately break any dishes," Ben said.

"In my father's hall it was done as a sign of appreciation," Eleonore said, face flaming hotter. "Though our mugs were made of metal or wood, so they didn't, ah, shatter like that." In retrospect, she probably could have determined it was a bad idea if she'd paused to think for a single second, but thinking things through in advance had never been her strongest skill.

"You're doing your best," Ben said. He looked like he was biting the inside of one cheek, though. Was he secretly laughing at her?

Eleonore crossed her arms and sat back with a huff. "What is rule number two of modern dining?"

"Well, you probably shouldn't call our server a wench."

Yes, he was secretly laughing, although clearly trying to restrain it. Eleonore's battered dignity appreciated the effort.

"Server is short for *serving wench*, isn't it?" she asked.

"I . . ." He coughed into his fist. "No, I don't think it is."

Christ's fingernails, this was annoying. She scraped the toe of her boot against the floor, trying to pretend she didn't notice all the people looking at her and whispering. "What should I call her, then?"

"*Waitress* would work. Or *Miss* or *Ms.*, maybe. Or you could ask her name."

"Any other rules for modern dining?"

Ben's lips quirked. "I hope it goes without saying that disemboweling people at the dinner table is frowned upon."

She gave a half-hearted hiss at that. "Very funny."

At the sound, the table nearest her abruptly returned their attention to their own plates.

"The best practice is to enjoy your meal and try not to do anything . . . destructive," Ben said.

Easier said than done. The world was full of breakable things.

A second IPA was set down gingerly at her elbow. Seeing how nervous the wench—the *server*—looked, Eleonore bit down her bruised pride and attempted to make amends. "I apologize," she said. "I regret throwing the glass."

The server's doe-brown eyes met Eleonore's. "Not the weirdest thing to happen here," she said. "We do live in Glimmer Falls, after all. And . . . are you an immortal, by any chance?"

What an odd question. "In a way," Eleonore said. "I was imprisoned in a crystal six centuries past—"

"Right," the waitress said, nodding. "Immortal. Totally get it." She was smiling again, for whatever reason. "Never a dull moment when one of you is around."

She moved away, leaving Eleonore confused. "Why did she ask me that?" she asked Ben.

He shrugged. "No idea."

Well, at least Eleonore's faux pas had apparently been forgiven. The mention of Glimmer Falls intrigued her, so she pushed Ben for more details about the "weird" things that happened in town. He warmed to the topic quickly, and by the time their meal arrived, Eleonore had learned about everything from public nudity to midnight blood orgies to tentacle wrestling. Compared to the time Diantha Spark had teleported a colony of raccoons into a town hall meeting or the time the Human-Centaur Polo League had consumed a few too many prematch drinks and ended up galloping through the library, one vampire succubus throwing a glass on the floor didn't seem so bad after all.

The steak arrived, thick and so succulent-looking her mouth watered. Eleonore grabbed her knife and stabbed the chunk of meat, lifting it to her mouth.

"God's tits!" she declared around the mouthful of meat. "This was seasoned well."

A man and woman at the nearest table looked at her oddly, then nudged their chairs farther away. She was going to question why when she saw the dogs seated at their feet. They weren't as lean or muscled as the hounds from her father's hall—weren't lean or muscled in the slightest, in fact—but perhaps they had been bred for a special purpose. They had curling gray-brown hair and sweet eyes and were small enough to hold in a lap, although two at once might overflow.

"What kind of hounds are those?" she asked Ben, pointing at them.

He was cringing again for some reason. "Schnoodles, I believe," he said, looking between her and the animals. "So, uh, in modern day we generally eat with a fork . . ."

Eleonore was familiar with forks, but what was the point? There was no need to slice a steak into tiny pieces when teeth would do the job. She ate another bite of succulent meat off the tip of her knife. It was good of the restaurant to provide one—during the medieval era, guests had carried their own knives to the table.

It did seem she was the only person eating in this manner, though, and perhaps it would benefit her to blend in. So she put the steak down, speared it with a fork, and commenced trying to pry the meat apart.

Ben sat frozen with his own carefully sectioned bite halfway to his mouth, watching her attempts. She managed to rip a piece off, though it flew off the table. The hounds swarmed it immediately. These so-called schnoodles might have an undignified name, but they had retained their predatory instincts.

"Rupert! Wesley! No!" the neighboring diner said, tugging on the dogs' leads. The pups ignored him, as well they should. Eleonore smiled, already planning to drop another piece of meat on the floor. Feeding the hounds had always been a particular delight of hers.

She finally managed to wrestle the steak into submission with her fork and knife. *What a waste of time to eat in this way*, she thought as she chewed a bite. They'd already consumed the garlic bread, so there was nothing to sop up the drippings—how was she supposed to clean her plate with a fork?

Food had never been wasted in her father's hall. Though these hounds would be pleased to polish the plate with their tongues, their owner might stop them, and Eleonore had always liked drippings anyway. She shoved her chair back, preparing to stand so she could inquire after more bread.

The chair collided with something. "Ow!" a man said. "Watch it, lady!" A heavy hand landed on her shoulder.

Sudden touches were never good for a lifelong assassin.

Eleonore was on her feet in an instant, knocking the man's hand away before she jammed her forearm into his throat and pinned him against the wall. Her heart raced as hot rage blazed through her, narrowing her field of vision until all she could see was the man's flushed, terrified face. She could almost hear the witch's voice in her head.

Kill the enemy. Kill him.

"Touch me and die," she said, baring her fangs.

And people began screaming.

SEVEN

Ben's fork was halfway to his mouth when Eleonore abruptly disappeared out of her chair. An instant later, she reappeared, pinning the man who'd grabbed her shoulder to the wall. Her mouth was wide open, displaying shiny white fangs.

"A vampire!" someone cried out. "A daywalking vampire!"

The other patrons began screaming.

Ben dropped the fork, stomach plunging and pulse spiking. "Eleonore—"

"No one touches me without permission," she told the man in a deadly voice. "I should rip out your throat." To punctuate the threat, she snapped her fangs inches from his face.

The man had gone from cocky to terrified in an instant, and a wet patch appeared on the front of his jeans. "Jesus, lady, I didn't mean anything by it."

The hysteria was spreading as people babbled about vampires. Multiple patrons had gotten their phones out and were documenting the scene. Ben needed to do crisis management, and fast.

He stood, nearly knocking the table over. His body was too big for this damned furniture. He hurried toward Eleonore, holding his hands out placatingly. "Please let him go, Eleonore."

Her head whipped around and she pinned him with a hard stare. "Are you ordering or asking?"

"Asking," he said, hoping a softer touch would calm her. "He definitely shouldn't have touched you without permission, but you can't murder him in the middle of the restaurant."

"I absolutely can," she said. The man whimpered, and she grabbed his hair to jerk his head to the side. Even Ben could see the frantic flutter of the man's pulse in his exposed neck. "See?" she asked, fangs hovering over his jugular. "It would be so easy."

A cacophony of voices filled the air.

"I've never seen a vampire before."

"Is she going to kill him?"

"If she does, I'm recording for GhoulTube!"

This needed to stop for everyone's sake. Ben took a deep breath and edged closer. He didn't dare touch Eleonore's shoulder to try to pry her off the man—he liked having his windpipe *inside* his body, thank you very much—but he had a responsibility to fix this situation, since he was the one who'd ultimately caused it by bringing her here. It was time for a more direct approach.

"Eleonore," Ben said with all the firmness he could muster. "Let him go."

She released the man instantly, though she snapped her teeth one last time. Then she turned on Ben, rage burning in her eyes. "I thought you were asking, not ordering."

He looked over his shoulder at the people watching avidly and scowled. "Stop rubbernecking," he told them. Then he shifted to put as much of his body between her and the room as possible. "I'm sorry," he said, lowering his voice. "I know he frightened you."

Eleonore stiffened. Her mouth opened, then closed again. The blind fury receded, replaced by a look of consternation. "I wasn't afraid," she finally said. "I'm not afraid of anything."

There was something haunted in her green eyes now, though, a shadow he recognized. Maybe she wasn't truly afraid, but she had been triggered by the sudden touch. A tremor raced over her arm and settled in her right hand, which twitched at her side.

Compassion joined the chaotic stew of Ben's emotions. "I know," he said softly. "You thought there was a threat and you reacted accordingly. How about we get you home, away from all these people?"

She blinked, looking like she'd just remembered there were other people on the patio, then leaned to look around him. He heard her soft inhale. "They're all staring."

"Let's get you out of here." Ben fished in his pocket for his wallet, then threw a clump of bills on the table—way more than the meal cost, but hopefully enough to convey his apology. He reached for Eleonore, then hesitated. "May I?" he asked.

She looked at his fingers for a moment, then nodded.

Ben gently took hold of her upper arm and brought her close. He steered her out of the restaurant, angling his body as best he could to shield her from curious eyes. His own cheeks burned with embarrassment—as a rule, he tried not to involve himself in anything that might qualify as a "scene"—but he was more worried about Eleonore.

That had looked an awful lot like a PTSD reaction. And if she'd truly been trapped for centuries, forced to commit assassinations at the whim of a wicked witch, he couldn't imagine the depth of that trauma or how to even begin tackling it.

◆ ◆ ◆

BEN PACED BACK AND FORTH IN HIS BEDROOM, SMACKING HIS forehead with his palm. Now that they were back at his house and the immediate crisis was over, he was free to freak out properly.

What had he been thinking, taking Eleonore out to dinner in public? He barely knew her, and what he did know should have prepared him for some sort of calamity. She was angry, violent, and traumatized, with no knowledge of the modern day. Of course she'd been overwhelmed.

Eleonore was currently holed up in his spare room with the door shut. The wind had kicked up, whipping past the windows, and Ben twitched at the slightest creak of the house, wondering what Eleonore was doing. Was she shredding his best pillows? Baring her fangs at passersby who spotted her through the window? Sharpening her knives in preparation for gutting him?

Or worse . . . was she sad?

Her eyes had looked so haunted as he'd guided her out of the restaurant, and she hadn't spoken on the drive home. When it came to fight, flight, or freeze, Ben generally fell into the freeze category, but Eleonore's instincts were firmly in the fight camp. Perceiving danger, she'd lashed out. Once the danger was proven inconsequential, she'd probably felt as ashamed as he did after recovering from one of his panic attacks.

His phone buzzed in his back pocket. He pulled it out and grimaced at the sight of Gigi's name on the caller ID. Not that he didn't love Gigi, of course, but he could use a few hours of quiet.

He lifted the phone to his ear. "Hey, Gigi."

"Benjamin Handel Rosewood, what the hell are you doing?"

Her tone was . . . strident. The use of his unfortunate middle name didn't bode well either.

"Ah, come again?" Ben asked.

"It's all over social media. You and some *vampire* tried to murder someone at Brittany's!"

He winced. "Oh. That."

"Yes, that!" She was increasing in volume, and he imagined steam coming out of her ears. "Putting aside the ethics of public execution by vampire, you know I'm running for mayor. My image has to be squeaky-clean."

He sat on the edge of the mattress, rubbing his temples. The rug beneath his bare feet had been hand-tufted by his mother, the colors a spray of springtime over the hardwood floor. He dug his toes into the worn fabric—right foot, left foot, right foot, left foot. "I fail to see what your image has to do with what happened tonight."

"It's a small town, dumbass. Everyone knows we're related." There was a commotion on the other side of the line—the low, familiar voices of his parents saying something unintelligible to Gigi. She sighed and asked, "Who was that vampire, anyway?"

There was no way to explain without looking pathetic, incompetent, or of questionable sanity. "A . . . friend," he said weakly.

That set off a flurry of hushed arguing and another minor commotion before a new voice took over. "That's wonderful!" Ben's mother, Violet Rosewood, said. "How did you meet her?"

He groaned. "It wasn't a date, Mom."

"If you say so, honey. What's her name? What's she like?"

"She tried to kill someone, Mom," Gigi said in the background.

"Oh, hush. All I saw was a woman protecting her personal space."

"By threatening to *rip his throat out*?"

"Your father's said worse after the full moon."

"That's different. Everyone's aggressive on the full moon. She's a *vampire*."

"So? It might be nice to diversify the Rosewood-Levine bloodline. Get a few new species in there to liven up the holidays."

"We are not dating," Ben said loudly to interrupt the argument. "Much less reproducing."

"You've never mentioned a vampire friend before, though," his mother said.

His father's voice sounded in the background. ". . . the café?" was all Ben caught.

"Oh, that would make sense." Violet sounded disappointed. "Is she one of the contractors for the café?"

If it would end this line of interrogation, Ben would agree to just about anything. He loved his parents dearly, but they'd been getting broody about the lack of grandchildren. "Yes," he said, seizing the excuse. "She's, ah, a consultant."

"You need a consultant to serve coffee?" Gigi asked skeptically. "Or are you putting bloodletting on the menu?"

Inspiration struck—a way to explain Eleonore's presence and her . . . dramatic . . . tendencies. "It's for the theatre," Ben said. "You know, that stage I'm putting in? I want to start hosting stand-up comedy, open mic nights, some solo shows. She's a performance artist, very experimental." He wasn't typically a great liar, but this was sounding pretty good, so he forged on. "Tonight's scene was actually supposed to help promote her latest show. Viral advertising through found footage, that sort of thing." He prayed that actually was the sort of thing an experimental performance artist would do to advertise.

There was a long pause. Ben clenched his jaw and fidgeted, hoping they'd buy it.

"You're already booking shows?" Gigi asked. "That's awesome! Weird way to advertise it, but you can workshop that."

Ben exhaled a sigh of relief. "Yeah, I'm meeting with a few people. I thought about adding the stage later, but I think it would be great to celebrate the café opening with the Emporium's first artist-in-residence."

Damn, this was good. He mentally high-fived himself.

"You know, this actually sounds like a great opportunity," Gigi said. "Have you read my manifesto yet?"

Her list of campaign goals and promises was sitting in his inbox, unopened. "Not yet, but again, I think you should probably call it something besides a manifesto."

"It's a little serial killer, huh? Well, part of my platform involves increasing access to the arts for lower-income members of the community."

That sounded like Gigi. She'd always loved music, even if she couldn't carry a tune in a bucket. "Great, we can definitely host a few campaign events at the Emporium, if you like. Get you up on-stage to make some speeches." He heard a noise from the other room—footsteps padding over the floor, then the creak of the door—and stood, preparing to say goodbye to his sister so he could figure out next steps with Eleonore. "Hey, so—"

"It'll be the perfect opportunity to announce my candidacy," Gigi said, barreling on as she often did when excited. "The opening night of the café is going to be a big draw anyway, and after I talk about my campaign promises, people can watch the show."

Eleonore was moving around the apartment. "Uh-huh," Ben said distractedly, the majority of his attention fixated on whatever Eleonore was doing in his living room. It sounded like she was muttering to herself, and there was a metallic sound he hoped didn't involve weaponry.

"It's brilliant, actually," Gigi said. "Proof that my promises aren't just words. I can say I support the arts, but if I'm not actually in person supporting the arts, it doesn't count, right?"

"Right," he said, not having processed a word. That clanking made him think Eleonore was in the kitchen. Did she need more blood? She was talking again, though he couldn't tell what she was saying except that it was one word or phrase repeated over and over with increasing levels of irritation.

"Thank you so much," Gigi gushed. "This will kill two birds with one stone. Explain away the scene tonight while providing a platform for my campaign announcement. Three birds, I guess, because it's extra publicity for the café's opening and the show. I'll make sure there's a crowd!"

"Sounds good—wait, what?" His attention snapped back to the conversation in time to realize what she'd said didn't make sense.

"You're the best, Ben. This is going to be *awesome*." Then Gigi made a startled sound. "Shoot, I'm late for dinner with my fashion adviser. Got to go!"

"Your what?" He was still trying to catch up with whatever conversation she'd been having with him while he was tuning out. A banging noise started emanating from the kitchen.

"When you get the chance, can you email over her name and the title of the show? I'll chat with the team about how best to promote it. Love you, bye!"

Gigi hung up.

Ben stared at the phone in his hand. He considered himself an intelligent person capable of following most conversations, but Gigi was like a tornado when she was on a mission: whipping through life, rearranging everything and everyone as she saw fit, and Lycaon help the storm chasers who tried to keep up.

He ran the conversation back through his mind to hopefully piece together the missing narrative.

Gigi's platform involved supporting the arts.

She wanted to announce her mayoral campaign.

She also wanted to kill a number of birds with one metaphorical stone.

"Oh, fuck." Ben sank back onto the bed, hand clapped to his mouth as he realized what he had inadvertently agreed to.

Gigi wanted to announce her mayoral campaign and passion for the arts at the official opening of the Emporium's new café and theatre . . . after which her supporters would be treated to a live theatrical performance.

By Eleonore.

EIGHT

"T EA," ELEONORE REPEATED, STARING AT THE REPLICATOR.
"Earl Grey, hot."

The replicator remained silent. No tea appeared.

Frustration simmered in her veins. She'd already tried ordering warm blood, warm milk, and a bottle of whiskey to no avail. At the very least it had to be familiar with tea, right? But no, the infernal box sat smugly on the countertop, refusing to produce a single thing she wanted.

Her chest felt too tight, and her stomach was full of knots. She kept replaying the moment the man had grabbed her arm. "Watch it, lady," he'd said, and she'd felt a wave of such blinding fury she hadn't realized she'd moved until he was pinned to the wall. She'd even temporarily forgotten where she was, living out memories and instincts that ought to have remained buried.

Was she going mad?

Eleonore made a frustrated sound and whacked the top of the replicator with a wooden spoon. It had come from a jar that held an array of kitchen implements arranged like flowers. "Computer, listen to me!"

"Ah . . . why are you hitting my microwave with a spoon?"

She turned to find Ben standing in the entrance to the kitchen, looking perplexed. "Your replicator is broken," she said, feeling foolish and flushed.

He'd changed into pajama pants and a T-shirt, and his feet were bare. His toes scrunched rhythmically against the border between the living room floorboards and the kitchen linoleum: one foot, then the other. "A replicator," he repeated slowly. "Like . . . from *Star Trek*?"

"Yes!" Finally, they were speaking the same language. "I've requested blood, milk, whiskey, and tea, and it refuses to produce a single thing." She glared at the black box. "I think it's mocking me."

Christ's toes, she needed a drink. Something warm or alcoholic enough to loosen the tension in her throat.

Ben looked between her and the replicator. His eyes reminded her of a puppy dog's, a bit wide and lost. "How do you know so much about *Star Trek* but nothing about microwaves?"

She smacked the black box with the spoon again. "Whatever it's called, can you make this work?"

"What are you trying to heat up?" He padded over, shoulders slightly curved. She'd noticed he adopted that posture more often than not. He ought to stand up straight—there was no ignoring his height, even if he did slouch.

"Anything," Eleonore said. "I want to drink something hot or something that will get me drunk." The leftover blood in the refrigerator was cold or she'd have plugged her fangs into it already.

He reached for the handle on the black box and tugged it open, revealing a round glass plate inside. "This is a microwave, not a replicator. It doesn't create anything the way it does in *Star Trek*. It just heats things up."

"Oh." Eleonore looked at the microwave, embarrassed. It seemed she would never stop making herself a fool in front of him. "Can you make it function so I can have hot blood?" She hadn't finished dinner, and her fangs itched with the memory of how close she'd come to killing that man.

What must Ben think of her?

"I have a better idea," he said, closing the microwave.

A few minutes later, the blood from the refrigerator sat in a saucepan on the stovetop. Eleonore watched carefully as Ben fiddled with the dials, explaining this would heat more gradually and evenly than the microwave. She'd seen ovens before, obviously, but this one had perplexed her—there were no metal rings or other visible heating elements, so it was a surprise when concentric orange circles glowed to life on the smooth black surface.

Ben grabbed a flat rectangular packet and unwrapped it before placing it in the microwave. When he pressed a button, the machine whirred to life, noisy and bright through the glass door.

Supposedly that packet contained popcorn. Eleonore watched, fascinated, as the popcorn turned on its glass pedestal. When the first pop of a kernel sounded, she let out a startled laugh. "Marvelous." The witch had always summoned food for the two of them, so she was unfamiliar with technology like this.

"When was the last time you left the witch's cabin again?" Ben asked.

"Nineteen sixty-nine," she said, bending to study the gradually inflating bag. *Pop pop pop* it went, the noise cheering her.

"They had microwaves back then, didn't they?"

She shrugged as she straightened. "Maybe. It was a brief visit. I abducted my target and brought him straight to the witch." Seeing the uncomfortable shift in Ben's expression, she felt the urge to explain herself. "I didn't kill that one. The witch did. And he was a bad man, anyway."

That was one small comfort she'd seized upon. Eleonore didn't shy away from violence, but it needed to be justified, and she hated being someone else's sword. The witch had made sure to detail the crimes of her enemies before each mission, though, which had made it easier to kill them. Even the humans Eleonore abducted for the witch every fifty years or so—which the witch herself drained of life to prolong her own life span—were carefully selected. *Human monsters*, the witch had said while watching Eleonore dig a grave for the man from 1969. *The world will not miss them.*

Eleonore had been too disgusted by the actions of those humans to fuck them. She had fucked the witch's less-objectionable enemies in the past, though. Not because the witch had ordered her to—for all her crimes, forcing Eleonore to have sex against her will would have horrified even that foul sorceress—but because Eleonore had hungers that needed sating. She'd long since resigned herself to a life without true love or lasting passion, but premurder sex was as valid as hate sex. Like scratching an itch.

She eyed Ben's broad shoulders. Were she to succumb to the temptation to explore this werewolf's body, it would be no different.

Ben cleared his throat. "Want an introduction to the other kitchen gadgets?" he asked.

Relieved at not having to explain her murders further, and not wanting to think too much about Ben's shoulders or the differences between sex and passion, Eleonore nodded.

Ben took her on a tour of the cabinets as the popcorn began popping more urgently. She was introduced to a toaster, a coffeepot, a blender, and a slow cooker. For anything she didn't recognize, he briefly explained how it worked.

Her ignorance was still mortifying, but Ben managed to educate her in such a way that she didn't feel he was judging her. When she praised the convenience of an automated dishwasher, he smiled, the skin beside his eyes crinkling agreeably. "I'll show you everything," he promised. "I'm sorry I didn't realize earlier that you wouldn't be familiar with most of these things."

He wore a soft expression she didn't totally understand. It had better not be pity.

"Can I borrow your PADD, too?" she asked. At his confused look, she clarified. "Your device. Phone. You said you can look things up on it."

"Oh, yes." He reached for his pocket, then hesitated. "Let me give you a tutorial before I let you borrow it. I want to make sure you don't accidentally dial Gigi or something."

The microwave beeped, shrill and insistent. The air smelled delicious, and Eleonore's stomach rumbled. She grabbed a mug and poured heated blood into it, then turned the stovetop dial to the off position. Ben nodded in confirmation she'd done the right thing before grabbing a large bowl and pouring popcorn into it. "Feel free to dive in," he said, handing it over. "I'm going to make myself some hot cocoa."

Eleonore took the bowl and mug of blood to the living room, placing them on the low table before the couch. She settled in cross-legged on the brown leather and tugged a blanket over her lap. It was the same blanket he'd laid over her earlier, and she liked the feel of it.

She liked the taste of hot blood even more. Though she wasn't thirsty in the survival sense, there was comfort in the coppery warmth sliding down her throat. Following a swig with a handful of greasy popcorn was even better. She munched, watching the purpling sky outside the window lose its last streaks of light.

Ben appeared with a mug in his hand and a plastic bag full of white objects in the other. "This might be a terrible idea," he said, holding the bag up, "but marshmallows improve hot cocoa, so I thought I'd bring them out in case you want to try them with blood."

Eleonore eyed the bag with interest as he settled in on the other end of the couch. He didn't sit too close, which she appreciated, but there was something nice about the casual companionship.

Ben opened the bag, then handed her a marshmallow. Eleonore studied the fluffy white object, then gave it a tentative lick. Her nose crinkled. "It's sweet."

"Like I said, it may not go with blood—I just figured I'd give you the option."

Eleonore shrugged and plopped the marshmallow into her mug. "Let's find out."

Blood laced with sugary sweetness was . . . odd but interesting, she decided on the first sip. The second sip was better. By the time she was halfway done with the mug, now a raspberry pink from the mix of blood and sugar, she was a convert.

"It's the strangest combination of flavors," she told Ben around a mouthful of popcorn, "but somehow it works."

"I'm glad." He'd eaten popcorn along with her at first, but his pace had slowed, and his mind had seemed to wander to places that cast a shadow over his face. Now he sat with his mug in his lap, staring down at the liquid. He fiddled with it, biting his lip, and his toes were rubbing against the floor again.

"What is it?" Eleonore asked.

He lifted his head. "What?"

"You look like you want to say something."

He blew out a breath. "Am I that obvious?"

She eyed him, from the tips of his scrunching toes to the wrinkle in his brow. Eleonore had met many liars over the centuries, and Ben was either the greatest one in history or pathetically bad at it. Her bet was on pathetically bad. "Yes."

His chuckle was strained. "You do like saying what you think."

"I'm told it's a refreshing trait." She had been told nothing of the sort. She waved a hand, motioning for him to get on with it. "So? What is it?"

He closed his eyes, and his chest expanded on a deep breath. Eleonore eyed that chest, thinking how useful it would be to have lungs of that scale. Wondering what it would feel like to lie atop his chest and feel his breath lifting her, too.

"There's a bit of a situation," he said.

When he didn't immediately clarify, Eleonore prodded for more. "What kind of situation?" Did her knives need to be involved?

He set the mug on the table, then shifted to face her, hands clasped in his lap. "My sister's running for mayor," he said. "Apparently what happened tonight at the restaurant showed up online, and she called me. The video is gaining traction."

The gods-damned internet again, which Eleonore really needed to learn how to use. She flushed to think about strangers watching a recording of her outburst. "And?"

He raked a hand through his shaggy hair. "Well, I kind of panicked when she asked me what was going on, and I . . . uh . . . might have told her you're an actress who's going to put on a show at the Emporium's café and what happened at the restaurant was an advertisement for that."

Eleonore blinked at the sudden rush of words, which he'd spat out like maybe if he said them quickly enough, she wouldn't notice their content. "That was very creative of you." Though why he seemed so nervous about it, she couldn't say.

Honestly, it was a relief to have her actions excused away by something like the theatre. Yes, acting was technically lying, but it was using the skill for a positive purpose. She'd loved puppet shows, pantomimes, and the stray stage performances she'd been able to sneak away to watch. The time she'd managed to get in on the ground floor at the Globe Theatre in 1607 was a fond memory amid a slew of unwelcome ones.

Ben winced. "Yeah, well, Gigi's platform apparently involves supporting the arts, so she decided to announce her candidacy at the café's opening. Followed by a stage performance."

This didn't seem like news worthy of the way he was squeezing his fingers together so tightly the knuckles were white. "You don't approve of her plan?" she asked.

"The stage isn't built yet," he said. "And there are no shows in the works. Which means Gigi's expecting a performance . . . by you."

Eleonore stared at Ben, waiting for an indication he was joking. Not that the werewolf seemed overly inclined to jokes so far—or else Eleonore simply didn't understand his sense of humor—but a statement that absurd couldn't possibly be taken at face value.

His hands were clasped in his lap, and he was squeezing them together in rhythmic pulses. It reminded her of his foot fidgets.

"You aren't serious," she said.

Ben winced. "I am, unfortunately."

And the werewolf didn't like lying.

"No," she said.

"Please just hear me out," Ben said, as if she hadn't made her intentions clear. "Any negative publicity about Gigi's family—me—could hurt her mayoral campaign."

"Why does that require me to perform on your stage?" She wasn't even sure what such a show would entail. If he expected jokes, he was talking to the wrong person—a lifetime of imprisonment and murder hadn't left her with a wide comedic repertoire.

"I told you, it explains what happened at the restaurant. We can say it was a viral stunt to drum up publicity."

Eleonore wasn't sure what viruses had to do with anything, but surely there were other possible explanations that didn't involve her becoming an actress. "Another explanation is that the man annoyed me and I retaliated."

Or the man startled me and I temporarily lost my mind.

Ben sighed. "Please, Eleonore. Gigi really needs to win. Our current mayor is awful."

"Most political leaders are." She shrugged one shoulder. "I fail to see how that's my problem."

"Because you were the one who nearly killed someone in Brittany's on camera!"

It seemed like an uncharacteristically vehement exclamation from him, but then again, she'd known him for less than a day. Most men ended up shouting eventually.

Eleonore also ended up shouting sometimes. Frequently. Too often, perhaps. She shifted, looking down into the bowl of popcorn as her skin flushed hot with embarrassment again at the reminder of her near-crime. "I wouldn't have actually killed him," she said. "Probably."

He pinched the bridge of his nose. "Even if you wouldn't have, people are talking. And Gigi asked me—you—to do this." There was a pause. "Or at least she told me it should happen."

Eleonore shoved the popcorn back onto the table and stood, beginning to pace. "So you want to pretend what happened at the restaurant was a stunt to draw attention for a theatrical performance. And then you want me to act in said performance so your sister can say she supports the arts and ask people to vote for her for mayor."

He winced. "I know it's not ideal, but it's just one night. Surely you can come up with something. Even a short monologue would work."

Eleonore scoffed and looked out the window at the blue-black night. The warm, salty-sweet taste of blood, marshmallows, and popcorn lingered on her tongue. She should have known the food wasn't an earnest offering but a trick to get her to agree to this absurd plan. No outstretched hand could be trusted, no matter what rewards it contained. A second hand was always behind the giver's back, holding a weapon.

"I will not do this," she said.

Ben sighed and bent forward, propping his elbows on his knees and looking up at her beseechingly. "You have to, Eleonore."

She stiffened. So far he'd avoided turning the request into an order, but that wording had done it. She felt a mystical tug in her chest, the invisible urgency of a task that needed to be accomplished. "As you command," she said softly.

He had sad puppy eyes again. Connard. "It's just one night," he said softly. "I'm sorry, but Gigi's my family. I would do anything for her."

Then why wasn't he donning a costume and parading around onstage? *Because he hadn't been the one threatening violence in public*, a more reasonable inner voice replied, but Eleonore had no patience for reasonable voices at the moment, inner or outer. Ben had volunteered her for something without her consent, then ordered her to complete it. She was a prisoner to the crystal and to him, and he had decreed her first act of servitude would be putting on a one-woman theatrical show at his coffee shop.

Fury burned in her chest, and bile rose in her throat. It wasn't the nature of the task that infuriated her—a monologue was better than murder, after all. It was that Ben had commanded her to do it.

"I thought you didn't like lying," she said.

"I don't." He switched to rubbing his temples; she spitefully hoped he had a headache. "Things are a mess right now. I'm trying to open the café, Gigi sprung her campaign on me, and now you're here, and I have no idea what to do. I'm just trying to hold things together."

Bold of him to blame part of his struggle on her. She hadn't just shown up, after all—he had deliberately sought her out. Purchased her, in fact! Accidental or not, this was his doing.

Ben Rosewood might be bashful and a terrible liar, but he was also proving to be like everyone else she'd ever met: determined to get his own way, with Eleonore relegated to nothing but a tool for his ambitions.

She straightened her shoulders and took a deep breath. Now that she'd been commanded, she had to carry out his mission, but that didn't mean she couldn't seize some measure of control—or revenge—from it. As the witch had learned early on, specificity was important when giving Eleonore orders.

"Very well," she said, holding out her hand. "Give me your PADD so I can research modern theatre." In addition to everything else she needed to research in order to survive in this time.

He handed it to her gingerly, as if expecting her to hurl it against the wall. Did he think her foolish? No one in her position would refuse the key to decades of missing knowledge.

"Thank you," he said after telling her the passcode and showing her how to access the internet on the device. "I'll make it up to you, I promise."

As if she believed that. She left the room without a word.

So Ben Rosewood wanted her to put on a theatrical performance to help promote his sister's mayoral campaign? Eleonore would deliver . . . and then some. She wasn't familiar with modern theatre yet, but she'd seen enough over the years to know a theatrical performance could involve any number of alarming, questionable, or embarrassing things.

She pulled up the internet browser and typed in *strangest theatrical shows in history*.

Ben, his sister, and everyone else who showed up to the performance were about to be very, very uncomfortable.

NINE

B EN SAT AT THE FRONT COUNTER OF HIS SHOP, FROWNING with concentration as he repotted an azalea. Its pink flowers trembled as he lowered it into its new, larger pot. This would likely be the last bloom of the year, and he hoped he could get it to bloom again next year. Mariel's magic could bring it back, of course, but azaleas were fickle, and he liked the challenge of gardening the old-fashioned way.

The shop bell tinkled. He looked up to see Mariel, as if his thoughts had summoned her. He straightened, brushing off his hands. "What are you doing here?" he asked. "I thought you were on your honeymoon."

She grinned, rosy-cheeked and looking blissful in the way only a newlywed could. "We're heading out shortly. I just wanted to stop by and see if any plants need magic, since I won't be back for a few weeks."

She and Oz were going on an extended trip, starting in the de-mon plane, then heading to the elven plane for a few days before returning to Earth for a week in France. Mariel had never been out of the country other than the occasional visit to the demon plane, and it had been nice seeing her excitement grow in the months leading up to the wedding.

Ben looked around, trying to think if any plants had been struggling lately. "There's a canna lily that could use some encouragement," he said, pointing. "Nothing dire, it just hasn't been thriving the way I hoped."

As Mariel headed for the plant in question, the construction forewoman stuck her head around the corner. "Hey, boss. We're about to start putting the stage in, so it's gonna be loud."

At the mention of the stage, Ben's stomach dropped. Ever since last night when he'd told Eleonore he needed her to perform, she'd been giving him the silent treatment. She spent her time holed up in her room, glued to a spare tablet he'd borrowed from Themmie after realizing Eleonore didn't want to return his phone and the knowledge it gave her access to. He heard her muttering periodically, a mixture of curses, exclamations over world events from the past half century, and the occasional snippet of Shakespeare.

He felt horrible about asking her to cover for his lie, but what else was he supposed to do? Gigi was counting on him, and the future of Glimmer Falls was counting on Gigi. Besides, Eleonore had finally agreed, even if she hadn't looked that happy about it.

He'd get Eleonore something special to thank her, he decided. Maybe a top-shelf bottle of bourbon-spiked blood. Then she'd forgive him and they could be on friendly terms again—as friendly as terms could be when he was essentially her prison warden.

"Sounds good," he told the forewoman. "Thanks for being willing to add it last minute."

The woman grinned. "Not a problem. I've been looking for a new venue for my stand-up, anyway."

Ben suppressed a wince. Having been to a few comedy shows around town, he knew the quality of that particular act was . . . questionable. But if it meant getting a stage put in before the café's opening—and Gigi's mayoral announcement—he'd offer her a headliner spot every night of the week.

When the builder left, Mariel popped her head around a shelf. "Why are you adding a stage now?" she asked. "I thought that was going to wait for the next stage of construction."

"Uh . . ." Ben's brain stalled out. "I thought—well, my sister likes the arts, you know? And it just . . . ah . . . it's because . . . because . . ."

There were a lot of reasons he didn't like lying. One of them was that he was generally terrible at it.

Mariel crossed her arms, adopting a determined expression. "Out with it," she said.

Ben exhaled, shoulders slumping. Well, everyone would find out about Eleonore sooner or later, if they hadn't already seen the viral video. And besides, it might be a relief to tell someone how colossally he'd complicated his life. "You're not going to believe it."

Mariel laughed and settled onto a stool next to the counter. "Ben, I once accidentally summoned a demon instead of a bag of flour. Trust me: whatever's going on can't be weirder than that."

Ten minutes later, Mariel stared at him with wide eyes and a slack jaw. "I take it back," she said. "That's weirder."

He winced. "Yeah."

"I didn't even know you could buy succubi on eBay. Surely that's against their terms and conditions?"

Ben hadn't considered that. Maybe he could contact customer service and arrange a return? Except then Eleonore would be stuck again with the witch who'd imprisoned her.

No, he couldn't.

"I need to find a way to break the curse tying her to that plastic crystal," he said. Then she'd be free to do whatever she liked, far away from Ben, his anxiety, and his terrible online shopping choices.

Mariel whipped out her phone. "Mind if I text the Scooby gang? Someone might have encountered this before."

"The Scooby gang" was a relatively new term Themmie had chosen for the boisterous group chat that included the pixie, Mariel, Oz, Calladia, Astaroth, Ben, and Rani. Ben sat out about eighty percent of the group's activities due to scheduling challenges, social anxiety, or the after-work urge to sink into his couch and stare at a blank wall, but he enjoyed the time he did spend with them.

"Sure," he said, swallowing his embarrassment at having gotten himself into this situation to begin with. If there was one undeniable truth, it was that he needed help.

"Great," she said, thumb tapping over the screen. Her eyes flicked up to him. "Curse aside, let's also talk about this theatrical performance you've strong-armed Eleonore into giving."

He frowned. "I didn't strong-arm her."

"You told her you wanted her to do it."

He opened his mouth, about to argue that she could have refused outright if it mattered that much, then shut it, feeling another surge of guilt. She had refused, but he'd kept pushing. It was uncharacteristic behavior from him, and even though he'd been freaking out at the time, that didn't excuse it.

"What am I supposed to do?" he asked. "The *Glimmer Falls Gazette* already published a gossip item naming me specifically. They said I was an active participant in a possible murder attempt. The only reason I'm not in jail right now is because it didn't escalate further."

In a supernatural town, traditional law and order had to take certain things into consideration. Witches were always cursing one another and engaging in duels, centaur jousting was a beloved sport that frequently put people in the hospital, and inappropriate summonings, orgies, and brawls were the norm. During one infamous town hall, Mayor Cynthia Cunnington had teleported a journalist to Antarctica. The main question in criminal issues was: "Is this reversible?" With magic users abounding everywhere, the answer was usually yes, but murder was its own category. Even if the town had had a necromancer in residence to reverse it, killing someone would always be illegal.

Mariel patted his hand. "I sympathize, but whether or not this performance goes forward, there's one thing you absolutely have to do."

He clung to her certainty like a life raft in a turbulent sea. "What?" he asked, praying she had the perfect answer to his dilemma.

"Be gentle with Eleonore," Mariel said. "Apologize for putting her in this situation and then cook her dinner or something."

Ben envisioned Eleonore's fury-filled eyes and snapping fangs. "I don't know if dinner will help. She's practically feral, and I'm pretty sure she hates me right now."

"She isn't used to this time. And frankly, it sounds like she's working through a lot of historical trauma. Wouldn't you be freaked out and combative if you were plopped into a random point in the future with no friends or frame of reference?"

He'd been feeling guilty already, but at that, the feeling condensed into a thick ball in his chest, heavy and awful. Mariel was right. Eleonore might be semiferal, but she had ample reason to be.

The vampire succubus could be aggressive and frightening and had no compunctions about delivering threats, which was so far removed from Ben's temperament that he hadn't truly questioned the reason for the behavior. Some people were tougher and more assertive than others, right?

Maybe it wasn't that simple, though.

Ben cleared his throat. "Do you think . . . she's afraid?"

Mariel nodded, hazel eyes full of sympathy. "Some people lash out when they're scared or cornered. Calladia, for one, if you consider all the fights she's been in. Even me sometimes, though I'm less violent about it." She made an embarrassed face. "I snapped at Oz a few times when he first showed up because I was freaking out, but at least I apologized afterwards."

Ben rubbed his chest over the hard knot of guilt. He should have considered this earlier. He'd been operating in panic mode instead of thinking clearly. "Thanks, Mariel. I'm going to make her dinner and bring her some flowers."

Mariel hugged him. "You can do this," she said, patting his back. "And as someone who once had a semiferal surprise house-guest myself, you can always come to me for advice."

"After your honeymoon," he said. "You're going to turn your phone off and enjoy that without any interruptions from me or anyone else."

She grinned and saluted him. "Aye aye, boss."

A few bouts of plant magic later, Mariel left with a flurry of waves and assurances that Ben would be fine and had this totally under control.

Did he have this under control? Not even remotely. But he at least had a place to start.

He turned his eyes to the racks of plants, trying to determine which would be the best apology gift for a secretly scared vampire succubus.

TEN

Work No. 227: The lights going on and off.

Eleonore wrinkled her nose at the Witchipedia article she'd accessed on her new PADD. Or digital tablet, she corrected herself, since that was apparently this era's term for the device. The image accompanying the text showed an empty, dark room. Then the image changed, the lights in the room coming on. Eleonore twitched, startled.

Right, a GIF. She'd learned about those earlier, though she still wasn't sure how to pronounce the acronym. She'd learned about a *lot* of things that day. Accessing the internet was rather like opening her mouth beneath a waterfall and attempting to sip.

She was addicted.

Having researched odd experimental theatrical performances, she was now investigating the strangest works of art of the modern era. Martin Creed's 2000 installation had to be near the top of the list—it was just an empty room with electric lights set on a timer.

"How is this worth one hundred ten thousand pounds?" she asked herself incredulously.

It was good fodder for her brainstorming session, though. Perhaps her performance at Ben's Plant Emporium could involve her standing stone-faced at a light switch, turning it on and off.

She scribbled the idea down in a notebook Ben had given her. He'd supplied her with paper and pens from his desk, along with the tablet, which was helpful for plotting her revenge against him.

Was he being helpful in terms of acclimating her to the modern world? Yes. But when he'd just ordered her to perform a one-woman show at his café, that helpfulness was negated.

Eleonore had several other spite- and internet-generated ideas written down already: "setting fire to stage," "sitting in silence with paper bag over head," "incoherent screaming." Maybe she should actually bite someone onstage.

It wasn't that Eleonore hated the idea of someday getting to perform in a play. When she'd been young, the main path open to her had been fighting for their clan, and then she'd been stuck in a career rut for six centuries. If she could break free of the curse, she didn't know what she would do, but it certainly wouldn't involve as much violence. Acting might be just the thing.

The issue was being forced to do it after she'd refused. The werewolf must know she was mystically bound to obey his every command. The eBay listing hadn't gone into detail about that, but it had to be obvious, right? That was how enchantments of this sort worked. Even if he didn't know, though, he'd still ordered her to come up with a show with only two weeks to prepare.

Ben had returned from work approximately an hour ago, but Eleonore hadn't felt like facing him. She was still stewing, and anger aside, she was confused about how to feel about him. He'd fed her and provided her with modern technology, which was helpful and possibly even kind. He'd also put new sheets on the guest bed and had mentioned taking her clothes shopping so she didn't have to stay in her current outfit. (The witch had failed to ship Eleonore's small wardrobe with the crystal.) He owned a large bathtub she had full access to, and his shampoo smelled delicious.

It was so far from what she was used to, Eleonore had no idea how to act or what to think.

A clatter came from the kitchen. Her stomach rumbled, and she eyed the bedroom door. It was close to dinnertime, and though she'd made herself a sandwich for lunch, she was getting hungry again.

The rhythmic sound of vegetables being chopped tempted her. Curious what Ben was making and wanting to learn about any additional kitchen gadgets (the internet had taught her about air fryers and waffle irons), she slid a fluffy robe over her clothes and headed for the kitchen.

The robe was dark blue and designed for someone much larger. It trailed behind her like a monarch's cloak, whispering against the floorboards, and the sleeves dangled over her hands. She lifted the lapel to her nose and sniffed, then let out a secret sigh. The fabric smelled like Ben's shampoo and a whiff of the cologne she'd sprayed in the air out of curiosity earlier, but her vampire senses were sharp, and she knew that wasn't the sole reason it smelled good. His skin and the blood beneath were naturally delectable, calling to her predatory impulses.

She found Ben sautéing onions and garlic while a pot of water heated on the stove. His glasses were fogged. "Hello," he said, looking up from the skillet. His tone was warm, though she could sense his cautiousness. "How are you liking the tablet?"

With food and continuing access to the internet at stake, she decided to be conciliatory, at least on the surface. "I like it," she said cautiously. If she seemed too excited, would he take it away? She hadn't had many things of her own over the centuries—a weapons collection, a few outfits, and some *Star Trek* bobbleheads the witch had insisted on summoning after their *TNG* marathon, all of which presumably still resided at the cabin in the woods.

"Learn anything interesting?" Ben asked.

Eleonore had learned a lot of very interesting facts over the course of the day. "I don't know where to begin," she said. "The Cold War, the International Space Station, Roger Federer, the Great Molasses Flood of 1919, the Interplanar Song Contest, emojis . . ." It had been like being trampled by a herd of centaurs, information pummeling her with such detail and immediacy she'd hardly been able to process one fact before compulsively clicking a link to discover another.

Ben paused in his sautéing. "The Molasses . . . what?"

He didn't know? This would be the first time Eleonore had knowledge about recent history he didn't, and she was excited to explain. "Twelve thousand tons of molasses broke out of a storage tank and flooded the city of Boston," she said enthusiastically. "Twenty-one people died!"

Ben blinked. "Wow. That's . . . a lot of molasses."

"Many more people were injured," she said. "What a fascinating problem for a city to have, don't you think? Supposedly the neighborhood smelled sweet for decades afterward."

Ben looked like he was biting the inside of his cheek. "You like morbid facts, don't you?"

"I like all facts," Eleonore said. Then she considered. "But yes."

Life could be very dark. She'd known that before she'd been chained to the crystal, when the vampire clans had engaged in frequent territorial warfare. When confronted with a foe or an unpleasant situation, Eleonore preferred to face it directly. Knowledge was, if not power, at least armor. And sometimes the darkest facts were the most interesting.

Ben stirred the onions again, then set the wooden spoon aside. "I have something for you," he said, wiping his hands on his apron.

The fabric was stamped with the words *KISS THE CHEF*, and Eleonore's thoughts briefly fixated on the idea. Curse her residual succubus hunger. If she could just spy on a decent orgy . . . As it was, she'd need to find a source of carnal energy within the next week or so, lest she become tired and listless.

Catching the direction of her gaze, Ben winced. "The apron is from my parents. They're eternally optimistic."

He turned to fuss with a vase of flowers on the counter before Eleonore could ask what his parents were optimistic about. The flowers were nice—roses with a sunset look to them, pink bleeding into orange. They smelled good, too. Maybe she could ask him to place them on the table before the television so the aroma would waft through the house.

He turned and held the vase out to her.

Eleonore looked at it, then back at him. "Do you want me to do something with that?" Maybe he would issue another order, she thought, spitefulness rising again.

Ben shifted from foot to foot. "They're for you."

"For me to . . . put somewhere?" she asked, puzzled.

"No. I mean yes, I suppose. If you want." Ben bit his lip, then thrust the flowers out more forcefully. "It's a gift."

A gift. Other than the *Star Trek* bobbleheads, which didn't count even if she had been secretly fond of Commander Data, she hadn't received a gift in a long time. "Oh," she said, hesitantly accepting the vase. The glass was ridged and cool under her fingers. "Why?"

Ben was scrunching his toes against the floor. Nervous. "Because I shouldn't have told you to do the show. I mean, I would still like it if you did, but I went about it the wrong way." He grimaced and looked down, rubbing the back of his neck. "I said that wrong, too. The point is, it's not fair of me to put you in an uncomfortable position. You're probably freaked out right now, and I'm really sorry, and I want to make you more comfortable in this time while we figure out how to free you."

A strange unfurling sensation happened in Eleonore's chest, like a snowdrop opening its petals at the end of winter. "You're—sorry?"

He nodded. "Sometimes I get stuck in my own head and don't think about what other people are going through. You must be scared—"

"I'm not scared," Eleonore interrupted. That would be confessing a weakness.

Except . . . she was scared. A bit. A very minor bit.

"Even if you aren't scared," Ben said, "this time and place is new to you. I should take better care of you." He gestured awkwardly at the stove. "So . . . pasta. And flowers. And I'll listen better going forward."

This was unprecedented. It would have been *unimaginable* if she hadn't just heard the words fall from his lips. Eleonore clutched the vase to her chest, staring at him.

A burning smell wafted to her nose.

"Shit. I mean, shoot," Ben said, grabbing the pan off the stove. "I forgot about the onions."

Eleonore was too flabbergasted to speak. She stared as Ben scooped burnt items out of the pan.

He was sorry?

He wanted to take care of her?

He'd given her flowers?

Eleonore brought the vase to her nose, breathing in as the petals brushed her nostrils. It smelled like happiness.

Was Ben actually being genuine?

She stayed unmoving as he dumped a box of dried pasta into the boiling water and added a can of tomatoes to the skillet.

Ben looked at her. "Want me to put those flowers somewhere?"

Eleonore shook her head and backed away, holding the vase closer. Vampires were territorial, and these were *hers* now.

"Okay," Ben said, eyes flicking between her face, the flowers, and the skillet. "You can do whatever you want with them."

There wasn't much to do with flowers. She could dry them out and paste them in a scrapbook if she were the sentimental type, which she was not. She could put them in the living room to make the house smell nice, as she'd originally thought, but no. This was Eleonore's gift, and right now, she didn't want to be parted from it.

"Thank you," she said cautiously.

He smiled in response, a grin that lit up his face and made his eyes crinkle agreeably. "You're welcome."

Eleonore kept the vase with her throughout dinner preparations. When Ben brought the bowls of pasta to the coffee table in front of his couch, she set the vase next to the food, close enough that she could snatch it up if needed.

Ben provided a plastic tub of shredded Parmesan cheese, which she dumped liberally on the pasta. Her first bite tasted like heaven.

Maybe Ben was forgiven.

Then he said, "Pass the cheese."

The mystical pull in Eleonore's chest sparked to life, along with familiar resentment at being given an order. Her rage had worn a deep path in her brain over the centuries, one she slipped back into without thought. Fury and instinct collided, and with a screech, she threw a handful of cheese at him.

Ben flinched as Parmesan bounced off his forehead. Some of it stuck to his hair and beard like snow. They stared at each other for a long moment, and then Ben set his fork down and cleared his throat. "May I ask why you threw the cheese at me?"

Eleonore's brain caught up with her body, and she felt mortified at the loss of control. "Sorry," she said. "It was instinct."

"Instinct," he repeated. "Throwing cheese is a vampire instinct?"

He was being very reasonable for someone who was the victim of her seesawing moods. Eleonore's cheeks felt hot. She shook her head, looking down at her lap. Her first flowers and a nice meal, and she'd ruined it. "You ordered it, so I had to obey. I don't like orders." And she was apparently the equivalent of a feral street dog, snapping at anyone who came too close.

"It wasn't exactly an order," Ben said, brushing cheese out of his hair. "People say 'pass the salt' all the time." When she peeked up at him, she saw his forehead furrow. "Wait, what do you mean you *had* to obey?"

So he truly hadn't known the details of owning the crystal. Eleonore felt a bizarre urge to laugh and cry at the same time. She scrubbed her hands over her face. "It's part of the spell," she said. "The curse. If the person who owns the crystal issues me a direct command, I'm mystically compelled to obey."

Realization washed over his face, quickly followed by horror. "You can't say no, no matter what I tell you to do?"

"So long as it's worded like an order and not a request, no. I can't refuse." He could tell her to strangle someone or jump in front of a car or run for two days straight without stopping, and she'd have to do it, no matter the cost to her health or sanity. "Why do you think I killed so many people for the Witch in the Woods? Because I wanted to?"

Ben covered his mouth with one hand. His eyes widened behind his glasses. "My God . . . Eleonore, I had no idea. That's barbaric."

"How could you not have at least guessed?" she asked. "That's how spells like this tend to work."

He shook his head. "I've never even heard of a spell like this, and I guess I didn't think about the details that much. It's only been a day, and there's so much going on . . ." His breath hitched. "So when I said you had to perform at the café, that counted as a mystical order?" At Eleonore's nod, his eyes grew watery. "That's why you were so angry. I mean, you were right to be angry at me, but it's not just because I asked you to do something you didn't want to. It's because you're being forced to do it by the magic."

Eleonore nodded again.

Ben's breathing was growing agitated. "I violated your consent," he said. "With that order and with . . . Lycaon, have I commanded you to do anything else?"

"Not much," Eleonore said. "Just the performance. And leaving the restaurant. And passing the cheese. And telling me to stop drinking your blood."

He braced his elbows on his knees, breathing so fast it was more like panting. "I'm so sorry. You don't have to do the performance or anything else. Can I revoke the command? I revoke it. I'm so, so sorry. I've been such a villain."

That was taking it a bit far, but Eleonore knew all about taking things too far. She had flung a handful of Parmesan at him in a fit of rage, after all. "Hey," she said when his breathing began to sound not just rapid but unhealthy. "Take a deep breath. You didn't know."

He did not take a deep breath. When he raised his head to look at her, his cheeks were wet with tears. "This whole situation is so stressful. I never should have clicked on that eBay listing. I never should have told that stupid lie to Gigi or taken you to Brittany's or ordered you to give me cheese or any of it. Lycaon, what are we going to do?"

Eleonore gingerly patted his back. "Can you try some deep breathing? This is growing alarming."

He sucked in a breath, then another, but it didn't seem to help. "Sorry," he said. "I get anxiety attacks sometimes. You can leave me to wait it out—wait, that's an order, shit, fuck, I don't mean it, I'm so sorry."

It wasn't technically an order—"leave me" would have counted, but the addition of "can" turned it into a statement of possibility—and she was glad of it. Not just for her sake, since orders sent her rage to uncontrollable heights, but because she didn't want him to suffer through this alone. She looked around, her own anxiety spiking as she tried to figure out what would soothe a werewolf having a panic attack. "Stay here," she said, standing up.

She returned in seconds with a glass of water from the sink. He jolted when she set it in front of him. "I forgot how fast you move," he wheezed, hand pressed over his heart.

Right. If she was trying to soothe him, she probably shouldn't give him a jump scare. She moved with excruciating slowness to grab the blanket on the back of the couch and wrapped it around him like she was swaddling a baby. Then she sat next to him, staring in what she hoped was a nonmenacing manner. She patted his back again. "There, there," she said, trying to remember how her parents had soothed her when she'd been upset as a child. Not that Ben was a child, but the things that were most comforting often had roots in those formative years. "There, there."

Over the next few minutes, Ben's breathing gradually grew slower. Eleonore lifted the glass to his mouth and helpfully tipped it, since he remained swaddled. He coughed—perhaps she had been overly enthusiastic in pouring water down his throat—then extricated an arm from the blanket to take control of the glass.

Once he was done drinking, he set the glass down and slumped back, closing his eyes. "Thank you," he said. "And I'm sorry. For the orders and for making you see me like this."

She frowned. He sounded ashamed. "You don't have to apologize for having anxiety."

He winced. "That's what my parents always said when I was growing up, but I can't help it. What kind of werewolf has panic attacks?"

"I'm sure plenty of werewolves have panic attacks."

"Maybe." He didn't sound convinced, though.

They returned to eating pasta, an awkward silence falling between them. Eleonore took the time to think.

Ben wasn't anything like she'd expected him to be when she'd first been summoned. He was anxious and thoughtful, and he'd given her flowers, then cried over violating her consent. He wasn't a complete villain after all. Maybe not any kind of villain.

And he was under a great deal of stress between her arrival, his café opening, and his sister's expectations. Having been the cause of a lot of that stress, Eleonore decided to be the solution as well. "I'll still do the performance," she said.

"No," he said instantly. "I don't want you to do it because you were ordered to."

"You took the command back," she pointed out. "That means if I do it, it'll be of my own free will."

He chewed his lip. "But—"

"But nothing," she said. "The performance goes on."

He looked at her with tentative hope in his eyes. "You would do that? I thought you hated the idea."

She shrugged. "I didn't like being surprised by it or ordered to do it, but if I get to choose? It could be interesting. Maybe even . . . fun." Not a word she used often.

He finally smiled again, a small curve of his lips that made the inside of her chest feel warm and soft. "Thank you, Eleonore. I really appreciate it. You have free rein to do whatever you like, of course, and anything you need . . ."

"I'll let you know."

The silence this time was easier as they finished dinner. Eleonore's mind churned over possibilities. She wouldn't be flicking a light switch on and off or setting fire to anything anymore. No, she was going to put on a real, meaningful performance, the kind that would be talked about for years.

She looked at her roses and smiled. Ben wasn't going to regret trusting her with this.

ELEVEN

THE TWO WEEKS BEFORE THE OFFICIAL OPENING OF THE Annex were hectic. Ben spent most of his time at the Emporium overseeing final details while also managing the existing nursery business, with breaks to chat with Gigi about her campaign. Exhaustion hung heavy on him, but when sleep did come, it was limited and sporadic, dotted with nightmares of espresso machines exploding and plants trying to strangle him.

One silver lining to the stress was that Eleonore had proven herself surprisingly helpful since his meltdown on the couch. Granted, her support often took the form of sudden, startling appearances with blankets or mugs of hot chocolate that nearly made him soil his pants—accompanied by intense staring, since she didn't seem familiar or entirely comfortable with the position of caregiver—but he appreciated the gestures.

Eleonore was also catching up on history and current events very quickly. She'd taught Ben all manner of morbid or odd facts over breakfast or dinner, like that platypuses had venomous spurs on their legs, that the shortest war in history lasted only thirty-eight minutes, and that hippopotamuses were responsible for more deaths annually than manticore stampedes. There was still tension between the two of them—how could there not be when he had a terrifying amount of power over her life?—but her wariness seemed to diminish every day.

His guilt over the situation didn't. "When all this stress is over," he'd promised her, "we'll find a way to release you from the curse." He still felt awful, though. It was unethical to keep her bound to the crystal, but he didn't have the bandwidth or expertise to find a solution for that right now. So he worked carefully on his phrasing, trying to catch inadvertent commands before they left his mouth. When he did issue an accidental command, her widened eyes, flared nostrils, and violent looks quickly alerted him so he could rescind the order.

A week before the café opening and mayoral campaign announcement, Gigi called a postdinner meeting of her "team." She'd assembled what she called the best minds in Glimmer Falls, but when Ben walked into Gigi's living room to discover it full of their mutual friends, he resisted the urge to snark that she must not have looked very hard for help.

Truthfully, even though no one had experience running a political campaign, Gigi had them working to their strengths. Themmie was the Communications Officer, of course, busily drafting copy for a social media and email calendar. The demon Astaroth was the Branding Officer—Branding Master and Commander, he'd first tried to label himself, which Gigi had informed him made no sense on LinkedIn—responsible for crafting a consistent, appealing image and persona from both Gigi's closet and her personality (and her eccentricities, Ben felt allowed to say as her older brother). Ben's employee Rani, a naiad who had briefly dated Gigi during college and was still good friends with her, was her Hype Woman and Event Planner. ("How is Hype Woman LinkedIn-appropriate?" Astaroth groused to unsympathetic ears.) Ben had been bestowed the vague yet ominous title of Logistics Manager. Calladia was at the meeting, too, though as she'd said, "You don't need a Bar Fight Officer, so I'm an all-purpose assistant." Oz and Mariel would eventually step in to help as well, though not until they'd enjoyed newlywed bliss for a while.

"Here's the proposed campaign logo," Themmie said, passing around her phone. She'd engaged centaur Hylo as a graphic designer.

When the phone made it to him, Ben squinted at the pink image. It looked like a circle with some random jagged lines. "What is it?"

Themmie rolled her eyes. "Obviously a moon, since she's a werewolf, and the mountains represent our city's connection to the natural world."

Below the mocked-up logo was a tagline: *Gigi Rosewood: Howling for Change.*

Ben guffawed.

"Hey," Themmie said, snatching her phone back. "Constructive criticism only."

"Sorry," he said. "It's just . . . *Howling for Change?*"

"I think it's good," Astaroth said, surprising Ben. "It's succinct and snappy and positions her as both a werewolf and a progressive. Voters know they'll get exactly what it says on the tin."

While the rest of the group were merely sitting on Gigi's couches and chairs, Astaroth was somehow *lounging* in a casually cool way Ben could never hope to aspire to. His gray suit was pristine, and he was toying with a cane topped with a crystal skull that ought to look ridiculous but didn't.

Calladia sat next to her partner in a tank top and leggings, her ponytail askew from a day of work as a personal trainer. She elbowed Astaroth in the ribs, eliciting a *whuff* that diminished the demon's coolness a bit. "I still like *Gigi Rosewood: Taking a Bite Out of Government Corruption,*" she said.

"Also good," Astaroth acknowledged. "But it's long for a T-shirt and does sling some mud at Cynthia Cunnington. Mudslinging is deserved, of course, but I've been doing some market research, and while anger is effective at getting clicks, positive emotions elicit a better response rate when there's a call to action."

Ben was in over his head. "Call to action?" he asked. "Is that . . . voting?"

The look Astaroth gave him dripped with condescension. "We want people to sign up for Gigi's newsletter and donate to her campaign first," he said. "Voting is the end goal, but there are a lot of steps that need to happen first."

"*Taking a bite out of corruption* will be a good sound bite for social media," Themmie said, thumb flying over her phone screen. "Let's make it part of a speech."

The brainstorming continued, covering a swath of topics. Astaroth had decided Gigi's colorful pink Converse would be her trademark, especially in conjunction with Themmie's proposed door-to-door campaign to engage with the citizens of Glimmer Falls. Rani was working on rally decorations and a word-of-mouth campaign in conjunction with Themmie's social media efforts—they were teasing a Big Reveal at the Annex's opening night.

Ben sat back and listened, feeling ill-equipped to help. If Gigi had been starting a business he would have more to contribute, but the world of marketing was foreign to him. Thankfully, he was only in charge of the event space and catering for the campaign launch, which basically meant telling the kitchen to make extra food (which Gigi was paying for, having refused to accept it as a gift).

"So this performance artist," Gigi said. "What's her background?"

Ben's stomach dropped. Gigi wasn't part of the group chat in which Mariel had posted the "Ben bought a vampire succubus on eBay when he was drunk" update—an update that had earned him a lot of well-deserved razzing. He'd sworn his friends to secrecy, and if he told his sister the details now, he'd have to admit he'd lied about the situation at Brittany's. "Uh," he said, tired brain struggling to come up with anything.

Thankfully, Themmie intervened. "Eleonore's new," the pixie said. "Just moved to the area, and this is actually going to be her world premiere performance. I think giving new talent a chance is a great way to emphasize your message about expanding access to the arts to communities who historically haven't been given opportunities or resources."

It was all—technically—true, and far better than anything Ben would have come up with. He sent a grateful glance Themmie's way, and she winked when Gigi wasn't looking.

"I hear she's very avant-garde," Astaroth drawled. "It's going to be a *bloody* good time."

The damn demon. Astaroth had been delighted by this development, which appealed to his chaotic nature. Once he'd learned straightlaced Ben had acquired a half-feral vampire succubus assassin he had no idea how to interact with, he'd declared it the funniest thing he'd heard all year. He was now making vampire puns at every opportunity.

"I hope the show isn't terrible," Gigi said with a frown. "Since it's her first one."

Ben shrugged. "It's Glimmer Falls, not Broadway. I think people will enjoy it even if it isn't the best show they've ever seen. And she's excited about the opportunity."

Opportunity was a strong word for the clusterfuck he'd thrust Eleonore into the middle of, but at least she really did seem excited about the performance now. He had no idea what she was planning, but he knew she was taking it seriously. She'd confessed that her original plan had been to embarrass him with something truly bizarre—which he had to admit was funny now that he knew it was no longer going to happen—but she'd assured him this would be a carefully thought-out performance in the best tradition of experimental theatre. He heard her muttering to herself in the guest room late at night, accompanied by thumping and the occasional soft shriek.

"Well, I look forward to seeing it." Gigi smiled at Ben and reached out to ruffle his hair, eliciting an eye roll from him. "Thanks, bro. I appreciate you letting me co-opt your café opening."

"It'll bring in more customers," he said. "So it's a mutually beneficial arrangement."

Gigi high-fived him. "Rosewood clan for the win! Speaking of which, Mom and Dad are *so* excited. Can we get them front-row seats?"

"Shit," Ben said, shooting to his feet on a wave of adrenaline. "I forgot chairs!"

The group laughed as he sprinted out of Gigi's house. He waved over his shoulder, muttering to himself about the sheer incompetence it took to construct an entire stage without thinking that maybe the audience would like somewhere to sit.

Thankfully, chairs were easy to source. He'd get some proper ones custom-made down the line from a woodworker he knew in neighboring Fable Farms, but simple folding wooden chairs—the same ones Mariel and Oz had rented from a local restaurant for their wedding—would suffice for the launch. A phone call later, he had arranged for them to be delivered first thing in the morning in exchange for a fire lily the cyclops restaurateur had his eye on.

His phone chimed after he hung up—a notification from Moon-Cycle, a versatile period/moonshift-tracking app used by both werewolves and menstruating people. Tomorrow night would be the full moon.

Ben swore at the reminder. With the chaos of the last few weeks, he had lost track of the waxing moon. He didn't have *time* to transform into a wolf and run around terrorizing rabbits.

Shifting wasn't optional, though, at least not with current

technology. The moment scientists came up with a shift suppressant, Ben would be signing up. For now he sighed and mentally reviewed his schedule. He'd be out of commission for roughly seven hours, which meant the holiday knitting he'd planned to catch up on would need to be postponed yet again. He could grab a few hours of sleep after shifting back before heading to the Emporium to open shop.

Not ideal, but manageable, so long as he remembered to program the coffeepot.

Back home, Ben found Eleonore watching TV. He recognized the program as that trendy show with dragons he could never remember the name of. He'd tried to get interested in the previous dragon series, but there were a few too many beheadings for his taste.

"How was the meeting?" Eleonore asked, pausing the show. She'd grown adept with modern technology in a shockingly short amount of time. It was like she was a sponge; after being starved of knowledge for so long, she was absorbing everything she could.

"Fine," he said distractedly as he hung his coat up and put his wallet and keys in the bowl next to the door. "I realized I have to shift tomorrow night, so I'll come home very early in the morning. I'll try not to wake you up."

"Cool," she said.

He made a face. "Not really." Then, realizing her tone had been lackluster, he took a closer look at her. Her complexion looked wan, and there were shadows under her eyes. "Hey, are you all right? You look . . ." He cut off that sentence immediately, having learned that one should never tell a woman she looked tired or sick. *Oh my God*, Gigi had exclaimed once. *A girl skips makeup for one day and suddenly she's Baba Yaga.* A tad overstated, but he had taken note of the misstep and vowed not to do it again.

Eleonore blinked slowly, as if it was taking her a few moments to process the words. "Oh. Yes. I'm fine."

"Can I get you something? Blood, water, tea, whiskey? Something to help you sleep?"

Her full lips tipped up in a small smile. "Stop fretting, wolf. I'm all right, truly."

If she said she was, he would believe her. He nodded. "I'm going to get a shower, then. I hope you enjoy the show."

She didn't reply, instead sinking back into the couch and grabbing the remote.

Once he was under the hot spray of water, Ben sighed and leaned his head against the tile, tension slipping out of his muscles. The tub was large, custom-built for his height the same way he'd needed to order a custom bed. Being tall got expensive, but in moments like this he was glad he'd invested in comfort rather than forcing himself to squeeze into smaller spaces the way he did in the outside world.

The hot water was divine, pinkening his skin and slicking his hair to his scalp as it worked magic on the stress held in his body. If he wasn't so exhausted, he'd have considered a bubble bath, but he didn't want to drown, and he had a feeling the moment he got horizontal it would be lights out—assuming he could get his brain to stop running through logistics, worrying about the vampire succubus in his living room, or reliving embarrassing memories from a decade ago, that was.

Ben had long ago perfected a nighttime routine for when he needed sleep and working himself into exhaustion hadn't calmed the brain gremlins. First, a hot shower and a quick masturbation session to relax him. Then a cup of tea, a melatonin pill, and a CD of soothing whale sounds to lull him to sleep. Except on days his anxiety flared out of control, that would put him out like a light.

His dick was flaccid, but that could be rectified. Ben handled himself with the efficiency and expertise of nearly thirty years of practice, closing his eyes and rifling through fantasies until he settled on a scene from a paranormal romance novel he'd discovered in the library at a formative age.

This time, though, he couldn't envision the particulars—or rather, they kept changing. The brunette's hair turned fiery red, her curves grew more voluptuous, and at the moment when she was supposed to drop to her knees, she instead bared her fangs and *hissed*.

Ben's hips jerked. "Shit," he muttered under his breath, even as his hand moved faster. Masturbating to Eleonore was wrong on . . . God, probably a million levels . . . but he couldn't stop. This wasn't a perfunctory wank anymore, designed to release tension with all the efficiency and passion of a sneeze. He was *into it* in a way he hadn't been in a long time.

Ben groaned as he stroked himself, unable to stop the flood of images. Eleonore baring her fangs at him. Sucking his finger while grinding against him. Calling him *wolf* in that French accent. He imagined her bare breasts, how the weight of them would feel in his palms. She'd have a fiery thatch of hair for him to nose through on his way down, and when he licked between her legs, she would groan and order him to keep going or else she'd rip out his spine.

He finished startlingly quickly, muffling a shout with his free hand. When he was spent, he leaned back against the wall, legs shaking.

What was *that*?

Ben hadn't dated in so long, it had seemed like the sensual part of him had atrophied and died. Yet here he was, head spinning from the best orgasm he'd had in years, thoughts tangled around Eleonore. Eleonore, who he'd brought here unwillingly. Eleonore, whom he held a terrifying amount of power over. Eleonore, who would probably rather eat his liver than suck his dick.

"Fuck," he whispered, running a hand over his face.

He finished the shower quickly, then brushed his teeth and

shrugged on a black bathrobe. Eleonore didn't need to know what was going on in his head; he would treat her the same way he had before, with a mix of politeness, consideration, and wary respect. They would work to release her from the spell, and then she'd be free to go her own way and never think of Ben again.

It took about one second and two steps into the living room to realize Eleonore had undergone a drastic change. While before she'd been tired and sickly looking, now she was alert and rosy-cheeked. Her skin seemed to glow, and even her lips looked redder as she smiled at him. "Good shower?" she asked.

Shit.

Shit shit shit.

Vampire succubus, emphasis on the *succubus*. She seemed so wholly vampiric most of the time he'd almost forgotten what she'd told him that first day in the kitchen after sucking blood from his finger.

I could sense your arousal.

She totally knew he'd been jacking off.

Mortification washed over him in hot, dizzying waves. Wishing it was possible to disintegrate and become one with the floor-boards, Ben nodded.

"Good," Eleonore said, beaming at him. "Thank you."

Thank him? For . . .

Realization hit.

I feed on that, too.

Ben had fed her regularly that week and provided more blood from NecroNomNomNoms, but he'd forgotten about the other part of her hunger. She needed to dine on sexual energy as frequently as she drank blood.

Ben's cheeks were burning. "Can you . . . ah . . . tell what . . ." He trailed off, incapable of saying the words out loud. If he did, he thought he might actually die from humiliation.

"What you were fantasizing about?" Eleonore asked with her usual bluntness. She was still grinning. "No, I'm not psychic. It felt like a good one, though."

If his cheeks could spontaneously combust, he would be a human torch right now. This was embarrassing on a level he'd never before experienced. He opened his mouth to apologize, but she looked so damn pleased he couldn't get the words out.

She'd been hungry, he told himself. It was just like needing food or blood. Still, he needed to check. "If I . . ." He cleared his throat. "If I do that, I don't want to sexually harass you. Since you can sense it."

It wasn't a question, but she understood. "I do not feel harassed," she told him. She'd coiled the length of her hair and was toying with it, and he tried to block out memories of how her hair—and the grip he could take it in—had featured in his shower fantasies. "What you do is your business, Ben. And if it makes you uncomfortable and you want me to leave the house when you do that, I will."

"How would you feed, then?" he dared to ask.

She shrugged one shoulder, looking effortlessly French in a way he'd only seen in movies. "I'll find a way."

Someone as savvy as Eleonore—and as beautiful—could find many ways to feed in Glimmer Falls. A tight, unpleasant feeling squeezed Ben's throat. "I'm not uncomfortable," he lied. "And I'm your host. Feeding you is my responsibility."

Her auburn lashes brushed the delicate skin above her cheekbones. "As you—and I—wish, then."

Her wicked smile was doing things to him and Ben only had so much bandwidth for processing simultaneously sexy, confusing, and mortifying things, so he nodded. "Cool," he said, inwardly cringing. "Cool cool cool."

Then he hurried to his bedroom, wondering once again what the hell he had gotten himself into.

TWELVE

BEN'S LIST OF THINGS TO AVOID IF AT ALL POSSIBLE FEATURED one absolutely impossible-to-avoid thing. Every twenty-nine days the moon completed its cycle, having marched through the eight phases of new, waxing crescent, first quarter, waxing gibbous, full, waning gibbous, third quarter, and waning crescent. He'd learned that sequence in werewolf day care, where it was given the same import as learning shapes or letters or how not to blunder into traffic.

To be fair, it did control the werewolf existence. And how ridiculous was it that a celestial object 238,900 miles from Earth could wield that kind of influence on an entire species? But just as its gravitation pulled the tides, something in that white glow pulled a beast from inside him. It was the one night he truly lost control—not just in the panicked way of his brain trying to fight itself, but real, physical control.

It terrified him.

He stood at the window, hands braced on either side of the frame and fingers tapping agitatedly as he glowered at the rosy sunset. He should be working late at the Emporium, but since he didn't want to transform into an animal with fangs and impulse control issues in a room full of fragile plants and terra-cotta pots, he'd come home to prepare. Once moonrise was thirty minutes away, he'd get in his car and head into the thick forest north of town. It was emptier than the woods on the hills rising to the east of Glimmer Falls, which housed the area's famous hot springs and were frequented by visitors at all hours.

If Ben was going to end up rolling around in mud, persecuting the local wildlife, and shamelessly scratching his balls, he would rather do so far away from witnesses.

"Will you shift soon?" Eleonore asked from behind him.

He cringed. It had been less than twenty-four hours since the Masturbation Incident, and going on past experience, it would take at least twenty-four years to get over an embarrassment of that magnitude. The previous night he'd tossed and turned, having added "accidental public masturbation" to the litany of sins that ran through his head at two a.m.

"Unfortunately," he muttered. Lycaon, why was he like this? Other werewolves loved the moonshift, which made this one more thing that was wrong with Ben.

He looked over his shoulder in time to see Eleonore plop onto the couch and cross her legs beneath her. Her notebook was open on the coffee table next to her tablet, the pages filled with bold scribbles about her upcoming performance. Having already overstepped massively, Ben had diligently avoided looking at her brainstorming notes.

"How's prep for the show going?" he asked. "Do you need anything?"

"A cloak and something colorful to wear underneath it," she said.

Right. Performers generally needed costumes. "Sorry, I should have thought about that." He held out his hand. "May I have your tablet for a moment? I can log you in to my account so you can buy whatever you need online."

She looked intrigued. "Anything I need?"

He hesitated. "Anything you need under a budget of, say . . . one hundred dollars?"

She laughed outright at that. "Please, Ben. How much could a cloak cost, five dollars?" She handed the tablet over. "I can't imagine going over that budget, but I promise I won't."

Clothing prices had increased since the 1960s, but Ben trusted her to keep her word. He logged into an all-purpose online retailer and then walked her through how to search, put things in the cart, and check out.

A familiar tingle started beneath his skin—the itchy feel of his wolf-self rousing in anticipation of the full moon. Thirty minutes to go. He handed the tablet back, then hurried to the front door. "I'm heading out," he said. "I can't operate a cell phone while in wolf form, so if there's an emergency, please call 911."

She nodded, already immersed in online shopping. "Good luck," she said distractedly.

Ben hurried to the car. He needed to get to his normal shifting place in time to strip naked, otherwise his clothes would be shredded. While he had an emergency backup shirt and pants in the back of the SUV, he'd rather not destroy these ones. Public nudity was on the list of things Ben would prefer not to engage in, but after a few mishaps as a teenager—werewolves started shifting during adolescence—he'd learned to get naked beforehand.

Traffic was heavier than usual, and his fingers drummed over the steering wheel while his left foot tapped a staccato beat. "Come on," he said, eyeing the clock. He had the exact time of moonrise memorized, but he also felt it coming in the tightening of his skin. Shifting into a wolf inside his car would be unfortunate.

Thankfully, traffic eased, and soon he was speeding out of town on a narrow road that wound into the trees. Pines and western red cedars clustered close, and the air was crisp and fresh through the lowered window. September was a liminal month—hot on some days, with cool nights that would lengthen into a cold, dark winter.

At his usual pullout, Ben parked, then hiked into the woods. He stripped next to a stream, folding his clothes and placing them on a rock. Then he closed his eyes and waited.

A cool, shivery sensation raced over his exposed skin. It was followed by heat and the sound of bones grinding as his body rearranged itself. Shifting didn't hurt, but it was strange and uncomfortable. There was an element of body horror to seeing his skin stretch over a new form before growing thick brown fur, so he kept his eyes squeezed shut. His face narrowed and elongated, nose becoming a snout and teeth sharpening. When he could no longer stand on two legs, he dropped to four paws.

Ben opened his eyes to a new world. Colors were no longer so vibrant, but he could detect the faintest quiver of leaves overhead. The wind carried the scent of earth and running water, along with a whiff of fresh scat and broken stems where a prey animal had passed. His stomach rumbled. The evening's stir-fry hadn't filled the ache, and saliva pooled as he identified the scent of rabbit.

No, came the distant protest of his human self. *Not the rabbits!*

Ben whuffed and bounded into the underbrush, wolven instinct drowning out thought. His muscles bunched and lengthened in turn as he ran, and the moon brushed his fur with its silvery caress.

A mouse skittered over the root of a tree, and Ben's jaws closed on it before he processed the urge. It was a small mouthful, but the meat whetted his appetite. He crunched the tiny bones and spat out the tail, then kept running.

Alive. Hungry. Wild.

The rabbit posed no challenge. It was dead in an instant, neck snapped, and then Ben settled under the sheltering branches of a bush to consume his prey. Faint distress lay behind his delight at the taste, but it was impossible to focus on anything but the filling of his stomach.

A distant howl echoed over the hills—a werewolf calling for others to join the hunt. He cocked his head, listening, then returned his attention to the rabbit. He was a loner by instinct, and he had no desire to leave his territory.

Ben paused to scratch himself with his hind leg, then rubbed against a tree to mark it with his scent. This was his patch of land, no one else's, and every month he marked the perimeter to keep it safe. His land, his trees, his stream, his rabbits.

Ben ran for hours, pausing only to mark trees and howl at the fat white moon overhead. His muscles burned, and the air came crisp and sharp in his lungs. He met no other wolves, just one startled midnight hiker who shrieked at the sight of him. Ben bared his teeth and stared the man down, raising a leg and pissing on a stump right then and there to indicate his thoughts on having his territory breached. The man backed away sweating, then turned and ran.

Good.

Ben howled his triumph at having driven off the intruder, then padded to the nearby stream. He jumped in, sending water splashing, then rolled around, letting the current carry away the dirt from his coat and the blood from his muzzle. Then he stood with his paws on the rocky bottom and drank.

Belly full of meat and water, Ben flopped on the bank of the stream for a few minutes. The forest moved and chattered around him, ever alive. His head felt empty and full at once—thoughts came distant and more in images than words, but the impulse to movement pressed on the inside of his skull. Despite the tiredness of his limbs, he pushed back to his feet and loped off again.

Hours passed like this. So long as the moon was high in the sky, its energy lent him strength. But eventually it began its retreat, and Ben returned to where he had started, feeling tired and cold. He curled up next to his clothes with his tail covering his nose, wishing someone was there to wrap him in a blanket instead.

When Ben woke, he was human-shaped, naked, and absolutely freezing. The sky overhead held the deep navy hue of the silent hour before dawn, and wind whipped the treetops. He staggered upright, cursing as he tugged his clothes back on with cold, clumsy fingers.

Rational thought returned in a rush, like the dam constraining it had crumbled, and he was flooded with the knowledge of what he'd done all night. One mouse and two rabbits had fallen to his fangs, and his mouth had a nasty coppery aftertaste. He groaned, covering his face as he remembered aggressively pissing in front of the stranger he'd startled. Christ, he hoped that wasn't one of his customers. Reason said even if he was, the man wouldn't recognize Ben's wolf form, but panic said every horrible thing was possible.

He stuffed his feet into shoes, then staggered toward the car. It took a few minutes with the engine on and heater blasting to warm him up after his nap on the cold ground. His eyes were bleary and his head throbbed, and Ben white-knuckled the wheel as he drove back into town.

Once home, he tiptoed toward the bathroom for a much-needed shower and toothbrushing. His sense of smell was good even in human form, though, and when Eleonore's uniquely luscious scent wafted down the hallway, he stopped in his tracks.

Hot, lustful blood surged, stiffening his cock, and he had a brief vision of flinging Eleonore over his shoulder and carrying her off to ravish her in the woods. Ben closed his eyes with his hand on the doorknob, struggling with the sudden impulse. *It's the moon*, he told himself. *The moon makes you aggressive and out of control.* It would take hours for the final effects of it to fade.

Lycaon, he wanted Eleonore.

But Ben wanted all sorts of things he couldn't have: a calm mind, a billion dollars, an extra five or six hours in each day. A future that involved no more public urination or dismembered rabbits.

And Eleonore deserved better than a self-loathing werewolf.

So he shook his head and headed into the bathroom, wishing shame washed away as easily as dirt.

THIRTEEN

B EN DID NOT SEEM HAPPY AFTER THE MOONSHIFT.
Eleonore perched on the kitchen counter, shoving hand-
fuls of cereal into her mouth. Ben had made a sour face when he'd
entered the kitchen that morning, rubbing his stomach and saying
he was regrettably full, and though he'd offered to make her breakfast, Eleonore had declined. She liked the way he cooked eggs, but
she disliked being seen as needy. Plus, he looked very glum.

She'd heard him return in the dark hours of the morning and
had been curious enough to rouse from bed and crack open the
bedroom door to peek at him. He'd been covered in dirt and leaves,
his face lined with exhaustion. He'd stopped outside the bathroom, hand on the knob, and she'd wondered if he'd sensed her
presence. His energy had flooded with enough lust to make her
catch her breath, but he'd just shaken his head and entered the
bathroom, so Eleonore had forced herself to return to bed.

She'd sensed the carnal beast beneath his skin on that first day,
when she'd tasted his blood. There was a wildness to him that he took

great pains to conceal. But why? And why was he so unhappy this morning? The werewolves she'd met over the centuries loved shifting. It was the highlight of the month, a chance to be utterly free.

"Hey," he said, poking his head around the doorframe. "I'm heading to work. Do you need anything?"

His eyes were reddened, with shadows beneath them. She cocked her head. "You don't look fit for work."

He squinted at her. "Gee, thanks." His gaze shifted to the box of cereal. "You know, people normally pour cereal into a bowl and eat it with a spoon."

Eleonore hopped off the counter, casting the box aside. "Did you not enjoy the moonshift?"

He made a face. "I don't like shifting."

Curious, she stepped closer, eyeing him from head to toe. He had the typical burly werewolf build, complete with a thick head of hair reminiscent of a pelt, but maybe he wasn't a full-blood werewolf. "Are you a hybrid?" she asked.

"What?"

"I thought werewolves liked shifting. But if you aren't a full-blood werewolf, maybe you take after another species." Like how she took after her vampire sire more than her succubus mother, even though she had traits of both.

His shoulders slumped, and he looked more tired than before. Eleonore felt a twinge of regret at having asked so bluntly. "No," he said quietly, "I'm not a hybrid. I just don't like it. It wastes so much time, and . . ." He bit his lip, hesitating.

"And?" she prompted.

"I already feel out of control," he said, tapping his temple with a forefinger. "On a bad day I can spiral and it's like I have no control over my thoughts or emotions. Shifting is like that. All of a sudden I'm in a new form, feeling all these powerful instincts, and I have no say in it."

Surprisingly, that made perfect sense to Eleonore. "You don't get a choice whether or not you shift," she said. "It just happens to you." Like being ordered around *just happened* to Eleonore, and she had no say in the matter.

Maybe they had more in common than she'd realized.

Ben nodded. "It's also so undignified. There's all that scratching and howling and . . . well, urges."

The pregnant pause and subsequent embarrassed look intrigued her. "What sort of urges?"

He looked even more embarrassed as he scratched the back of his neck. "Well, ah, wolves are very primal. So anything in that category. Eating, fighting . . . other stuff."

Her succubus instincts honed in on that subtext. "Do you fuck as a wolf?"

The blunt question had him hiding his face in his hands. "No! Some people do, but I don't like the idea of it. But some of that animalistic energy lingers after I shift back, and it translates into . . . and it's embarrassing, you know? I have to take a cold shower and meditate to get back to normal. If I can ever be called normal."

Aha. That explained the sudden surge of lust when he'd arrived home, if not what had sparked it. His bestial instincts lingered past the physical transformation.

Eleonore wasn't ashamed of sexual desires. People throughout history had been driven to find food, water, and shelter, and many of them pursued sex just as instinctively. Ben was no different. "You don't need to be ashamed of having carnal urges," she said.

He winced. "Can we please stop talking about my carnal urges?"

It wasn't an order, but Eleonore respected the boundary. "Of course."

"Thank you." There was a pause while he chewed his lip, and then he blurted, "And then there are the animals."

"The animals?" she asked, not following.

"I ate two rabbits and a mouse this time," he said glumly. "Last month it was only one rabbit."

"You don't like hunting?"

He rocked on his heels, back and forth and back and forth. "No, I do not. I thought I ate enough stir-fry beforehand to fill me up, but then a rabbit hopped in my path and . . ." His gesture implied helplessness.

Disliking hunting was an unusual werewolf trait, but it sounded like a classic considerate Ben Rosewood trait. This glimpse beneath his surface was intriguing. "Is there anything you do like about shifting?"

He ran a hand over his face. "What's with the interrogation?"

His tone was rarely so snappish. Eleonore didn't want to push too far, but she was hungry to know more about the wolf she was trapped with. "I've only met a few werewolves before. I'm curious."

He exhaled gustily. "Of course you are. I'm sorry, I'm in a bad mood this morning."

"Bad moods are normal," she said. "I have them all the time."

"Yeah, well, you definitely have more reason for them than I do." His mouth tipped up slightly. "Being able to see, smell, and hear better is interesting, and I do like running around and exploring. There's something freeing about it, and it's nice to take a break from my thoughts. But it's also like being a totally different person. I couldn't balance a checkbook as a wolf if I tried."

Eleonore had encountered checkbooks in 1969. An object that small ought to be easily balanced on a snout or paw, but perhaps he was uncoordinated in wolf form. She wouldn't insult him by suggesting so, though. "So you like being free and active," she said, "but you don't like killing the things you eat or temporarily being worse at business. That makes sense."

"Does it, though?"

She sensed Ben's veins dilating as he blushed. He was embarrassed when he had no need to be. "I don't like draining people to death either," she said, offering a slice of kinship to him.

His eyes widened and he took a half step back. "You drink people to *death*?"

"Only when the witch orders me to," she hurried to clarify, disliking how he was looking at her. "Or ordered, rather." Past tense. It was still strange to think she was free of that foul woman. "Normally feeding is a consensual arrangement both parties are happy with, and no one dies."

"Huh." He opened his mouth as if to ask a question, then closed it again and looked at his watch. "Shoot. I need to get going. Do you need anything before I leave? The Annex opening is Friday night."

As if she could forget. There was nothing left to shop for—her costume had been ordered with overnight shipping and would arrive later that day—but she could use more time in the space. "Can you take me with you? I've been corresponding via internet with the theatre students, but I would like to meet them and investigate the stage and lighting in person." Ben had put her in touch with two high school thespians who were eager to gain technical experience, and they'd been writing back and forth about Eleonore's music choice, the props she needed, and how the scene would be lit. Everything was arranged, but she would feel better if there was a chance to speak with the students in person beforehand.

Ben slapped a hand to his forehead. "Of course. I'm so sorry, I should have thought of that earlier." He dug his phone out of his pocket and started typing. "Amy and Caitlin have theatre for fourth period, so I'm asking the teacher if they can come by to help out."

Eleonore nodded. "Thank you."

"Thank *you*," he said fervently. "You're really saving me here." Then he gave her a soft, crooked smile that made Eleonore's heart flutter in appreciation. Now that she no longer despised him—and since he'd fed her so well with his orgasm in the shower—she could appreciate how handsome he was without blaming it on hunger. "And thanks for listening. Most people don't understand how I feel about shifting." He shook his head. "Actually, I haven't even talked to anyone about it in years."

That meant he trusted her with both his secret and his embarrassment. Eleonore's heart did another giddy little dance. Feeling daring, she brushed his fingers with her own. "I am grateful you shared with me."

A spark seemed to jump between them at the touch. Ben's pupils dilated, and Eleonore caught her breath. They stood close together, fingers barely grazing as silence stretched between them. Eleonore inhaled his scent, gaze tracing from the warm brown of his irises over the bold line of his nose and down to his mouth. His lips were full and pink, framed by his beard. She wondered how he used them in the bedroom—if they were always gentle, or if he let some of the beast out in private. She wondered if his beard would feel soft or coarse against her inner thighs.

She wondered what it would be like to take blood from the throbbing pulse at the side of his throat and what his moan of pleasure would feel like against her tongue.

She listed forward . . . just as Ben cleared his throat and stepped back. "Let's get going," he said, rubbing the back of his neck as his eyes danced away from hers. "We've only got a few days left to prepare for your theatrical debut."

Eleonore followed him to the car, this time wondering at the depth of disappointment she'd felt when he pulled away.

FOURTEEN

Ben's Plant Emporium was packed for the opening event on Friday night. Between the people browsing the plant selections and those gathering next door at the Annex to sample coffee, tea, wine, beer, and a range of pastries and sandwiches, they were nearing full occupancy.

A great problem to have, but Ben was about to sweat through his dress shirt, and his body was torn between extremes. His pulse raced and nausea gripped his stomach, but the thrill of seeing people turn out filled his chest with sparking fireworks of excitement. He manned the plant counter himself for the first hour before turning it over to Rani so he could circulate among the guests.

"Heck of a place you've got here," his cousin Avram said, slapping his back. The tall, good-natured werewolf lived in nearby Fable Farms, and since the two of them were the same age, they'd grown up together. Avram's thick brown hair matched Ben's and they both had the Rosewood jawline, but Avram's sparkling hazel eyes and easy smile were all Levine.

"Thank you," Ben said. "It's been a lot of work. It's hard to believe it's actually happening."

He looked at the venue with pride. He'd knocked down a section of wall between the nursery and the adjoining building so people could circulate freely, and the windows and roof beams were festooned with white holiday lights. The overall aesthetic was warm, homey, and handmade, with a rustic bartop and furniture commissioned from the same carpenter who had constructed the stage. Local artisans had provided woven rugs, pillows for cozy seating nooks, and art to adorn the walls, and he'd built display cases for them to sell their work. The local elementary schoolers had a corner display full of colorfully painted terra-cotta plant pots for purchase—maybe Ben's favorite detail, since a customer could walk out with a plant and a one-of-a-kind adorable piece of art, and a small child would end up thrilled as a result.

"The sandwiches are amazing," Avram said. "I had the turkey pesto and . . ." He kissed his fingers. Then he spotted someone over Ben's shoulder and waved. "Oi, Kai! Get over here and tell Ben how amazing this place is."

Kai was a good friend and another member of the Fable Farms pack. A transplant from New Zealand, the charming black-haired werewolf also captained the Fable Farms Furies rugby team. With a roguish smile, a primal love of the moonshift, and an incredible amount of self-confidence, he was the quintessential werewolf Ben often wished he could be.

"This is ace," Kai said, joining the group. "Amazing job, mate. What do you think, Lili?"

Speaking of an incredible amount of self-confidence, Kai had his arm around a short, beautiful redhead—his girlfriend of the past two years, Lilith. Her black horns were smaller than her son Astaroth's and she might not look physically imposing, but if Ben had to bet on anyone in a fight, it would always be the Mother of All Demons.

Tonight the demoness's smile was eerily wide, and her pale blue eyes had an unfocused look that meant she was probably a million miles away, thinking of heavens only knew what. Her attire was, as usual, vaguely piratical, and she had an actual cutlass strapped to her hip. "I tried to eat a cactus," she announced.

Ben blinked, then looked over his shoulder at the plant nursery portion of the store. Rani was standing at the counter, shaking her head as she cradled a pot containing a small barrel cactus. Catching Ben's gaze, the naiad rolled her eyes, pointed at Lilith, and mimed gnawing on the plant.

"The plants aren't for consumption," Ben said, returning his attention to Lilith. "The only food is in this half of the shop."

Lilith pouted. "So I was informed. But what's the point of immortality if you only eat safe things?"

Ben wasn't sure how to respond to that. He had his own temperamental, odd, immortal-ish redhead to deal with, but Eleonore was of sound mind—though traumatized—and he was no longer afraid she'd eat his liver. Lilith was a stick of dynamite no one knew was lit until it went off. "That's an interesting perspective," Ben said cautiously.

Kai leaned in and winked. "That's why she likes me so much. Not a safe bone in my body." He flexed, showing off his tattoos.

Avram snorted. "You're about as dangerous as a pillow fight, Kai."

Lilith looked Kai up and down disdainfully. "Silly puppy. Are you due for a flogging?"

"Absolutely," Kai said, clapping a hand to his chest dramatically. "I live to tremble at your feet, my beautiful demoness."

"Jesus Christ," Avram muttered.

Lilith's lips curved in a smile reminiscent of Astaroth's when he was feeling wicked, and she slapped Kai's ass. "Good wolf." Then she grabbed him by the belt buckle and dragged him away.

Kai tipped back his head and howled to the ceiling, then shot Ben a thumbs-up. "Back soon! Maybe!"

Ben shook his head as the pair vanished out the door. "Kai's a braver man than me."

Avram snorted again. He and Kai were the kind of friends who constantly took the piss out of each other. "He's been waiting for a pretty woman to walk all over him for ages. I just don't understand what Lilith gets out of it."

"A willing and eager victim?" Ben suggested.

"Good point."

Thoughts of Lilith receded as a stream of new guests descended on Ben to deliver congratulations. Somewhere amid the chaos, Calladia pressed a glass of champagne into his hand, and then Themmie insisted on taking interminable pictures of him with guests, plants, the wine rack, and an espresso machine manned by Hylo, whom he'd poached from Le Chapeau Magique to manage the Annex and the new employees on that side of the business. Ben smiled gamely, following Themmie's instructions. He'd long ago learned that avoiding photos with the pixie was an impossible task and that no matter how awkward he felt, she'd somehow manage to come up with a brilliant, flattering image he could use for his website or text to his parents to elicit a flurry of delighted emojis.

Speaking of his parents, they had arrived with the latest throng of well-wishers.

"Benjamin, I am so proud of you," his mother said, wrapping him in the best hug known to mankind. Even though he'd topped her five foot ten inches by half a foot twenty years ago, her warm embrace still made him feel cozy.

Ben was grabbed in a bear hug from the side, this time by someone nearly his height. "Atta boy," his father said, clapping his back. "You've done wonders with the place."

Ben grinned. "Thank you both so much. I'm glad you could make it."

His parents were a coordinated pair as always, wearing matching shades of blue. They were both over seventy but had the energy of people much younger. Violet Rosewood wore her silver hair in a ponytail, and her skin was creased with lines from a lifetime of smiling. Loren Rosewood had sun-coarsened cheeks from working in his garden and dramatically peaked eyebrows. Both of them were sturdy in the way of people who lived life hands-on, as eager to build a house for the needy as they were to cook a feast for the neighbors.

Some of Ben's tension relaxed at seeing them. *Come heck or high water,* his mother had always said, *we Rosewoods stick together.* His parents were no longer as robust as they'd been in his youth—age was wearing its unwelcome way over them, leaving arthritis and stooped frames in its wake—but they still loomed large over Ben's existence. Introverted Ben might be an exotic species amid the rambunctious Rosewood-Levines, but Loren and Violet Rosewood's exuberant brand of love had been the bedrock he'd built a life upon.

"When's the performance?" his mother asked, looking around. "Will there be singing?"

"I'm not sure," Ben said. "I gave her total creative freedom." The least he could do after ordering Eleonore to perform.

There was a hurried consultation between his parents, which they whispered at a volume he could absolutely hear. He braced himself for the coming interrogation.

"This is your supposedly not-girlfriend, right?" his father asked, not at all casually.

"She is not my girlfriend, that's correct."

"Kind of interesting, don't you think?" Loren mused, stroking his white-bearded chin. "You said the stage would be put in next year, and then suddenly you started calling in favors and paying extra for the builders to set it up early."

Damn this town's love of gossip. "I changed my mind about timing."

His dad cackled. "Yeah, just in time to host a pretty redhead's debut show." He clicked his tongue. "Don't think you can trick me. I was young once; I know how this goes."

Ben rolled his eyes. "Stop badgering me about my nonexistent love life and go find some champagne." Spotting one of the staff passing by with a tray of chicken wings, he pointed. "Free appetizers!"

"Free, you say?" His father was already on the move.

Violet Rosewood wasn't so easily distracted, though. She slapped Ben's arm lightly and gave him a reproving look. "You know your father can't resist free food."

"Exactly." It was Ben's trump card because it always worked.

She sighed. "We just want to see you happy."

"And I am happy," he said. At this moment, anyway. "So go eat and give me another hug later."

His mother popped up on her toes to kiss his cheek, then straightened his tie before joining her spouse.

Ben looked around, wondering if he could slip away for a breather. He was proud and excited to share the results of his hard work at long last, but this was also . . . a lot.

Astaroth approached, holding out a small box. "Congratulations," he said.

Ben took it hesitantly, unsure what the half demon could possibly have brought him. Ben had gotten off to a rocky start with Oz and demons in general, and though Astaroth was fun to hang out with, the two men were completely opposite in personality and taste.

Inside the box were silver cufflinks—a pair of beautiful, undoubtedly expensive full moons. Ben's jaw tightened, but he forced himself to smile and be appropriately grateful for a kind, thoughtful gesture. Astaroth couldn't know Ben didn't particularly love the full moon, since Ben was too embarrassed to tell people, and he probably thought every man had a suit in his closet just begging for fancy cufflinks. "These are incredible," Ben said, giving the demon a brief hug. "Thank you so much."

Astaroth nodded and tapped his skull-topped cane against his boot. If Calladia was to be believed, it contained a sword. The apple didn't fall far from the tree when it came to Lilith's offspring. "You're doing a good thing for this town," Astaroth said, ice-blue eyes sweeping over the room. "People need more places to gather and feel welcome."

It was a surprising sentiment from the witty, sarcastic demon, who wielded words like both weapon and armor. But he'd softened considerably since meeting Calladia and giving up his power-hungry ambitions as a member of the demonic high council, and he seemed earnest now.

"Thank you," Ben said. "I agree."

Then Astaroth popped on his charming grin and winked, raising his champagne. "And they always need more places to drink."

Ben laughed and clinked his glass against Astaroth's. "Cheers to that."

The music faded, and Gigi stepped onto the stage, tapping the microphone. "Is this thing on?"

The microphone was, indeed, on. The speaker emitted a shrill squeal, and everyone winced.

Ben looked toward the soundboard, where one of the high school thespians was turning dials frantically. She gave a thumbs-up.

"Check check," Gigi said. This time her voice was an appropriate volume, and the assembly cheered. "Great," Gigi said, grinning. "And thank you, sound wizard. I have no idea what was wrong and I have no idea how you fixed it, but you are the hero of the evening." She clapped in the direction of the soundboard, and others followed suit until the girl was blushing.

Gigi looked great. Her brown hair was put up in some kind of fancy knot that was presumably Themmie's work, and she wore a pin-striped gray pantsuit with sparkles on the stripes, as well as Astaroth-mandated pink Converse. She looked professional with a fun, approachable edge.

"Isn't this space amazing?" Gigi gestured around the room. "I'm so proud of my brother, Ben Rosewood, for not only killing it in his plant nursery business but expanding it to give people room to eat, drink, mingle, and watch live theatre. It's too easy to end up glued to our phones or laptops, working too hard and interacting with our loved ones from a distance." The room was silent, the audience hanging on every word. "Glimmer Falls is a rich, diverse community," Gigi continued, "and spaces like Ben's Plant Emporium remind us of that. None of us are alone, and there are places where we are always welcome. So let's give it up for Ben!"

The guests applauded, turning appreciative smiles his way. Ben bowed his head, feeling like his chest might burst from pride, assuming his flaming cheeks didn't kill him first. Gigi had tried to convince him to make a speech, but he'd refused, instead letting Rani give a brief welcome earlier when he'd cut the ribbon between the Emporium and the Annex.

The curtain behind Gigi shifted, drawing Ben's eye. The backstage space was laughably small—maybe two feet deep and spanning the width of the stage, with an access point through a former janitor's closet—so that must be Eleonore, preparing for her show.

The attention thankfully moved away from Ben as Gigi launched into a rousing speech about community, so he focused on the black velvet curtain. There was a slight gap on the right—left? He always forgot how stage directions worked—and he smiled when he saw a slice of pale face appear and vanish just as quickly.

Was Eleonore nervous the way he'd been nervous about the

Annex opening? He suspected the answer was yes, given how jumpy and brooding she'd acted all day, but he hadn't been about to ask or suggest such a thing. Funny, how quickly he'd come to understand her pride and some of her quirks, but becoming inadvertent roommates had provided them with a rapid education. Besides, Eleonore was not a particularly subtle person.

"And that's why I'm running for mayor!"

Ben snapped back to attention when the room burst into a cacophony of cheers and applause. Gigi was beaming under the spotlight. It was a very hastily assembled spotlight, manned by another high schooler from the Thespian Club, but the teen managed it with very few wobbles. Ben decided on the spot to offer the stage free to the high school as a place for students to gain experience and get comfortable with an audience.

The stage might not have become a staple of the Emporium and the Annex so quickly if it weren't for Eleonore and Gigi, but even with the added stress it had caused, Ben didn't mind. In fact, he was glad. He might never set foot on the boards, but he respected people who did, and he vowed that Ben's Plant Emporium would always be a place for fledgling creators—whether elementary school artists, high school theatre students, or aspiring comedians—to spread their wings safely.

As Gigi detailed her goals for public office and the future of Glimmer Falls, Ben watched the crowd, assessing their reactions. It was clear the room was in her thrall.

Ben had to admit it was impressive. He was used to thinking of Gigi as his wild, social butterfly younger sister, but she presented herself and her campaign with a mix of wit and earnestness that would have had him sold even if he wasn't related to her. He would never in a million years be able to talk in front of people like that.

It wasn't that Ben hadn't known Gigi was smart, funny, insightful, and on a mission to better their community, or that he in any way believed her incapable of changing the world. He loved her unconditionally, and no matter how much he razzed her (and she razzed him back, far more viciously and articulately), he had faith she would do whatever she set her mind to and the world would be better for it.

But this was still his little sister commanding the room. The girl who had insisted on wearing her favorite sequined shirt to elementary school for an entire month, claiming she was a world-famous pop star. The girl who, as a teenager, had driven her car into a fire hydrant because she'd been texting. The one who had needed to be picked up from a rave in college *by their parents*.

Watching Gigi speak with articulate, inspiring passion, Ben felt a lump in his throat.

His little sister had grown up. And yes, he'd already known that, but still. This was something special.

When she finished her speech with "Let's get out the vote!" Ben hollered and clapped louder than anyone. And cried, too, sniffling and wiping his eyes on his sleeve.

"If you aren't registered to vote yet, go see the volunteers in the back," Gigi said. "They'll be happy to help out. And if you feel like volunteering your time or skills for the campaign, Rani at the front desk has all the info." She grinned and swept out a hand. "Now, we have a very exciting performance to christen the stage of Ben's Plant Emporium. Please welcome the world debut of actress Eleonore Bettencourt-Devereux!"

Cheers broke out, then faded with the lights as people hurried to claim available seats. The twinkle lights still shone on the outer windows, but the stage was a murky gray expanse. The curtain moved, and a female silhouette took center stage.

Ben clenched his fists, instinctively flexing his toes inside his dress shoes. This was the performance that would set the tone for the rest of the Emporium's performances. It would also give credence to Gigi's campaign.

And yet the question currently top of his mind was . . .

Was Eleonore scared?

She had never performed before, though she'd told him she liked the idea. She also wasn't used to this time and place, and it didn't take a therapist to figure out she was dealing with PTSD on top of that. Though Eleonore should probably see a therapist. Ben should, too. It had been a few years—he'd once gone regularly, hoping to corral his buzzing thoughts, but the business had become too demanding.

"You've got this," he said under his breath, gaze pinned on the shadowy figure onstage.

The stage lights came up.

Eleonore stood at the microphone with a bucket by her side. She wore a voluminous cloak, and the effect was eerie. Black cloak, porcelain-pale skin, flaming red hair that had been combed in some sort of way to make it look tangled.

"In the beginning," Eleonore said, raising a fist, "we were dust. Stardust, fallen to earth to mix with the baser elements and create life." She tipped her hand over and opened it, letting a fine spray of sand form a small pyramid on the stage. "When we die, we become dust, too."

Ben nodded. He'd heard that metaphor before, but it was a good poetic image and a fine start. Optimistic about the cycle of life, death, and rebirth. Thematically appropriate for electing a new mayor.

Eleonore flung the rest of the sand away violently, and an audience member in the first row flailed at their face and started coughing. "Before we become dust, though," Eleonore announced, "our corpses bloat and rot. We do not dissolve peacefully. Just as we crawled out of a primordial soup once, when our lives are ended, we *ooze*."

Ben nearly choked on his tongue. What in the name of—

He looked around, terrified people were about to start fleeing for the exits.

Though a few audience members shifted and muttered to one another, they remained in their seats. For now, at least.

"When I was thirty years of age many centuries ago," Eleonore said quietly into the microphone, "a witch found me and chained my life to a crystal. My hands became hers. My words became hers. My free will became hers."

Maybe this wouldn't be so bad, Ben told himself. There was something compelling about her intense, serious expression, something that demanded he lean forward and give her his full attention. The intro had been weird, but maybe that had been a fluke and this would be the bulk of the piece: a monologue about what Eleonore had endured. It would make him sad and upset about her past and guilty about his ownership of the crystal, but he could handle it, and maybe other people would be moved by her story, too.

"She used my hands for killing her enemies, of course," Eleonore said. "Have you ever watched the light leave a person's eyes?" She produced a musical triangle from a pocket in the cloak and struck it. *Bing.* "If you had, you would know it isn't a light at all. It's something that can only be defined by its absence."

Bing.

Bing.

Bing.

Ben scratched his neck and shifted from foot to foot. His pulse was speeding in a familiar and unpleasant way, and sweat beaded at his hairline. This hadn't gone completely off the rails yet, but it was getting close.

Eleonore's face was solemn as she bent to stick her hand in the bucket. It came up coated in red liquid, which she dragged over her face, leaving finger streaks like something from a haunted house.

"Oh, no," Ben whispered.

"The true virtue of a killer," Eleonore said into the microphone, eyes gone wide, "is in what they're willing to watch. Our mortal shells are mere sacks of meat, ripe for the slaughter, and there is nothing beautiful in death. During my years of servitude my hands were not my own, but my eyes were, and I can tell you now . . ." She paused dramatically before a vicious whisper left her red lips. "I watched."

Ben's stomach dropped—or rather, continued the trajectory it had begun when she'd first thrown sand in some poor customer's face. He could sense Gigi's eyes burning into him from where she stood at the back of the crowd. When his sister started heading his way, he knew he was in deep trouble.

Eleonore suddenly beamed. "And now," she said, throwing off the cloak to reveal a rainbow-sequined jumpsuit, "an interpretive dance!"

Music piped in from the speakers, loud and sudden enough to make him jump. Was that . . . "Barbie Girl" by Aqua?

Yes. Yes, it was, and Eleonore was now capering around the stage, smearing bloody handprints over her jumpsuit. She'd produced a knife from somewhere and was holding it clenched between her teeth as she flailed and spun. The audience stared silently, faces frozen in a range of expressions, shock and horror chief among them, though an ancient woman in the front row was beaming and bopping her head in time with the beat.

"Hey, Ben," Gigi said way too casually when she reached his side. "Quick question: What the fuck is this?"

Onstage, Eleonore began acting out the dramatic stabbing of invisible enemies, periodically pausing to strike the triangle and make odd, warbling vocalizations. Ben felt faint. "I . . . have no idea."

It's experimental, visceral, and dynamic, Eleonore had told him when he'd asked about her planned show. *Think Joan Jonas meets Ana Mendieta with shades of Isadora Duncan and Kesha.* Not knowing who those people were, he'd nodded and told her that sounded good. She'd clearly done the research, after all.

He really should have looked up those names.

"This is . . ." Gigi flinched as Eleonore howled and poured the remaining liquid in the bucket over her head. "Jesus fuck."

That about summed it up. At least Ben's sensitive werewolf nose could tell the liquid wasn't real blood. He hoped it cleaned up easily.

The music abruptly stopped, and Eleonore froze in position, staring at the audience. "If you were the one wielding the knife," she whispered, "would you watch?"

She moved so quickly his eyes couldn't track it, striking a new dramatic pose at each corner of the stage. And then, making Ben's heart lurch into his throat, she moved in a blur up the wall and appeared *on the ceiling*, clinging to it upside down like Spider-Man in a way he hadn't even known vampires were capable of. Her fake-blood-soaked hair dangled in clumped strands as she bared her teeth, hissed, and then let out a primal scream.

"Oh, God," Ben said, jerking backward and nearly knocking over a table.

The lights went out.

When they came back up, Eleonore was standing back on the stage, grinning. She swept a bow. "Thank you for watching!" she said. "And don't forget to vote for Gigi Rosewood in November."

◆　◆　◆

BEN . . . CLAPPED.

Other people were clapping, too, which was a good sign. Maybe. They were also talking in hushed voices, though, and no one looked particularly happy except the grandmother—now spattered with fake blood—and the two high school theatre kids, who were hooting and high-fiving.

Eleonore took another bow, dripping more fake blood onto the floor. She looked like Carrie at the prom, except with more sequins.

When she disappeared behind the curtain and the rest of the café lights came up, Ben sank into the nearest chair, hands pressed to his mouth as he tried not to hyperventilate.

He'd fucked up. Lycaon, how he'd fucked up. Gigi had asked him to put together a performance that would get people excited about the arts and voting, and he hadn't asked a single question when Eleonore had assured him she had come up with something "in the finest tradition of experimental theatre." He'd been too busy obsessing about the million other things he barely had a handle on.

Gigi sat next to Ben. She stared blankly at the stage, which one of the Thespians was now mopping. It was almost enough for Ben to forgive the kids for helping Eleonore pull off that horrifying display in the first place.

"That was . . ." Gigi said, trailing off.

"Yeah," Ben replied.

"A lot."

"Yup."

A string quartet he'd hired to wrap up the event launched into a lively ditty. A few customers had already left, but as the sound of violins wound around the tables, the atmosphere relaxed.

He hoped. It was hard to tell when his pulse was pounding in his temples and he felt like beating his head against the nearest wall. He swallowed the urge to vomit.

Ben's parents chose that moment to appear in front of him. They looked . . . well, about how he imagined he looked. "Wow, that was sure something!" his mother enthused, pasting on a wide smile. "Such an original choice. Very daring."

"She's very pretty when she's not dripping with blood and shrieking," his father offered.

Ben groaned and covered his face with his hands. "I . . . don't know how to process this yet. That wasn't what I expected."

That earned him two more hugs and a peck on the cheek from his mother, and then his parents were thankfully out the door. His mother had always seemed nearly psychic about what her children needed, and in this case Ben needed space to have a meltdown.

"Ben Rosewood, right?"

Ben flinched, dreading whatever was about to follow that inquiry. Melting down would have to wait. "That's me," he said, standing and turning to face his judgment.

A short, rotund man with pointed ears, horns, and backward-jointed knees stood before him. A faun, hiding his furry haunches beneath a purple velvet suit.

The man held out a hand. "I'm Cornelius Crabapple, arts and entertainment journalist at the *Glimmer Falls Gazette*. A pleasure to make your acquaintance."

Ben gave a tentative handshake. Inside he was screaming, though. Of all the people who could have witnessed Eleonore's performance, this had to be one of the worst. Just imagining the headline in the *Glimmer Falls Gazette* made him sick: "Vampire Succubus Unleashes Shrieking Reign of Terror on Horrified Patrons of Ben's Plant Emporium and It's All Ben's Fault." "Sorry," he said. "That show was . . ."

"Brilliant!" Cornelius exclaimed, clapping his hands.

Ben blinked, taken aback. "It . . . was?"

Cornelius nodded happily, making his silky ears bob. "Glimmer Falls used to welcome more edgy shows in the seventies, but for decades now we've been subjected to the same wholesome community theatre shows year after year." The faun winced. "I can't tell you how many times I've been forced to endure *Hello, Dolly!* at the theatre guild. This is a daring departure and, dare I say, bold enough to put Glimmer Falls on the national experimental theatre map."

Next to him, Gigi looked as baffled as Ben felt. When he didn't reply, though, unable to summon words, she quickly took over. Her expression smoothed into a smile, and she shook Cornelius's hand. "We're so glad you feel that way," she said warmly. "I believe strongly that there's a place for all art in Glimmer Falls, from family-friendly musicals to daring, experimental pieces that push the limits of what audiences are comfortable with."

Ben suppressed the urge to snort at that line of bullshit. She was definitely developing into a politician.

"Exactly," Cornelius said, snapping his fingers. "The feelings elicited in the viewer are as much a part of the art as what happens onstage. I know I'll be thinking about this show for a long time." He looked around the room. "Is the actress available? I'd love to get a few quotes from her for my review."

Ben was about to say, *No, Eleonore's long gone, please don't allow her to make this any weirder*, but she took that moment to pop out from the old janitor's closet, face freshly scrubbed and fake-blood-soaked hair clipped up. She'd changed into normal clothing, and Ben wondered at the state of the sequined jumpsuit. Could it be dry-cleaned?

"Ms. Bettencourt-Devereux," Cornelius called out, waving frantically as he hurried toward Eleonore. "A moment of your time!"

As he engaged Eleonore in conversation, Ben looked at Gigi again. They stared at each other blankly for a long moment, then simultaneously burst into laughter.

"Oh my God," Gigi wheezed, bending over at the waist. "Did that just happen?"

"Do you mean," Ben replied between great, shoulder-shaking laughs, "d-did the most horrifying thing I've ever seen just im-impress a theatre critic so much he says—he says—oh God—it's going to put us on the national experimental theatre map?"

He was losing it. Going through so many emotions in the course of an hour couldn't be healthy.

"Heavens," Gigi said, fanning her red-tinged cheeks. "I knew theatre people were odd, but *wow*."

Other people were clustering around Eleonore, peppering her with questions. When Ben looked around, he realized not that many customers had left after all. The majority were chatting or drinking or perusing the plants, and the bright sound of laughter rang over the gathering.

Hope swelled behind the last few wheezy chuckles. Maybe he hadn't messed up as badly as he'd thought. "Am I forgiven?" he asked Gigi.

"That was the fucking weirdest thing I've ever seen," his sister said. "But you know what? I'm not mad at it." She grinned, then punched his shoulder. "You at least keep things interesting."

FIFTEEN

P ERFORMING ONSTAGE WAS *AMAZING.*

Eleonore beamed as she accepted a glass of champagne from one of her new fans.

"That was some crazy shit," the dryad said. "I think the old man in front of me nearly fainted." She looked to be in her early twenties, with bark-brown skin and hair. Eleonore wouldn't have necessarily known she was a dryad if she hadn't popped out of the wood-paneled wall, nearly scaring Eleonore into an inadvertent stabbing. Thankfully she'd restrained herself, since murdering one of her fans would have been unfortunate.

"Thank you," Eleonore said, bowing her head. "I wasn't sure it would be experimental enough."

Her research had emphasized that the point of experimental theatre was to push the boundaries of what was comfortable and acceptable in public. To create a space so far from the ordinary, one could explore both the profane and the sacred, free of traditional limits. But since Eleonore wasn't using real blood, actively harming herself or anyone else, or engaging in public acts of sex or defecation, she'd feared she hadn't brought enough of the profane into her performance.

"Oh, believe me, it's going to be the talk of the town." The dryad raised a hand. Eleonore hesitantly raised her own, mirroring it as she'd seen Tarzan do in an animated movie earlier that week. The woman smacked their palms together, making Eleonore jolt with surprise. "Please tell me you're performing again," the dryad said.

That was what the theatre critic, Cornelius Crabapple, had requested, too. "I don't know," Eleonore said, looking toward Ben. "That's up to the proprietor."

She hoped he'd let her perform again, though.

She'd been painfully aware of Ben's presence all night, watching him from behind the curtain. He was obviously not comfortable in large social settings, choosing to linger near the walls, but he'd been beaming with pride.

Most of the time, anyway. Immediately after her performance, he'd looked so distressed she'd had a terrible fear she had disappointed him.

Thankfully, he was now laughing with his sister and their friends, so apparently all was well.

"I want to bring my stepmom next time," the dryad said, drawing Eleonore's attention again.

"Do you think she'll like it?" Eleonore asked. She sipped the champagne, enjoying the play of bubbles over her tongue.

"Not in the least." The woman grinned. "But I'll have a hell of a good time."

Another well-wisher approached. Eleonore wasn't practiced with casual conversation after so many years, but it was surprisingly easy to fall back into the rhythm of it. People congratulated her; she thanked them. Sometimes they had questions about the performance, the costume, or the fake blood recipe, which she'd been happy to share. The Glimmer Falls High School students Ben had connected her with for lighting and sound—Amy and Caitlin—had been enormously helpful on all accounts. They'd created this batch of fake blood and taught her how to make her own from common household ingredients.

She glanced toward Ben again, nibbling her lower lip. What had he thought about the performance? Had it been interesting and significant enough to give a boost to Gigi's campaign?

He met her eyes across the room, and Eleonore's heart sped up. She pressed her fingers to the throbbing pulse in her neck, wondering at the visceral response to nothing but a look. Then Ben started making his way toward her through the crowd, and her stomach dipped in a pleasant yet alarming way.

The werewolf looked especially handsome tonight in gray slacks and a forest-green dress shirt with a silver tie. His thick hair had been brushed and styled by Themmie earlier, and it looked smooth and shiny under the light. Her fingertips itched as she wondered what the strands would feel like gripped in her fists. His cologne wafted toward her as he approached, and she inhaled deeply, seeking the scent of his skin and blood beneath.

Stars, he smelled edible. Her fangs lengthened at the temptation.

Ben waited for a gap between fans. "Hey," he said when he was finally able to step close.

"Hey," she replied, tipping her head back to look up at him. She suddenly felt too warm, and anxiety skittered up her spine to burrow into her brain. What if he'd hated the show? What if it hadn't been daring or original enough?

What if she didn't smell as good to him as he smelled to her?

He cleared his throat, then pulled his hand from behind his back to reveal a small pot filled with red-and-yellow pansies. "For you," he said.

Eleonore took the pot. The petals trembled, and she realized she was shaking slightly. "Thank you, but why? You already gave me flowers once."

His mouth quirked up. "Flowers aren't a once-in-a-lifetime gift, Eleonore. People give them to each other frequently to say thank you or sorry or congratulations or just because they're thinking about someone."

"Oh." Her face felt even more flushed. "But I don't have any for you."

"I wasn't the one performing," he said, shrugging. "Besides, men don't usually get flowers."

She frowned. "That doesn't seem fair. Why shouldn't men deserve flowers as well?" In fact, she felt bad for neglecting this apparent tradition. It was the opening night of his café—he deserved something pretty to congratulate him.

"I agree," he said. "Maybe that can be your next campaign after revitalizing the Glimmer Falls theatre scene. Equal access to floral arrangements." He had such a nice smile, the kind that crinkled the skin beside his eyes and creased his cheeks. His face was lived-in, which she liked. It made her want to know the story behind each small line. Made her want to deepen those lines, too, knowing she was the cause of his smiles.

She rubbed her chest over her pounding heart. Her mortal, succubus heart, which was beating for a new possibility—one she wasn't sure she could fully face yet.

"Was it truly okay?" Eleonore asked quietly. "The performance?" It had been a long time since she'd craved someone's approval, but she craved his.

Ben bit his lip. He had normal canines, not sharp like hers, but his teeth were nice and mostly straight except for a few charmingly snaggled ones she liked the look of. "It was very original," he said.

Her shoulders relaxed. "Thank goodness. I was worried it wouldn't be groundbreaking enough."

At that, Ben chuckled. "Ah, no, it was plenty groundbreaking," he said. "Glimmer Falls is full of oddities, but I can safely say no one has done precisely that before."

"And you liked it?" she pressed. The audience clearly had—or at least those who hadn't seemed to enjoy it had been appropriately dazed and contemplative afterward—but his opinion meant the most.

Why that should be, she didn't care to analyze at the moment. As a habit she tried not to ruminate on her emotions.

"It was amazing," Ben said. "Very weird and kind of scary, but that's what you were going for, right?"

Amazing, he'd said. Pride swelled in her breast. "I wanted to challenge the audience's perception of beauty, appearances, death, and truth," she explained, echoing her artist's statement. "Juxtaposing music and glitter with the bloody reality of killing or being killed reminds us that life is fleeting, and that there's something raw and ugly underneath even the prettiest of surfaces."

"Oh," Ben said, smile dimming. He nudged his glasses up his nose, and light bounced off the metal frame in a starry flash. "You really think everything is ugly underneath?"

She shrugged. "It doesn't have to be in a bad way. Vampires think blood is beautiful, after all, even when it's pooled beneath a corpse."

Ben's eye twitched at that. He wasn't used to seeing things from the darker perspective she'd been raised with. The medieval era hadn't been a gentle one, and she'd been raised in a band of warriors before she'd had to put those lessons into practice as an ensorcelled assassin.

Eleonore wanted him to understand, though, so she cast about for better words to explain why she'd chosen this message and why it wasn't as dismal as it sounded. "It's more that . . . Most people end up in the ground anyway. Pretending otherwise doesn't change that, and there's freedom in knowing that and fighting anyway. Choosing to face the truth beneath life, no matter how bloody or strange, is always better than fooling yourself into thinking the sparkles on the surface are what's real."

It was something she'd thought about often over the years, not only as someone who had been raised to face the dark and thrive in it, but as someone others viewed a certain way. Eleonore was beautiful—there was no point denying that. She'd inherited her mother's looks and a bit of her succubus magnetism. Often, the best way to carry out the witch's orders had been to let Eleonore's prey assume the pretty surface was the sum of her substance and that they had nothing to fear.

It had bothered her to act vapid and flirtatious. It had bothered her that when people who misjudged or harassed her died, she felt guilty that she hadn't shown them the truth from the start. Better to face death knowing it was coming than be surprised when something you thought was safe turned out not to be.

And if you were the one dealing the death, it was essential to face what you had done. She hadn't been able to defy the orders of the Witch in the Woods, but she had been able to control how she viewed her own actions. Lying to herself was even worse than lying to others.

That train of thought was enough to bring her mood down, as always, but this time Eleonore didn't want to let the anger and sorrow in. She shook her head sharply, dispelling the memories and musings. Tonight was a celebration, and if the performance had pulled an uncomfortable emotion out of her, that was the nature of impactful theatre.

"Enough about the play," she said, waving away whatever question was hovering on Ben's lips. "People love the café. How do you think the opening went?"

Ben looked around at the happy guests, and pride washed over his features. "I almost can't believe it's real and that so many people showed up."

"They like this place," Eleonore said. "And they like you."

Ben shifted, looking down at his toes. "I don't know about that," he said, rubbing the back of his neck. "They like free food and booze."

Did he truly not see how people looked at him? They watched him with affection and respect, and he'd barely had a moment alone all night. "They do like you," Eleonore said firmly. "You are not allowed to be self-deprecating."

His head popped back up, and his eyebrows rose. "I'm not?"

"No," she said, crossing her arms. "Tonight is a celebration, and I insist you accept everyone's praise and appreciate your own hard work making this happen."

Ben chuckled, biting his lip for another of those rueful, thoughtlessly charming smiles. "Is it the vampire part or the succubus part that likes giving orders?"

"It's the Eleonore part," she replied. Then she poked him in the arm. "Now go mingle and let people praise you."

He hesitated, eyes darting over the crowd. "Will you go with me? Social events aren't really my thing."

He wanted her to be his support? That was . . . nice. She hadn't had anyone rely on her on the field of battle in a long time. Perhaps this wasn't a traditional battlefield, but nothing about the situation she'd landed herself in was traditional.

"Yes," she said. "I will make sure no one accosts you or otherwise jeopardizes your person."

He chuckled and shook his head, then extended his elbow. "Then let's go do that horrible activity known as socializing."

Eleonore looped her hand through his arm, feeling warm and flustered and as if, for the first time in a very long time, something good might be beginning.

SIXTEEN

WHEN BEN OPENED HIS EYES, THERE WAS SOMETHING ON his nightstand.

He blinked away sleep, trying to orient himself. It was the morning after the Annex opening, and by the sunlight streaming through the crack in the curtains, he'd slept later than usual. The light caught the petals of a handful of black-eyed Susans near his head, their roots encrusted in dirt.

He sat up, forehead furrowed. There was only one person who could be responsible, but why had Eleonore ripped them out of the ground to leave next to his bed? And where had they come from?

There was a piece of paper next to the yellow blooms with one word written on it: CONGRATULATIONS.

"Oh," he said softly, rubbing his chest where a sweet ache had started behind his breastbone.

Eleonore had given him flowers.

Sure, she had done it by invading someone's garden, then sneaking into his room in the dead of night—which was a bit unsettling considering her long career as an assassin—and crumbs of dirt were now spread over his nightstand and the surrounding floor, but it was the thought that counted.

Why shouldn't men deserve flowers as well?

She'd been indignant about the injustice, but he'd shrugged it off at the time. He ought to have known she wouldn't leave it at that. Eleonore was a vampire succubus of action, for better or worse. She had discovered a wrong that needed righting, and so she had done it as quickly and aggressively as she did everything else.

He was beginning to suspect that beneath her prickly exterior, Eleonore was rather . . . sweet.

Ben picked up the flowers and cradled them close, not caring that he was getting his T-shirt dirty. He inhaled, taking in the fresh, sweet, earthy smell. His eyes grew blurry.

"Ridiculous," he whispered, rubbing away the tears that were tempted to fall. They were just flowers, nothing to cry over.

But they were *his* flowers.

He remembered how Eleonore had looked when he'd given her flowers as an apology gift. Baffled at first, then surprised, and then she'd clutched the vase like a dragon hoarding treasure, hesitant to put them down even to eat.

He understood how that felt now.

Ben slid his feet into slippers and padded into the living room, where Eleonore was glued to the television, mouth agape. "Good morning," he said. "What are you watching?"

"An interview show full of horrible people," Eleonore replied. A mug of blood sat before her, steam wafting upward. "Can you believe this man cheated on his wife with the nanny while she was cheating on him with the gardener and none of their combined thirteen children are his?"

Ben took one look at what was on TV and hurried over to block her view. "Oh, no, no, no. This is not good content to represent modern times." He considered. "At least, I hope not. But these shows are staged, anyway."

"It's fake?" Eleonore frowned. "They shouldn't pretend it's real, then."

"Wait until you discover *The Bachelor*." It was Gigi's guilty pleasure, which Ben had been forced to watch with her the season a werewolf had been looking for love. She'd tried to convince him to apply, but that had been a hard no. Dating one person was daunting enough—dating multiple people on camera would be a nightmare. The only possible redeeming feature was that it would all be scripted—no matter what Gigi thought, he could not be convinced otherwise—which meant he wouldn't have to come up with witty conversation or smooth compliments on his own.

Eleonore turned the TV off, then turned to face him. "You found your flowers." She looked expectant, if a bit wary. Worried about what he would say?

Ben was still hugging the flowers to his chest. "I did," he said. "They're wonderful. Thank you, Eleonore."

She shrugged, but a smile tugged at her lips. "Someone has to rectify the world's injustices."

Her smile hit him in the chest. It was soft and genuine, and he took it as a sign that she was coming to trust him. It was a trust he would always do his best to honor.

Ben busied himself trimming the stalks and finding a vase from the hall closet. Then he set the flowers on a bookshelf by the front window where the light would catch their petals.

The sight of a plastic-wrapped bundle on the driveway sent him hurrying out. The *Glimmer Falls Gazette* had arrived, likely containing a review of Eleonore's performance and hopefully some good words for both Gigi and the Emporium's expansion. He ripped the plastic off on his way back in, and his sensitive nose twitched at the crisp, appetizing smell of newsprint paper and ink.

"Surprise Mayoral Development!" was the headline on the front page. Beneath it was a photo of Gigi onstage at the Emporium. Ben skimmed the article, which introduced the new challenger for Cynthia Cunnington's position and detailed a few campaign promises. The article didn't take sides—with Gigi an unknown and Cynthia quite frankly terrifying, Ben hadn't expected it to—but it was a decent write-up Gigi ought to be pleased with.

Columnist Artemis Crumpet was the reporter responsible for updates on local events and venues, and Ben fist pumped when he saw "Local Spotlight: Ben's Plant Emporium" featured in her weekly column.

> *Ben's Plant Emporium, long a destination for those green in thumb, has expanded both its venue and appeal. An adjoining café termed the Annex now offers coffee, tea, wine, beer, and scrumptious sandwich and pastry options. The opening night was raucous and delightful, and this reporter was surprised to see the christening of a small stage that will host theatrical performances. Far be it from me to review the play at hand—Cornelius Crabapple has the details of that—but it's safe to say that, having witnessed a performance I never could have anticipated and have no words to describe, I'm excited to see what wild happenings Emporium proprietor Ben Rosewood plans to host next.*

Ben grinned as he skimmed the rest of the piece, which touched on a few specifics of the new menu and praised the Emporium's Annex as a great addition to the local gastronomic scene.

"What are you reading?" Eleonore asked.

Ben had been so absorbed he hadn't moved past the front door. "The local newspaper," he said. "They're discussing the Annex and Gigi's campaign."

Eleonore was at his side instantly, but this time Ben wasn't as badly startled as usual. Her vampire hyperspeed was becoming routine. They still needed to address the ceiling-crawling she'd debuted during her performance, though, which he hoped she never did late at night when he wasn't expecting it. "Is the performance review in there?" she asked.

"I'm looking for it," he said, flipping pages.

Eleonore was nearly standing on his toes, so impatiently was she scanning the paper. Her arm pressed against his, and he could smell the conditioner she'd used on her long red hair—*his* conditioner, he thought with an odd sort of pride—and the naturally sweet spice of her skin. His pulse kicked up a notch. Eleonore slid a glance up at him, undoubtedly able to hear or sense his heart rate, but thankfully didn't say anything.

"Here we go."

"A Bold New Talent" read the headline.

Gentlefolks of Glimmer Falls, I bear exciting news. In an era when our entertainment options are often limited to reality television reruns or the same goddamn musical year after year—no offense to the talent of our Glimmer Falls Theatre Guild, which is of high caliber but should really consider saying "Goodbye" to Dolly—our city has been blessed with an art piece so unique, so daring, so visceral, we have not seen its like before. Experimental theatrical performer Eleonore Bettencourt-Devereux, a vampire succubus of mysterious origins, unleashed a fury of a performance onstage at Ben's Plant Emporium and Annex last night. It is impossible to fully explain the show's appeal in words—some things must be experienced to be understood.

"This is great," Ben said. The photo accompanying it had been taken in the interpretive dance section before she'd dumped the bucket over her head. Eleonore had been captured midmovement: her fake-blood-streaked torso was twisted, her hands outspread and head flung back as she balanced on one leg. Starbursts of light shone from the sequins, and her hair trailed behind her like a fiery banner.

She looked . . . joyous.

"He really did like it," Eleonore said wonderingly. She tapped the page with one fingernail. "See here? He says I am 'beautiful and fearsome to behold' and 'a true original.'"

"You are," Ben said. "In every way."

Eleonore looked up at him like he'd hung the stars in the sky. Her green eyes were bright with feeling, and a pretty pink flush crested her cheeks. "That's the nicest compliment I've ever gotten," she said in a hushed voice.

Ben felt dizzy looking at her. She'd already been the most beautiful woman he'd ever seen, but happiness gave an ethereal glow to her features. His stomach dipped, and every inch of his skin seemed to light up at once. He was hyperaware of the soft press of her arm against his and the way one of her long, waving locks tickled his skin; he fancied he could even feel the shift of molecules in the air as she exhaled.

Oh.

Oh shit.

Ben had been single for a long time and was, historically, rather dense about women, but he could tell when he was about to be in a boatload of trouble. No one had caught his eye in years, yet here he was, tumbling headfirst into infatuation with the scariest, strangest, most captivating woman he'd ever met.

Ben swallowed hard. "I'll need to compliment you more often, then," he said in a rough voice.

Eleonore's gaze flicked to his lips so quickly he might have imagined it. "Compliments aren't mandatory."

He huffed in amusement. Practical, blunt Eleonore. "I know," he said. "Neither are flowers."

The silent message hung between them. They had both given

each other flowers, not out of obligation, but because they'd wanted to. Because they cared.

Eleonore's lips curved in a secret smile. "You know, I think—"

Whatever she was thinking was lost, though, because his phone rang suddenly and shrilly. It was his house phone, which only his family had the number to—"A *landline*, Ben? In the era of Our Lady Taylor Swift?" Themmie had mocked when she'd found out—which meant someone had tried to call his cell phone first and wanted to talk to him badly. "Sorry," Ben said, forehead furrowing as he hurried for the receiver. "No one calls that number unless it's important."

When he picked up, he'd barely started to say hello when Gigi's voice burst over the line.

"Cynthia Cunnington wants to meet me. What do I do?"

His sister thought this was important enough to interrupt his . . . flirting? Was that what he'd been doing?

Ben pinched the bridge of his nose. "Did you think you'd get through the whole campaign without seeing her? She probably wants to set up a debate."

"Not a debate," Gigi said. "She wants to meet me alone in an abandoned warehouse on the south side of town. In an hour."

"Oh." That admittedly didn't sound great. "Maybe it's an informal meet and greet, since you're her only opponent."

"Yeah, and maybe she's going to murder me where there are no witnesses."

"She's not going to murder you."

"She *might*."

"Who is committing murder?" Eleonore asked from right next to Ben, where she had arrived with her usual abruptness.

Ben put his hand over the receiver. "Cynthia Cunnington wants to meet Gigi in an hour," he told Eleonore. "She's nervous about it."

"Oh my God," Gigi said so loudly anyone within five feet of the phone could have heard her. "Do you have *a woman* over at your house?" She sounded scandalized and delighted, and Ben groaned, knowing the news would spread to his parents and then the rest of the Rosewood-Levine clan with shocking rapidity.

"Give me that," Eleonore said, snatching the phone from his grasp.

Ben blinked as Eleonore launched into a series of terse questions. Where was the meeting? Was Gigi worried for her safety? Had Cynthia Cunnington murdered many people before? No? Well, that was no guarantee she wouldn't start now.

"Tell her you'll be happy to meet but will be bringing security," Eleonore ordered. She handed the phone off to Ben without waiting for a response. "I'll go sharpen my knives." She disappeared into the spare room.

Ben gaped after Eleonore until a burst of sound from the receiver reminded him Gigi was still on the line.

"That was Eleonore, wasn't it?" she asked. "Are you sleeping with her? Does she moonlight as a security officer?"

Ben winced. "I'm not sleeping with her, not that it's any of your business. And no, not to my knowledge, but she seems to have volunteered herself for the task."

Gigi made a shrieking noise. "I knew you were into her."

"Shhhh." He had no idea how sharp vampire hearing was. "It's not like that."

It was totally like that. It was also almost certainly one-sided.

"Yeah, sure." He could almost hear her eye roll. "We'll talk more about this verrrry interesting development later. I need to pick an outfit suitable for meeting my new enemy. Are you part of my security detail, too?"

The alternative was letting both Gigi and Eleonore confront Cynthia Cunnington, the ice queen mayor of Glimmer Falls, alone, and neither werewolf curiosity nor Ben's natural protectiveness would allow that to happen. Cynthia wasn't a killer, but she wasn't exactly nice either. "Obviously," he said—even though the first and only time he'd interacted directly with Cynthia had resulted in him being harangued and insulted before Cynthia had magically blasted Oz across the Emporium and destroyed one of Ben's plant displays. He swallowed hard. "Wear shoes you can run in, okay?"

"Sure thing," Gigi said. "Lycaon, now I'm actually excited. See you and your totally-not-girlfriend Eleonore soon! I'll text you the address."

She hung up, and Ben sagged against the wall, feeling like he'd been churned up and spit out by two tornadoes in a row. What vindictive deity had saddled him with so many domineering women?

His lips twitched. And why wasn't he remotely upset about it?

SEVENTEEN

B EN'S SISTER WOULD HAVE BEEN INSTANTLY RECOGNIZABLE
even if Eleonore hadn't seen her the previous evening. She
had the same thick, slightly unkempt hair as Ben, the same warm
brown eyes, and a tall, sturdy build. She was also fidgety, though
in a less nervous-seeming way than Ben: she was bouncing on her
toes, hands in her coat pockets while she watched passersby with
avid curiosity. She wore the same pink shoes as the previous night.

"Hey!" she said, hurrying over once she'd spotted them. They'd
decided to meet at a café a few blocks from the warehouse. She
hugged Ben, then extended her hand to Eleonore. "Nice to officially meet you, Eleonore. I'm Gigi."

"I know," Eleonore said as she shook Gigi's hand. Did Gigi think
she was forgetful enough not to realize this was the same person
she'd seen the previous night?

Gigi took Eleonore's bluntness in stride. "So you're my security
detail, huh? Do you have a bulletproof vest under there?"

Eleonore looked down at her attire—black jeans, sturdy boots,
and a leather jacket. After Ben had taken her to buy clothes, he'd

used a sewing machine to add hidden pockets at her request, so her knives were well concealed. "Why would I need a bulletproof vest?" she asked, having learned of the invention on the internet. "I'm faster than some witch." Besides, guns were a clumsy, unsophisticated weapon, and no witch or warlock she knew would stoop to using one instead of spellcraft.

"Love the confidence." Gigi cocked her head. "So, uh, do you have a background in stage combat or something? No offense, but you're not exactly what I envision when thinking about bodyguards. Not that that's a problem, of course. I'm grateful for the help."

Ben must not have shared Eleonore's credentials with his sister. "Don't worry about my capabilities," she reassured her. "I have been killing for six centuries."

Ben winced for some reason.

"Oh." Gigi blinked. "That's . . . Wait, I thought that was just part of the performance." Eleonore shook her head, and there was a long pause. "Six centuries, wow," Gigi said. "Sorry, I guess I forgot vampires are immortal. The Middle Ages must have been something, huh?" She made a few stabbing motions. "All that feudalism and stuff."

"I'm only half vampire and therefore not immortal," Eleonore said. "Technically."

That elicited an even longer pause. Gigi looked at Ben and widened her eyes. Eleonore didn't see what expression Ben made in response. She was too interested in watching Gigi's face. She'd been all smiling professionalism last night, but in this more informal setting she was more expressive, thoughts and feelings flying across her features with little effort to disguise them.

What a safe time people lived in now. They could hug strangers without fear of gutting. They could say what they liked and show what they were feeling on their faces without shame or consequences. Eleonore knew she was often an overly literal person, failing to understand subtext or the fast-paced jokes and references people made, but she could read the meaning in Gigi's expression easily. Gigi had never met someone like Eleonore before and wasn't sure how to react.

Eleonore didn't mind. She was a product of her time and lived experiences. And part of why she didn't mind was because, like Ben, Gigi took her blunt proclamations in stride and accepted her anyway. The young werewolf had started grinning again, eyes sparkling as she focused on Eleonore. "We need to go out for drinks sometime," she said. "I have a feeling you have some very interesting stories."

"Maybe next weekend?" Ben suggested. "This week's going to be busy with all the new business coming in to the Annex."

Gigi waved a hand. "Oh, you're not invited. This is a girls' night." She winked at Ben. "Just me and your *friend* Eleonore here."

Ben groaned. "Just what I need, the two of you collaborating."

Eleonore seized on the idea instantly. "Yes," she said. "We shall have a girls' night."

She hadn't socialized privately with someone who wasn't in possession of the crystal in . . . how long? And yes, Ben was far preferable to the Witch in the Woods, but there was still an edge of discomfort to their arrangement. He could alter the course of her life with a few words.

Eleonore was under no mystical obligation to Gigi. They could just be people together.

"Great." Gigi clapped her hands. "Let's work out the details later. Are we ready to face Cynthia Cunnington?"

"Tell me about her," Eleonore said, switching into mission mode. "What potential dangers will we face?"

Gigi grimaced. "Honestly, she's probably just going to be nasty and try to get me to drop out of the race. She's rich and snooty and friends with all the other rich and snooty people in town, and one of her ancestors cofounded Glimmer Falls in the 1800s, so her opinion holds extra weight in the community because of that. Oh, and she's a really good witch."

"She plays with her necklace before casting spells," Ben said.

Eleonore nodded. She was familiar with the ways of witches. Magic required a combination of spellwords and a physical ritual. Some witches drew runes, some danced, and others manipulated thread or other objects—whatever was most natural for gathering their focus and channeling it into mystical intention. "Does she know you're bringing protection?"

"Yeah, I emailed her back and mentioned I'd be bringing a few members of my team," Gigi said. "I didn't say bodyguards, though, because I don't want to start the meeting on a hostile note."

"Will Cynthia have protection with her?"

Gigi looked abashed. "You know, I didn't think to ask."

Eleonore had gone into far worse situations blind. "No matter," she said. "I will be more than capable of handling any threat that arises."

Ben lightly nudged Eleonore's hand, drawing her attention and sending a shiver down her spine. "Hey," he said softly, dipping his head toward hers as if sharing a secret. Historically, she wasn't a fan of people looming over her, but Ben's looming felt protective, not hostile. "Obviously if anyone's in real danger, you can protect us, but this is probably just going to be an awkward conversation. So maybe . . ." His mouth worked as he clearly considered his words. "Maybe don't . . ."

When he didn't immediately elaborate, Eleonore realized his concern. "Bite her throat out unprovoked?" she asked, raising her brows.

He coughed into his fist. "Well, yeah, but also . . ."

Also? Gods, what else did he think she might do? Yes, she was easily startled, but in six hundred years she hadn't once gutted or beheaded someone without good reason or mystical compulsion. "No random acts of disembowelment?" Eleonore joked.

"No unnecessary maiming in general," Gigi broke in when Ben just stammered. "Or, um, other . . . vampire stuff."

Christ's balls, they were serious.

Eleonore took in their solemn faces, then burst into laughter. Did they think she had the temperament and manners of a rabid dog? "I don't *enjoy* killing or maiming," she said, still chuckling. "I only kill when forced to or in cases of mortal peril. So unless Ben orders me to chop Cynthia's head off or she actively tries to hurt you, I will merely stand nearby, being quietly menacing." Another giggle slipped out. "*No unnecessary maiming*, really."

Gigi and Ben weren't laughing with her, though. In fact, Gigi was looking at her with consternation and Ben with some pensive expression she couldn't interpret. Eleonore's laugh trailed off. Had she committed a faux pas? The stars knew she wasn't aligned with this time and its social norms, but surely their concern about her committing unprovoked crimes had been a *bit* funny.

"What do you mean, you kill when forced to?" Gigi asked softly.

Oh.

Eleonore turned on Ben. "You haven't told your family why I'm here?"

Ben looked guilty. "It's a whole thing," he told Gigi in a low voice, as if Eleonore weren't standing right there. "I'll explain later."

"Why later?" Eleonore asked, humor slipping into irritation. Would he rather Gigi think Eleonore an unpredictably violent murderer? If Gigi truly thought she was a rabid dog with no mind of her own, girls' night was canceled. "Gigi wants to learn about the binding spell, and the primary source is right here." She turned to face Ben's sister. "I have been mystically tied to a crystal for six hundred years, cursed to obey any order the owner issues." The words were well-worn by now, but they still tasted sharp on her tongue. "Ben bought the crystal, so if he ordered me to behead Cynthia or jump off a cliff, I would be forced to do it."

Gigi's jaw dropped. "Like *Ella Enchanted*?"

Eleonore didn't know who that was. "Does this Ella also murder on command?" she asked. If so, she extended her sympathies.

Gigi's head whipped around as she glared at Ben. "Did you seriously buy that crystal? What the fuck, Ben?"

A gratifying response. Girls' night was back on.

"I didn't do it on purpose," Ben said quickly. "I was drunk and thought the eBay listing was a joke . . ."

"It was posted on *eBay*?" Gigi repeated. "Is that even legal?" She looked furious. "I need to look into this. As mayor, I will refuse to allow mystical entrapment in Glimmer Falls."

Girls' night was going to become a weekly event. "Thank you," Eleonore said. "I'm not enthused by the situation, as you can imagine."

"I'm going to figure out how to release her from the spell," Ben told Gigi. "It's just been so hectic lately I haven't had time to look into it."

Gigi didn't look mollified by that. "No offense, Ben, but when someone's destiny lies entirely in your hands, you should probably *make time*."

Ben made a frustrated sound, then looked at his feet. His toes were tapping in that anxious rhythm: right, left, right, left. "You're right," he said softly. "I dropped the ball on this one."

Eleonore frowned, thinking of Ben's late nights and red-rimmed eyes, how sometimes he was so tired he fell asleep during dinner. How he was on the phone all the time talking to vendors or Gigi's other campaign advisers, how she'd caught him staring at a half-made scarf in his lap at three a.m. one morning, muttering sadly that he'd dropped a stitch. The silver spikes hadn't been weapons, after all—they were knitting needles he was using to create gifts for his family members.

"Hold on," Eleonore said, putting her fists on her hips and

facing Gigi. "That's not fair. Ben has been working himself ragged lately, including on *your* campaign. He can't magically create more time when every minute of it is already taken up with obligations."

Ben looked up, surprise written over his features. Gigi, too, seemed taken aback. "Oh," she said. "Sorry, Ben. I didn't realize things were that hectic." She hesitated. "I can find someone else for the campaign . . ."

"I can handle it," he said instantly.

Gigi looked relieved. "Are you sure?"

He nodded. "Positive. One hundred percent." He jerked his thumbs at his chest. "Solid as a rock, this guy."

Eleonore narrowed her eyes at him.

He smiled a little. "Really," he said softly. "But thank you, Eleonore. And I promise we'll find a way to break the curse."

"Hmm." She recognized wounded pride when she saw it, understood how important it could be to cling to scraps of imagined control long past the point of reason. Her pride, battered and chipped as it was, was her most precious possession, like an old warrior's armor kept in a place of honor despite the dings and indents of battles lost.

Ben was too proud to admit he was overwhelmed. He would cling to his knitting and his obligations until he passed out from sheer exhaustion.

"Very well," Eleonore said, deciding to let it go. "Forget the crystal for now. We have a wicked witch to face."

◆   ◆   ◆

CYNTHIA CUNNINGTON STOOD ALONE IN THE MIDDLE OF THE warehouse, highlighted by a fall of sunshine from a broken skylight. The concrete floor was stained and dust floated in the air, though none of it seemed to settle on the witch. Her pulled-back hair was as golden as the sunlight, and she wore an iron-gray pantsuit with clean, sharp edges. A pearl necklace ringed her throat—the only visible weapon, but the only one she likely needed.

Eleonore considered the height of the witch's heels and how she'd positioned herself for maximum visual impact rather than strategic advantage in combat. Some of the tension left her shoulders. This wasn't the look of someone eager to start a fight—at least, not a physical one. This was someone who wanted to make a statement.

"I told you to come alone," Cynthia said as she watched the three approach. Her eyes touched on Eleonore briefly before lingering longer on Ben.

The first—and often last—mistake many warriors made was assuming the largest-looking threat was the most dangerous one. Eleonore smiled, feeling a rush of adrenaline. There was something intoxicating about battle that started in the tense, waiting moments before all hell broke loose. She remembered it from standing with her clan on the edge of a snowy field, knowing the white expanse would soon be churned and spattered with crimson.

She didn't miss killing, but she did miss that feeling, though she'd thought it lost after centuries of tedious, meaningless violence. But here it was again, pricking her nerves and sharpening her senses. She was here of her own accord to defend others; no one had commanded it.

That made all the difference.

"I emailed you," Gigi said brightly. "Generally I don't make a habit of lurking in abandoned warehouses alone, but to each their own." She stopped out of arm's reach of Cynthia, bracing her feet apart as Ben and Eleonore flanked her. Gigi didn't look as polished, but her footwear was far more sensible, and her smile expressed confidence.

Interesting, how easily Gigi shifted from the bright, expressive, ebullient woman they'd met on the sidewalk to this more contained, practiced version. There were no cracks in her composure for enemies to sink their claws into.

Cynthia's eyes were blue and cold. Her beautiful face was expressionless, but there was a thin quality to her skin and enough fine lines—though not smile lines—for Eleonore to put her age at somewhere in her fifties. Her posture was impeccable. "Why are you running for mayor?" she asked without preamble.

"Because I love Glimmer Falls and believe I can institute worthwhile change," Gigi replied. "Why are *you* running for mayor?"

Cynthia's pink lipstick–tinged mouth tightened. "I'm not running for mayor. I *am* the mayor."

"For the moment." Gigi was still smiling, though Eleonore's sharp eyes caught a tremor in the hand at her side. Nervous, then, but doing an admirable job of hiding it.

"You don't have experience in politics," Cynthia said.

"Neither did you when you ran for mayor."

"You don't have the required connections."

"Agree to disagree on that one."

"No one's going to vote for you. Look at you—you're like a child playing dress-up, desperate to fit in with her betters." Cynthia laughed, light and nasty. "Do you actually imagine you have what it takes to challenge me?"

Ben made a low, angry sound. "Watch it," he said.

Cynthia turned her cutting gaze on him. "I remember you. The flower seller, right?"

"Something like that."

Her disdainful once-over before she returned her attention to Gigi spoke volumes. "I looked up your family," Cynthia told Gigi. "As common as they come. Your father was a roofer, your mother a secretary, your brother"—she tipped her head toward Ben—"no one important. You're working-class stock, completely unsuited for public office."

Eleonore did not like this woman. "You are unpleasant," she said.

A tiny line formed between Cynthia's brows as she looked at Eleonore. "Is this another relative?" she asked. "Hecate knows werewolves breed like it's going out of style."

"I revise my statement," Eleonore said. "Vous êtes une connasse." She turned to Gigi. "People actually voted for her?"

"She pretends to be a lot nicer in public," Ben said. "But the elitism is part of the package for her supporters, and there wasn't a huge voter turnout last time."

"More people will vote this year," Gigi said confidently. "We're partnering with the Glimmer Falls Resiliency Project, the Environmental Protection Club, and local schools and nonprofits to launch a Get Out the Vote campaign."

Cynthia did not look pleased. "You can launch any campaign you like—you'll still lose. Which is why I'm giving you the opportunity to withdraw from the race now and save yourself a large amount of money and humiliation."

Gigi tipped her head back and laughed, and Eleonore's esteem for her rose even more. It took courage to laugh in the face of opposition. "What a generous offer," she said. "However, I must decline."

Cynthia's eyes narrowed. "You really insist on doing this?"

"I do."

"Then know this," Cynthia Cunnington said. "After I walk out that door, we will be enemies. And I give no quarter to my enemies."

Gigi raised two fingers to her brow and saluted. "See you on the campaign trail, Mayor Cunnington."

Cynthia brushed past, heels clicking on the concrete as she strode for the exit. She didn't look back.

"Well," Ben said when she was gone, "that went better than expected."

Gigi bent over, bracing her hands on her knees. "Damn," she wheezed. "She's intimidating enough from a distance, but up close she's terrifying." She glanced at Eleonore. "As our resident acting expert, how'd I do?"

Eleonore wasn't sure she could be termed an expert, but she liked the sound of it. "You did very well, and I believe you hit on exactly the right technique to anger her most."

"I did?" Gigi straightened. "And is that good or bad?"

"Good. A frustrated or angry opponent is more likely to make errors."

"What was the technique?" Ben asked. "She seems pissed off one hundred percent of the time."

"Gigi laughed at her," Eleonore said. "It's clear Mayor Cunnington takes herself very seriously and expects others to do so as well. She expects to earn respect or fear. Laughing at her hits her directly in her weakest spot: her pride."

"How very Jane Austen of you," Gigi said. "Something-something 'pride is always in good regulation'?"

"What?" Ben asked, looking baffled.

Eleonore had no idea either.

"*Pride and Prejudice*? Which I'm sure someone can quote way better than me." As the blank looks continued, Gigi sighed. "Uncultured swine."

"Pride isn't always a weakness," Eleonore said. "For some people it's a motivator, a reason to feel engaged with their cause. Something that comes from earned confidence. People who are truly proud of themselves and secure in it don't mind being laughed at." She tipped her head toward the warehouse exit. "She nearly burst a vein when you laughed at her." And oh, how nice that blood would have been to lap up. "When pride is that fragile, it's just aggression papered over insecurity or cruelty. It becomes a liability."

Eleonore liked to believe her own pride was in the strength

category, rather than a weakness. She was certain of her worth as a person and determined to have that worth be respected. That was the sort of pride that allowed her to hold her head high despite whatever indignities she suffered.

Cynthia Cunnington didn't sound like she'd suffered many indignities in her life—which was good news for Gigi. They could write up a list of Cynthia's weaknesses, then craft strategies to exploit them.

"I'm pretty sure Darcy said something almost exactly like that in the book," Gigi mused. "Maybe he was a six-hundred-year-old vampire succubus, too."

"Wouldn't that be an incubus?" Ben asked.

"Good point." Gigi pulled her phone out of her pocket and swiped her thumb over the screen. "I also definitely need to read some fan fiction about vampire incubus Fitzwilliam Darcy, so I'm putting in a request to Lilith."

Ben's eyes widened. "You're on a texting basis with Lilith, the Mother of All Demons?"

Eleonore listened with interest, remembering the demoness she'd met behind the newspaper box while stalking Ben.

"We're in the same fan fiction Discord server," Gigi said. "Themmie founded it. It's called the Smutty Smurfettes. We share prompt fills, and Lilith always picks the most outrageous ones." She tilted her head, chewing on her lip. "Maybe we can work in tentacles somehow? *Elizabeth Bennet, tentacle monster* has a nice ring to it."

Ben shook his head and started walking away. "I refuse to discuss tentacle porn with you."

Eleonore wouldn't have minded learning more about tentacle porn, but that was what Google was for, so she followed.

"Fine, fine," Gigi said, catching up with them. "No Austenian tentacles. Let's get out of here and start coordinating a kickass Get Out the Vote campaign."

EIGHTEEN

ARE YOU REGISTERED TO VOTE?" GIGI ASKED.

Ben stood at his sister's side, holding a clipboard on which they'd recorded five new voters so far.

The centaur who'd opened the door looked at Gigi mistrustfully. "Who are you and why do you want to know?"

Ben winced, but Gigi was unfazed. "Gigi Rosewood, candidate for mayor." She launched into her campaign spiel, which Ben had heard so many times at this point he almost had it memorized. He eyed a fountain in the centaur's front yard, wondering if he could sneak away to drown himself in it.

Door-to-door campaigning was the worst. In addition to the dreaded task of public speaking, it involved invading other people's territory, which had resulted in several hostile encounters. The last one had involved a scythe being waved in a threatening manner as a robed figure screamed he was *not* interested in joining their cult.

Extroverted Gigi had no problem knocking on doors not

knowing what was waiting on the other side, but Ben wasn't built like that. Could he handle difficult, unpredictable customers at the Emporium? Yes, because that was his territory and being the owner automatically made him an authority. This, though? Door-to-door canvassing ranked very high on the list of Things To Avoid If At All Possible, somewhere between stubbing his toe and testicular torsion.

The centaur was already registered to vote, but he took a pamphlet before shutting the door in their faces. The pamphlets were colorful and crisp, with Gigi's new headshot—courtesy of Themmie—smiling over the words *Gigi Rosewood: Howling for Change.*

They headed back down the driveway, but before they could turn toward the next house—a purple, turreted monstrosity that either contained a winged person or someone with a flair for the dramatic—Ben stopped in his tracks. "I can't take this anymore," he said, holding out the clipboard. "Please, I beg you—find someone else to help you bother total strangers."

Gigi wrinkled her nose. "I was wondering how soon the introvert juice would kick in and send you scurrying for cover."

"It's not about being an introvert," Ben said. "Who actually enjoys striking up conversations with strangers?"

Gigi laughed. "Me, for one, but I take your point." She patted his arm. "Thanks, bro. I know this isn't your favorite thing to do."

"It absolutely is not," he agreed vehemently.

Gigi made a shooing motion. "Go check on the Emporium or hang out with Eleonore or something. I can handle the rest of today's route on my own."

"You're not going to walk around alone and unprotected," he said, appalled at the suggestion. "You're a public figure now." His little sister had made herself a target for the whole world, it seemed, and both Ben's brotherly and pack instincts refused to leave her to fend for herself.

"Oh, yes, a very important public figure," she replied. "I can't even wipe my ass without a bodyguard's help, lest the toilet snakes try to murder me for my political views."

Ben ignored the snark and pulled out his phone, thinking of the most aggressive friend they both knew. "I'm calling Calladia for backup." He immediately reconsidered. "Wait, not Calladia."

As a personal trainer with a love of mayhem, Calladia had flexible hours and a mean right hook, which would normally make her an excellent candidate for some daytime bodyguarding. Unfortunately, Cynthia Cunnington was Calladia's mother, and though the two were estranged, he suspected having Calladia actively campaign for Gigi would cause major drama.

"I feel so bad for Calladia," Gigi said with a frown. "It's mind-boggling that horrid woman produced such an amazing person. And Cynthia doesn't even seem to realize how wonderful Calladia is."

"I know." Ben couldn't understand that family dynamic either. The stories he'd heard about Calladia's upbringing had sounded nightmarish, with an absent father and a demanding mother who had wanted her daughter to be another icy, pearl-wearing social-ite. Calladia was about as far from that stereotype as one could get, and Cynthia had been vocal in her displeasure over that fact. The two had basically had no contact for the last two years, and though Calladia seemed at peace with that choice, it couldn't feel good.

Ben's parents were kind and loving, and the extended clan was equally supportive. No one was forced to be someone they weren't, even if people enjoyed some good-natured teasing. If he needed help, he could dial any of a dozen numbers and have someone on their way immediately.

Speaking of which . . . "I'll text Avram," he said. "If he can't canvass with you, he'll know someone who can."

Fifteen minutes later, Ben's cousin arrived with Kai and Lilith in tow. Both werewolves were wearing their rugby kits—they must have come from a game—and Ben was amused to see that Lilith was wearing a Fable Farms Furies T-shirt and had pom-pom ribbons dangling out of her pocket. Of course, being Lilith, she also had a broadsword strapped to her back.

"Sorry about that," Avram whispered, jerking his thumb over his shoulder at where Lilith was sharpening the sword while cheerfully suggesting Gigi close her pitch with "Vote or die." "I only invited Kai, but those two are attached at the hip these days."

Dark-haired Kai was doing energetic push-ups next to Lilith. He hopped up and pumped his fist. "Three cheers for democracy," he declared. "Huzzah!" When no one joined in, he elbowed Lilith lightly. "Come on, Lili. Huzzah!"

She pinned him with an icy stare that would have sent most people fleeing. "My next pom-pom will use your intestines for ribbons."

Kai bit his lip and gave Lilith a flirty look Ben recognized from bar nights he'd been dragged to in years past. Kai had always had a way with the ladies. "Damn," he said, "it's hot when you threaten to maim me."

Ben shook his head, chuckling. The two were the oddest couple, but somehow it worked. Lilith's red hair and dramatic threats made him think of Eleonore, and he decided to go home rather than stopping by the Emporium as planned. "Good luck," he said, clapping Avram on the shoulder. "I've got my own menacing redhead to check in on."

The family all knew about Eleonore and the crystal situation by now, of course. Text messages had flown fast and furious all week, memes had been shared, and Ben had been razzed to hell and back for getting drunk and buying a possessed plastic rock. Everyone wanted to know if they were dating, of course, and no one believed him when he said they weren't. He now had about fifteen social invitations to pass on to Eleonore, which he was trying not to inundate her with all at once. He wasn't sure how she felt about spending time with strangers, and he wasn't sure he wanted her anywhere near people who knew his most embarrassing childhood secrets anyway.

Avram perked up. "Did you tell Eleonore she has an open invite to come play rugby?"

"I did. She wanted to know if knives are involved."

"Alas, no." Avram winked. "Not while the ref is looking, anyway."

Ben laughed, then waved to the group as he headed out. On the drive home, he found himself whistling and jostling his knee, in an oddly good mood for someone who had been forced to ask people about their voting habits. He couldn't wait to see what Eleonore had been up to today.

She was constantly surprising him. He might come home to find her reciting Shakespeare, or she might greet him with a flurry of bizarre facts she'd learned on Witchipedia about historical massacres or animal reproductive habits. One time he'd come home to a kitchen full of smoke and a vampire succubus shrieking gruesome threats at a ball of blackened cookie dough. Another time he'd found her practicing some sort of martial art with his knitting needles.

"I thought they were weapons at first," she'd admitted when he'd inquired about the needles. Amused, Ben had attempted to teach her to knit, which Eleonore had gamely tried for half an hour before pronouncing it *excessively complicated for something so boring*.

A curtain twitched when Ben pulled into the driveway. Had she been watching and waiting for him?

He felt a bit breathless at the thought.

"I'm back," he called out as he opened the front door. "And I am never going canvassing again—" He broke off, nearly tripping over his feet.

Eleonore stood in the living room wearing a sleeveless, high-necked dress. The emerald fabric clung to her breasts, waist, and hips before falling loose to the floor. Two slits reached high enough on her thighs to reveal the edges of leather knife holsters, and matching loops of leather ringed her waist and wrists. The bracelets covered her forearms like gauntlets, and when Ben spied the gleam of metal tucked into one—a tiny hidden dagger—he nearly whimpered.

Oh fuck. It was like some god had plucked an image out of his subconscious just to taunt him with his deepest, most untouchable desire.

"A live audience reaction," an unexpected male voice said. "Excellent."

Ben hadn't even noticed Astaroth, Calladia, and Themmie seated on the couch. He tugged at his collar, flushing at having been caught ogling. "I don't recall inviting you over," he told the demon, witch, and pixie, frowning at them and hoping his jeans were sturdy enough to disguise his response to Eleonore in that mind-blowing, earth-shattering dress.

Astaroth shrugged. "Hasn't stopped me before." The demon's lean frame was encased in a dove-gray suit, and his beringed fingers were interlaced on the skull top of his cane. His pale blond hair shone in the sunlight falling through the window, as perfectly coiffed as the rest of him.

Next to him, Calladia had her bare feet tucked up on the couch, as casual as her partner was formal. She wore teal workout spandex and a T-shirt that said *Punch Like No One's Watching*, and her long blond hair—a warmer, more golden shade than her partner's—was pulled up in the messiest bun Ben had ever seen.

Themmie rounded out the trio, a burst of chaotic color and patterns that were presumably fashionable, not that Ben would be able to tell. Privately, he thought it looked like she'd thrown a bunch of costume pieces in the air, closed her eyes and spun around, and selected things at random. Her top was black-and-white tartan, which contrasted with a fluffy pink skirt and chunky, rainbow-hued jewelry, and her hair had been bespelled bubblegum pink. Her brown cheeks were dusted with something glittery that for all Ben knew might be actual pixie dust, since it mirrored the shimmer of her wings.

Varying degrees of trouble, all three of them.

"So?" Themmie asked, gesturing at Eleonore. "What do you think?"

Was he supposed to be capable of thought? Ben held his breath, daring to look at Eleonore once more.

Breasts.

Yes, those were definitely breasts, he confirmed silently. Full breasts and wide hips, the contours of which were made very clear by the tight fabric. The neckline rose nearly to her chin, but despite the lack of visible cleavage—or maybe because of it—Ben couldn't stop thinking about the shape of her and how she'd feel under his hands.

It wasn't that her curves were news to him—far from it. But she was such a dynamic force, always moving or hissing or being outrageous, that ogling her generally took a back burner to adapting to her chaos. And besides, he went out of his way *not* to ogle her, eyes darting away whenever her lush curves and strong thighs caught his attention. Staring wasn't gentlemanly.

Now he was being asked to stare. So, cheeks hot and palms sweating, he did.

The green fabric was the perfect contrast to her pale skin and flaming hair, which hung unbound and waving to her waist. When she shifted, the fabric whispered, exposing more of one creamy thigh. The holster was digging slightly into her skin, and for a mad moment he contemplated unbuckling it—possibly while she held the knife to his throat—and then soothing the pink marks on her skin with his lips.

Astaroth cleared his throat. "Do you suppose he's had a stroke?"

Ben tore his gaze away from Eleonore. "Ah," he said, reaching up to rub the back of his neck. "It's a . . . dress."

Themmie winced.

"Spot on," Astaroth drawled. "I knew werewolves had heightened senses, but your powers of observation are unmatched."

Eleonore crossed her arms, and her lips turned down. "He doesn't like it," she announced.

"I don't think that's the issue," Calladia said, eyes sparkling with mischief.

Themmie was mouthing things at Ben behind Eleonore's back, and though he couldn't tell what the specific words were, he picked up on the general meaning when she started gesticulating passionately.

"It's a very nice dress," he hurried to say. "Very, ah, green. Yes, very green."

Themmie escalated to wringing an invisible neck—his, no doubt.

"Beautiful," he continued, trying to dig himself out of this horniness-induced hole. "You look beautiful. I'm sorry, I'm not always good with words."

Eleonore's arms loosened, then dropped to her sides. "You think it's beautiful?"

I think you're *beautiful, no matter what you wear.* "It's astounding," he said. "In a good way, to be clear. You look very . . . yes."

That slit was high enough that he could push the fabric aside to kiss his way up her inner thigh to that wet, sweet spot between her legs. Would she sigh at the touch of his lips? Moan? Or order him to put his mouth exactly where she wanted it? He got harder imagining it.

Her eyes widened. "Oh, you *do* like it," she said, reminding Ben of the unfortunate fact that she could sense his erections. He would have been more mortified if her frown hadn't vanished to be replaced by a look of delight. "Excellent," she said. "It's for any political events I need to attend as your sister's bodyguard."

"Oh." Ben revisited the staring situation, this time trying to figure out in what world this was a good outfit for a bodyguard. "Isn't it a bit . . . movement-restricting?"

Tight, he meant. Very, very tight up top.

"Not at all," she said. "Watch this." There was a blur, and then she stood still once more, looking at him expectantly. "Well?"

"Maybe drop out of warp speed and try that again," he suggested.

As always, *Star Trek* terminology made her face light up. "Aye aye, Captain." Then she went through a sequence of movements that involved spinning, ducking, punching, and kicking. She was right—the fabric was stretchy, her arms were unencumbered, and the high slits allowed her to kick and move freely. The slits also revealed quite a bit more of her, but thankfully—for Ben's cardiovascular health—she was wearing spandex shorts. She finished the routine by pulling both knives from her thigh holsters and flinging them across the room.

Ben stared at where the hilts stuck side by side out of the doorframe, quivering from the force of her throw. "Well," he said, mouth dry. "That explains the mysterious holes I've noticed around the house lately."

The long skirt swished as Eleonore strode across the room to retrieve the knives. "As you can see," she said, sliding them back into their holsters, "this dress will allow me to blend in at formal events while still being able to kill people if I need to." She grinned, brushing her long hair back over her shoulder.

Ben suspected nothing would help her blend in, especially not that miracle of a dress, but he was still stuck on the violence she'd apparently been inflicting on his walls. He wasn't planning on moving anytime soon, but a Realtor would have questions if he did. "How about I set up a target dummy in the backyard for you to throw knives at?" he suggested.

She stopped in front of him, eyes widening. "You would do that for me?"

Looking into her green eyes, Ben wondered if there was anything he wouldn't do for her at this point. "Of course. If you have any other weapons or equipment you want me to order, please let me know."

"Oh," she said softly. "Thank you." Her grin bloomed, bright and open, and a light flush dusted her cheekbones. A man could get addicted to that smile.

He was in so much trouble.

Ben was a practical man by nature. There was no world in which Eleonore, with all her strength and fire and passion, would return his feelings. He was an awkward, socially inept workaholic whose dating skills, if they could ever have been termed "skills," were beyond rusty, and that was before one considered the messy power dynamics involved. The plastic crystal was locked in a safe in his bedroom so no one else could get their hands on it, but he was aware of its existence nearly every moment of every day.

The curse was the only thing tying him to Eleonore, but though he already mourned the day she would walk out of his life, he wanted her to be free more than anything.

He wasn't her partner and never would be, but he was still going to spoil and care for her in his limited way for as long as she let him. If she wanted a jousting arena in his backyard, he'd build one. If she wanted a lance, he'd chop down a tree and carve one by hand. And once she was done jabbing the stuffing out of a dummy, he'd cook her dinner, pour her a mug of hot blood topped with marshmallows, and then go jerk off in the shower to keep her sexual hunger sated.

It was the least a good host could do.

She was standing very close, he realized. Close enough for his sensitive nose to pick up the musky undertones of her natural scent. Close enough to see the golden flecks in her eyes.

He was definitely staring, but so was she. The air between them felt thick and charged.

Why was she staring at him? Should he stop staring at her? Was this weird?

This was definitely weird. He should absolutely stop staring.

God, she smelled good.

A cleared throat made him startle, breaking the spell. He tore his eyes away from Eleonore to see Calladia stand, brushing off her hands. "Great job, team," she told Astaroth and Themmie. "Let's go get lunch."

"Wait," Astaroth said. "What about the other dresses we brought her to try on?"

"Leave them," Calladia and Themmie said in unison. The two women gave each other a significant look that made Ben feel paranoid. Could they tell he was infatuated with Eleonore?

Oh, who was he kidding. He might as well have hearts in his eyes like some cartoon character.

Astaroth looked like he wanted to argue, but Calladia tugged on his necktie and whispered something in his ear. "Oh," the demon said. "Right."

"Bye!" Themmie chirped, half walking, half fluttering to the door. "See you at the rally!"

Ben had no idea what she was talking about. "Sure," he said, giving a half wave.

Then he was alone with Eleonore.

The moment was gone, though. In true Eleonore fashion, she was now darting around the room, flitting between the mirror and the window, then trying out a few more kicks. She raced to the wall, scaled it like a lizard, and started crawling over the ceiling, red hair and green fabric dangling beneath her.

Ben's pulse spiked. He was still not used to that particular vampiric skill, which belonged in a horror movie and not his living room. "Please don't ever do that in the dark," he begged. "You'll give me a heart attack."

She stopped above him, head angled so she could grin down at him. Her hair was long enough to drape over his shoulder, and he unconsciously lifted a hand to brush the strands. Soft, so soft. "I would not wish to give my werewolf a heart attack," she said.

Her werewolf?

Before he could bask in the glow that induced, she skittered away and descended the wall headfirst. Once she was standing again, she grabbed a handful of her hair and frowned at the tangles in it. "I will have to text Themmie to ask what an appropriate hairstyle is for possible combat at political rallies."

This was the second mention of a rally, and he had the unpleasant suspicion he'd forgotten something. "Rally?"

"The one tonight outside City Hall."

Shoot. He had forgotten. A hasty consultation of his mental calendar made him realize today was Thursday, not Wednesday. And Thursday evening was, indeed, Gigi's inaugural rally. Friday would bring a meeting of the Glimmer Falls Resiliency Project at the Annex, then Eleonore's second performance—this time attended by a Seattle theatre critic, which was putting stress on both her and him. Saturday was a special discount day at the Emporium, for which he anticipated high turnout, followed by another outing of Eleonore's performance. Sunday . . . he didn't even want to get into the array of events the Annex would hold on Sunday.

Lycaon, he was tired.

"What is your bodyguard attire?" Eleonore asked.

Ben blinked. "Ah . . . what?"

She shook her head, then grabbed his arm and started dragging him out of the room. "Show me your closet and weaponry. We will outfit you appropriately."

Ben could have told her his closet was light on weaponry and bodyguard outfits, whatever those might be, but he kept his mouth shut. Eleonore was touching him and enthusing about all the things she'd learned about modern clothing from Themmie and Astaroth, and it was wonderful.

He might never be her partner, but if she felt like manhandling him, he felt like letting her.

NINETEEN

BEN'S WARDROBE COULD USE MORE PRACTICAL PIECES—IN no way was he prepared for an attack by frenzied jackalopes or a sword-wielding shape-shifter—but seeing him walking toward her with a cup of hot chocolate in each hand, Eleonore found she didn't mind. His khakis clung to muscled thighs, his dress shirt was rolled up at the cuffs to reveal delectable forearms, and the sweater vest clinging to his torso for dear life only accentuated his size. The poor thing seemed like it might rip at the seams with a sudden movement.

It wouldn't, though. Ben had knitted it himself, as he'd bashfully explained when Eleonore had held it up to his chest earlier that day, wondering at the usefulness of such an item. All of his knitwear was made by hand, as he had trouble fitting into standard store sizes. In addition to being formed on a larger scale, as most werewolves were, he'd built muscles through activity at the Emporium. Squatting to plant and tend flowers, carrying heavy potted palms, moving and rearranging furniture and shelving . . . Gardening was a surprisingly effective fitness activity.

The argyle sweater vest wasn't useful in a military sense, but she rather liked it. He looked so deliciously restrained and proper, she felt the urge to rip it off him with her teeth.

Succubus instincts . . . or something else?

"Thank you," she said when Ben handed her the hot chocolate. Warmth sank into her palms, and she raised the cup to her nose, inhaling the scent that rose from a narrow opening in the plastic top. She hadn't even mentioned wanting one; when they'd arrived at City Hall to find a few pop-up food stands, she'd merely looked at a stall with interest and Ben had announced he was in the mood for hot chocolate.

Had that been true, or was he being nice to her again? He was nice to her an awful lot, which was novel and strange and alarming in how much she liked it. Her defenses were crumbling, and though she knew she ought to shore them up, she couldn't seem to manage.

Ben smiled and raised his cup. "I like when the evenings get cool enough for hot chocolate. One good thing about the shortening days."

It was the end of September, a month that seemed confused between summery days and brisk nights, with spurts of rain coming at random. Weather in the Pacific Northwest United States was apparently hard to predict due to proximity to the ocean and an assortment of meteorological and technological factors she had begun to research before deciding that was best left to experts. Every weather station had a prognosticator who could cast bones to support a meteorologist's predictions, yet still the weather managed to surprise.

It struck Eleonore that if she actually broke the curse, she might end up staying in one place long enough to begin to predict its unpredictability.

She looked around with this thought top of mind. They were

among a small but raucous crowd in a park facing City Hall. The sun was setting, casting its orange rays over the odd building. City Hall's marble pillars harkened back to Greco-Roman times, but the colorful peaked roof reminded her of the Zsolnay-tiled buildings she'd seen during a mission in Budapest, and the construction was topped by a copper cupola that had its roots in Islamic architecture.

This mishmash of architectural styles seemed particularly common in Glimmer Falls, a town that took "originality" very seriously. Even when the buildings were similar in construction, they were unique in paint and decoration.

Odd things thrived here. Eleonore liked that.

One of those odd things was standing next to her, blowing softly into his cup of hot chocolate. The body of a berserker, the glasses and general demeanor of a librarian. Eleonore couldn't help but smile looking at him.

"What are you smiling at?" he asked.

Eleonore shook her head. "Hard to explain."

He raised his brows. "Now I'm just more curious."

How to explain a feeling like this? Her chest was warm and she liked looking at him and she sometimes wondered how heavy his testicles would be on her tongue, but as poorly socialized as Eleonore was, even she knew that wasn't something to admit in public. "I haven't met anyone like you before, that's all. And I like your sweater vest."

His face lit up with delight, as if she'd given him a flower. "Really? Gigi makes fun of the sweater vests. She says they're frumpy and nerdy, and I'm pretty sure the entire internet would agree with her."

Eleonore made a dismissive noise. "The internet is a worldwide system of interconnected computer networks and therefore incapable of holding opinions." Witchipedia had taught her that, though she still wasn't sure she understood it.

Ben barked out a laugh. "Okay, Spock, point taken."

Eleonore warmed at that compliment. She liked Spock, who was both rational and honest. Eleonore could acknowledge she wasn't particularly rational, so Spock had been more of an aspirational figure.

The reference to *Star Trek* made her wonder about the internet and the emotional state of computers again. "The Voyager probes haven't gained sentience, have they?" she asked, thinking of *Star Trek: The Motion Picture* and Captain Kirk's discovery that the massive artificial life-form V'Ger had originated as a *Voyager 6* space probe. *Star Trek* wasn't a documentary, so she'd been surprised to learn America had indeed launched two Voyager space probes in the 1970s.

"Not that I'm aware of . . . ?"

"Good," Eleonore said vehemently. Though Kirk had seemed excited about the birth of a new life-form after V'Ger had merged with Captain Willard Decker, melding machine with man, Eleonore stoutly believed that incident had been the origin of the Borg, and no one wanted that.

Ben looked at her oddly. "I can't say I follow all your thought processes, but they're always interesting." Then he smiled softly. "Thank you for saying you like my sweater vest." He raised a hand, hesitated, then rested it gently on her shoulder. "That means a lot."

Though the touch was blunted by the cardigan covering the green dress Themmie had termed Battle Formalwear, Eleonore shivered. A spark of awareness traveled from his hand through her body, lighting up her nerves and starting a pulse between her thighs. Big hands, gentle man.

He'd be precise and giving as a lover, constantly attuned to his partner's reactions. A treat to be savored before returning that attention with equal detail and care. But sex had many aspects, and Eleonore couldn't help but wonder what would happen if Ben were to let go of his tight control. Release a bit of the wolf he had such a tight leash on.

His thumb rubbed lightly over the spot where her shoulder met her collarbone, and Eleonore instinctively grabbed his hand, holding it against her. Their eyes locked, and it was as if the rest of the world faded away. She licked her lips, then slowly guided his hand to the back of her neck.

Ben inhaled sharply, and then his fingers were sinking into the woven strands of her braid, tipping her head back gently but firmly.

Gods, she hadn't had sex in so long. And though Ben had been feeding her succubus half with regular shower masturbation sessions neither of them acknowledged out loud, she was still . . . needy. Hungry for more than just sustenance.

His pupils dilated, making the brown of his irises seem to darken. The pulse at his throat beat faster, begging for her teeth, and she could sense his heightening arousal, as she'd sensed it when he'd first viewed her wearing the dress. His scent grew darker, muskier, spicier.

Eleonore's fangs throbbed in time with the hot need between her legs.

Was he going to kiss her?

She didn't like waiting for her pleasures. They were to be seized, because the good things in life could be fleeting. So she hooked her finger in the V-neck of Ben's sweater vest, pulled him closer, and—

"Good evening, Glimmer Falls!"

Gigi Rosewood's voice boomed through the speakers, startling Eleonore so badly she jolted backward and would have fallen if it weren't for Ben steadying her. Outraged at having the moment stolen, she instinctively whipped her head around to hiss in the direction of City Hall's front steps, where Gigi stood highlighted by portable lights.

"Easy," Ben murmured. His hands fell away, much to her displeasure, and he retreated a few steps. Whatever confidence he'd found had vanished, too, because now he couldn't even meet her eyes.

Maybe Eleonore should hiss at him, too.

"What an amazing turnout!" Gigi said into the microphone as the audience clapped. "Thank you all for being here." She wore a glittery gold pantsuit with her usual pink sneakers and her hair had been pulled into a bun at the nape of her neck. A pink sign propped next to her featured her name, her campaign logo, and a website URL where supporters could donate. "Our town is made up of people from so many different backgrounds and economic situations, but for the past few years, our city's leadership has prioritized the wants of the ultra-wealthy and those with personal connections to power. Anyone else remember the resort and spa debacle two years ago?"

That elicited scattered exclamations and boos. Eleonore looked to Ben for an explanation.

"There was a piece of contested land in the forest outside town," Ben explained to the air next to Eleonore's right ear. "Cynthia claimed the deed had been found and the land belonged to the city, and then she sold it to a developer to put in a resort and spa that would have destroyed the local ecosystem and the ley lines that make this place so magical. Without asking anyone, of course. And she and her cronies were shareholders in the business."

If Ben had been looking Eleonore in the eye, he would have seen her look of disdain. "Few monarchs deserve their crowns," she said.

"Power corrupts," he mused.

"Or the corrupt are those who seek power in the first place."

At that, he did finally meet her gaze. His brows rose, and he jerked his head toward the stage. "Gigi isn't corrupt."

"I said few monarchs," Eleonore said, glad he was at least facing her again. "Not all."

Truthfully, she didn't know what sort of leader Gigi would be. She barely knew the woman. But she respected passion, and Gigi seemed earnest about wanting to change the city for the better. The trick would be maintaining that idealism once the keys to the city were in her hand.

"Was the resort built?" Eleonore pressed.

"Mariel stopped the construction. It was when she first got together with Oz."

Eleonore had only seen Mariel and Oz in passing, as the newlyweds had recently returned from their honeymoon and were more wrapped up in each other than the outside world. Mariel had offered to help with Gigi's campaign, but the "Scooby gang," as Ben had called his friendship group—a strange reference that required research—was giving her space to enjoy her new marriage. And from what Eleonore had seen, Oz was a taciturn sort who was devoted to Mariel but had even less interest in canvassing than Ben did.

Ben was now dedicating his entire attention to Gigi's speech, eyes trained on City Hall's steps with laser focus. That was the expected behavior of a brother at his sister's political event, but Eleonore still felt stung and oddly off-balance. She'd thought they were about to explore the erotic tension between them, but now he was acting like it had never happened, even as the residual echo of his arousal lingered in the air.

Eleonore rubbed a hand over her heart. There was an ache there she didn't like. It was injured pride, she decided. She wasn't used to being rejected sexually, as mild as this rejection had been.

Was this just sexual, though? The question was quiet, spoken by a part of herself she hadn't allowed space for in a long time.

She sniffed dismissively. Of course it was. She was a sexual, violent being. It was her inheritance and her destiny to fuck and kill, simple as that.

But she remembered her father gently caressing her mother's

cheek and how her mother had taken up a sword to defend his memory, and her heart hurt worse. That love had been rare. How much rarer would her own be? Was it even possible?

People were clapping—Gigi must have said something inspirational. Eleonore clapped along with them.

"And that's why," Gigi said, "I plan to—"

The sign next to her burst into flames.

Gigi jumped away from the blackening cardboard, and just in time—the microphone was next, exploding in a burst of rainbow sparks. Loud bangs sounded overhead as fireworks burst over the crowd, sending embers raining over the gathering.

Ben grabbed Eleonore, tucking her against his chest. She struggled free, heart hammering. "Get to safety," she ordered him, batting at the sparks that had settled on his sweater vest.

"Eleonore—"

He reached for her hand, but she shook her head. "I'm security, remember?"

A centaur galloped past, tail flaming. Eleonore dodged panicked, screaming people as the explosions continued. She had her knives out, ready to throw, but there was no assailant in sight. This was clearly a magical attack, which meant the caster could be anywhere. Cursing, she shoved the knives back into their holsters. There would be no fighting today, only getting Gigi to safety.

Eleonore reached Gigi's side in an instant. The werewolf was slightly larger than Eleonore, but vampires were strong and Eleonore had centuries of combat experience, so she hoisted Gigi over her shoulder and ran at top speed away from the rally.

Gigi shrieked and thrashed, hammering Eleonore's back with her fists in what amounted to slow motion compared to Eleonore's pace. "Put me down!"

Not a chance. Eleonore had been given one duty—keep Gigi Rosewood safe. She grimaced as Gigi punched a kidney. Vampire strength didn't mean she was invulnerable, and it was hard to run carrying something that didn't want to be held.

Once they were five blocks away from the scene, Eleonore stopped under the awning of a deli and deposited Gigi on her feet.

Gigi staggered, catching herself on the wall. "What the—" She broke off, and a look of relief washed over her face. "Oh, it's you. You moved so fast I didn't know who it was."

"Are you injured?" Eleonore demanded.

Gigi patted herself as if checking to make sure she was intact. She frowned at a singe mark on her sleeve, then grabbed a hank of hair that had come loose from her bun. The ends were crinkled and blackened, and the acrid scent of burnt hair spiced the air. "Not injured," Gigi said, scowling at the hair, "just lightly barbecued. Is everyone else okay?"

"I don't know."

Gigi started to jog back in the direction they'd come from. "We have to go back. I need to make sure no one was hurt."

Eleonore blocked her progress. "Absolutely not. I'm not going to let you walk into danger."

Gigi tried to dodge around her. Maybe if she'd been in wolf form she could have done it, but as a human she stood no chance of outmaneuvering a vampire. "Please," Gigi said. "Those are my friends and supporters. My community. I can't run away."

"If you go back now, there's every chance you'll be blown up, and then what happens to your friends and supporters?" When Gigi started to argue again, Eleonore held out her hand. "Give me your phone. We will call Ben."

Gigi didn't hand it over, instead dialing her brother herself, but she at least put it on speaker mode.

"Gigi? Are you okay? Where are you?" Ben's voice burst from the speaker, full of panic. "Is Eleonore with you?"

"I'm fine," Gigi said, narrowing her eyes at Eleonore in a look of reproof. "And yes, Eleonore is here. She's not letting me go back to check on everyone." She said that like it was a moral failing, and Eleonore bared a fang in response.

"Good," Ben said vehemently. "Almost everyone's cleared out and the fire department is here, but that doesn't mean it's safe. Where are you? I'll pick you up."

Gigi looked around, seeming to notice their surroundings for the first time. "Outside cousin Maya's deli, actually." She frowned. "Ben, I need to check on everyone."

"We need to regroup first. I don't think anyone was seriously injured—just a few minor burns the paramedics are treating. You can check in on people once we're sure you're out of danger."

"Ugh." Gigi hung up and shoved her phone back in her pocket. "You and my brother, I swear."

Eleonore raised her brows. "Is it wrong to want to keep you safe?"

"You don't understand." Gigi jabbed a finger in the direction of City Hall. "Those people were there because of me. I asked them to be there. Which means if anyone's hurt, it's because of *me*."

"No, it's because of whoever attacked you." Eleonore didn't know many people in Glimmer Falls, but there was one obvious suspect. "Cynthia Cunnington, undoubtedly."

"It wasn't an *attack*," Gigi said, looking startled by the suggestion. "Some jackass set off illegal fireworks."

Eleonore shook her head. "It was designed to look like fireworks, but it was clearly magic. Your sign was targeted first, then the microphone. That's not random."

Gigi's lips parted, but she didn't argue. For the first time, she seemed to understand the severity of the situation. "You really think someone tried to kill me?" she whispered.

"Not kill you," Eleonore said. "If that was the goal, she wouldn't have started with your sign or sent explosions into the crowd. Even if you'd still been at the microphone when it blew up, your burns would have been superficial. That was a message."

Drop out of the race or else.

Fury washed over Gigi's features. "The conniving *bitch*," she spat. "Does she care so much about keeping power that she's willing to hurt her own constituents?"

"Yes," Eleonore replied bluntly. Sacrificing peasants in the name of kings was a time-honored human tradition.

"I can't imagine being such a horrible person." Gigi shook her head. "Maybe I should drop out of the race to keep everyone safe."

"Absolutely not." Eleonore grabbed Gigi's shoulders, looking her in the eye. "If you drop out now, she wins. And if she's willing to light her own people on fire, what else is she willing to do to this town?" Ben had told her about the resort, how it would have destroyed the ley lines. When magic was woven into a place as deeply as it was in Glimmer Falls, unraveling that mystical network would have catastrophic effects. "She can't win another term."

Gigi leaned against the front window of the deli, wrapping her arms tightly around herself. She looked shaken but angry, which was good. Anger could keep a body going in the face of many odds. Long after Eleonore's hope had died, her fury had kept her going.

"I don't want people to be hurt," Gigi said. "But you're right. I can't roll over and let her win. She's gone too far."

Headlights turned onto the street, and some of the tightness in Eleonore's chest loosened at the sight of Ben's familiar green car. Ben would help make this better. Eleonore knew how to fight and how to run, but Ben had a skill set she didn't. He would make hot chocolate with marshmallows and tell Gigi it would be all right, and Gigi would believe him.

Maybe he would tell Eleonore that, too. And despite years of seeing the worst of people, years of forgetting how to trust, Eleonore might believe him, too.

TWENTY

I T WAS TWO A.M. WHEN THE SCOOBY GANG FINALLY LEFT
Ben's house. They'd convened an emergency meeting to discuss
what to do next. While Astaroth, Oz, and Eleonore had discussed
various means of retribution and Calladia had paced furiously,
muttering about how she'd known her mother was corrupt but not
that corrupt, Ben had made hot chocolate and cookies for everyone. Mariel and Themmie had eventually talked Eleonore and the
demons down from their more dramatic suggestions, and ultimately they'd decided to release a statement condemning the attack on democracy. Gigi would make the rounds, checking on the
injured, and they would hire more security for future events.

"We don't back down," Gigi had said, clutching her mug to her
chest. It had upset Ben to see his sister so shaken, but she was
tough, and his concern had warred with pride as she'd vowed to
keep fighting the good fight.

Ben had tried to honor that courage with his own, keeping his
shaking fear locked up until he could let it out in private.

Astaroth and Calladia had offered to escort Gigi home. Ben

waved from the doorway as they piled into Calladia's red truck. As soon as the taillights disappeared around the corner, Ben exhaled shakily and sagged against the doorframe, pressing a hand to his heart. His finger brushed the edges of a singe mark that had melted the fibers of his sweater vest. His favorite sweater vest, he thought deliriously. Blue-and-gray argyle. He'd worn it to impress Eleonore, and now it was ruined.

Eleonore was at his side in an instant. "Sit down," she ordered, grabbing his elbow.

Ben let her lead him back inside. She shoved him onto the couch, wrapped him in a blanket with efficient, aggressive movements, and disappeared into the kitchen. A few minutes later she was back with a mug of tea on a saucer, which she planted on the coffee table in front of him. Then she crossed her arms and stared at him with unblinking intensity.

Ben blinked bleary eyes, looking between her and the steaming tea. She'd bundled him up so tightly he couldn't move his arms. "Um?"

"Drink," she ordered. "You are distressed."

As a nursemaid, she lacked a delicate touch, but Ben smiled for the first time since the disastrous rally. Eleonore approached life like a general facing a battlefield, and now she was deploying her forces—tea and a blanket—to comfort him.

His rigid control over his emotions unraveled and he started crying.

Eleonore's eyes widened. She sat next to him and patted his shoulder. "There, there," she said. "We will defeat the enemy."

Ben couldn't help it—he laughed wetly at her attempt to be soothing, sniffling through his tears. "Sorry," he said, wiping his eyes. "I was trying not to freak out in front of Gigi." Gigi had been freaked out enough—she hadn't needed Ben falling apart in front of her. Now that she was gone, though, he was free to cry out the fear of seeing his sister narrowly escape danger.

Ben had always been a crier. At sad movies, when his family and friends were upset, when he was overwhelmed . . . He'd been bullied for it at school, but he didn't mind so much now. This was who he was, and he'd rather love deeply and cry than feel anything less for his family.

Eleonore looked consternated at his distress. She hadn't cried once about her situation, he realized, and he wondered if she ever did. Her eyes darted between his teary face and the tea, and she nudged the saucer closer.

Taking the hint, Ben extricated his arms from the blanket and grabbed the mug. There were five tea bags in it. Maybe Eleonore thought the bigger the distress, the bigger the ammunition needed to combat it. He sipped the almost unbearably pepperminty brew and made an appreciative noise. "Very nice," he choked out. "Thank you."

She nodded, still watching him like a hawk. Under that piercing green gaze, Ben choked down the rest of the tea as quickly as possible. Then he set the mug back on the saucer. "Delicious," he said, wondering if his taste buds would ever recover. At least the tea had shocked him out of his tears.

"You were very good with Gigi," Eleonore said, surprising him. "She was afraid, but you stayed calm, and it made her feel better."

"Only on the outside," he said. "Inside I've been screaming incoherently for a few hours."

"Are you still screaming internally?" she asked, auburn brows drawing closer together. "I can procure more tea—"

"No," he said forcefully. "No more tea, thank you." At her continued expression of concern, he fumbled for something else that might make her feel like she was being helpful. "There's whiskey in the cabinet over the stove."

A short while later they were both slightly tipsy and wearing pajamas, watching an episode of *Star Trek* together. Eleonore's pajamas consisted of one of his shirts and a pair of his flannel pants rolled up at the waist. Ben knew he should probably get her some-thing that fit better, but after the first time seeing her swimming in his clothes, he'd been too delighted to offer anything else. It touched a strange, possessive place in his heart. She was here, wearing his clothes, watching her favorite show on his TV, looking relaxed and content.

He didn't think Eleonore had much experience being relaxed.

"I don't think Q does enough interesting things with omnipo-tence," she said.

"Hm?" Ben realized he hadn't been watching *TNG* for a few minutes, instead letting his eyes trace the pale curve of neck that had been revealed when she'd tied her hair up in a messy bun.

"I mean, he does interesting things," she said, gesturing at the TV, where Q was playing the trumpet as part of a mariachi band on the bridge of the *Enterprise*, "but he's very focused on the crew of the *Enterprise* when he could be shaping the fate of the uni-verse."

"Maybe he's tired of shaping the fate of the universe," Ben said. "Maybe he wants to feel accepted by normal people."

Eleonore's head whipped around. She looked struck by the thought. "He's lonely."

"Maybe." Ben's eyes were still stuck on Eleonore's neck. The whiskey had softened the edges of the world, but he wasn't drunk yet, just loose enough to ask a question he'd been wondering. "Does being bitten by a vampire hurt much?"

Eleonore's spine went rigid. Her pupils dilated so fast her eyes turned from green to black in an instant. "What?"

Ben tapped his neck with the tips of two fingers. "Being bitten. You said it feels good for the, ah, prey, but . . . does it hurt, too? I thought vampires preferred drinking that way."

Her lips parted. Though she was sitting perfectly still, the air around her seemed to vibrate. "We do like drinking that way, yes," she said, her accent stronger than he'd ever heard it. "It is intimate."

Her fangs had lengthened as they did whenever she drank, and she dug one into her lower lip, indenting the plush surface. "I have never been bitten, obviously, but I hear it doesn't hurt. Our saliva numbs the skin. There's a slight pinch, and then the greatest pleasure."

The greatest pleasure sounded . . . interesting. Ben shifted on the couch, making room for his growing erection. "Do you drain people when you bite them?" he asked. He'd never been so aware of his own pulse before.

"No, we drink only until we are sated."

Ben shivered at the word *sated* in her French accent. If Eleonore rarely relaxed, he imagined she was truly *sated* even less frequently. "Do you want to?" he asked.

She stiffened even further, but now he could see fine tremors racing over her limbs. "Ben, are you offering your neck?" she asked quietly.

Was he? He thought of the bagged blood in his fridge. Even heated up on the stove, it couldn't taste as good as fresh blood. She hadn't drunk deeply in nearly a week; she must be thirsty.

She was sitting on his couch, in his clothes, watching his TV. He wanted her sated and sleepy on his blood, too.

Ben sat up straight, running a hand through his hair. "Are you drunk?" he asked. "I'm not, just a little tipsy, but I don't want to do this if you're drunk—"

In a flash, Eleonore was straddling his lap. She cupped his cheeks in her palms. "I'm not drunk," she said. "So tell me—do you want this?"

Oh God.

She felt incredible on top of him, strong thighs squeezing him as he gripped her waist. Ben's heart raced. He felt alive, invigorated—*desperate.* To have her lips on him even in this way . . .

He nodded. "Yes," he said, tipping his head to the side to expose his jugular. "I do."

A shuddering breath escaped her red lips. Ben braced himself, expecting her to strike like a snake, but instead she leaned in until her breath ghosted over his pulse. Then came the soft, wet stroke of her tongue dragging over his skin.

Ben groaned. He was hard from nothing but anticipation and her weight in his lap.

Eleonore must have felt it. Must have sensed it with whatever succubus instincts she had, too, because she settled further into his lap and gently rocked her hips, moving over his erection in slow, incremental movements that were going to drive him mad. Her tongue dabbed his skin again, and he squeezed her waist, nearly out of his mind from anticipation.

There was a sudden sting, but the pain vanished instantly, replaced by a wave of heat that traveled from his neck over his entire body. Her fangs were in his neck, he realized hazily. Then she sucked for the first time, and he came utterly undone.

"Oh—my—" Ben couldn't finish the sentence. Pleasure spun through him, hot and tingly and beyond anything he could have imagined. Goosebumps peppered his skin, then were soothed away by more waves of heat, and each draw of her mouth roused a new pulse of arousal. His fingers dug into her waist as he bucked, grinding against her without restraint. Distantly he wondered if he was bruising her with his hands and the force with which he was humping up against her, but Eleonore didn't seem to mind. She ground against him just as hard, then moaned against his neck. The sound vibrated through his veins before setting up camp at the base of his skull.

"Lycaon, Hecate, Jesus, *fuck*—" Ben didn't believe in any particular deity, but their names spilled from his tongue regardless. Pressure built in his dick, and his balls tightened. He was going to come from this.

Eleonore sucked one more time, hard enough to make his head swim, then drew back and licked the puncture wounds. "So good," she moaned, continuing to rock against him. Her fingers dug into his hair, holding him in place so she could look into his eyes.

Ben had never seen anything sexier. Her lips were ruby-red with his blood, and a trickle dripped toward her chin. Her pale skin had grown flush with the life he'd poured into her, and her eyes were dark and hazy with desire. She panted as she rubbed her clit over his cock in short, sharp circles that told him she was getting close.

Then she tipped her head back and cried out, and that was all it took. Ben orgasmed in his pajama pants, a burst of sensation that had him shouting and clutching her closer. He crushed her to his chest as he thrust, riding out the spurts.

When he was spent, he collapsed back against the couch, chest heaving like a bellows. He forced himself to release his death grip on Eleonore, instead stroking gently up and down her back. She shivered, then tucked her face into his neck and licked the bite mark. Soothing him or savoring the last bit of flavor, he couldn't say, but he adored it.

He adored *her*.

Dizziness swept over him, and he blinked up at the ceiling. It felt like he'd taken an axe to the trajectory of his life, splitting time into a before and an after. *Before* her mouth had been on him. *After* he'd known the mind-spinning, impossible pleasure of her bite.

"You drink from me from now on," he said roughly. Then, realizing his error at the stiffening of her spine, he clarified. "Only if you want to, of course. It wasn't an order. Sorry."

It wasn't in his nature to give orders, even without the curse making him extra cautious, but something primal and possessive had risen with her bite. He had the sudden thought that he would rip out the throat of anyone who tried to take Eleonore from him.

This primal need and fury . . . this wasn't him. Not a version of him he recognized, anyway, but the alarm he should have felt was distant in the postorgasmic haze. He'd heard other werewolves talk about the instincts of the wolf, but he'd never understood what they meant before.

Now he did.

Eleonore had relaxed after his clarification, and now she lifted her head. He braced himself for her anger at being commanded, even inadvertently and with the order quickly rescinded, but she smiled lazily. Her cheeks were flushed, and her skin had the dewy glow it took on every time he masturbated in the shower. He'd fed her twice over tonight. "I would like to drink from you from now on," she told him, accent still thick. Then her lashes fluttered and she yawned hugely.

Ben had orgasmed so intensely he shouldn't have been capable of movement, but his brain had been overrun by animal instincts. He'd fed his mate, and now she was tired. He shifted her in his arms, then stood to carry her to the bedroom. His bedroom, because he wasn't willing to let her sleep away from him after what they'd shared.

"Here," he whispered, setting her down on his dark blue sheets. "Will you stay with me tonight? Please?"

Eleonore nodded, cheek moving over the pillow. Her eyes were closed, and as he watched, her breathing grew slow and even.

Something unbearably tender bloomed in his chest. He rubbed his breastbone, marveling at the sleeping vampire succubus in his bed. What trust it took to fall asleep next to him while he was still awake.

He made a brief detour to the restroom to clean up, then changed into fresh pajama pants, climbed into bed beside her, and turned out the light. Letting his instincts take the helm as his thoughts receded into the haze of sleep, he tucked her against his chest and curved his body around her, a bulwark against the world that had been so cruel to her.

She trusted him.

He would never violate that trust.

TWENTY-ONE

Eleonore was clinging upside down to the ceiling when Ben entered the kitchen the next morning.

"I have an idea," he said. "Let's—wait, what are you doing?"

Eleonore waved down at him. "We should repaint your house!"

He looked sexy, and that wasn't just because Eleonore had drunk his blood the night before. His T-shirt and pajama pants were rumpled, his hair was tousled in an appealing way, and stubble had grown in around the edges of his beard. She liked seeing him all messed up.

She'd liked feeling his body against hers last night, too. What a delight her werewolf had turned out to be!

Ben blinked up at her. "What?"

"The whole house could use a coat of paint, but your ceiling is especially bad." The white paint was peeling in spots and yellowed in others. Eleonore poked one of the ridges, wrinkling her nose when a flake of paint fell away.

"I guess," he said, heading for the coffeepot. "It's one of those things I don't think about. Too much else going on." He made a pleased sound when he found the pot full. "You made coffee?"

Eleonore nodded, red hair swinging beneath her. "It took a few tries, but I think I figured it out."

A few tries was the mild term for her battle with the coffee machine that morning. She'd seen Ben use it, so she'd felt prepared, but faced with all the bits and pieces, it had been confusing. First she'd forgotten to fill the machine with water. Then she'd forgotten to put the carafe back in after cleaning it, which had resulted in a torrent of brown water pouring over the kitchen floor. She also wasn't sure how many scoops to put in the filter, so she'd guessed, but finally the pot was full of a hot liquid that looked appropriately coffeelike.

After drinking one mug, she was currently plastered to the ceiling inspecting the paint, so she figured it had done its job of waking her up.

"It's a lovely day," she said. Her fingers quivered, and her leg kept jogging so fast it was almost vibrating. "So much sun! Maybe we can install a training dummy in the yard today. Or maybe we should hunt down Cynthia Cunnington and break her arms?" She giggled. "So many possibilities! I'm already having a great time."

She clung tighter to the ceiling so she wouldn't collapse as her fingers twitched in a random sequence. The thought of plummeting to Ben's kitchen floor made her giggle again. How dramatic that would be!

Even upside down, she could tell Ben was looking at her oddly. He poured a mug of coffee, took a sip . . . and spit it out into the sink. "Good God," he choked out. "How much ground coffee did you use?"

Eleonore thought back to her calculations. With eight cups of water she ought to use . . . "Twenty-four scoops," she said proudly.

Ben was running the faucet and cupping water in his palm to rinse out his mouth. "Too much," he said. "Way too much."

"Was it?" Eleonore frowned. "It tasted like horrible brown sludge, but isn't that the point?" Coffee tasted bad and felt good, and right now Eleonore felt like she could single-handedly fight an entire army so long as her heart didn't explode first.

Ben straightened, then leaned against the counter, looking up at her. "You're caffeinated up to the stratosphere, aren't you?" he asked.

Eleonore didn't know that term yet—*stratosphere*—but she would look it up. She laughed again. "I feel like I could fly!"

Ben rubbed a hand over his nose and chin, avoiding his glasses. "Right," he said. "You're going to have a bad comedown."

Eleonore didn't know how that was possible when she'd never been so excited in her life. "I love coffee!" she pronounced.

"I'm sure you do." Ben held out his arms. "Care to join me on the ground?"

The thought of falling into his grip was appealing, but she didn't want to injure him, so Eleonore scuttled over the ceiling like a crab and headed down the wall. She popped up on her feet, then swayed. "Oh," she said, pressing a hand to her chest. "My heart is going very fast." Her head spun, too. Being right side up didn't feel so good.

"Water," Ben said. He filled a glass, then handed it to her.

Eleonore chugged it as her eyelid twitched. She had started sweating, and anxiety surged. "Did I poison myself?" she asked. "Am I dying?" After six centuries, this would be an embarrassing way to go.

"No," Ben said, "but let's see how you do with water. If you don't feel better in a bit, I'll take you to the doctor."

Eleonore bared her fangs and hissed. "No leeches," she said. "I hate leeches."

"They don't do leeches anymore." Ben looped an arm around her, then guided her to the couch. "Why don't you sit down and keep drinking water while I make us some breakfast?"

Breakfast sounded good. Eleonore was suddenly starving.

The sound of the refrigerator opening and closing was followed by the cracking of eggs. As something delicious started sizzling, Eleonore threw herself down on the couch, trying to force her racing thoughts and heart to still.

Maybe she should work this alarming sensation into her show. Her second performance was tonight, and she'd decided a true avant-garde artiste would vary the content of the performance each time to create a unique experience. The underlying dance of bloodlust, free will, and coercion would remain the core of the piece, but perhaps there was room to expand it. Explore new facets of the situation she'd been thrown into.

By the time Ben appeared with a plate of bacon and scrambled eggs, she was practicing a full-body movement designed to evoke the feeling of too much coffee. She let a shiver climb her body from ankles to fingertips, escalating into full-body flailing, and then she mimicked the feeling of her head exploding with what the internet had informed her were *jazz hands*.

Ben's steps paused slightly before he made his way to the coffee table to deposit the plate. "I can't tell if it's a good sign that I don't even question half the things you do anymore."

"Bacon!" she exclaimed, skipping over and plopping herself down in front of the plate. "Do you have some as well?"

He grunted in confirmation, then retrieved his own plate and sat next to her, bringing with him another large glass of water. Thankfully, the combination of food and water helped calm her a bit, though an ache had started in her head.

"How many scoops should I have put in the coffee machine?" she asked, rubbing her temples.

"Eight or so."

"Oh." A third of what she had used. "And that is sufficient to wake you up?"

Ben chuckled. "Depends on the day." He checked his watch. "I need to head to the store. Are you good to stay here, or do you want to come with me?"

Normally she would go, but considering the escalating pain in her head . . . "Stay," she decided. "I need to practice my routine anyway."

"Right," he said. "The second show. I told you it's sold out, right?"

"Yes!" Given the interest from theatrical critics and the glowing newspaper review, Ben had decided to sell tickets, with a small percentage going to the Emporium for use of the space and the rest going to Eleonore herself. She liked the idea of having her own money.

He shook his head, smiling. "I never would have guessed bloodsoaked interpretive dance was the latest in theatre, but I haven't seen a show in years, so what do I know?" He widened the spread of his legs until his knee nudged her thigh. "You're a phenomenon, Eleonore."

She felt flustered at the praise and delighted by the physical touch. After last night, she'd half expected Ben to emerge from his room embarrassed and apologizing for orgasming in his pants, but it seemed removing the physical barrier between them in such dramatic fashion had made him more comfortable with casual contact.

Speaking of casual contact . . . "I was thinking," she said, setting the fork down.

"Yes?" he asked before biting into a strip of bacon.

"You liked me sucking your blood. Can I suck your penis, too?"

The bacon flew across the room as Ben made an explosive wheezing sound. He clapped a hand to his mouth, then whipped his head around to stare at her wide-eyed. A strangled sound emerged from behind his palm.

Eleonore frowned. "Was that too forward?" Admittedly, she hadn't dated in six centuries. Not that this was necessarily dating. But her carnal encounters over the years had mostly been one-time affairs when she could sneak away from assassination missions—or the intro to said assassinations—so she didn't know the politics of asking the man she was living with if she could put his penis in her mouth.

Yes, the situation with Ben was complicated, but he tasted nice and supported her theatrical endeavors and made her breakfast, and she liked all of that. And for the first time in a long, long time, it felt like she could have something for herself. A pleasure, freely given and freely taken.

She would like fucking him, too, but that was a line she didn't want to cross yet. Not until everything was equal between them and no command could shape her will.

Ben dropped his hand to his lap, but his mouth worked soundlessly for a few moments before he spoke. "Why would you want to give me a blow job?"

That must be what the act was called these days. She shrugged and scooted closer. "I like you," she said. "I'm sure I'll like blowing your job, too."

His mouth quivered, and she wasn't sure if he was trying not to laugh or about to run away screaming. "I, ah—" He cleared his throat, shifting on the couch. "I haven't done that in a while. A long while."

"I can fix that." She reached for the waistband of his pants, then hesitated when he scooted away. "You don't want it?" The rejection speared her in the chest, sharp and unpleasant. She'd thought they were on the same page. That maybe he liked her, too, and wanted to reciprocate. She dropped her hand to her lap.

"It's not that," he said hurriedly. "I do want it. Lycaon, how I want it." He groaned, and the rough edge to his voice did a lot to help with the rejection. "But you're not here by choice. It wouldn't be right."

"We get to decide what's right," Eleonore said. "No, I didn't come here by choice, but I'm staying with you now and I don't have to. I don't have to blow your job either, but I want to."

He nudged his glasses up his nose, and she realized his cheeks had turned red, the blush visible at the edge of his beard. "*Blow job* is a noun. Instead of *blowing the job*, you would say, ah . . ."

"Yes?" she asked. When he didn't immediately answer, she pushed for more. "I like vocabulary lessons. And it's important to blend in in this time, right?"

Oh, the wolf was a delight when embarrassed. This wasn't the stressed, taut look of anxiety but something earnest and sweet. It made her want to tease him every chance she got. "You could say *blowing me*, if you wanted," he said. "Or, ah, *sucking my cock*. Or *dick*." He made a face. "Not *penis*, though. That sounds very clinical."

The vulgar words fell from his tongue hesitantly, which made them seem even naughtier. She was absolutely going to suck his penis, and she was going to make him put on a sweater vest before doing it.

"So it's a yes to sucking the cock?" she asked.

He groaned again. "I'm not awake enough for this discussion."

"Should have had the coffee," Eleonore pointed out.

Ben stood and paced halfway to the TV, then turned to face her again. "I need to think about this. I felt bad enough losing control last night." His brow furrowed. "Did I hurt you, by the way?"

Eleonore had a few bruises on her hips and waist from his fingers, which was exactly how it should be. "You were perfect. And you don't have to be embarrassed about losing control. That's the fun of it." Not that she had lost control with a partner since her mystical entrapment—that required trust, which she'd long since decided herself incapable of.

"I'm not . . . good at losing control," Ben said. His stubbled throat bobbed.

Eleonore patted the couch next to her. "I won't maul you," she said when he hesitated. "I only want to do this if you're comfortable." Consent was the most important thing to her. If Ben was nervous or hesitant about a blow job, she would never push him into it.

Maybe she should make her own boundaries clear, too. "I'm only talking about mouths and hands," she said. "No penetrative sex until the curse is broken." It wasn't that penetrative sex was somehow better than hands and mouths—she'd had lovers with no penises and some with penises who were unable to use them or who didn't want to, and it had never mattered to her—but she wanted to have something to look forward to. Not just for her, but for him.

It's a reason to make him eager to lift the curse, the wary part of her whispered. Some men would promise anything to have sex and then break those promises the moment the act was done. She didn't think Ben was one of those men . . . but it didn't hurt to hold something back.

Ben finally returned to sit next to her. "Something's wrong with me," he said, pushing his glasses to the top of his head so he could rub his face. "What kind of man wants to wait when the most beautiful woman in the world offers to suck his dick?"

The most beautiful woman in the world. Eleonore preened at that, but she didn't want him flagellating himself. "I did suggest it rather suddenly," she said. Possibly the caffeine's fault, at least a bit. "Don't feel bad, Ben. I mean it. Take time to think."

In response, he reached for her hand and laced his fingers through hers. Though the caffeine and her impulsive nature tempted her to launch into a barrage of questions about his past experiences, what he wanted, and when he might make a decision about her offer, she forced herself to stay silent and wait for him to answer.

"I do want to take some time to think today," he said at last. "We're in a tricky situation with that crystal."

She nodded.

"And even if we do . . . do that," he said, "I don't want it to be rushed. I have to be at work in twenty minutes, and that's not nearly enough time."

Oooh, that was promising. Eleonore shifted, liking the idea of a leisurely session with Ben—assuming he planned on returning the favor. "Would you lick me back?" she asked, feeling the need to clarify.

He gave her a look that said *obviously*. "I don't receive without giving, Eleonore. If we do this, I'm going to be thorough."

Very, very promising. Her nipples tightened and arousal began to pulse between her thighs. "I like thorough," she said.

He squeezed her fingers again, then huffed and shook his head, smiling a little. "You never stop surprising me." Surprising her in return, he leaned in to press a quick kiss to her forehead. "I need to get to work. Feel free to call if you need anything."

She remembered surprising him by being on the ceiling that morning, and it reminded her of something. "When you first came to the kitchen, you said you had an idea. What was it?"

"Oh!" He snapped his fingers. "I know a private investigator—a friend of my third cousin's. I was thinking he could look into the Witch in the Woods for you. See if we can find out who she is and where she is." He got up to grab a piece of paper from his desk, then handed it to her. On it was scribbled a name and phone number. "You can give him a call and let him know everything you remember about the witch. I've already given him a heads-up, and I'll pay for it, of course."

At last, a step toward resolving the issue of the Witch in the Woods, though the part of her that questioned anything good couldn't help but wonder if it was because sex had been brought up. She told that wary, paranoid part of herself to be quiet and accept the gift. "Thank you, Ben."

He gave her a fond look, then tucked a loose lock of hair behind her ear. "I'll see you at the show tonight."

TWENTY-TWO

*C*AN I SUCK YOUR PENIS, TOO?

Ben couldn't stop replaying the conversation from that morning. Between finding Eleonore on the ceiling, tasting the coffee equivalent of battery acid, and receiving such an abrupt and explicit offer, it was like he'd hopped straight from bed onto a roller coaster.

He was now sitting at the Emporium's front desk, supposedly balancing the books, and though he'd been staring at the same account ledger for twenty minutes, he couldn't have described it if someone had held a sword to his throat and threatened imminent decapitation.

He fingered the remnants of Eleonore's bite. The two tiny wounds had already healed over, which research had taught him was normal for vampire bites. Whether it was something in their saliva or an aspect of whatever magic animated them, vampires had developed quite the evolutionary advantage. Their prey not only loved the bite but recovered quickly—the better to drink from again.

He couldn't wait for her to drink from him again.

Did he want Eleonore to give him a blow job, too? Obviously yes, very much. Way, way too much, as evidenced by the fact he'd had to duck into the bathroom for a furtive masturbation session not even an hour into his shift. But he was out of practice and she was mystically bound to obey his every command, and that seemed like a recipe for disaster.

Ben also had to admit he was worried about disappointing her. She was a succubus and had probably had more partners than he could imagine. He didn't care who or how many she'd been with—that sort of insecurity was patriarchal bullshit that treated female pleasure as something to be ashamed of—but she probably had high expectations for a partner's performance. Ben had been with six women over the years, and though he fancied he'd left them all satisfied, how could that possibly compare to a sort-of-immortal's experiences receiving cunnilingus?

But to have her mouth on him and his between her legs in return . . .

"Any reason you're staring at the Peter peppers like you want to take them out to dinner and then back to your place for a quote-unquote 'nightcap'?"

Mariel's question jolted him back into the present. He had zoned out while staring in the direction of a plant on display next to the desk, one that was currently fruiting bright red peppers. And not just any red peppers, he realized with dismay—no, they had to be Peter peppers, which had the misfortune of resembling penises in shape.

Great. Blame Mariel and Rani for that display choice. He'd suggested highlighting some of their edible peppers earlier that morning, so of course they'd found the most phallic ones possible.

"Just thinking," he said, cheeks heating.

Mariel gave him a skeptical look from where she was watering a tray of African violets on the other side of the desk. "I would ask what about, but we don't have an HR department to help me process the inevitable trauma."

"Or an HR department to question your pepper choices," he shot back.

Mariel grinned. She'd returned from her honeymoon a week ago, the day after Eleonore's first performance. Her freckled skin was lightly tanned and she radiated happiness. Oz had the same glow whenever he came into the Emporium for a quick kiss from Mariel—which was often. Newlywed bliss agreed with both of them.

Mariel and Oz hadn't always been so cozy, though. "How did you know getting together with Oz was the right thing to do?" he asked, shoving the ledger aside. There would be no focusing on numbers until he'd decided what to do about the blow job situation.

"What do you mean?" Mariel asked.

Ben's fingers drummed an uneasy tempo against the desk. "It had to be awkward, since you'd summoned him and he couldn't leave without taking your soul." A conundrum that had been resolved through some clever spellcraft on both parts, though they'd already been an item by that point. "So how did you know it was . . . okay?"

"Ah." Mariel set down the watering can and gave him a knowing look. "This is about your succubus."

The group text remained, as ever, far too active when it came to speculating about his personal affairs. "Vampire succubus," he corrected. "And she isn't mine."

According to eBay she was, though, which was the root of the problem.

Mariel shrugged. "With Oz . . . I guess I was horny."

Ben nearly choked on his laugh. "You're very lucky we don't have an HR department." He didn't mean it, of course. Mariel and Rani were his friends. Maybe that wasn't a wise way to run a business, but Ben wasn't some corporate dictator. He couldn't imagine putting distance between himself and the people he spent most of his time with, especially when they were so delightful. He leaned in, clasping his fingers together on the desk as his feet took up the drumming motion. "But really. Were there any questions about . . . consent?"

Mariel's expression turned thoughtful. "Yes, a bit. I'd summoned Oz by mistake, but the result was the same regardless of my intention. He was stuck with me until I gave up my soul."

Very similar to the eBay issue. "And?"

"Look, I knew hooking up with him was probably a bad idea when I did it." She squinted. "Maybe. To reiterate, I was very horny. But the point is, even if he didn't consent to being summoned, he could still consent to a relationship—and sex, if that's what you're asking about."

Ben buried his face in his hands. Yes, that was what he was asking about. No, he didn't want to say it out loud.

"Is she trying to escalate things or are you?" Mariel asked.

He shook his head, still hiding his face.

"Her, then. Not that I'm surprised."

At that, Ben dared a peek at her between his fingers.

"You're very . . ." Mariel paused, clearly thinking through how to say whatever came next. "Gentlemanly, of course, but you don't put yourself out there dating-wise. So it makes sense she made the first move."

"I work a lot," he said, feeling like he needed to justify his lack of romantic entanglements over the years.

"I know," Mariel said, making soothing gestures that would have rankled if he hadn't been so desperate for advice. "And it wasn't a judgment. I'm just saying that as far as I've seen, you put your business and your family and friends first, even above your own personal happiness."

He didn't quite know what to say to that. "Uh . . ."

"How many family knitting projects do you have going on right now?" she asked bluntly.

He winced. "I'm running so behind. Things have been hectic—"

"Exactly." She pointed at him. "You're probably castigating yourself because you haven't finished eight thousand hats and a million scarves in time for the holidays when you've also been working yourself to the bone on the Annex."

More like two scarves, one hat, and a baby blanket, but he supposed he could see her point. "I love my family. And I'm not great with words, so this is how I show them."

"I'd argue you are great with words," she said. "You just say them more quietly than anyone else in your family."

His family was very loud, that was true. "The issue right now isn't my knitting or how I communicate with my family. What do I do about Eleonore?"

Mariel crossed her arms, leveling him with a serious look that, funnily enough, channeled Oz. "Do you want to hook up with her?"

"I mean . . ." He gestured aimlessly.

"Use your words, Benjamin."

He grimaced. "Yes, obviously. She's—she's amazing." He remembered her clinging to the ceiling, babbling about breaking Cynthia Cunnington's arms, and smiled. "I've never met anyone like her. She's brave and exciting and really, really strange, and every day I wonder what new, odd thing she'll be up to."

"Ah." Mariel grabbed a stool and dragged it over, plopping herself down opposite him. "So it's not just a physical attraction."

"No, but obviously that's part of it. I mean, you've seen her."

She nodded. "Holy Jessica Rabbit. Total bombshell."

Ben rubbed the back of his neck, wondering if he should share this next detail with Mariel. He wasn't used to talking about his feelings with anyone except the occasional therapist. But in for a penny, right? "She bit me last night," he confessed. "Consensually, obviously."

Mariel made a squealing sound. "How was it? I hear vampire bites are freaky hot."

He swallowed, determined not to think about how "freaky hot" it had been while at his place of work. "It was good. Yes. Very . . . good. But that's what started this whole thing. Now she wants to take it further."

"And you clearly like her, so what's the issue? Bang it out, babes!" Mariel held up a hand for a high five he was absolutely not going to give.

"She's mystically compelled to do anything I order her to," he said. "It's not an equal power dynamic."

"Ah." Mariel dropped the hand back to the desk, looking thoughtful. "Would you order her around in the bedroom, though?"

"No!" he said, horrified by the thought. She could order him around all she liked, though.

"Then so long as you don't ever break that promise, what's the harm? And you're trying to figure out how to break the spell anyway, so this might not even be an issue for very long."

"You're very eager to see me hook up with her." Ben's leg jogged beneath the desk. Maybe he shouldn't have brought this up with Mariel in the first place—sure, she was his friend, but he also felt embarrassed, like he'd been caught leaving the house with no clothes on. This wasn't a part of him he'd shown many people over the years.

"I'm eager to see you happy," Mariel retorted. "As long as I've known you, you've worked insane hours and spent most of your free time doing things for other people. You deserve to be loved up a little, Ben." She laid a hand over his and gave it a squeeze. "If you're worried, set some ground rules. Talk about what you'll do if it doesn't work out. Talk about whether this is just physical for the both of you or means something more."

It meant more to him, but he couldn't *say* that. To look Eleonore in her beautiful eyes and confess that he was falling for her meant risking her telling him he was just a bit of fun. Or a literal snack. Or worse, a way to alleviate her boredom, since he wasn't sending her on high-stakes missions.

"Maybe," he said after a pause.

Mariel rolled her eyes. "Men. Oz can be just as pigheaded, though thank Hecate he's gotten better about communicating." She stood, reaching for her watering can once more. "Give it some thought. Write down some pros and cons." She nudged her chin toward his ledger, which was filled with painstakingly handwritten numbers. "You like doing things the analog way anyway."

"Yeah, yeah," he grumbled. "You've only made fun of my paper records a million times."

She grinned. "It's charming. And has Eleonore seen your handwriting? It's gorgeous. That'll win her heart for sure."

He scoffed, then waved her off. "Go be helpful to a plant." Before she could get far, he spoke again. "And hey. Thanks for the advice."

She raised her watering can in a toast of sorts. "I'm here anytime you want a female perspective."

As she moved away, humming and watering plants and occasionally stroking leaves to impart a spark of magic into the greenery, Ben reflected that maybe talking about feelings wasn't the worst thing ever, after all.

TWENTY-THREE

ELEONORE LET OUT A FINAL TRIUMPHANT SHRIEK FROM HER position on the ceiling and dropped back down to the stage as the spotlight went dark. The main lights came up a moment later, and she beamed at the clapping audience in their rows of folding chairs. "Thank you," she said, bowing. Her hair swung with the movement, crimson with fake blood and matted in long tangles that would take forever to comb out, and her skin was sticky and itchy, but it was all worth it. She'd never felt a rush like performing before.

It was the third outing of her one-woman show and the Saturday night crowd was even more raucous than Friday's had been. Cornelius Crabapple was in the front row again, beaming as he applauded.

Ben brought two chairs onto the stage. He gave her a smile that launched a giddy fluttering in her chest. "You did great," he mouthed.

"Thank you," Eleonore said, wondering if her cheeks were as pink as they felt. She unhooked the microphone from its stand and sat in one chair. Cornelius trotted up to take the other, hooves clicking on the floorboards. Ben handed the faun a second portable microphone, then vacated the stage with another flutter-inducing smile for Eleonore.

"What an amazing performance!" Cornelius said into the microphone, eliciting further applause. "I got chills when you screamed at the end."

The faun was taking his role as the discoverer of what he'd deemed "an important new talent" seriously and had decided to host a moderated question and answer session about her art.

"Good," Eleonore said. "It's meant to be visceral." She crossed her legs at the knee, foot jogging with excitement. The sequins covering her jumpsuit glittered, flashes of light peeping from beneath the blood spatters. This costume wouldn't survive many more shows—already some of the stains had been impossible to get out—but she had decided her show was going to be an evolution. Whatever she replaced it with would be colorful in a different way.

"Your show is abstract, but the theme of pointless societal violence and the importance of individual free will to combat it comes through clearly in the metaphor of an immortal assassin doomed to kill again and again for a faceless master." Cornelius leaned in, eyes sparkling as he gave her a charming smile. "Can you share the inspiration for this piece?"

"Well," Eleonore said slowly, "I have been chained to a crystal for six centuries, forced to do the bidding of whoever wields it." She shrugged. "There was a lot of murder."

Cornelius blinked, smile fading. "What?"

"And I drew inspiration from Kesha, the movies *Carrie* and *Cats*, and performers like Ana Mendieta, Joan Jonas, and Isadora Duncan," she continued. "All raw performances in their own ways. I think there's a lot to be explored at the intersection of sequins and blood." She was obsessed with Kesha's eclectic fashion and message of surviving and thriving despite trauma, and Eleonore certainly wasn't the first artist to gyrate oddly or douse themselves in blood, real or fake, to make a point.

Cornelius chuckled, face relaxing. "I see. You don't want the audience to draw a distinction between the artist and the art. As far as we and your message are concerned, you might as well be the character of the assassin."

She squinted at him, confused. "Is that a question?"

A chuckle went through the audience. She wasn't sure why, but she smiled at them anyway.

"Fair point," Cornelius said. "Here's a question: Why 'Barbie Girl' by Aqua?"

Ah, the song choice. She'd thought it a perfect metaphor. "Dolls have no free will—they are mere objects to be played with," she explained. "'I'm a Barbie girl in a Barbie world' sounds fun and upbeat, but there's a dark truth beneath the synthesizers. A Barbie girl has no say in her fate. In fact, the singer addresses her unknown master directly in the lyrics: 'life is your creation.'" She paused to let that sink in. "*Your* creation, she says, not *my* creation."

It had infuriated her the first time she'd heard the song courtesy of Amy, the high school thespian running the sound booth, who had shared her music library to help Eleonore choose a song to accompany her dance.

Cornelius's jaw dropped as his gray eyebrows rose. "Brilliant," he exclaimed. "I hadn't even considered the lyrics. I thought you were just trying to startle the audience with the contrast between blood and sequins, as you said earlier."

She nodded. "'Make me walk, make me talk, do whatever you please.' Isn't that a sinister lyric?"

One of the visiting journalists was scribbling notes on a scroll while another was softly dictating into a recording device. Eleonore looked offstage toward Ben, feeling nervous. What if they wrote horrible things about her?

He was leaning against the wall, arms crossed, but at her look he straightened and gave her two thumbs up. He looked cozy in jeans and a frankly incredible green shirt apparently called a Henley that highlighted his shoulders and chest. He'd pushed up the sleeves to reveal his forearms, and she sighed at the sight of them. What a treat he was.

Feeling better, Eleonore looked back at Cornelius. "Next question?"

The rest of the question and answer session flew by with Cornelius asking about her dance training (none, though she'd incorporated sword fighting movements and studied GhoulTube videos of high school show choirs), her theatrical training (it was mainly instinct), and plans for future shows (no plans at present, though she would be delighted to have a full-time theatrical career). Even saying the word *career* into the microphone gave her a buzz of excitement. A career implied stability, the time to stay in one place and dedicate herself to something for her personal, financial, and artistic enrichment.

The Witch in the Woods owed her a lot. Time and sanity and a life, yes, but also compensation. Now that Eleonore was earning money from her performances, she felt a burst of outrage that none of her kills or human-acquisition quests had been rewarded with money. The internet had informed her that Americans shared a countrywide hobby of "suing" people. Maybe she could sue the Witch in the Woods for back wages.

Then she'd disembowel her.

When the session ended, Eleonore bowed again, thanked Cornelius for his time, and hurried backstage to wipe her face. The fake blood had started to itch under the spotlight.

She was standing in the small dressing room closet, scrubbing her cheeks with a wet wipe, when her ears caught a familiar voice amid the conversation beyond the door.

"How embarrassing," Cynthia Cunnington said. "I would be

surprised at your choice of entertainment, but I already know your family lacks class."

Eleonore stiffened. What was that despicable witch doing there?

Ben's voice followed, low but firm. "Don't talk about my family or Eleonore like that."

"Don't tell the truth?" Cynthia laughed, light but ugly. "Do you really think these people enjoyed that performance? They're here to laugh."

Hurt arrowed through Eleonore's chest. She crumpled the wipe in her fist, glaring at the door.

"I said," Ben repeated, "don't talk about Eleonore like that. People like her performances. Her shows are sold out for the next month."

"People are laughing at your sister, too," Cynthia said, undeterred. "So young and inexperienced, yet so sure she stands a chance of being elected." She scoffed. "How humiliating it will be when she fails."

"Is there a reason you're here?" Ben asked with more patience than Eleonore would have mustered in his place. Yes, he sounded angry, but Eleonore would probably have the mayor pinned to the wall by her throat by now.

"Since your sister won't take my calls," Cynthia said, "you can tell her I'm prepared to offer her one last chance to withdraw from this race. After what I've seen tonight, I'm certain the lot of you are only going to embarrass yourselves worse in the next two months."

"That's it," Ben said flatly. "Get out. You are no longer welcome in the Emporium."

"And what will you do?" Cynthia asked, sounding amused. "Your hands are shaking. Do I make you nervous?"

That's it, Eleonore whispered to herself, echoing Ben's words. Cynthia Cunnington could insult Eleonore all she liked, but she would not stand for the woman making Ben upset. She marched toward the closet door—all of two steps—and flung it open. "If you don't vacate this establishment right now," Eleonore announced loudly, "I will rip out your spine and beat you with it."

Ben and Cynthia were facing off five feet away. Ben looked distressed, while Cynthia seemed smug. Considering her lack of surprise at Eleonore's sudden appearance, she'd known Eleonore could hear each insult.

Most of the audience had filed out, but a few curious onlookers remained. "You, too," Eleonore said, pointing at a young man who was aiming his phone in her direction. She'd learned her lesson about antagonistic encounters being filmed and placed on the internet. "Out." She emphasized the order with a snap of her fangs.

The remaining onlookers fled. After the shop bell tinkled a final time, Eleonore strode forward and inserted herself between Cynthia and Ben.

"Hey," Ben said, resting a hand on her shoulder—no doubt preparing to take her place confronting Cynthia, but Eleonore was having none of it. His hands *were* shaking, and he was too kind for a confrontation like this one.

Eleonore wasn't.

She grabbed his hand from her shoulder, but instead of tossing it off the way she would have if anyone else had tried to stop her from engaging in a fight, she found herself lacing her fingers through his.

Cynthia's blue eyes darted down to their interlaced hands, then back up. "And so the reason for your ridiculous show being allowed onstage becomes clear." She wore a pale pink pantsuit today, and her blond hair was put up in the same chignon she'd worn at their first meeting. "I suppose it's in character, considering the Rosewood lack of taste."

God's right tit, this woman was annoying. Eleonore was tempted to punch Cynthia hard enough to take away *her* sense of taste, but she took a deep breath. *Be more like Ben*, she told herself. *Think this through.* Ben had somehow managed to maintain his composure in the face of this provocation.

She remembered what she'd told Gigi after that first meeting. A woman like Cynthia had one deep vulnerability.

"Now look here—" Ben started, but Eleonore looked at him and shook her head.

I'll handle it, she mouthed. Then she tipped back her head and forced herself to laugh.

Predictably, Cynthia stiffened, the amusement dropping from her face. "What's so funny?"

"You are," Eleonore said. "So afraid you'll lose the election that you feel the need to come in here with your insults and threats."

"I'm not afraid I'll lose," Cynthia gritted out. "I'm just giving Gigi—and the two of you—an opportunity to save yourselves future humiliation. Political campaigns are high-profile. It's not going to reflect well on the Rosewood name."

Eleonore shrugged one shoulder, clutching Ben's hand tighter. "All I see is an insecure woman with no compassion and even less sense. Do you think you reflect well on the Cunnington family name? Your sabotage of the rally aside, this is a pathetic display."

Cynthia's nostrils flared. "That is *slander*," she spat. She grabbed the beads of her pearl necklace and started rolling them in her fingers, muttering something.

Eleonore yanked Ben out of the way just in time to avoid a concussive blast of air that made the open closet door slam shut so hard it rattled. If Ben had been standing there, he would have been thrown into it.

Fury blazed through her, hot and unforgiving, and she gave up trying to think things through. Eleonore didn't have magic, but she did have warp speed and good upper body strength. In an instant, she was holding Cynthia off the ground by her throat.

The woman kicked and struggled, clawing at Eleonore's hand, but Eleonore didn't budge. She carried Cynthia to the front door of the Emporium, opened it, and threw her out on her ass—straight into a puddle.

"I'm going to be laughing at this all night," Eleonore called out as Cynthia sputtered and thrashed. "Maybe Ben should hire you as entertainment next. A comedy show!"

Then she yanked the door shut, bell jangling in an agitated cacophony, and flipped the lock.

When she turned, Ben was gaping at her. Was it a good gape or a bad gape?

She heard Cynthia shrieking through the glass, and a look over her shoulder showed the muddied mayor screaming into her cell phone as she stomped toward a car. Eleonore bared her fangs. "Good riddance," she muttered.

"Eleonore," Ben said, drawing her attention. "That was—" His throat bobbed, and then he began striding toward her, an intense expression on his face.

"Are you angry?" she asked, unable to interpret the feeling in his eyes. "She had it coming—"

She broke off when Ben yanked her into his arms. "That," he growled, "was one of the sexiest things I've ever seen."

Then he lowered his head and kissed her.

Eleonore gripped Ben's upper arms for support as he kissed her with mind-scrambling thoroughness. His lips were soft, though they moved over hers with purpose. His beard was softer than she'd expected, too—there was no rasp against her skin, only a pleasant friction that added to the sensation.

She'd wondered if he'd be a tentative kisser, but he wasn't. He seemed downright *hungry.*

Eleonore pressed into him, reveling in the sturdy strength of his body. Her nipples stiffened, and she rolled in a sinuous wave, seeking more contact.

In response, Ben groaned into her mouth and pulled her tighter against him.

This was what she wanted, she thought hazily as lust built between them. A person who could be soft and strong. A person who didn't care that she had hard edges or her own strength. A person who kissed her like both offering and demand.

She groped upward from his arms to sink her fingers into his hair. It was thick and slightly coarse, perfect for gripping. Their height difference meant he was leaning over her, spine stooped slightly, so she stood on tiptoes to meet him.

Stars, she loved this. The slick slide of his tongue, the nip of his teeth, the soft puff of his breath. The feel of another living person so close and so caught up in the attraction burning between them. Eleonore widened her mouth, meeting his tongue with hers. She gently nibbled his lower lip, careful not to pierce him with her fangs. The thought of drinking blood from his mouth while their tongues tangled caused a fresh surge of wetness between her thighs, but she would never do that without asking first and she didn't want to stop kissing him.

Ben broke away with a gasp, and Eleonore made a noise of complaint, following his mouth to nip at his lower lip.

"Sorry," he said.

"Don't you dare apologize," she growled, grabbing his shirt collar to keep him from escaping.

He let out a breathless laugh. "I'm not sorry for kissing you," he said. "But I think we should probably go back to my place so we can shower and change into something less . . . sticky."

Oh. Eleonore noticed the state he was in after kissing her. His shirt and pants were wet with the gooey fake blood she'd been covered in, since she hadn't changed out of her costume before confronting Cynthia. "Good point," she said. She would have liked licking real blood from his skin, but this corn syrup concoction was not an adequate replacement.

Still, loath to let go and figuring the shirt was already compromised beyond help, she tugged him against her once more, sliding her tongue into his mouth.

He groaned and returned the stroke with one of his own. Oh, she liked the way he kissed. Bold but not too forceful; sweet but still sexy.

His hands slid into her hair, and then he grunted and pulled them back out. Eleonore laughed when he grimaced at the red, sticky fluid now coating his fingers.

"Didn't think that one through," he said.

She grabbed his sticky hand. "Take me home? We can shower together."

Ben's eyes widened, and then he was tugging her toward the door, long legs eating up the space. "You don't have to say that twice."

Eleonore grinned as she followed, excitement sparkling through her like fireworks. Her werewolf had apparently concluded his thinking from the morning, and she couldn't wait to taste every inch of him.

TWENTY-FOUR

B EN COULDN'T BELIEVE THIS WAS HAPPENING.
He drove like a maniac, ten miles an hour over the speed limit and only coming to rolling stops. His knee jogged as he glanced over at Eleonore.

Ben had never imagined a sticky red sequined jumpsuit would be the pinnacle of erotic attire, but he suspected anything Eleonore wore would turn him on. The jumpsuit hugged her curves, and he kept envisioning the moment she'd choked Cynthia Cunnington and thrown her into the street.

Should he find her violence that arousing? Did it say something about him that Freud would have written a paper on?

Ben didn't care. He'd kissed Eleonore's beautiful lips and held her in his arms, and now he was going to shower with her. It didn't even matter that both of them were leaving red stains on the seats of his SUV. Cars could be cleaned and seats reupholstered; getting to soap down a succubus was a much rarer experience.

He parked in his driveway and nearly strangled himself on the seat belt trying to get out of it. Eleonore was waiting for him outside the house before he could even get to the passenger side to open the door for her. Her use of vampire speed might limit his ability to be a gentleman, but at least it showed she was as eager to get this started as he was.

Ben backed her against the front door, kissing her again. He fumbled with his keys, trying to unlock the door without taking his lips from hers. Eleonore giggled—had there ever been a sweeter sound?—and turned in his arms to take control of the keys. There was a new red streak on his front door, but he'd been thinking about adding a pop of color anyway.

He planned to kiss her all the way to the bathroom, but Eleonore was apparently too impatient. She moved in a blur across the living room, vanishing down the hallway that led to the bedrooms and bathroom. When Ben caught up with her, she was already shimmying out of her jumpsuit.

He held out a hand, and she tossed the garment over. He absently folded it and set it on the counter without taking his eyes from Eleonore. She wore blue cotton underwear and a sexy, sturdy-looking bra—not something with underwire and forcibly overflowing cups, more akin to a sports bra that had been custom-tailored for large breasts. He didn't know if she'd always had it or if she'd picked it up online shopping or if it had come in the same delivery as the devastating green dress.

Eleonore reached behind her back and unhooked it, then sent the bra sailing. Ben snatched it out of the air and placed it next to the jumpsuit. The fabric was warm under his fingertips. She shimmied out of the panties next and kicked them away, and then she was standing nude and unashamed before him.

Had any goddess been formed with such care? Ben stared and stared, taking her in one miracle at a time: the dramatic curve between hips and waist, the strong legs, the fiery curls between her thighs. Her breasts were heavy, with large rosy nipples that tipped up as if volunteering to be sucked. There were red marks on her skin from the bra, and he wanted to soothe them with his tongue.

His eyes reached her face, familiar by now but still breathtaking: high cheekbones, a stubborn chin with a small divot in it, wickedly smiling lips. Her long hair was tangled and matted with fake blood, though, which reminded Ben she couldn't feel entirely comfortable. He shook himself and moved to the shower to start the water. "Eleonore," he said as he dabbled his fingers in the stream, "you are so beautiful I'm speechless."

"You just spoke," she pointed out.

Ben would have laughed if his dick hadn't been so hard he was getting light-headed. "Well, please imagine there are reams of poetry dedicated to your nude body in my head." With the water at an ideal temperature, he swept the curtain aside to usher her in.

Eleonore hopped in, humming and wriggling as the hot water hit her. Steam began rising, and her skin flushed before his eyes until the fog began to encroach on his glasses.

"Ben." She snapped her fingers. "Get naked."

He blinked. "Right." They would be showering *together*, and thank goodness he'd sprung for an expanded tub to fit his height. He kicked his shoes into the corner next to hers and stripped off his clothes, flinging them into a haphazard pile. He looked down at his erect dick, silently praying she would find it acceptable. Then he set his glasses on the counter and joined Eleonore in the shower.

The heat was a jolt to his system, making him suck in a breath. He cupped water in his palms and dumped it on his head and face, then shook his hair out.

Eleonore let out a startled laugh as droplets hit her. "How wolf-like," she said. She stood facing him under the spray, fake blood trickling in rivulets from her hair and tracing her curves.

"Can I wash you?" Ben asked.

Eleonore looked surprised, but then she smiled. "Be my guest," she said, turning to face the tiled wall.

He swallowed hard as his eyes traced down her muscled back to her round ass. She was magnificent, and thank goodness his vision was decent enough to make out the details at this close distance.

Ben was a big man. He'd worried he was *too* big in the past. He needed custom clothing and custom tubs and a big car, and if he was walking at night and spotted someone ahead, he crossed the street to avoid alarming them. It was a strange dichotomy—a nervous brain housed in a tank of a body—and he'd often worried about being too much for a romantic partner in more ways than one.

Eleonore didn't seem to mind his brain or his body. She was strong and sturdy, tough enough to kick his ass and blunt enough to let him know if anything he did upset her.

The knowledge unraveled something in Ben's chest. He didn't need to worry about anything but pleasing her.

He exhaled, then reached for the shampoo.

Eleonore hummed as he scrubbed her scalp with his fingers. "That's nice," she said.

Ben grunted in response, focused on washing fake blood out of her hair. The red locks darkened under the water, draping over her breasts to her waist. He washed carefully, not wanting to snag the tangles with his fingers. When the water ran clean, he traded shampoo for conditioner.

"How do you know so much about hair?" Eleonore asked as he combed the product through with a wide tooth comb.

"We always had conditioner at my house growing up," he said, carefully untangling a snarl. "I was surprised when I got to college and realized a lot of other guys didn't condition separately or use beard oil." No, the majority of them had used horrifying three-in-one shampoo, conditioner, and bodywash that smelled like a diseased pine tree. He'd also learned he was an oddity for moisturizing his face and filing his nails after clipping them.

His hygiene had earned razzing from other guys, which had baffled him. Why shouldn't he want to smell and look nice? Why shouldn't he make his fingernails smooth in case he actually got to touch a woman?

Speaking of touching . . . Ben took a break from combing to run his hands over Eleonore's curves. Her skin was so soft. He drew her hair over her shoulder and bent to press a kiss there.

She tipped her head to the side. "Mmm. Are you done washing me yet?"

"Almost." Ben turned her around and rinsed the conditioner out of her hair, then poured bodywash onto a sponge and ran it over her skin. It wasn't the most thorough scrubbing, but there was only so much patience a man could be expected to exhibit when the object of his desires was naked under his hands.

He cast the sponge aside and cupped her breasts, savoring the soft weight of them. They overflowed even his broad palms. He thumbed her rosy nipples, and Eleonore hummed before lacing her arms around his neck. She toyed with the ends of his hair, and the scratch of her fingernails against his scalp sent a pleasurable shiver over him.

"Are your nipples sensitive?" he asked.

"Not that sensitive," she said. "I like to have them pinched."

Ben could do that. He gently squeezed her nipples between thumb and forefinger. "This much pressure?"

She covered his hands with her own, pressing his fingers harder against her skin. "That much."

Ben obeyed her direction, alternating between massaging her breasts and pinching her nipples until they were rosy and stiff. He lowered his head to suck them, and when he lightly bit at one straining tip, her head kicked back and she let out a breathy gasp. "*Good* wolf."

Oh, Ben liked that. Determined to earn more of her praise, he set himself to exploring what made her tick. Kissing her neck earned him more soft sighs, and she shivered when he traced his fingers over the delicate skin of her inner elbows. When he touched her hips with the same light touch, she made a growling sound and clapped her hands over his, encouraging him to grip more forcefully.

She explored him, too, dragging her hands in long sweeps over his chest and arms, scratching lightly at his back. They panted into each other's mouths, tongues tangling and lips stroking in an increasingly frantic rhythm.

He learned she liked rough touches in expected places and soft touches in unexpected ones. A kiss behind her ear produced the same moan that pinching her nipples did, and when he gripped her ass and hauled her against him, she let out a guttural *yes* that was going to play in his memories for the rest of time. Her lush ass overflowed Ben's grip, and he groaned into the curve of her shoulder as she nudged her hips forward, grinding against him.

She grabbed his buttocks, too, squeezing them in a covetous manner before lightly spanking one cheek. "Bon arrière-train," she said.

Ben chuckled breathlessly. "What does that mean?"

"You have a good posterior."

That was the oddest way anyone had ever said "nice ass," but he was into it. "You also have a bone . . . error train." When she snorted, he shook his head. "You can teach me how to say it properly later."

There was one place he hadn't explored yet. His fingers coasted over her hip, and then he slid his hand between their bodies, toying with the shower-wet curls before delving lower. When he parted her labia with his finger, he groaned to find her slick with more than just shower water. "Fuck, Eleonore. You're so wet."

"Yes," she gasped. She gripped his cock with her usual directness, and he let out a choked sound at the feel of her fingers curving around him. "And you are deliciously hard," she said, stroking up and down the shaft.

Ben wasn't circumcised, and the skin moved under her grip in an exquisite slide. He wasn't going to last long with her touching him, and he refused to orgasm first, so he bit down on his inner cheek and focused on learning her contours. He played with her labia, circled the stiffened nub of her clit, gently pressed the tip of one finger inside her. Shower water wasn't the best lubricant, but she was so wet she accepted him easily. Still, he went slowly, sinking his finger into her a bit at a time. He crooked it when he dragged back out, massaging her inner wall, and Eleonore made a filthy hot noise and squeezed his dick in response.

Ben buried his face in her neck. "How do you like being touched?" he asked against her skin.

"Two fingers," she told him. "I like the stretch."

Ben closed his eyes as he obeyed her order. *Don't come*, he told himself. *Don't come.* Because now he couldn't help but imagine her spreading her legs for his cock, moaning about the *stretch* as he thrust into her.

He nudged her clit with his thumb, and she issued another hissed *yes* that made his hips jerk.

"Direct touch?" he asked, barely able to string together words.

"Oui," she breathed.

Thankfully, if there was one word Ben knew in French, it was that one. Encouraged, he focused on rubbing her clit, keeping his fingers sunk inside her and flexing them rather than thrusting in and out. Giving her both the stretch and the direct clitoral stimulation she craved.

Eleonore was panting now. When he pulled his head back to study her face, he saw her biting her lower lip, fangs indenting the plush surface. Her eyes were hazed with desire, and her skin was pink from heat and passion.

"Ne t'arrête pas," she said.

"Is that—"

"Don't stop," she ordered. "Don't you dare stop." She jerked him faster and more aggressively, occasionally swirling her thumb around the exposed tip of his cock, and her other hand came into play, cupping his balls.

Ben wouldn't stop. He anchored her against him with his free hand, fingers digging into the plush skin of her ass, while he continued rubbing and rubbing and rubbing her clit. Soon Eleonore was gasping and twitching, and then she let out a long, broken moan as her pussy squeezed his fingers rhythmically.

Thank fuck. Ben lowered his head to bite the side of her neck as the pressure building in his cock released all at once. His cum spurted over her lower belly and coated both of their hands, but she didn't stop tugging until he groaned and gently nudged her fingers away from his too-sensitive dick.

He sagged back against the tile, head spinning. Eleonore popped one of her fingers into her mouth to suck it clean, and he nearly fainted dead away at the sight. "Woman," he said in a ragged voice, "you might kill me."

"I would never wish to kill my wolf," she said solemnly. Then her naughty smile peeped out. "Unless it is la petite mort."

He chuckled. He knew that phrase, too: the little death. Thankfully, that was the sort of death that allowed for resurrection, even if his refractory period wasn't what it had been in college. He looked down at his softening cock, wondering how soon he would be able to orgasm again.

Then Eleonore yawned, and he revised his plans. The water was lukewarm now and getting colder, so he quickly washed the remnants of passion away and turned off the shower. He wrapped Eleonore in a towel before grabbing his own. To his delighted surprise, she plopped a hand towel on his head and scrubbed vigorously, helping dry his hair. He returned the favor, then detoured to the bedroom to grab pajamas for both of them.

Within five minutes they were cuddled together under his blankets. Ben spooned her, enjoying the feel of her pressed against him. "How was it?" he asked.

"The shower?" She turned her head to look at him over her shoulder. "Very thorough."

The sparkle in her eyes said she was teasing. Ben lightly tapped her nose. "You know what I mean."

"The conditioner?" she asked, blinking innocently. "It smells very nice."

He groaned around a laugh. "You're going to make me beg for this compliment, aren't you?" Then, not wanting her to feel pressured if, in fact, it hadn't been up to her standards, he hurried to clarify. "You don't have to compliment me, of course. And if there are any areas I can improve in, I'd love to hear it. I can practice, make sure I'm doing exactly what you like—"

"Hush." She kissed his fingertip. "The orgasm was delightful."

He exhaled in relief. "Whew. Okay. Good. But I'm always open to feedback."

"Noted." She nuzzled into the pillow. "I have no criticisms whatsoever. But it's just like sword fighting. We should both make sure to practice frequently to keep our skills sharp, don't you think?"

He grinned. "Eleonore Bettencourt-Devereux, are you propositioning me?"

"Yes."

He laughed at her bluntness. "Then I accept. We can practice whenever you want."

He drifted to sleep soon after that, still smiling.

TWENTY-FIVE

"WHAT DO YOU MEAN, DO I HAVE MORE INFORMATION?" Eleonore demanded into the phone. "Isn't it your job to find that?"

On the other end of the line, the private investigator let out a weary sigh Eleonore didn't think was merited. "So far," the investigator said, "the only things you've told me about this witch are that she wears a hooded cloak, has pale skin and dark hair, likes *Star Trek*, and lives in an isolated house in the woods. You haven't even given me a street address."

"Of course I haven't," Eleonore said. "There are no streets in the forest."

She drummed her fingers on Ben's kitchen counter, which she was sitting on. A few feet away, Ben was preparing grilled cheese sandwiches. He gave her a sympathetic look as he closed the portable griddle on the first sandwich.

Her eyes skated down his frame, landing on his ass. A very fine posterior, the werewolf had. Round enough to sink her fingers into—which she had, happily, during their absolutely delightful shower the previous night.

It was hard to stay irritated when Ben was so big and handsome and grilling sandwiches, so Eleonore forced herself to look away from him so she could properly intimidate the investigator.

"Look, lady—"

"I am not nobility," Eleonore said crisply, "and my knives have drunk too much blood over the centuries for me to lay claim to any such genteel titles."

"Christ," the investigator muttered. "I hate having immortals as clients. Everything's always so vague and weird and threatening."

"I'm not technically—"

"Yeah, yeah," he said, cutting Eleonore off, which was a sure way to learn what *actual* threatening behavior was. "You're not technically immortal, you were mystically entrapped hundreds of years ago by a witch who wears a cloak and lives in an unknown forest somewhere in the world."

"She's lived in several forests over the centuries," Eleonore said, biting down on the urge to threaten his spleen with a good chomping. "Which, as I said, is why she goes by the Witch in the Woods." Honestly, had he even been listening? "The most recent one she lived in resembles those in the Pacific Northwest and the crystal was shipped domestically, so that narrows down the location."

Ben had taken her on a drive into the forest surrounding Glimmer Falls a week ago. The winding road had led up wooded hills dotted with hot springs. They'd stopped at a lookout point that provided an unobstructed view of Glimmer Falls and the undulating green land and sharp, snowcapped peaks beyond, and she'd marveled at how beautiful this slice of nature was.

It had also been oddly familiar. The precise shades of green, the height and breadth of the trees, the moss hanging like fairy chandeliers from branches in the dampest depths of the woods . . . it had reminded her of the forest where the Witch in the Woods had taken up residence during the past century, which had given her hope that perhaps the witch was somewhere nearby.

"I guess it's something," the investigator said glumly. "But I still need more information to go on."

Eleonore opened her mouth, ready to hiss, but the most delectable smell was coming from the griddle. She sniffed the air, then let out an appreciative sigh—Ben had included onions and thin slices of turkey in the sandwiches. He didn't look her way, but his lips quirked in a half smile.

Eleonore narrowed her eyes, realizing she was being managed. "Tricky wolf," she said with no true ire. "You know I can't be angry when faced with grilled cheese."

Recently, his sandwich-making had mysteriously begun to coincide with her particularly cranky moods. This lunch was earlier than normal, but she wouldn't have thought anything of it if he hadn't begun prep work the moment she'd announced she was going to call the private investigator to see if the previous day's labors had yielded any fruit. A professional ought to be able to provide *some* information after nearly twenty-four hours.

"What?" The confused question came from the phone.

"I'm talking to my werewolf paramour, not you," she informed the investigator.

He sighed again. "Of course you are."

"But really, how many nigh-immortal-life witches can there be?" Eleonore asked, returning to the issue at hand. For whatever reason, witchcraft blossomed only among mortals who were human or had human ancestry—it didn't manifest in other species or true immortals. But each witch or warlock had areas of spellcraft they had a natural affinity for, and a very few could manipulate life itself, prolonging it to extremes. The Witch in the Woods had

managed to extend her life span to at least six centuries by draining mortals of life and adding it to her own.

"You'd be surprised." The investigator heaved yet another
heavy sigh—he certainly did that a lot. "I'm sorry, but I'm going to
have to return the fee for this one. You need someone with more
of a magical specialty to find this witch."

"You're quitting?" Eleonore asked, dumbfounded.

Ben shoved a sandwich into her hand.

"Thank you," she whispered to him. Then she sank her fangs
into the cheesy interior of the sandwich in lieu of biting the phone
in half.

God's ovaries, that was delicious.

"I'm sorry," the man repeated. "Being imprisoned in a rock for
six hundred years sounds like it sucks."

"It was a sequence of rocks culminating in a plastic embarrassment," Eleonore said. "And no, I do not recommend it."

"But it wouldn't be right to waste your money and time on
something I can't help with," the investigator continued. "I'm
deadly with a Google search and some moderate stalking, but you
need someone with magical expertise. Maybe try asking around
some ritual ingredient shops? Or see if Diantha Spark has any
recommendations—she's as good a witch as Cynthia Cunnington
and loves giving advice."

Diantha Spark—Mariel's mother—was a terror if rumors were
to be believed. She was also Cynthia Cunnington's frienemesis,
according to Themmie—a word Eleonore had never heard before
that apparently meant a nemesis one pretended to like for unknown reasons.

Perhaps the Witch in the Woods considered Eleonore a frienemesis. She'd often said nonsensical things like *You're my best
friend* or *You're like a daughter to me*, but what kind of person imprisoned someone they cared for?

"I'll ask," she said. And then, because this man hadn't done anything truly terrible and because the first bite of grilled cheese was settling in her stomach, she softened her tone. "Thank you for being honest."

"It's a dirty business, but you gotta preserve your honor somehow, right?"

"Right," Eleonore repeated, feeling like that, at least, she could understand.

Once she hung up the phone, Eleonore turned her attention fully to the sandwich. She was still frustrated and angry in a way that felt like there was a bubbling hot cauldron between the base of her breastbone and her stomach, so she forced herself to eat methodically and slowly, giving her irritation room to settle.

She'd always been quick to anger, but it had only gotten worse over the centuries with the witch. The internet had taught her *fight or flight* was the term for a person's primal instinct when faced with trauma, but Eleonore had never been able to flee. Instead, she'd put all her resources into fighting however she could, even if it was with nothing but her words and her rage.

Now that she wasn't living under the constant threat of being forced to murder someone—or forced to spend time drifting through an unpleasant haze inside the crystal—her reactions were out of proportion to her new existence. She recognized this. But knowing the cause of the behavior and changing said behavior were two different things.

Still, she was trying to work on it—partially because whenever she succumbed to those bursts of temper she felt like a monster in comparison to even-tempered Ben. He made her want to be a better person—an impulse she hadn't felt in so long, she'd forgotten what it was like.

Thus: chewing slowly.

Very, very slowly.

"Thank you again," she said when the sandwich was finally done and the urge to shriek had faded. "Food calms me down."

He smiled, showing those adorable eye crinkles. "My mother taught me that trick growing up. Gigi gets hangry, too."

"Hangry?"

"Angry because you're hungry," he clarified.

"Ah." This was another word like *frienemesis*, smashed together out of two separate concepts. "Well, I am no longer hangry, even if it's disappointing the investigator can't help."

Ben held out his arms, and Eleonore only hesitated briefly before walking into them and burrowing her face against his broad chest. He smelled so nice.

"I'm sorry," he said. "We'll ask the gang for any other leads tonight."

They were going to a barbecue at Mariel and Oz's house, which was the first group social event not involving Gigi's mayoral campaign that Eleonore would attend. She wasn't sure if she was excited or nervous at the prospect of socializing. "All right," she said, voice muffled.

The word *frienemesis* was still pinging around her head. Ben probably didn't have one of those. No, he had a collection of friends who did normal things like host barbecues and who had probably never once considered kidnapping or imprisoning one another.

She didn't like thinking about the witch, much less talking about her, but she felt the sudden urge to unburden herself.

"The witch pretended to be my friend," she said.

Ben had been rubbing her back, but he stilled at that. She could almost hear his brain whirring as he tried to follow her thought process. "How so?" he asked—not understanding the origin of the thought, perhaps, but willing to see where it led.

Eleonore didn't want to be restrained while talking about this, so she pulled out of his embrace and paced to the window. She crossed her arms, looking out at Ben's lawn and the flowers blooming by the sidewalk. "Whenever she summoned me, she seemed excited to see me. She sometimes gave me gifts—a trinket, a new knife, a *Star Trek* bobblehead." Eleonore swallowed, no longer seeing Ben's yard but a cascade of memories. "She'd say she missed me or that I was her only friend. Once she said I was like a daughter to her."

Ben made a low noise. "That's bullshit."

He didn't swear as frequently as others in this time, she'd noticed. She liked that he would swear for her. "Yes, but it bothered me. Given a single moment of freedom, I would have ripped her throat out, but she thought I was her *friend*." The witch had seemed so certain in their bond that Eleonore had sometimes wondered if the witch was the mad one or if *she* was.

"Was she saying it to manipulate you?"

Eleonore shrugged, ill at ease. "Maybe. She was also insane. But if she really believed we were friends . . ."

"What?" Ben asked after she trailed off.

"I don't know." Every time she tried to think about it, her head hurt and she felt sick to her stomach. How was she supposed to feel about a person who hurt her with one hand and offered gifts with the other?

"If I can speak plainly," Ben said, "I don't think it matters if she believed you were friends or not. That doesn't change what she did to you."

"I know," Eleonore said, turning to face him again. Ben's forehead was furrowed, and she could read both anger and pity in his expression. The pity made her want to snap her teeth. "I'm not saying it changes anything or that I won't rip her throat out. I look forward to ripping her throat out." She shook her head. "I don't even know why I started talking about this."

Ben cocked his head, eyes trained on her like he was looking under her skin and into her brain. He was the one with the complicated thoughts and reasoned words; maybe he could pull some meaning out of her jumbled confession. "You can talk about whatever you want," he said. "It's good to let things like that out rather than stewing on them."

Eleonore wasn't a stewer by nature. Perhaps that was why she struggled to pull apart these tangled threads of fury, grief, and discomfort. Her waking hours over the centuries had been spent in rage and violence, with occasional odd lulls for *Star Trek* or confusing gifts from the witch. Her time in the crystal had been a hazy sleep of half-formed dreams and memories. Now she was awake and alive in a peaceful time with no immediate target for her rage, and she had too much time to think.

"I don't like ruminating," she declared.

Ben exhaled at that. "I don't either, but it's what I spend most of my time doing."

"That means you're good at it."

He blinked a few times. "You know, I never thought about it that way." There was a pause, and then he shook his head. "Now you're going to have me ruminating about what it means to be good at anxiety."

There was too much ruminating in this room in general. Eleonore clapped her hands. "Let's do something."

Ben took her abrupt announcement in stride. "Hmm," he said, rubbing his bearded chin. "How about online shopping for a target dummy to throw knives at?"

Eleonore wanted a target dummy, but scrolling the internet wasn't physical enough to get her out of her head. "Something more active than that."

His smile turned naughty. "How about an orgasm?"

Oooh. Clever wolf. "Yours or mine?" she asked, bouncing on her toes.

He chuckled. "I was thinking yours."

It would be nice to have his hands on her, but if there was one thing that would put her in an excellent mood, it was feeding off the delicious energy of his orgasm. "I would prefer to suck your pe—I mean, blow your dick." She waved a hand. "Whatever the act is called."

Eleonore could sense Ben's veins dilating as his heart pumped blood to both his blushing cheeks and his penis. A werewolf who blushed while erect; how charming. If she hadn't drunk his blood a few nights ago, she would have asked to sink her fangs into him. Thank goodness a succubus could never be too "full" of sexual energy.

"You would rather suck my dick than have me go down on you?" Ben asked.

Well, when he put it like that . . .

"I have an idea."

Five minutes later they were entwined naked on his bed, kissing passionately. Since they were saving penetrative sex for after the curse was broken, she got to be as creative and thorough as she liked with her hands and mouth, and Eleonore couldn't wait to express the full range of her creativity all over that brawny body.

Eleonore obviously hadn't invented the position she had in mind, but it was a good one. She repositioned herself, turning in a half circle until her hips hovered over Ben's face and her mouth was within striking distance of his dick. Kissing distance, she corrected herself, because though she'd love to taste blood directly from the throbbing vein winding up his shaft, that was the sort of thing that ought to be negotiated ahead of time.

He gripped her hips and tugged her against his face, and she jolted and slapped a hand against the mattress. "Oh," she gasped as his tongue started stroking over her. No hesitation here.

Ben was good at oral, direct and thorough in his approach, and she suspected it was because he genuinely liked doing it. He mixed licks with deep groans, and that primal delight couldn't be faked. When he flicked his tongue against her clit, she was tempted to abandon her plans and just ride his face straight toward the orgasm he'd been so eager to give her.

This was supposed to be an equal exchange, though, so Eleonore leaned forward to suck his dick. Or tried, anyway. He was eight inches taller than her, and she hadn't calculated the physics of aligning their mouths and crotches in this manner. She licked a circle around the head of his cock, but when she shifted forward to suck him deep, her pussy lifted away from Ben's face. He tugged her back onto his mouth instantly, preventing her from getting the right angle.

"I can't suck you properly like this," she complained.

His response was a chuckle that vibrated against her clit. Eleonore whimpered, grinding against his face for a moment before forcing herself to return to her mission. Vampire speed gave her an advantage, and she managed to take him to the back of her throat before he'd realized she'd moved.

"Oh, *fuck*," he shouted, fingers digging hard into her hips.

She would have smiled if her mouth hadn't been better occupied. Ben was so proper that when he let loose, it felt like an *event*. She bobbed her head, enjoying the stretch of her lips around his thick shaft and the feel of him plunging deep in her mouth. He tasted divine, musky and sweet with his natural flavor, with the spice of blood beneath his skin teasing her nostrils.

Moments like this were why she was happy with the gifts of her heritage. Other people tasted their partners, but not like she did. They didn't feel the humming psychic energy of arousal, neon and saturated in her mind's eye, nor could they smell the sultry cocktail of hidden blood and pheromones. They couldn't nourish themselves on their partners' bodies and would never know the deep joy of being offered that nourishment.

Ben tried to shift her back onto his face a few more times, but once she put her hands to work cupping his testicles and stroking the spit-slick base of his shaft, he gave up with a ragged cry. Eleonore bobbed her head faster, working her tongue over the prominent vein. Then she squeezed and twisted lightly at the base of his cock while the fingers of her other hand pressed the sensitive skin behind his testicles, and he exploded with a shout.

Eleonore drank him down, savoring the flavor. Energy hummed through her from his release, making her head spin and her skin flush with excitement. She was crackling with energy, as if a lightning storm had swept through her body and struck every pleasurable nerve on its way.

She swallowed the last drops, then looked over her shoulder with a smirk. Ben's hair was mussed, his face was red, and with his glasses deposited on the nightstand, there was nothing disguising the dazed look in his eyes.

His grin was drunken. "You look so smug."

She tossed her hair as she shifted to face him. "That's because I am."

"As you should be." He lay for a few moments before sitting up with a groan. "All right, time to turn the tables." Then his arms seemed to give out, and he flopped back to the pillow. He let out a breathy laugh, then tapped his lips. "You'll need to hop on, I'm afraid."

"Oh, no," Eleonore said dryly as she scooted forward and straddled his face. "What a terrible fate." Then she grabbed his hair in one hand, slapped her other against the wall, and began to rock over his generous, gifted mouth.

Ben hummed happily and gripped her hips and ass, fingers digging in as he helped her ride. His beard rubbed her inner thighs as he kissed her pussy with open-mouthed enthusiasm. Eleonore often liked a finger or two inside her during oral, but she was so keyed up from tasting his orgasm—both physically and psychically—that she wasn't going to last long enough to escalate past grinding. Her fingers curled against the wall as tension built low in her belly. It peaked sharply and she cried out, hips jerking as the orgasm blew through her in hot, clenching waves.

Ben was still lapping at her when she felt sane enough to move. She lifted off his face, thighs trembling, then collapsed next to him.

Ben slid an arm under her so she could rest her head in the juncture between his chest and shoulder. He was looking at her with such obvious pride that Eleonore cackled.

Ben raised his brows in silent inquiry.

"You look so smug," she said, mirroring his words from earlier.

He gently tapped her nose. "If you could see your face right now, you'd feel smug, too."

She could imagine. Her cheeks felt tight from how widely she was grinning, and she was undoubtedly bright red. Her werewolf was a gifted lover.

"Well," she said, nestling deeper into his hold, "you deserve to feel as smug as you like."

He chuckled, and warmth filled Eleonore's chest. It felt like a bubble of happiness was filling behind her breastbone, iridescent and shimmering.

Happiness was a trap. She knew the truth of that somewhere in her brain; the voice of caution was impossible to silence even if the orgasm and sandwich had muted it. Pain was inevitable in this life, and it only hurt worse when joy had preceded it. A reasonable woman would guard her heart, knowing nothing this pure and good could last.

But Eleonore had never been reasonable. So she closed her eyes and breathed in the smell of Ben's skin. "That was a good idea, werewolf."

TWENTY-SIX

M ARIEL SPARK GREETED THEM AT THE DOOR WITH A GRIN. "I'm so glad you could make it!"

Eleonore thrust out the bottle of wine Ben had bought on the way over. "I'm told gifts of alcohol are customary for modern social gatherings," she said.

Inwardly she winced, recognizing that wasn't the most natural way to enter a party, but nerves were twisting her stomach and making her hands sweat. It wasn't just the prospect of socializing in a context other than being Gigi's bodyguard that worried her—it was interacting with the people Ben cared about without any buffers.

Mariel didn't seem to mind her awkwardness. "Thank you," the brunette witch said, accepting the offering. Her hazel eyes were bright, and her dress was a riot of spring colors under a mint green cardigan. "Are you a hugger?" she asked Eleonore.

Eleonore blinked, having never been asked that question before. "I . . . don't know." Ben hugged her, but that was different.

Mariel's smile gentled. "Then let's start with a handshake." One firm handshake later, Mariel turned to Ben. "Thanks for stopping by," she said as she popped up on her toes to give him a tight hug.

All right, that did look rather nice. But Eleonore wasn't sure about anyone but Ben touching her yet, so she resolved to watch how the others interacted and decide if she wanted a hug later.

"Come on in," Mariel said. "Oz just fired up the grill."

"Sorry we're late," Ben said, casting a guilty look at Eleonore that nearly made her guffaw. They were late for an important reason that had involved the back seat of his SUV in the grocery store parking lot. *It's like being a teenager again*, Ben had said after their frantic kissing session. *I can't get enough of you.*

She couldn't get enough of him either, and it was nice to find a man who didn't require an orgasm or sex to enjoy intimacy. Sure, orgasms were lovely, but there was a whole universe of sensation to be explored and more than one way to be close to another person. They'd done nothing but kiss in that back seat and he'd seemed as delighted as if she'd given him head again.

Mariel waved away the apology. "There was no real start time for this. Honestly, I'm amazed Themmie's already here, but I guess there weren't any other parties tonight."

"Hey! I turned down five other social engagements to be here, thank you very much. *And* I brought lumpia." The pixie's voice came from deeper in the house, and then she appeared in the archway leading to the kitchen. Her hair was now crimson at the roots and orange at the tips, and she wore glasses with blue frames.

Eleonore's brow furrowed. "Has your vision deteriorated?" she asked, concerned. There had been no spectacles the previous times she'd met the pixie.

"What?" Themmie looked puzzled, and then realization washed over her face. "Oh! No, these are just decorative." She took the glasses off and waved them around. "Nerd chic is officially in."

"Now you tell me," Ben grumbled. "When I was growing up, people made fun of me for being a nerd."

Eleonore now knew what *nerds*, *geeks*, and *gatekeeping* were thanks to a few *Star Trek* message boards. A lot of the people commenting on those posts seemed inexplicably upset that other people enjoyed their hobbies without being persecuted for it. Ben didn't sound truly upset, but still—"You don't gatekeep geekiness, do you?" Eleonore asked.

"I don't . . . what?" Ben clearly had no idea what she was talking about.

Themmie bent over, resting her hands on her knees as she let out a loud laugh. "Eleonore, you are the best."

"Am I?" She wasn't sure why.

"I'm not laughing at you, to be clear," Themmie said, straightening. "I just love seeing you learn about modern times, and it's amazing how quickly you've picked up the lingo. Gatekeeping geekiness! That's so real, though I promise Ben isn't guilty of it. I bet you already know more about American pop culture after a month than he does after a lifetime."

Ben looked sheepish. "That's probably true," he said, rubbing the back of his neck.

Themmie fluttered closer. "Come on," she said, looping her arm through Eleonore's. "I want to hear all about you."

Eleonore barely had time to wave at Ben before she was towed away. Themmie couldn't be taller than five feet, but pixies were surprisingly strong for how delicate they looked: like rainbows that could strangle someone if they felt like it. Eleonore had a healthy respect for the species, having tangled with a few pixies in her day.

Themmie took her down the hallway past a living room and into the kitchen, which was warm and bright, and smelled pleasingly like cookies. From there they headed into the backyard, which was lit by strings of small electric lights. Fruit trees lined the fence and a glass-walled structure containing plants sat in the back corner.

Oz stood at the grill, scowling at hunks of raw meat like they had done him personal injury. At his side was Astaroth, who was providing Oz with loud tips on how best to handle his meat. Calladia and Rani were drinking beer and laughing nearby.

"I don't know why this is taking so long," Oz grumbled as they approached, poking the meat with a pair of tongs.

"Did you tenderize the steak before putting it on?" Astaroth asked. In contrast to Oz's casual, all-black attire, he wore a pristine white suit with a silver waistcoat and tie—a daring choice for a backyard barbecue, which internet research had indicated could be a messy experience. Eleonore would have to look up more details about the modern marvel of "dry cleaning" to determine how much danger the suit was actually in. She pulled a small notebook and pen out of the pocket of her leather jacket and added *dry cleaning* to her ongoing list of things to research.

Oz hesitated. "Is this going to be another innuendo?" he asked, deep voice dripping with suspicion.

Eleonore found the contrast between the two demons interesting. Astaroth might be the elder by centuries, but he spoke with a mortal British accent, while Oz's accent was pure demon: lilting, with some vowels clipped and others lengthened compared to American or British English.

She wondered if she would finally stick around one time and place long enough for her own accent to evolve as vampires' always did. Already she was using more slang, and it wouldn't take long for the remnants of France in her voice to disappear.

Astaroth widened his eyes. "Innuendo? Me?" he asked innocently. "Never. Besides, tenderizing steak is a well-known cooking technique."

Oz eyed him warily. "No, I did not tenderize the steak."

Astaroth gasped and clapped a hand to his chest. "Oz, Oz, Oz," he said, shaking his head. "How many times must I tell you the importance of *beating your meat*?"

Themmie burst into bright cackles, Rani snorted, and Calladia spit out a mouthful of beer. Eleonore might not be familiar with that particular slang, but there was enough context to figure it out.

Oz leveled his former mentor with a damning look and raised the tongs, snapping them menacingly. "If you don't leave me alone to grill, you won't have any meat left to beat."

Astaroth winced and backed away with hands held up. "I shall retreat with my dignity and manly parts intact."

Calladia hauled him in for a deep kiss that involved roving hands and a lot of tongue. "It's cute," she said when they finally parted.

"What?" Astaroth panted, having clearly forgotten everything in the wake of that kiss. Eleonore didn't blame him—her succubus senses were afire with the couple's lust for each other. The evening air was cool enough that her leather jacket was welcome, but she was tempted to fan herself.

Calladia patted the demon's ass and winked. "That you think you have any dignity left."

That elicited more laughter from Themmie and Rani, and Oz joined in, his joy booming across the yard. Even Eleonore found herself smiling, though she barely knew these people.

She barely knew them, yet she already liked them. On the grand scale she barely knew Ben either, and she liked him even more.

It was dangerous to get attached, like daring the universe—for she no longer believed in the gods of her youth—to take them away. Yet here she was, growing attached to this place and these people anyway.

"Want a beer?" Ben asked her.

Eleonore nodded. "The pine tree one, if they have it."

He grinned. "One IPA coming up, so long as you promise not to throw the bottle once you're done with it."

Her cheeks felt hot at the reminder of how she'd embarrassed herself on her first night in Glimmer Falls. "No smashing bottles," she promised. "Or threatening anyone."

Mariel came out with a tray of cookies and set them on a plastic table. "Are you still grilling?" she asked Oz.

He scowled at the steak. "It's not cooking."

Mariel took one look—then started to laugh. "The grill isn't on, you doofus."

That elicited an explosion of hilarity from everyone assembled, punctuated by Astaroth's exclamation, "Oz, you have to get *turned on* before you can properly handle your meat!" Which was followed by the tongs flying through the air and narrowly missing Astaroth's head.

Eleonore accepted a glass bottle from Ben, grinning at the antics of his friends. "I like this," she said.

"Me, too." Ben clinked his own bottle against hers. "Santé."

"Santé," she repeated, pleased he'd remembered.

The evening unrolled pleasantly from there. Once the grill was lit, the meat cooked quickly, and soon they were eating delicious steak, roasted vegetables, Themmie's pork-stuffed lumpia, and Mariel's cookies. Eleonore had feared she'd be out of place, but everyone seemed friendly and genuinely curious about her life. She relaxed, letting the IPA, food, and company loosen her tongue until she was sharing stories of her youth she'd long since thought forgotten.

She found herself standing next to Rani at one point while Oz cleaned the grill and Calladia, Astaroth, Mariel, and Ben played a game with the unusual name of "cornhole." It involved throwing small bags at a plank of wood while Themmie drunkenly heckled from where she was perched in a tree.

"Your friends are funny," Eleonore said, sipping her second beer.

"Hilarious," Rani agreed. The naiad was gorgeous, with smooth brown skin and long black hair. Her scales were barely visible at her hairline, their rainbow colors muted away from water. "And so nice. I was nervous when I first got invited to one of these, but now it feels like I've known them forever."

"I was nervous, too," Eleonore admitted. "My social skills are not always . . . modern." One way to put it. "But they don't seem to mind."

"Your social skills are fine."

"Even when I said the steak knife was sharp enough to disembowel someone quite neatly?" She'd meant it as a compliment, but the pause before Mariel had said, "Wow, I never thought about that before!" had made her realize perhaps they had different ideas of what made for a good knife.

Rani snorted. "Don't worry about it. We're all weird, and Oz and Astaroth say things like that, too. You're from a different time and worked as an assassin; everyone gets that." She nodded toward Ben. "I haven't seen Ben this happy in a long time. He likes having you around."

Eleonore blushed. "I like being around," she said softly. Words that hid a deeper confession.

"He's a good guy," Rani said, "but he worries too much and runs himself ragged trying to help everyone. He needs someone who gives him the care he gives everyone else. Someone who can help protect him."

It was a message—and a question. Eleonore nodded. "I would gut anyone who harmed him," she said seriously.

Rani's lips quirked, and she clinked her bottle against Eleonore's. "Cheers to that. But he also needs someone who can help protect him from his own generous impulses. He doesn't know how to say no, so he ends up knitting a million scarves and cooking for people and helping with home repairs even if he doesn't have the time for it."

"Or he helps his sister with her mayoral campaign while

opening a café." Ben's perpetual desire to be useful hadn't been lost on her.

Rani nodded. "Exactly. He won't ever admit he's overcommitted, so I'm glad you see it."

Guilt pricked Eleonore's breast. "It doesn't help that I showed up at the same time as all that. Now he's driving me around and making me sandwiches and introducing me to his friends when he should be focusing on everything else going on." And he was researching the curse in his spare time; she'd caught him face down on the keyboard late one night, snoring softly with *how to break magical compulsionnjkjknnnnnkjkjnnnnnnnnnnnnnn* typed into the internet search bar.

Eleonore had done plenty of internet searches on that same topic and the Witch in the Woods with no results. It was frustrating that even in a time when a world full of information could be accessed from anywhere, the witch still managed to remain an enigma.

"Maybe he is spending a lot of time on you," Rani said, "but you know what else he's doing?" She pointed at where Ben was laughing, head tipped back to expose the strong line of his throat. "He's smiling and talking more than he has in ages."

Eleonore rubbed her free hand over the soft ache in her chest. "I should start making him sandwiches. Or knit him something." Knitting was simultaneously dull and complicated, but it would be far from the most objectionable thing she'd ever done.

"I mean, don't go all fifties housewife," Rani said with a laugh. "He enjoys knitting and cooking. And really, every good couple should have a soft one and a stabby one."

A soft one and a stabby one. Eleonore liked that—almost as much as she liked hearing herself and Ben described as a *couple*. Mariel was obviously the soft one in her relationship, but she wasn't sure of the others. She pointed at where Calladia and

Astaroth were high-fiving to celebrate their cornhole victory. "Which one is the stabby one?"

"Oh, that's a special case," Rani said. "They're both stabby." She considered, head tilted. "But if I had to pick . . . Astaroth is the soft one."

Eleonore chuckled. "I suspect he wouldn't like to hear that."

"Soft for her, anyway," Rani said. "He does have a literal sword in that cane."

Eleonore had noted the skull-topped cane Astaroth carried with him everywhere. She'd already accounted for its usefulness as a bludgeoning implement, but this was an interesting development. "Noted," she said, eyeing the cane with new respect. Then she sobered. "So how do I best protect Ben? Besides gutting his enemies."

Rani shrugged. "Just show him you care. Little gestures will go a long way. And maybe help him set some boundaries so he doesn't work himself to death."

Eleonore nodded, memorizing the instructions. "Thank you," she told the naiad. "For helping me with Ben. I really do like him." Her throat felt thick with how much.

Rani grinned. "I can tell. And hey, he's waving at you."

Eleonore turned to see Ben gesturing at her. "Want to help me get revenge on these two?" he called out, pointing at Astaroth and Calladia. Mariel was kissing Oz at the grill, apparently done with the game.

"I don't think even an ancient assassin can help your aim, mate," Astaroth said.

Eleonore narrowed her eyes at the demon. Oh, she was going to make him eat those words. She jogged over, stripping off her jacket. "I can pierce a cyclops's eye with a knife from twenty paces," she said. "This so-called 'cornhole' doesn't stand a chance."

TWENTY-SEVEN

B EN LAUGHED AS HE COLLAPSED INTO BED. HE'D GOTTEN A bit too drunk at the barbecue, so Eleonore had driven them home. She'd required little instruction, having studied his driving, and though they'd gotten off to a bit of a lurching start, she was soon handling the vehicle like a pro.

"Cornhole victors," he proclaimed when Eleonore appeared in the doorway in a large T-shirt and his rolled-up pajama pants. "May our names echo through eternity."

They had kicked Astaroth and Calladia's asses five times in a row, mostly due to Eleonore's excellent aim and ability to distract her opponents by hissing. Even Ben had gotten a few good shots in, the alcohol and his delight at her militant approach giving him confidence.

"We deserve laurel wreaths," Eleonore said. "Chisel our names in marble."

She crawled into bed, leaning against the headboard and propping herself up with pillows. She'd brought her tablet and a small notebook with her, and Ben watched with interest as she opened a browser search tab.

"What's that?" he asked, pointing at the notebook, which held a handwritten bulleted list.

"My list of things to look up." Eleonore tapped the screen as she inputted a search query. "There's so much to learn about the modern day that I'll lose track if I don't write it down."

He leaned over to look at the list. Several items had been crossed off already.

- *Sesame Street*
- *giant slalom*
- *wine aerator*
- *cum quoi it (correction: kumquat)*
- *the Wright brothers*
- *unsinkable Molly Brown*
- *Henry VIII codpiece armor*
- *multitool*
- *REI*
- *co-op*
- *poutine*
- *dry cleaning*
- *where to buy sword cane*

It was an . . . interesting combination of topics. "When did you start making this list?" he asked, charmed by her eccentric, insatiable curiosity.

"Yesterday," Eleonore said absently as she scrolled through images of poutine. "I was trying to keep it all organized in my head before then."

His brows rose. "You researched all of this in one day?" He'd never even heard of Henry VIII's codpiece armor, and he wasn't sure he wanted to.

"More than that," she said, clicking on a recipe. "These are just the things I was curious about while away from the PADD." She shook her head. "Tablet, I mean."

"You can call it a pad if you like," he said. It wasn't an iPad, but it was functionally the same.

"*Tablet* does sound unpleasantly biblical," Eleonore mused. "Personal Access Display Device is better."

"Ah," Ben said, understanding the origin and spelling of her preferred terminology at last. "That sounds like something from *Star Trek.*"

She smiled, and his heart, clichéd organ that it was, skipped a beat. It was hard to pinpoint exactly what had changed about her over the past weeks. Her face was still as devastatingly beautiful, but it struck him as softer somehow. She smiled more easily every day.

Eleonore returned her attention to the tablet—or the PADD, he supposed he ought to call it. His eyes traced affectionately over her full lips, her auburn lashes, and the opinionated divot in her chin. She wound a strand of long hair around her finger as she read, mouth moving soundlessly. A few tangles had snarled the wavy strands, whether from the wind or too much cornhole celebration, who could say.

"Can I braid your hair?" he asked.

She blinked and returned her attention to him. "What?"

"Your hair," he said, motioning to the gorgeous red fall of it. "My mom taught me to braid, but I never get to practice." When she still hesitated, he tried to make the motivation sound less desperate than *I want my hands on you however I can get them.* "It's important to practice core skills, right?"

Her eyes might have twinkled at that. "Of course," she said, shifting on the bed to present her back to him. She shook her hair over her shoulders until it fell in a curtain to her waist. "An unpracticed swordsman has already lost the battle."

"Stay there," Ben said, scrambling to get a comb from his bathroom. He was nearly out the door when he realized with a jolt that he'd issued a command without meaning to. "Only if you want to, that is," he said hastily. "Sorry. It was a wish, not an order."

Eleonore had tensed up, but now she relaxed and nodded at him, a smile brushing her lips again. He had gotten much better at catching commands before they left his mouth—adding *please* or *what if* or other qualifiers—but mistakes still happened. He was just grateful Eleonore was giving him grace when he did slip up.

Gigi had left a pack of hair ties for Eleonore on one of her visits after she'd realized Eleonore was using rubber bands—and what a reaming Ben had received over that oversight—so he grabbed one of those from the bathroom as well. When he returned, Eleonore was just as he'd left her, sitting cross-legged while she researched. Not because she'd been ordered to stay, but because she wanted to.

Ben settled in behind her, a lump of gratitude and something more in his throat. He'd touched her hair before—had shampooed it and sunk his fingers into it to angle her head back for kisses—but as he gently ran the comb through the long strands, it felt different. Like meditation in a way. The same calm came over him that he felt while knitting, and his breathing slowed.

He hadn't braided a woman's hair in . . . how long? His last girlfriend had had short hair, so it must have been the one before. He was still on good if distant terms with all his exes; there had been no high drama, just mutual realizations that they didn't suit.

It used to trouble him that he didn't seem able to feel the raw passion for a partner that his werewolf friends spoke about in the same glowing terms they spoke of the moonshift. He'd felt stuck and inadequate, remaining largely single as the people around him fell in love, got married, and started families.

Maybe he hadn't been stuck, though. Maybe he'd been waiting for the right person.

It was a big, scary thought. He'd known Eleonore for little more than a month, and already she felt like an essential part of his life. Not the quiet, gentle woman he'd long imagined he'd end up with, but a vibrant, complicated, hissing goddess.

And oh, how he wanted to worship her. On his knees and with his mouth and with his hands in her hair, gently braiding the silky strands.

Eleonore made a humming sound and wiggled. "That feels nice."

"Good," he said, voice gone rough from the intensity of his thoughts. He secured the hairband around the end of the braid. It wasn't totally even, but it would do for now, and he would practice every night until he got it perfect.

So long as she was here. So long as she let him.

She grabbed the braid and inspected it, then twisted to give him a bright grin. "You're a man of many talents."

And you're the woman I want to use those talents to serve, he thought. But Eleonore was new to this time and new to him, and he didn't want to frighten her with the intensity of his feelings, especially with the curse still hanging over them.

So he grabbed her in a hug from behind and kissed the top of her head. "Will you tell me the most interesting facts you've learned?" he asked, careful to word it as a request and not an order. He rocked her back and forth slightly, and she melted into his arms.

"Of course," she said, yawning. "But there are quite a few of them."

Good, he thought. "Then how about you tell me one new fact a day, if you like?"

She nodded. "Let's start with the mating practices of praying mantises."

As she launched into a disturbing tale involving beheading and insect necrophilia, Ben settled his cheek on her hair and reflected that he'd never been so happy to be horrified in his life.

TWENTY-EIGHT

"Y OU'RE GLARING AT THE SKY," ELEONORE POINTED OUT ON
the evening of the October full moon.

Ben scowled. He was. The sun was setting, and moonrise would
soon be upon them. He couldn't believe how fast the days had been
passing, but between his business, Eleonore's shows, and Gigi's
rapidly escalating mayoral campaign, there had been little time to
catch his breath.

There had been a few moments, though—pauses for dinner and
Star Trek and morbid facts, an afternoon installing a training
dummy in the backyard, sweet interludes for kisses. The famed
Glimmer Falls Autumn Festival had begun, and he'd been delighted to escort Eleonore to baking competitions and magic shows
around town. They'd gone to an outdoor craft fair that morning,
and she'd inadvertently become a hit with the local schoolchildren
when she'd gotten a fang stuck in a caramel apple—the sight of a
ferocious vampire struggling with sweets had been hilarious to
the under-ten crowd, and though he wasn't sure if she'd deliber-

ately played up her distress for them, he'd spied a secretive smile on her lips afterward.

It had been a fun, hilarious morning, but then he'd had to go to work, and now the day was slipping away, and with it Ben's good mood.

"Shifting is a waste of time," he said. "All that running around and howling at things." He could be balancing the books at the Emporium or finishing a scarf or kissing Eleonore until her eyes were hazed with desire.

Those eyes were fixed on him now, sharp and alert from where she sat on the couch. He'd arrived home a few minutes ago to find her stuffing paper-wrapped objects into a soft carry-on bag. Assuming it was part of her performance, which evolved in new and surprising ways each week, he hadn't asked questions.

"Glaring won't make the moon rise any faster," she said.

Ben sighed gustily. "I wish it would make the moon not rise at all." He glowered at the bloody streaks painting the sky to the west.

"I suspect that would have a detrimental impact on the planet," Eleonore said. "Though I have not researched it."

"Maybe this time the rabbits will know better than to hop in front of me," he said with no real hope. If there was one constant he'd noticed over the years, it was that rabbits were shockingly stupid.

She nodded. "Yes, you told me you prefer your meat prekilled."

Well, that made him sound like a hypocrite. "It shouldn't bother me," he said. "I eat meat from the store. Isn't it more ethical to do the hunting myself?" Except a package of chicken breasts didn't have soft, innocent eyes. It didn't quiver in terror when he popped out of the bushes. It didn't shriek when he bit into it.

He rubbed his stomach, feeling sick.

The best nights were when he didn't catch anything at all, instead nibbling on berries and seeds. It was why he tried to eat a full meal before shifting to make his wolf stomach less empty. He'd reheat some leftover pasta soon and eat as much as he could stand.

"Not everyone is a hunter." Eleonore's shrug was reflected in the window, and he turned to face her again, putting his back to the oncoming night. "We would be a limited society if that's all people were skilled at."

"Unfortunately, my wolf instincts don't love the idea of sitting and quietly knitting."

She nodded, then raised the bag. "I've been researching wolf diets, and I've created something you should be able to eat without feeling sad."

He blinked. The bag . . . was for him?

Eleonore busied herself taking out the things she'd stuffed into it, laying a series of paper-wrapped objects on the coffee table. "These contain venison," she said, pointing at three thick rectangles loosely tied with twine. "I figure your claws or teeth will get through the paper."

He gaped at her. "You cooked venison for me?" He'd smelled an ominous hint of smoke in the air when he'd returned from work, but he hadn't expected *this*.

Eleonore grimaced. "I tried, but it was . . . not successful. Raw meat is probably better for wolves anyway."

He rubbed his sternum, feeling a rush of warm, nearly unbearable affection. "Eleonore, this is so sweet. Thank you."

She was still fussing with paper-wrapped packages. "This one has a mix of nuts and seeds," she said, "and this one has apples, carrots, and assorted fruit." She gave him a tiny smile. "And I did manage to cook a can of chili successfully so you can have dinner beforehand."

Ben was going to do one of several different things, though he wasn't sure which: cry, laugh, or throw himself at her feet. Possibly a combination of all three.

He was moving before his mind had made itself up. He didn't fling himself on the ground, but he did wrap her in his arms and lift her off the couch, squeezing her tightly as he rocked back and forth. Then he buried his face in her hair, breathing in her scent as his eyes prickled. "You listened when I told you about the moonshift."

"I always listen to you," she said, voice muffled in his neck.

And she did. She drank in his lessons about the modern world and remembered details about his friends he'd forgotten he'd told her, and now she had created an entire werewolf care package to send him into the forest with.

"You are the absolute best," he said.

She squirmed, and he finally put her down. "Definitely not," she said, though she looked pleased, "but I'm glad you like it. Next month I'll try to rig up a harness so you can carry the food with you when you're running." She cocked her head, considering. "Or maybe you could take me with you so I can plant food at strategic points throughout the night."

He grinned, all of a sudden liking the idea of running if it meant pursuing the flash of her red hair through the woods. "We'll brainstorm. Either way, having a stash of food to return to is a great idea. I'm not sure it'll stop me if something darts in front of me, but it will definitely help." He hesitated. "I still wish I liked shifting more."

Eleonore sat on the couch and patted the cushion. "Talk to me."

"I already talked to you about this last time," he said, joining her. "We won't be covering new ground."

She shrugged. "Maybe not, but you were the one who told me it's important to let things out rather than stewing on them."

Hoisted by his own petard . . . whatever that meant. But she was right, and it was easier to have someone else give you permission to let out frustrations. Maybe they wouldn't cover new ground, but it was nice to talk about his hesitations openly after so long pretending he was a typical werewolf.

"You know I'm anxious," he said.

There was no judgment on her face as she nodded.

"Well, it's not just an occasional thing," he said. "I have panic attacks, but it's more than that. It's why I stay so busy—if I'm always working, my brain has so much to think about that there's less room for bad thoughts."

"What kind of bad thoughts?" she asked.

He had jumped straight past the moonshift, he realized. Well, maybe that was for the best. It was one thing to say, "I don't like to lose control," and another to admit that his brain was actively sabotaging him almost every day of his life. He bit his lip, embarrassed, but she deserved this truth if she was going to stay in his life.

Lycaon, he hoped she wanted to stay in his life.

"I often think I'm a fraud or a failure," he said through a tight throat. "Like everyone hates me or there's no point to my existence. Or that I'm not enough of a man or a werewolf, that there's something wrong with me for not enjoying brawling or hunting or one-night stands." Intrusive thoughts that played like a song on repeat, and the frustrating part was that even though he knew they weren't true—well, sort of knew, most of the time—that didn't stop them from ringing through his head.

Eleonore's expression stayed patient and understanding, so Ben kept going, even though it mortified him to do so.

"If I'm not exhausted when I go to bed," he continued, "I end up lying awake in the dark for hours, worrying about everything from the Emporium to stupid things I did twenty years ago." On nights like that the past was paved with regret, while the future spread out before him in a tangle of twisting paths, any one of which might drop him off the edge of a cliff.

His brain had always been like that, even when he was a child. He'd worried about the thousand horrible outcomes that were possible if he made the wrong choices. The wrong classes, the wrong school, the wrong job, the wrong place to live, the wrong everything.

The wrong Ben Rosewood.

"You aren't a failure," Eleonore said. "And no one hates you."

"Cynthia Cunnington does."

She waved a hand. "She probably hates the clouds for raining on her. I'd be more worried if she liked you."

He cracked a smile at that. "True."

"You're a complicated man," Eleonore said. When he grimaced, she clarified. "In a good way. You're thoughtful and diligent, and you don't force yourself to fit the stereotype of the overly aggressive macho man."

"Thanks?" He found toxic masculinity abhorrent, but a small part of him might have liked to be considered a "macho man" nonetheless.

Eleonore's mouth tipped into an expression of distaste. "I've spent too much time around petty tyrants—people with huge egos and small hearts who take their misery out on others. Battlefields are full of men who would tear apart the world to prove their strength."

Her eyes had gone distant, and he wondered what memory she was revisiting. She had lived a life of violence, too, but she didn't puff up her chest and brag about it. It hadn't even been a choice for much of her existence.

"Those men's lives are brief and bloody, and they die as small and alone as they always were inside," she continued. "There's nothing unique in that. I think true strength is in breaking from the stereotype to be a complex, thoughtful man." Her eyes refocused on him, and she smiled gently. "The kind of man who enjoys knitting and deep conversations. One who can admit he doesn't like harming woodland creatures."

"I don't think my friends and family *like* harming woodland creatures," he said, feeling the need to defend other werewolves who hunted on instinct. "I just don't think they worry about it the way I do. They see it as part of the cycle of nature. It's like how people who hunt their own food and use every part of the animal are living more sustainably than people who only buy factory-farmed beef at the grocery store." His parents lived in that deliberate manner, bringing home whatever was left of their prey to be repurposed so the sacrifice of a life didn't go to waste. Ben couldn't even go fishing without feeling guilty about the fish flopping on the line yet had no problem buying prepackaged salmon—albeit sustainably sourced—so didn't that make him worse than his werewolf brethren?

"And they are free to hunt down rabbits and deer if they choose," Eleonore said. "Just as you are free to eat prepackaged meat and berries if you choose." She shrugged. "The world is too large for everyone to be the same."

What she was saying made sense, but he still felt the sting of shame. "Diet aside, I wish I could enjoy being a werewolf as much as everyone else."

She tucked her legs under her. "Besides the hunting, what about it bothers you?"

He spoke slowly, trying to explain a feeling he'd never confessed to another person. "I told you I work constantly to wear myself out so I can't think about the wrong things. It's my way of controlling my brain. I have a schedule and habits and I try to think rationally whenever I can. But when I'm a wolf . . . there is no schedule. There's no rational thought. There's just this aggressive energy, and part of what's scary is that it feels good. I run for miles under the moonlight and howl like a maniac and can't resist sniffing things and scratching inappropriately. It's all instinct, and while I'm transformed, there's this primal joy. But after I shift back, I feel sick."

"Sick?"

It was frustrating trying to explain this when he didn't

understand it himself. He ran a hand through his hair, one leg jogging rapidly. "I feel embarrassed that I lost control. Or maybe afraid. What happens if I do something horrible as a wolf? What if I . . . I don't know . . . piss all over City Hall or trample an endangered species or eat a baby or something?"

Eleonore looked taken aback for the first time during this conversation. "Is eating babies a common werewolf behavior?"

"Not even slightly," Ben said with a ragged half chuckle. "But see? That's how my thoughts spiral. I start seeing the absolute worst outcome, even if it's ludicrous." If he spent the moonshift publicly scratching his balls—something human Ben would *never* do—he worried he would end up accidentally eating an infant. If his business didn't turn a profit one week, he was certain he'd end up dying alone in a gutter.

"Have you talked to anyone about this?" Eleonore asked. "Besides me, that is."

"I've gone to therapy. It's been a few years, though—I got too busy with the Emporium. And I was able to tell the therapist how my anxiety manifests at work or with my family, but I was always too embarrassed to talk about being a self-loathing werewolf." He didn't know a single pixie who regretted their wings or a centaur who would trade galloping for walking on two feet. "Do you ever mind drinking blood?"

Eleonore shrugged. "No, because I couldn't live without it. I have my own problems, though."

"The curse," he said, feeling guilty for complaining about something so minor when she had been mystically entrapped for centuries. "I'm sorry, you must think I'm so selfish—"

Eleonore reached forward and lightly pinched his lips closed, cutting off the sentence. "I will speak to my own thoughts, thank you."

He subsided at her authoritative tone. She released him, and when he didn't speak, she nodded approvingly. "I also fear losing control," she said. "Or not fear it, but despise it in myself. When I lash out or get angry beyond reason, it feels like there's some vicious, small creature in my chest I have no control over."

"That's a trauma response, though," he said. "You only lash out when you get triggered."

She shrugged. "I also naturally have a temper. It isn't my finest trait."

"But I have no *reason* to be anxious," he persisted. "My family is great. My life is great."

"I don't think you have to have a reason. You can be born that way, or maybe life has shaped you that way, but it's nothing to explain away or be embarrassed about." She worried her lower lip with one sharp fang. "My father was prone to dark moods," she said after a pause. "Weeks or months where he would feel despair over everything and nothing in particular. His father was the same, and some of his cousins as well. It was a private battle they all fought. Eventually the joy would emerge again—it always did—but we never judged him for those dark periods. We loved him through them."

We loved him through them. "Oh, Eleonore," he said, struck by the simple beauty of the phrase. "That's downright profound."

She tossed her hair over her shoulder. "I know." Then she smiled, softening the declaration into a joke. "The point is, we're all fighting invisible battles. My father struggled with sorrow—clinical depression, I believe you term it now. I have problems with rage and acting on impulse. You're full of worries." She shrugged. "I don't think it means any of us are broken."

How shrewdly she sliced to the core of the issue. Because yes, that was exactly what Ben had told himself. That he was broken. That he was *wrong*.

What she told him felt like absolution.

Except maybe she was right, and there was nothing to be

absolved for. Maybe it was okay that he wasn't like every other werewolf.

The moon was tugging, calling him to the forest. He needed to scarf down the chili and run out the door, but he needed to let her know how much her support meant first. "You've given me a lot to think about," he said, cupping her cheek. He kissed her, soft and slow, eyes closed against the setting sun. "Thank you."

She patted his shoulder briskly once the kiss was over. "Better you introspecting than me." Then she snapped her fingers. "Oh! I had another idea."

All her ideas had been amazing so far. "Yeah?"

"If you have an excess of carnal urges when you get back, would you like me to bite you?"

He blinked, startled. She hadn't fed from him since that first time, and he'd been quietly dying wondering when it would happen next. "Why specifically then?" he asked. "Obviously the answer is yes, but I might smell bad." He grimaced. "Sometimes I roll in things I shouldn't."

"You were unhappy after the last full moon," she said. "So this time I'll bite you and drink your blood until you're happy, and then you can fall asleep easily." She nodded decisively.

A brilliant idea. Way better than self-loathing combined with melatonin and whale noises. "Absolutely," he said.

With that to look forward to, he actually *wanted* the moon to rise.

TWENTY-NINE

ELEONORE WAS DOZING ON THE COUCH WHEN THE DOOR opened. She came awake instantly, rising to a seated position.

Ben stood in the doorway, looking exhausted. A streak of dirt crossed his forehead, and his clothes were rumpled.

"How was it?" she asked. She'd been nervous, wondering if her werewolf care bag would actually be helpful.

To her relief, Ben smiled, though the expression was a tired one. "I filled up on venison and didn't eat a single woodland creature." He shucked off his coat, hanging it up before tossing his keys and wallet in the bowl. "I did chase a few, but that was more for the fun of it."

Eleonore clapped her hands. "Excellent. How are your carnal urges?"

He laughed, running a hand over his face and smudging the dirt further, then gestured at his bulging crotch. "Very present."

She'd sensed the lingering wildness under the surface, tinged with lust. As he stared at her, the lust grew stronger. "Good," she said. "I'm going to bite you now."

She had him pinned to the wall in a flash, one hand at his shoulder and one in his hair. Her stomach cramped and her fangs lengthened. She was thirsty, and she couldn't wait to have his delectable blood coursing through her.

Ben grunted and cupped her ass, then hoisted her into the air. Eleonore wrapped her legs around his waist, then tipped his head to the side, licked the vein throbbing in his neck, and plunged her fangs into it.

Hot, decadent bliss.

Ben's blood roared through her in a wave of pulsing energy. She swallowed eagerly, moaning at the taste. Chocolate and spice lingered under the rich, coppery top notes. It was like drinking electricity, bright and invigorating.

"That's it," Ben said roughly, tipping his head back against the door. "Take whatever you need."

It was an order, but not one she could be angry at. Not one issued consciously either, she'd wager. She clutched Ben closer, vampiric instincts telling her to keep her prey immobilized. Arousal pumped through her in time with her pulse. *Their* pulse now, because her bite had put their hearts in time. His pumped fast and strong as he gave, and hers matched its pace as she took.

When she was sated, she disengaged and licked his neck to help seal the punctures. Then she grabbed his face and kissed him, traces of blood lingering on her tongue.

Ben moaned, meeting her kiss lick for lick. He pushed off the wall and carried her to the couch, where he tipped her on her back. Then he was on top of her, rolling his hips to drag his cock over her cunt.

Someday Eleonore would have to get them naked before she bit him, because neither of them could stop long enough to strip now. Her climax was building fast, and her nerves sang with sensation everywhere they touched.

She cried out as the orgasm pulsed through her. Heat sparkled from her belly out to her fingers and toes as she clenched again and again, her body seeking what only he could provide.

Ben came with a great, groaning shudder, and the psychic energy of his orgasm sank into her. It was like drinking from a golden chalice filled with liquid starlight, each moment of his pleasure intensifying her own.

When they were both finished, Eleonore felt like she might melt into the couch. Her limbs were loose and heavy, and she was so sated physically and mentally she might never move again, even if Ben's weight was nearly crushing her.

He groaned, then slowly shifted off her and stood, swaying. "Fuck," he said. "You're going to make me like the moonshift after all."

Eleonore grinned, pushing herself upright with trembling arms. "Think you'll sleep well?"

He gave her a speaking look. "It'll be a miracle if I make it three steps without passing out." He reached out a hand to help her up. "I'll shower some of this dirt off, and then we can go to bed."

Eleonore let him help her up, though he seemed about as shaky as she was. "Are you going to the Emporium in the morning?" Gigi had another rally planned for the next evening, but it would be nice if he could sleep in with her.

"Not a chance in hell," he said with a crooked grin. "I'm turning off my alarm."

"Good," she said, pride suffusing her. She'd discovered one excellent way to protect Ben Rosewood from himself.

✦ ✦ ✦

ELEONORE KEPT A WARY EYE ON THE GUESTS AT GIGI'S RALLY. The election was less than a week away, and this would be a prime moment for someone to cause a scene. The polls showed a close race, and Cynthia Cunnington would not like that.

Eleonore was amazed how quickly time seemed to be moving. Gigi had announced her candidacy last-minute for such things, having launched her campaign in August for an early November election, but it felt like so much had happened. When Eleonore thought of how she'd first arrived in Ben's living room—hissing and defensive, ready to rip out his throat—it felt like she'd been a different person then.

Not that she didn't hiss anymore, of course. She still bared her fangs and reached for her knives when startled. She hadn't yet adapted to the hugging habits or casual trust that Ben's friend group employed. And the flash of a black cloak in her peripheral vision—of which there were more than a few in Glimmer Falls, especially around Halloween—would set her heart racing as rage suffused her. But it was never actually the Witch in the Woods, and the more time passed, the quicker Eleonore was able to regain control over that anger.

She still didn't fully believe everything would be all right in the end, because historically it hadn't. But for the first time, she was allowing for the possibility.

Once she found the witch and severed her head, of course.

The rally was being hosted by the Human-Centaur Polo League at their barn. The motto of this unusual sporting organization was *Twice the torsos, twice the fun*, which reminded Eleonore of something her Great-Great-Uncle Dragoslav might have said while showing off his skeleton collection. He had been beheaded in the vampire wars a decade before Eleonore's father, but she had fond memories of playing knucklebones while he regaled her with the history of each victim in his collection.

The barn was spacious and clean, smelling pleasantly of hay and lemon wood polish. Strings of festive lights hung from the rafters, and the walls contained racks of polo equipment.

Ben's Plant Emporium was catering the event, and the room

was lined with tables piled high with food that appealed to the tastes of multiple species. Gigi had tried to pay for the spread, but Ben had refused, saying this time would be his treat.

It was the sort of generous gesture to be expected from him, but Eleonore couldn't help but think of Rani's warning: *He runs himself ragged trying to help everyone.* Ben was happy to donate time and money to help his sister, but Eleonore would need to keep an eye on him. Make sure he didn't push himself so far he—or the Emporium—collapsed.

The barn doors were open to the chilly late October night, but Mariel, Calladia, and a few other witches and warlocks had summoned glowing orbs that circulated through the crowd, giving off heat. One passed over Eleonore and she tipped her head back, letting the warmth spill over her face before she resumed her bodyguard duties of looking for trouble.

A flicker of movement outside the barn doors made her stiffen, but she relaxed when a centaur galloped through, blowing a kazoo. On his back was a human waving a pink *Howling for Change* flag. They galloped up and down the center of the barn while people clapped, howled, cheered, pranced, or undulated with delight.

How marvelous this time was that people should interact so freely and give of themselves so openly. Riding centaurs was strictly forbidden without consent, of course, but Eleonore had known some who would rather have galloped over a cliff than allow a human on their back even in dire emergency. This group simply liked playing a game together.

The centaur was followed by Gigi herself, who strolled into the barn in a tailored gray suit that screamed of Astaroth's influence. "Welcome!" Gigi called as she stepped onto a makeshift stage. Her shoes, as always, were pink. "I'm so glad you could make it out tonight."

A cheer went up.

"I started this journey with nothing but strong opinions, hope, and the assurance of the election board's scryer that I am not, in fact, an agent of pure evil," she continued. Chuckles followed this. "So it's astounded me that in little more than two months, we've built this community. It's all thanks to you—both the people gathered here tonight and those who couldn't make it but have been helping in other ways." She grinned. "It takes a village to raise a mayoral candidate. So thank you for your help, large and small—the people who donated money or advertising space, who canvassed door-to-door, who called their friends or bought campaign merchandise or, hell, even gave me a smile on a day I needed it. When we win—and we *will*—you will be the real heroes of this story."

It was a good speech, but Eleonore was used to that by now. Gigi was charismatic and warm, and people loved her. Eleonore wasn't here to listen to pretty words, though—she was more interested in how Cynthia Cunnington might sabotage the event.

Nothing had been as dramatic as the assault on Gigi's first rally, but Cynthia's touch had been evident in more subtle ways since then. Conservative websites had denounced Gigi for being unable to protect people at her rallies—"Are Our Children Safe from Explosions with Gigi Rosewood?" had been a notably overwrought headline—and nasty ads aired on the TV and radio. The complaints were varied: Gigi was too young and inexperienced for office; Gigi would tear down the magical legacy Cynthia had worked so hard to protect; Gigi would be a liability as a werewolf since public service couldn't take a break for the full moon. As if Cynthia Cunnington never stepped away from her desk to eat or sleep or shit.

Eleonore studied the shifting crowd and exit points. Across the barn, Ben was doing the same. He looked rather ferocious, having traded his sweater vest for a long-sleeved black shirt that highlighted his muscles and the breadth of his shoulders. If she hadn't been on duty, Eleonore would have spent quality time ogling him.

Her skin prickled, which meant her intuition had picked up on a shift in the environment. She looked harder, trying to determine what had changed.

The barn doors that had been open a minute before were now closed.

It could have been done by someone wanting to keep the heat in, but Eleonore would rather be paranoid than caught off guard. She made her way along the wall, fingers hovering over the sheathed knives at her thighs.

Ben, always attuned to her, mirrored her movements. "What is it?" he asked when they met past the last row of spectators. "Did you see something?"

"The door is shut." Then, realizing the folly of having both of them investigating the same thing at the same time, Eleonore pointed toward Gigi. "You should stay near her."

He nodded and slipped away.

The barn doors had a gap beneath them—not large, but enough for something small to wriggle through. Eleonore crouched—and saw the flash of black scales. A narrow, pointed face emerged, no wider than two of her fingers put together. Its red eyes were slit-pupiled, and smoke rose in twin wisps from its nostrils.

A smoke adder. Known for the burning pain of its bite—which was usually not fatal, unless an excessive amount of venom was delivered—and its tendency to conceal itself in clouds of smoke. At the sight of her, it startled, and smoke began billowing from it in earnest.

Though the snake might be five feet long at most, it could fill the entire barn with black, acrid smoke in under a minute. People would panic, and with only one exit, the stampede could turn deadly.

Eleonore didn't make a habit of handling reptiles, but she knew the basics: grab the snake behind the head so it couldn't bite. She took a deep breath, then regretted it when she started coughing. The peppery smoke burned, and tears flooded her eyes.

She couldn't see the snake anymore. Within seconds, the smoke had thickened and spread. It was now climbing the walls and reaching dark fingers toward the interior of the barn. Behind her came the first scream of "Fire!"

Usually not fatal, Eleonore reminded herself, gritting her teeth. Then she plunged her hand into the smoke. Hot scales met her fingertips, the texture rough and soft at once. Eleonore wrapped her hand around the snake, hoping she was in roughly the right place.

She was not.

A shriek tore from her throat when a pair of sharp fangs sank into her forearm. God's throbbing knob, that hurt. The first spurt of venom pumped inside her arm, and it felt like being stabbed by a hot poker.

At least if the snake was biting her, it couldn't bite anyone else. She fumbled for the barn doors with her free hand, cursing under her breath. Finally, one swung open, and she staggered into the cool night.

How to get this thing off her? Chopping the snake in half wouldn't be enough—it bit down in its death throes, and its fangs would remain sunk in her arm for gods knew how long. Besides, it hadn't bitten her out of malice, only because it felt threatened. The one thing she knew could stop an enraged smoke adder was dumping it in cold water, which would put it into a torpor and release the bite.

Eleonore's head spun as the poison sent alternating waves of fire and ice through her body. She shuddered, then hissed when the pain intensified further.

There was a small pond down the hill she could jump into . . . but would she make it before the snake delivered enough venom to kill her?

THIRTY

E LEONORE!"
Ben's pulse thundered as he ran after her, choking on the black smoke that obscured his vision and burned his lungs. She'd screamed once from within that darkness before going silent, and terror clawed at his chest.

Was the barn on fire? He didn't feel heat, but what else could it be?

He'd aimed his feet in the direction of the exit, but he couldn't see where the opening was. Thankfully, a gust of wind parted the smoke long enough for him to catch a glimpse of the night sky—and Eleonore staggering down the slope toward a small pond. The smoke followed her, and he realized it was coming from something coiled around her arm.

He shoved the second barn door open. People were running and screaming, but he only had eyes for Eleonore.

What *was* that on her arm?

He gained on her quickly, feet churning up mud and grass. "Eleonore!" he shouted.

She tripped, falling onto hands and knees. Then she crawled forward through a veil of smoke . . . and tumbled face-first into the pond.

Ben leaped into the pool after her with an enormous splash. His feet hit bottom when the water reached his neck. *Damn*, that was cold. Ben's muscles cramped, but adrenaline kept him moving. He fumbled around, trying to find Eleonore beneath the water.

His fingers touched soft skin, and he pulled her upright.

Eleonore emerged coughing and spluttering. Her feet kicked his shin before she stepped on his boot to gain purchase, chin barely topping the water.

"What happened?" Ben asked, frantically patting her underwater. "Were you on fire? Are you hurt?"

In response, Eleonore lifted her arm out of the water . . . revealing a snake wrapped around it. The reptile slid off and sank into the water.

"F-fine," Eleonore said, teeth chattering.

Bull*shit* she was fine. Ben hauled her into his arms and waded toward shore. The smoke was receding now that the snake—which had apparently been the cause—was gone, and a crowd of shocked people surrounded the pond. "Someone call a doctor," he shouted.

"Call a w-warlock for p-poison n-negation," Eleonore corrected, clinging to him with her left arm. Her right hung limp at her side. "That was a s-smoke adder."

Ben's stomach dropped. He'd seen those on a nature documentary, and his memory said they were highly venomous.

"I'm calling Alzapraz," Themmie said. "If anyone knows how to fix this, it's him."

Ben hoisted Eleonore out of the pond before clambering out himself. An icy whip of wind lashed his skin, and he shivered. Eleonore was shivering worse, though.

"Is she okay?" Gigi asked, crouching beside them. "What was that?"

"Smoke adder," Ben said tersely. "Someone must have planted it to sabotage the rally."

Gigi made an outraged noise, then stood and moved away to make a phone call, presumably to the police. She shot worried glances over at Eleonore every few seconds.

Eleonore glanced at her arm, then grimaced and closed her eyes. When Ben followed her gaze, he wished he hadn't. Her skin was red and swollen around the puncture wounds, resembling an overcooked sausage on the verge of splitting.

"Stay with me, sweetheart," Ben said, wet hand trembling on her forehead. "Please." If he could order her to heal, he would, but his commands only affected her actions, not the inner processes of her body.

"N-not dying," Eleonore said through gritted teeth. "I think, anyway."

"You'd better not be," he said vehemently. When she groaned, he looked around wildly. "Does anyone have a first aid kit? A blanket? Anything?"

Astaroth shucked off his suit coat, and Ben wrapped it around Eleonore, who moaned at being jostled. "I'm sorry," he said. "We need to keep you warm."

"This hurts like a *bitch*," she spat.

"I can confirm," Astaroth said, forehead furrowed. "One of those bit me in Andorra a few centuries back. It hurts, but it isn't fatal if you disengage the snake quickly enough."

How quick was quickly enough? Maybe twenty seconds had passed between Eleonore's scream and her tumble into the water.

"Ben?" Eleonore asked without opening her eyes.

"Yes?" He stroked her wet hair back from her face.

"Don't let anyone kill the snake. It doesn't know any better."

"Oh, sweetheart." Ben's eyes blurred with tears at the gesture of kindness to something that didn't deserve it. He might dislike hunting during the full moon, but he would gladly smash that snake with a rock right now.

When he didn't say anything further, Eleonore slitted her eyes open. "I mean it," she slurred. "Can't b-blame something with t-teeth for biting."

A lump filled his throat. "All right, I'll keep the snake safe." Assuming it hadn't already drowned. "Please just focus on getting better."

"I'll get the snake," Calladia said, pulling thread out of the pocket of her leggings and heading to the pond.

His friends were clustered around them. Oz consulted with Astaroth while Themmie flitted back and forth, making air drops of various helpful items: a horse blanket, a water bottle, a sweatshirt. As Ben dragged the blanket over Eleonore, Mariel crouched and pressed her finger to Eleonore's forehead. "I'm going to try a pain relief spell," she said. Her finger traced runes as she whispered.

Eleonore opened her eyes more fully when Mariel was done. "Thank you," she said, voice raspy with smoke. "That helped."

"Good." Mariel smiled. "It doesn't look any better, but that should keep you feeling okay for a few minutes."

Eleonore shivered.

"Let's get you warmed up," Ben said. He looked at Mariel. "Do you have a spell for that?"

"No, but I bet Calladia does."

Calladia had returned from the pond with the snake floating midair beside her in a cage woven of light. Ben glared at the creature, wishing he had wolf fangs to bare at it.

"Yeah, I've got something," Calladia said. She pulled thread from her pocket again and started tying knots. "*Ayorva en corporiyil.*"

A wave of heat rose from Eleonore's prone form, and her hair instantly dried. A moment later the same heat hit Ben, expanding outward from his core. Even the droplets on his glasses vanished.

He exhaled in relief. "Thank you."

"Alzapraz was drinking two blocks away," Themmie announced, buzzing into view. "He'll be here soon, and he told me the ingredients he needs for a poultice. Mariel, can you summon them?"

"Absolutely." Mariel went to consult with Themmie.

Alzapraz Spark was Mariel's ancestor and an expert in many types of magic, chief among them life magic. But the warlock's mastery was incomplete, and his physical body had aged despite his immortality—which meant Ben had doubts about how "soon" the decrepit man would be able to get there. He gritted his teeth against the surge of impatience and shifted to put Eleonore's head in his lap. "You're doing great," he told her.

"I know I am," Eleonore snapped.

Ben was going to take her peevishness as a good sign. He stroked her hair, pressing his lips together to suppress their trembling.

Mariel returned with an armful of ingredients. She knelt down and started mashing a mixture of bananas, toadstools, herbs, and milk in a copper bowl. Ben forced himself to match his frantic breathing to the steady grind of the pestle. Eleonore needed him to be her rock right now.

Her free hand caught his, and she squeezed his fingers. She didn't speak, but her eyes shone with fear. Ben's own eyes prickled with tears as he raised her knuckles to his mouth. "It's going to be okay," he said roughly.

"Here's Alzapraz," Mariel said, standing and brushing grass off her knees.

The ancient warlock took Mariel's place, kneeling with a cacophony of groans and clicking joints. He had long white hair, a scraggly beard, and age-spotted skin so wrinkled it looked like he'd been twisted up and wrung out, but his eyes were bright and intelligent beneath caterpillar eyebrows. "Smoke adder, eh?" he said in a voice like a creaking floorboard. "One of those bit my testicles once. Not fun."

Astaroth and Oz made matching noises of alarm. Ben would have, too, if he didn't have more pressing things to worry about.

"H-how did a snake get near your testicles?" Eleonore asked.

"You haven't lived until you've played the Russian roulette of sex games with a bevy of kinky snake shifters," Alzapraz wheezed. "It was still worth it."

"Can you please stop talking and fix her?" Ben asked. He wouldn't normally be so rude to Mariel's relative—or anyone else—but this was a dire situation.

"Yes, yes," Alzapraz said, waving a hand. "All things in their time." The warlock grabbed the bowl, then daubed the mixture onto Eleonore's arm. "*Genezserpil o' corpora*," he muttered. Then he pulled a strip of linen from the sleeve of his purple velvet robe and tied it around the wound. "Keep that on for a few hours," he said. "At midnight, go outside and light a candle to Hecate, then remove the bandage and bathe the wound in moonlight. You'll be good as new."

Eleonore already looked more relaxed, and Ben was pleased to see her arm was shrinking back to its normal size. "Thank you," she said, sitting up.

"You have an ancient sound to your voice," Alzapraz said, inspecting her closely. "When do you hail from?"

"France, some six centuries past."

He coughed. "I haven't met anyone that close to my age in a while. You're much better preserved than me, though."

Eleonore cocked her head, looking curious. "How old are you?"

"Older than that," he said dryly. He started to stand, got a few inches off the ground, then sank back down. "Curse it, I'm going to have to lose more of my dignity, aren't I?"

"I'll help you up," Themmie said. She ignored his glower, deftly raising him to his feet with one flap of her wings.

Eleonore was staring intently at Alzapraz. "You're a life warlock," she said, and Ben instantly understood her train of thought.

"Guilty as charged," Alzapraz said.

"Do you know another life witch who goes by the moniker the Witch in the Woods?" Eleonore asked. "A few inches shorter than me, pale skin, long dark hair, likes *Star Trek*, and has a habit of mystically enslaving assassins?"

Ben was tempted to smack his forehead. Of course they should have asked Alzapraz first. How had he not thought of that? Vast age and experience aside, Alzapraz might be familiar with other practitioners of life magic. Maybe there was a directory of sorts.

"*Star Trek?*" The wrinkles deepened into canyons as Alzapraz's forehead furrowed. "Can't say about that part, but the Witch in the Woods, sure." He let out another wheezing chuckle. "I told her that was a boring name, but she insisted simple was better to be remembered over the centuries. Guess she was right."

Eleonore shot to her feet instantly, and her fists clenched in the old man's robe. "Tell me where she is," she hissed, baring her fangs. "I will rip her heart out, eat it, and floss my teeth with her veins."

Ben winced at the words as he clambered to his own feet. Not everyone was as accustomed to Eleonore's dramatic threats as he was.

Alzapraz didn't seem alarmed, though. "I'm beginning to understand the assassin portion of your question."

"Eleonore," Ben said, gently laying a hand on her shoulder. "He did just save your life."

"I'm not going to floss with *his* veins," Eleonore pointed out as she released the robe. Then she eyed the ancient warlock. "Sorry. Thank you for saving my life."

Alzapraz waved a hand. "Never get offended by someone else's centuries-old blood feud, that's what I always say." He tipped his head to the side, and his neck cracked loudly before he put his hand to it with a grimace. "Funny you should mention the Witch in the Woods. Astaroth and Calladia went to see her a few years back."

Eleonore whipped her head around to glare at Astaroth. "What?"

Ben mirrored the movement and the question. "*What?*"

He liked Astaroth, but if the demon had known about the Witch in the Woods this whole time and hadn't said anything . . .

Astaroth's jaw dropped. "Isobel?" he asked. "*She's* the witch you're looking for?"

Isobel. The villain had a name at last.

"Oh, shit," Calladia said, eyes wide as she looked between Eleonore and Astaroth. "I knew I didn't like her even before she tried to have us killed."

Eleonore snapped her fangs. "Why didn't you tell me earlier?"

"Yeah," Ben echoed, crossing his arms and glaring. "Why didn't you?"

Astaroth held his hands up. "In my defense, she didn't call herself the Witch in the Woods or skulk around in a cloak when we met her. It was a brief encounter, really. I tried to regain the immortality she'd stolen, she called my nemesis to have him murder us . . ." He shrugged. "Just business."

Ben couldn't believe it. Astaroth and Calladia had fallen in love during a road trip to find an infamous witch two years ago, seeking the return of Astaroth's immortality and advice for defeating his enemy on the demon high council. The witch had been less than helpful and had promptly sold them out to said enemy.

Had Eleonore been in the cabin on that day two years ago, watching *Star Trek*? Or had she been trapped in the crystal, dreaming cold, lonely dreams?

"Where is she?" Eleonore demanded. She was trembling head to toe, and Ben couldn't imagine the intensity of what she must be feeling.

"About two days' drive from here," Astaroth said.

Ben's heart raced. He could hardly breathe. Two days? That was nothing. He grabbed Eleonore's hand. "We can leave first thing tomorrow," he promised.

Eleonore's lips quivered as she looked up at him. Then she buried her face in his chest and began to cry.

THIRTY-ONE

E LEONORE SOBBED INTO BEN'S SHIRT, BODY SHUDDERING
with the force of it. He'd picked her up the instant she'd begun
crying and was carrying her to the parking lot. Good. She didn't
want anyone else to see her like this.

She hadn't cried in centuries.

It was like discovering a lost art—the ability to weep. When
hate had been her armor, there had been little room for tears.
She'd forgotten how her eyes squinted and her nose tingled or how
her throat felt raw from the choked noises she was making. It was
an ugly feeling but also a relief—like a dam had burst and some
horrible pressure had finally been released.

The witch was two days from Glimmer Falls. And Ben was going to take her there.

"Sit in the car or go home?" Ben asked as he set her down next
to the SUV.

"Home," she gasped.

It didn't escape her that she'd thought of his house as *home*. As
she leaned her forehead against the window, the raw cries in her

throat turning to soft hiccups, she wondered if that was dangerous.

But she hadn't had a home in so long. And when she thought about where she wanted to curl up and hide from the world, that house with its earth tones and sturdy furniture and the peeling paint in the kitchen was the first choice.

He drove silently, though he kept a hand on her knee. A big hand, but one capable of tending to the most delicate orchids. Eleonore wasn't delicate, but it was nice to feel like it every once in a while. Or not delicate, but . . . protected. Like she could put down her weapons and rest and someone would be there, keeping watch.

Her clan's war camp hadn't been a soft place, but there had always been someone on the lookout. Succubi or other daytime species when the sun was up, vampire warriors at night. It had been easy to fall asleep at those fires with meat and blood in her belly and warm furs keeping the cold at bay. Despite the stereotype of the aloof, mysterious loner, vampires were clan creatures—they weren't meant to be alone.

By the time they reached the house, her tears had stopped. She rubbed her wet cheeks, tasting salt on her lips. Her head throbbed and her eyes felt swollen, but a feeling of peace had settled over her.

Ben set her up on the couch under a blanket, then retreated to the kitchen to make tea. "Need blood?" he called.

Eleonore took stock of her body. This was early to need sustenance, but the snake bite had taken a toll. "A small mug, please."

His head popped around the corner, and he tapped two fingers against his neck. "Want it from the source?"

That would be delicious, but—"If I drink from you, I'll get aroused, and I'm too exhausted for that." Even a succubus had her limits, and Eleonore felt wrung out. If she tried to grind on Ben's lap, she'd probably topple over.

"Fair enough. Just know it's on offer whenever you need."

Sweet wolf.

Eleonore closed her eyes while he bustled around the kitchen. The witch was two days away, but how would they break the curse?

A mug clinked on the table, and she opened her eyes to the welcome sight of steaming blood dotted with marshmallows. Ben sat next to her as Eleonore grabbed the mug with murmured thanks. She drained it in a few deep gulps.

Much better. Her foggy head was clearing, and the exhaustion weighing down her limbs had begun to lift. Even the sore throb of her bitten arm was diminishing as the blood nourished her.

"Did they catch the person who left the snake at the rally?" she asked, realizing she'd forgotten that aspect of things. "And was anyone hurt?"

"No one else was hurt," he said, tucking a lock of hair behind her ear. "Thanks to you. Gigi texted me that someone saw a car speeding away afterwards, but they didn't get the license plate. It had to have been Cynthia, though."

She thought of the smoke adder and how unfair it was for any creature to be used like that. "Is the snake all right?"

His expression softened as he looked at her. "I'll text Calladia to double-check." He typed on his phone, and a minute later it chimed with an incoming text message. "Yes, she got some wildlife researchers from the college involved. They'll rehabilitate it and figure out what to do with it after that."

"Good." With that question resolved, she could focus on the most important issue: what to do about Isobel. Eleonore knew a bit more about the witch now, but she didn't know nearly enough. "Do you have Alzapraz's phone number?"

He nodded. "Want me to call him?"

"Please."

Ben dialed and put the phone on speaker. It rang twice before the warlock answered. "Hello?"

"This is Eleonore Bettencourt-Devereux," she said.

"The vampire succubus who got bitten by the snake?"

"The same. Thank you for healing me." She eyed the clock—three more hours until midnight, when she could remove the poultice and bathe the wound by moonlight. "Since you know Isobel, I was wondering if you're also familiar with a binding spell for eternal servitude. I'm not immortal, but centuries ago she tied my life to a crystal. After that, she could summon or banish me at will, and I was mystically compelled to obey her orders."

"Oof, that's a nasty one." Alzapraz sighed. "Isobel never was overly burdened by morals."

"No," Eleonore agreed. "She usually ordered me to murder her enemies or source the humans she drained life from." She frowned, struck by a thought. "Do you extend your life span that way, too?"

He made a startled noise that evolved into a coughing fit. "So that's how she's doing it," he said when he'd regained his voice. "And Hecate, no. Though ask me again on a day when the arthritis cream isn't working."

The witch's hands had looked young throughout the years, not gnarled and spotted with age. "Is that why you look so old?"

Ben winced.

"What?" she whispered to him. "He must have a mirror."

Alzapraz had apparently overheard that, because he burst into wheezy chuckles. "I look like shit, I know. There's always an exchange with life magic—in my case, I traded my physical health for extra years of life. Thank goodness for Viagra."

"Oh, wow," Ben said. "Let's not mention that to Mariel."

"Why not?" Alzapraz asked. "I'll never understand why young people treat their elders like naive infants. Do you imagine you've invented a single sexual activity we haven't done before?"

Eleonore was starting to like this Alzapraz. "That's a good point," she said. "My Great-Great-Uncle Dragoslav claimed he introduced the Romans to anal plugs."

Ben made a choking sound.

"Oh, I'm sure anal play predates that," Alzapraz said. "I'd esti-mate it happened around the time humanity discovered fer-mented fruit. If there's one constant across the years, it's that people love getting drunk and stuffing inappropriate objects up their bums."

Ben cleared his throat. "Can we return to the topic at hand?"

"Yes, let's," Eleonore said. There would be time to tease her proper werewolf about anal play later. "Ben bought the crystal from the witch, so he can control my actions now. We want to break the binding spell, but we don't know how."

Alzapraz hummed. "How was the spell cast to begin with?"

The memory was burned into her brain indelibly, and shame tightened her throat as she revisited how foolish she'd been. "We were in battle against the clan who murdered my father." It had been a frozen, moonlit night, and blood had stained the snow while screams filled the air. Eleonore had shrieked her fury into the frigid sky as she battled toward the vampire who had slain her father. "During a lull when the enemy retreated to regroup, the witch approached me and said she had been watching me for a long time and admired my skill and ruthlessness. She said she could offer what I craved most: vengeance."

Isobel had been a strange, surreal figure in her black cloak, face shadowed and pale hands upraised as she promised Eleonore the head of her father's killer. Or what Eleonore had *assumed* was the head of her father's killer.

Ben nudged her hand with his, and she took it. It was nice to have something to hold on to while she shared this horrid mem-ory. "I was naive and had never met a witch before," she continued. "I was unaware one might offer trickery." Battle lust had been hot upon her, and with her heart pumping furiously and the wrong sort of pride surging at her combat talents being praised, Eleonore hadn't paused to think. "I said yes, and she cut her palm, dripping the blood in a circle around her."

"A blood binding," Alzapraz said. "That's an intimate spell. She must have really liked you."

"Don't say that," Eleonore snapped, jerking away from the phone. "There is *nothing* of affection in what she did to me."

There was a pause while she breathed heavily, glaring at the phone.

"I don't mean to say she was correct," Alzapraz said more gently. "Or sane, for that matter. I just mean that a blood binding connects the spellcaster with their target on a more personal level. You would have been in her thoughts often."

Eleonore bared her fangs. "Well, she ended up selling me on eBay, so I can't have been that important."

Ben squeezed her hand.

"How did the ritual proceed?" Alzapraz asked.

Eleonore closed her eyes, revisiting a night of stark colors: black and white and red and the uneven flicker of torchlight. "She had me cut my palm and clasp my hand with hers. Then she started chanting and drawing runes in the air, and wind and light came from nowhere." She shook her head. "I wish I could remember the words."

"They would have been customized to the moment," Alzapraz said. "Spellwork like that is very advanced—there's no all-purpose spell to bring someone under your thrall. She would have needed to combine multiple incantations and modify the language to the precise situation."

Well, that made her feel marginally better about not memorizing it. "When the light vanished, she was holding a piece of quartz. She said, *'I banish you to your vessel,'* and the world went away."

Eleonore shivered and opened her eyes to look at Ben. She hadn't told him what sort of command would return her to the plastic crystal, and it made her nervous to say the words out loud. He might be able to say many things and achieve the same effect, but as Alzapraz had pointed out, sometimes spells were specific. Maybe the precise words mattered.

If they did, she should never have spoken them before her new captor, no matter how unwilling he was or how she felt about him.

Ben wouldn't betray her, she told herself. But there were ways a person could be influenced—threats, torture, etcetera—and if he spoke the words, willingly or not, she would be banished back to her prison. And then what? How long would the gray haze last this time? Would she ever see this era or these people again? What if someone slew Ben and stole the crystal from him while she was unable to help?

His expression was compassionate as he rubbed his thumb over her fingers, and Eleonore told the paranoid part of herself to quiet down. He was here, he was alive, and he'd sworn not to command her again. It was enough for now.

"Well," Alzapraz said, "the good news is, the spell can be reversed."

Eleonore gasped, hope bubbling up in her breast. "It can?"

"The bad news is, Isobel has to reverse it herself."

Eleonore's stomach dropped, and the fragile hope splintered into bitter anger. There was no way the witch would do that. If she'd had any intention of freeing Eleonore, she'd had her opportunity when putting the crystal up for auction.

"Why can't I get another witch to do it?" Ben asked. "Since I own the crystal now."

"She sold the crystal to you, but that doesn't change the base nature of the spell." Alzapraz clicked his tongue. "Think of it like land someone gets to occupy only as long as they're alive. When they die, it goes back to whoever gave them possession. So you may possess the crystal—and Eleonore—for now, but rights revert to Isobel. If you were to die without selling the crystal to someone else, she would reclaim it."

"Oh, gods," Eleonore said. She hadn't realized. "So if we can't break the spell ourselves, even if I were to grow old with Ben . . ."

A thought she hadn't truly let herself entertain before realizing that future might be ripped away. She shook her head, refusing to accept it. "Maybe I'll die before him."

Ben looked distressed. "I don't like that."

"Unfortunately, spells like this are designed to be impossible to break by others," Alzapraz said. "It's dark, complicated, nasty magic most people would never touch, but I've seen it a few times over the centuries. You may age, but because Isobel tied your existence to hers, that connection will last until she releases you."

Her stomach felt tighter and sicker with every revelation. So Eleonore could age alongside Ben, but the moment he died she'd become Isobel's servant again, and she would linger until the witch was done with her.

It was a horrific thought.

Eleonore had never stopped fighting, though, so she reached for another possibility. "What if she dies? Will I be free then?"

"I'm not sure," Alzapraz said slowly. "My best guess is yes, but it depends on the wording used in the initial spell. She would have needed to include an end provision no matter what—most likely something like *Lygaria a' servidail casglir liberum oula mortium*, which roughly means 'the bond of your service to end with my release or my death.' But if she was feeling particularly cruel, she could have said *casglir liberum oula mortiuz*—'to end with release or *our* death.'"

It took Eleonore a few moments to parse the words, and then she stiffened. "Wait—"

Ben spoke at the same time. "You're saying it's possible that if the witch dies . . . Eleonore does, too?"

Please, no, she thought. Ben squeezed her hand hard, and she squeezed back until her bones ached.

"Possible, yes," Alzapraz said. "Likely? I struggle to believe even Isobel capable of that. And she may have used entirely different wording. The language of magic is complicated, which is another reason she has to be the one to break this spell. Only she knows the stipulations she put in place."

"Putain de bordel de merde," Eleonore whispered. She stared at the black rectangle of Ben's phone, wishing the answer to their predicament was as easy to look up as any other information on the internet. Her head ached, and a heavy, painful feeling pressed against the inside of her ribs.

She couldn't go back to the existence she'd lived before. She *wouldn't.*

"Can I at least torture her?" she asked. "I couldn't hurt her before, but since she sold the crystal . . ." She obviously hadn't tried hurting Ben, but she instinctively knew she wouldn't be able to, and not just because she cared for him.

"Probably!" Alzapraz said with the forced cheerfulness of an auctioneer trying to point out the finer traits of a racehorse with three legs. "The mystical compulsion is tied to ownership of the vessel, so whatever protection she put in place probably is, too. What we're dealing with here is more the fine print—extended warranty, liability, reversion of rights, things like that."

Eleonore hissed.

"I'm sorry," Alzapraz said. "None of this is pleasant to say or, I'm sure, to hear, but it's the truth."

She wanted to cry again, but her eyes wouldn't produce tears. Perhaps she had used them all up.

Ben's jaw was tense. His feet tapped a rapid rhythm against the floor. "We'll find a way to convince Isobel to break the curse," he said. "Or trick her into doing it."

Eleonore appreciated how certain he sounded, even if he was just saying it for her benefit, but she was a blunt weapon. She approached things head-on and smashed them, and her experiences with trickery had largely been in service of others. If tricking Isobel into releasing her was the solution, she had about as much hope of that as she did of traveling back through time to stop her former self from speaking to the witch in the first place.

"I'll force her to break it," she said. "Even if I have to gouge out her eyes and feed them to her."

Ben's own eye twitched.

Alzapraz's rattling sigh came from the phone speaker. "Well, good luck. I'm not a fan of forced eternal servitude, and it's been disappointing to see Isobel's trajectory over the years. She used to be fun before she got so paranoid."

Eleonore made a face. Alzapraz must have known Isobel for a long time, then, because she had always been paranoid. "I hope you're not friends, because I may commission Ben to knit a hat from her intestines."

Ben blanched and leaned back, shaking his head.

Well, perhaps this was a good reason to give knitting another try.

"I've seen worse," Alzapraz said with the resigned calm of a true immortal. "And Isobel and I were never much more than fuck buddies." There was a pause. "She always found power in what she could take from others. If she took something from you, take it back. Oddly enough, she would understand that."

Eleonore dug the heel of her free hand into her eye, pressing against a growing headache. She had words for many things in many languages, but she didn't have a word for the sick, glistening hate that filled her guts like tar. She didn't know how to speak the feelings that made her want to scream.

Ultimately, her most well-practiced language was that of violence, so Eleonore let go of Ben's hand to grip the hilt of the knife holstered at her thigh. The leather wrap was smooth from her touch over the years, well-worn and waiting.

If the only way forward was to torture Isobel into releasing her, Eleonore would set herself to the task.

"I will take my life back," she vowed. "Whatever it requires."

THIRTY-TWO

"—So I'll be back in a few days," Ben told Gigi over the phone. He'd explained the upcoming trip to find Isobel and hopefully break the binding spell.

He felt guilty about backing out of his Logistics Manager duties while Gigi was so stressed, but this was more important. Learning Eleonore would end up with Isobel again if something were to happen to Ben had only added more urgency to their quest.

"A few days?" Gigi asked. "Ben, the election is next Tuesday!"

He was well aware. It was Friday morning, and with a prolonged day's driving, they'd hit Fable Farms for lunch and reach Griffin's Nest to spend the night. Saturday morning they'd drive a few hours more to confront Isobel, having presumably come up with a brilliant plan on the way, and if they finished that up quickly . . . "We might be back Sunday, if everything goes well."

A big *if*. Eleonore had switched into mission mode, abandoning uncertainty and declaring everything would be fine and she'd know what to do when they got there, but Ben wasn't able to discard his worries so easily.

"But there are rallies tonight and Sunday, and tonight's venue just backed out. So did the band and catering." Gigi sounded near tears. "They apparently got a tip I'm planning to bargain with a demon to win the election. Cynthia has to be behind it, but what do I do?"

Eleonore passed Ben on the way to the car, carrying the travel bag that had previously held his werewolf full moon kit. She gave him a questioning look. He winced and pointed to the phone.

Losing a venue was a big deal, and he could recognize when someone else was anxiety-spiraling. Gigi might not have the day-to-day struggles he did, but this was an acute situation. His temples were throbbing and a sick fear had been balled up in his gut since the conversation with Alzapraz, but what did it matter what he felt? He could help both Eleonore and Gigi if he focused.

Ben took a deep breath and started strategizing. "If you move the start time to eight p.m., you can have the Annex tonight." He grabbed a notepad and started jotting down ideas. "For entertainment there's a werewolf in the Fable Farms pack with a ska band. Or maybe we can try Gabriel. What's his folk band called again . . . ?" He snapped his fingers. "Dr. Salmerón and the Cartographers, that's it."

"Dr. Salmerón the *dragon*?" Gigi asked disbelievingly. "The one who accidentally burned down the town square holiday tree two years in a row?"

"Those were isolated incidents," Ben said, wincing at the memories. "I hope." Although now that he thought about it, the one show he'd been to had involved pyrotechnics better suited to a Rammstein concert.

"Isolated enough for you to trust him around your plants? His tail thrashes a lot."

"Well, maybe not." Ben sighed and rubbed his temples. "Look, I have to get on the road, but I'll do some thinking on the way. Make a few calls." He wrote more notes to take with him. "I'll need to take a look at the staffing schedule to see if we can manage catering, but if not, there are a few local options—"

Abruptly, the phone was yanked out of his hand. Eleonore scowled as she put it on speaker. "Gigi, this is Eleonore. Ben is bad at drawing boundaries, so I'm going to do it for him. He's busy and you can find someone else to manage your event tonight."

Gigi sputtered. "But—"

"No buts," Eleonore said. "He's been working himself to exhaustion on your campaign, running the Emporium, and helping me. He's maxed out, and he has been for a long time."

Ben felt like he had whiplash from how suddenly the conversation had shifted. "I don't mind doing any of that," he protested.

Eleonore narrowed her eyes at him. "I like you, Gigi," she said, "but you have an entire team willing to help. Yes, Ben is good at logistics. But that doesn't mean he's the only one who can arrange an event." She paused. "I can postpone this trip if I have to, but it's past time everyone stopped leaning on him so heavily. He gives and gives and gives of himself, and he's never going to say no until he actually falls down dead of exhaustion."

Ben gaped at her. No one had ever made a speech like that on his behalf. And he couldn't imagine how hard it had been to offer to postpone their quest. "We are *not* postponing," he said.

Eleonore kept going. "Did you know he's been knitting holiday presents in the middle of the night?" she asked Gigi. "He doesn't have time to do it during the day. I found him at four a.m. the other night, passed out over a scarf. He'd nearly stabbed himself in the eye with a knitting needle."

Wait, Eleonore knew he'd been sneaking out of bed to knit? Normally he would have spent the hours before bed on his projects, but with Eleonore in his bed—and his arms—he'd needed to reallocate time. Refusing to spoon her to sleep wasn't an option, so whenever he woke up in an anxious sweat, he got out of bed to knit.

That would explain how he woke up on the couch covered in a blanket the other day when his last conscious memory had been undoing a stitch.

Silence followed Eleonore's pronouncement.

Ben cleared his throat. "Hey. I—"

"Is it true?" Gigi asked. "You're that worn out?"

"I mean . . . It's a stressful time for all of us, right?" He forced a smile, even if she couldn't see it. "I'll be fine."

Eleonore gave a little growl.

Gigi seemed to be on the same page. "Benjamin Handel Rosewood," she said, tone turning authoritative, "did you nearly poke an eye out with a knitting needle because you've been working around the clock?"

"I . . . well . . ." When Eleonore raised her eyebrows and flashed a hint of fang, he gave in. "Yeah, I guess."

There was another pause. Then Gigi spoke more softly. "I'm sorry, Ben. I didn't realize you were maxed out, but I should have. I wasn't thinking."

"Don't apologize," he started to say, but Gigi cut him off.

"I'll apologize if I want to, and you can't stop me." She sounded so much like a bratty little sister that he smiled. "Really, though. I've been so focused on the election I didn't think about the toll it's taking on you. You've always been my number one, but it's not fair to heap responsibility on you."

"Number One can't always man the bridge," Eleonore said. "That's why there's a chain of command."

"I'm not sure what bridge you're talking about, but you're right," Gigi said. "Other people can help. Mariel probably knows caterers, and Themmie goes to live music all the time. And I'm sure Calladia would love to march around giving orders."

That she would. A tension Ben hadn't realized he'd been carrying lifted from his shoulders. "Oz and Astaroth would be great security," he said. "Astaroth is probably dying for a chance to use his sword."

"Go on the trip," Gigi said. "Help Eleonore break the curse. Fuck, even saying that makes me realize how selfish I've been. Of course that's more important than the election. I'm really sorry, both of you. And, Eleonore, thanks for the wake-up call."

"You're welcome," she said. "I will repeat the lesson as needed."

Gigi laughed. "Hopefully once was enough, but I appreciate that."

"Good luck this weekend," Ben said. "We'll be back in time for the election."

"Take as long as you need. It'll all be worth it when Eleonore is free."

"Yes," Eleonore said seriously. "It will be."

◆　◆　◆

ELEONORE WAS AN . . . INTERESTING . . . ROAD TRIP COMPANION.

After they'd left Glimmer Falls, she'd been glued to the window. She provided running commentary about the things she was seeing. "Ooh, a phoenix!" "That is a very large tree. Is it real?" "Look, two boots dangling from telephone wires! I wonder if a pixie dropped them while flying? Or maybe the pixie was electrocuted and that's all that's left . . ."

She also fiddled with the radio, growing absorbed by various programs. She'd adored *Wait Wait . . . Don't Tell Me!* and everything else NPR offered, and had hissed when reception had grown fuzzy, though irritation soon turned to delight upon discovering a staticky Canadian French radio station. She'd spent the next thirty minutes listening intently to the conversation and discussing pronunciation, vocabulary, and how the Middle French she'd grown up with had transitioned into Modern French. "I had many missions in France over the years," she'd explained. "It was interesting hearing the changes over time." Ben didn't speak French, Canadian or otherwise, but the discussion was fascinating, and he'd been as disappointed as she was when the static grew too unpleasant and another station was required.

After a while, though, Eleonore had grown restless. Fidgeting in her seat, pulling her seat belt out and letting it zip back, snapping her fangs in chattering staccato bursts as she stared out the window.

"Didn't you grow up when people traveled by horse?" Ben asked after the third time Eleonore had asked, "Are we close?" They were not even remotely close, since they'd just passed Fable Farms and would need to overnight at Griffin's Nest before finishing the journey the next day.

She gave him a look. "Yes, but horses made walking seem tedious, and now we are in an era with airplanes."

"Fair enough." He grinned at that. Road trips were soothing to him, personally—something about the mindlessness of it, the way his thoughts could wander as the view outside changed. This one was less soothing because of what lay at the end of it, but he wasn't crawling out of his skin the way Eleonore was.

But Eleonore was a vampire succubus of action, the way Ben's high school English teacher had proclaimed Shakespeare's Marc Antony a man of action while Brutus was a man of words. She didn't hesitate or stew on things to the extent Ben did. She saw problems and resolved them, from grabbing a smoke adder to confronting Gigi about Ben's boundaries. Now she was bouncing in the seat, practically vibrating with impatience to reach the end of their quest.

He loved her.

The thought was sudden, but it settled into his mind as if it had always been there. Of course he loved her. She was funny and insightful and strange and beautiful and complex. Six hundred years of words couldn't define her. Six hundred *languages* couldn't.

He rubbed his chest, not trying to suppress the sweet ache of his heart but acknowledging it. That steady organ had known the truth before he'd put words to it.

What did he do about it, though?

"Would you like a sandwich?" Eleonore asked, twisting to reach for the cooler in the back seat.

He smiled, feeling a ridiculous flutter of butterflies in his stomach. "Yes, I would. Thank you."

The question of what a werewolf in love should do next could wait. For now, the most important thing was freeing Eleonore. Then they could figure out a path forward together.

◆ ◆ ◆

"IT IS AN UNUSUAL ROOM," ELEONORE SAID.

"It sure is." Ben looked around with interest. The hotel room they'd selected was situated in the woods outside Griffin's Nest and had been carved out of the stump of an enormous western red cedar. The opening at the top of the stump was covered, and roof beams crisscrossed overhead. The walls were the original rough wood of the tree, but the floor had been smoothed and topped with fluffy rugs. A magic-powered refrigerator held water and tiny bottles of alcohol, and two armchairs were squished in on either side of an enchanted fireplace that emitted heat but no smoke.

The entire rest of the space was taken up by the bed. It was seven feet long and the reason they had booked this room rather than one of the others offered by Tansy, a griffin who managed multiple properties around the town of Griffin's Nest. Though there was barely room to navigate around the bed, Ben would be able to sleep comfortably—an important feature when one was confronting an evil witch in the morning.

Tansy had been delighted to have visitors from Glimmer Falls. The griffin had shrieked an excited inquiry about Astaroth and Calladia, who had apparently stayed in a different property managed by the griffin. "Frieeeeaaands are 'aaaappy?" Tansy had cawed, and Ben had informed them that yes, Calladia and Astaroth were very happy. In response, Tansy had pawed the floor and bowed their head in a traditional griffin gesture of goodwill.

Ben smiled as he watched Eleonore explore the space. She moved in a blur, appearing first at the fireplace, then the mini-fridge to inspect the tiny bottles, then hanging upside down from the rafters.

Apparently satisfied, Eleonore released the overhead beam and plummeted onto the bed, bouncing before settling onto her stomach. "I'm so glad we're finally out of that car," she said, nuzzling the pillow with her face.

"I hope you disarmed before doing that," Ben said.

She turned her head to squint up at him. "Knives are in the bag. I'll arm up properly tomorrow."

It was touching she didn't feel the need to be armed around him. Eleonore almost always had a knife hidden somewhere on her person.

Ben eyed the bed, tempted to pass out, but he felt grimy after a day on the road and he could still smell the fast food they'd grabbed for dinner. "I'm going to take a shower," he said.

Eleonore perked up. "Can I come?"

As if he would say no. "Of course," he said, grabbing towels and a zipper pouch of toiletries from their bags.

Eleonore put her shoes back on and followed him out. It was dark outside, but the path to the shower complex was lit by small lanterns, each with a glowing magic orb inside. The wind picked up, and a few drops of rain struck his cheeks.

Unsure what an "outhouse and outdoor shower" entailed, Ben was relieved to see two small stone buildings protected from the elements. In one was a composting toilet and sink with magazines, extra toiletries, and towels on shelves around the room. The other hut had a gravel floor—the pebbles smooth enough not to bother the feet—with a rain shower overhead and racks to place clothing on. There was an adjacent alcove big enough for one person to stand in. An inscribed brass plate over the entrance announced its purpose: FOR BATHERS' BODIES WET, LET MAGIC DRY THEE GET. BE-WITCHED BY ASHBO THE ASTOUNDING, 2008. A magic drying station before they had to go out in the cold again—what a marvelous invention.

While Eleonore used the restroom, Ben started the shower. The floor had been set up so water drained into a channel that disappeared underground. Tansy had told them the water was purified and repurposed to feed a vegetable garden.

At least, that's what Ben thought Tansy had said. Griffin beaks were better suited to shrieking than precise enunciation.

Eleonore appeared at the door. "It's getting cold out there."

Ben swept an arm out, gesturing at the spray. "For you, milady."

She grinned as she shucked off her boots, pants, shirt, and undergarments. He stared at her full breasts, mouth watering as a familiar heaviness settled in his groin.

She smirked before stepping under the spray. "Are you going to join me?"

"In a moment." Ben ducked out, hurrying to the restroom to take his turn. The temperature had indeed dropped, and the rain was a steady patter on his hair when he emerged.

Thankfully, the rock-walled shower was toasty warm. Eleonore was a sight in the midst of the steam, her pale skin flushed pink and water trailing lovingly over her curves. Of course, Ben only had a moment to appreciate it before his glasses fogged over.

"I'm so glad this time has hot showers," Eleonore said. "I could have been liberated during a time when people only bathed once a year."

She'd been speaking of breaking the curse tomorrow as a certainty, and although Ben didn't know precisely how they would go about it, he'd followed suit. The alternative was unimaginable.

But Eleonore was positive she would be able to convince Isobel to lift the curse, so he was trying to suppress his worries and follow her lead.

"You could have been free sooner, though," Ben said. "Smelly, maybe, but free." He set his glasses next to his clothes, then turned to face Eleonore.

"With so much time spent in a fog, it's not like I experienced the extra few hundred years in real time. And now I have hot showers, *Star Trek*, and my PADD." There was a pause before she murmured, "And you."

He needed to kiss her for saying something so sweet. He marched under the spray, wincing at the hot sting. Acclimating himself gradually would have been wise, but a lot of things would have been wise that Ben had chosen not to do during this odd courtship, and it had worked out so far. So he kissed her, letting his discomfort and worries wash away until he only felt warmth, joy, and the woman in his arms.

"Ben," she gasped when he broke away to breathe.

"Yeah?" He nosed her ear, nibbling on the lobe before kissing down her neck.

"Do you want to have sex?"

"Always."

"Penetrative sex," she clarified.

He groaned, hips pushing forward until his erection pressed against her belly. "I thought we were going to wait until the curse was lifted."

"Yes, but . . ." She gripped his cheeks, looking him in the eye. "I trust you."

His heart ached with a feeling too beautiful to put into words. It was a precious gift she offered: to lay her body and safety on the line, knowing he could issue an order at any time. He would never, of course, but that was easy for him to say. She was the one with everything to lose.

Well, he had his heart to lose, but that was already gone, wasn't it? She held it in her hands.

"Just promise me something," she said.

"Anything," he vowed.

Her eyes were wide and beseeching, the dizzying green of verdant summer forests. "You won't go back on our deal and change your mind about freeing me after we do this."

"Go back on our deal?" he asked, astounded she would even worry about that. "Never, Eleonore. I vow never, ever to give you a command again, and I promise I'm not going to change my mind about the deal. And I'm not saying that just to have sex with you—you deserve freedom, and I'll do anything to help you get it."

Her lower lip trembled before she bit it. "Good." She nodded. "Very good." Then she reached down and, with typical Eleonore directness, hefted his balls in one hand. "Should we do it here, then?"

Ben choked on a sound that was half laugh, half wheeze. It was impossible to think with her cupping him. "Ah, maybe not right here."

"Oh." She looked around. "I suppose the rocks could get precarious." She eyed the ceiling consideringly. "I wonder if I'm strong enough . . ."

"How about we make love in a bed?" Ben suggested. Logistics aside, he liked the traditional romance of it. There would be time to get more adventurous later.

After the curse was broken. Because it would be.

It had to be.

Eleonore blinked, long lashes spiked with water. "You called it *making love.*"

Busted. He shifted from foot to foot, scrunching his toes in the gravel. "Uh . . ."

"It sounds much sweeter than *fucking*," she said thoughtfully. "Sweet words for a sweet wolf." She nodded. "Very well. We will make love in a bed."

Thank Lycaon she hadn't pushed him for more details about his terminology. Ben would tell her he loved her if she asked, but he wasn't ready to make the confession unprompted yet. That sort of thing required flowers, a fancy dinner, maybe a night out dancing under the quarter moon. Or a celebratory cake—could one bake a red velvet cake with blood? Whatever he chose, it required pomp and circumstance, not a blurted confession in a hotel shower.

They washed quickly—though Ben tried to linger while soaping down Eleonore's curves, she was too amped up about the sex to wait. When she washed him in return, it was with a mix of normal speed and superspeed, and at one point he jerked and made a bleating noise when a washcloth swiped his ass with the speed and precision of a tactical nuclear strike. Being goosed didn't diminish his arousal, though it did make him laugh, and how wonderful was that? To find passion mixed with joy.

The mystical body dryer was efficient, bathing him in warmth before sucking the excess moisture away. When he ran his hands through his hair, it stood up like he'd stuck his finger in an electrical socket. Or maybe his dick, considering which part of him was taking the lead. He was nearly painfully erect with anticipation.

Eleonore cackled at the sight of his wild hair, but she was little better when she emerged. Strands of long red hair lifted on invisible currents of static. When he reached out to touch one, electricity leaped between them.

"I was going to suggest you install one of these at home," she said as she re-dressed, "but perhaps there are less-aggressive versions."

Home, she'd said.

Was she coming to think of his house as her home, too?

He hoped so. He'd gotten used to having her around. No, not just that. He *loved* having her around. Her weird antics and cooking misadventures, her blanket burritos and *Star Trek* marathons. She was vibrant, shining brightly in a way wholly her own.

The rain was pelting down, so they sprinted the short distance to the room. It was toasty warm from the fireplace, and Ben was glad they had dried off before rolling around on those soft-looking sheets.

Eleonore kicked the door shut, then wasted no time stripping again. He followed suit, and Eleonore planted her hands on his bare chest and shoved him onto the bed. She clambered on top of him and kissed him hard, hands cupping his cheeks and eyes squeezed shut.

Ben let his own eyes drift closed. He ran his hands over her waist to her hips, then kneaded the lush curve of her ass. Her thighs were spread around his, and he felt the feather-light tickle of her pubic hair on his lower belly. He reached down to position his cock so it was sandwiched between them, then pulled her closer, encouraging her to grind against him.

Eleonore moved her hips in a rolling rhythm. She was already wet, but she grew wetter as she moved, leaving slick, hot streaks on his cock. The friction was exquisite, and Ben bit the inside of his cheek, trying to think of anything but how she would feel around him.

That made him realize something. "Shoot," he said, eyes opening. "I don't have a condom." He hadn't expected this to happen yet, and he was long past the days of an aspirational condom stored in his wallet.

Eleonore grinned, rubbing against him in another mind-scrambling movement. "There are some in the nightstand."

Thank Lycaon. "How did you know that?"

"I asked Tansy," she confessed.

Which meant . . . "You were planning on this?" he asked, surprised.

Even more surprising was that she looked . . . shy. "Not really," she said, pausing in her movements. She sat up more fully, supporting herself with her hands planted on his chest. "But I was thinking on the way here that part of why I was holding back was just for that reason—to have something to hold back. In case you needed motivation to help me."

The words sent an arrow of hurt into Ben's heart. "That's— Eleonore, you know I would never—"

She nodded fervently, and the ends of her long hair tickled his abdomen. "Yes, I know. That was the paranoid part of me speaking, not anything to do with you." Her eyes darted away, and she made a face. "There's a part of me that can't believe in good things. A nasty little creature inside that tells me this will all go wrong."

Ben could understand that. He had his own nasty little creature. So he exhaled the pain of her suspicion away, instead embracing the gift of her honesty. "It makes sense you'd be scared," he said. When her eyes flashed to him, he clarified. "Maybe *scared* isn't the right word. But you've had a lot of bad experiences that are going to shape your expectations."

She traced a nail through his chest hair. "No, I think that is the right word. I've been afraid of having something so good it would destroy me if it were taken away."

"Oh, Eleonore." Ben reached up to cup her cheeks, feeling a flood of affection and desire. Maybe he shouldn't still be aroused with the conversation taking this serious turn, but she was naked and trusting him with her truths, and the intimacy of it was breathtaking. "I won't take it away from you," he said softly. "I'll be at your side for as long as you want me."

Her beautiful green eyes searched his, and then she smiled, soft and radiant. "I believe you." Then she wiggled her hips. "Should we get to the sex, then?"

Ben's chuckle turned into a strangled groan as she rocked against him. With her seated upright, he could see her labia parted around the underside of his shaft, the skin pink and glistening, and the sight nearly ended him. Still, he struggled to hang on to a shred of rational thought. "We can wait if you want to think about it more."

"No, I have concluded my ruminating." She licked her lips. "So what do you say, werewolf? Shall we make love in this bed?"

As if there was any other answer to give. "Yes, Eleonore."

THIRTY-THREE

ELEONORE LOOKED DOWN INTO BEN'S SMILING BROWN EYES. She was glad they were doing this. Not just because sex was fun, but because this was different from the other times she'd had sex. It wasn't just the give and take of bodies—it was an expression of trust.

She trusted him and she trusted herself. Not the small, paranoid creature that spoke doubts in her head, but the self she was becoming. The one who could offer without worrying someone might take too much. They were going into battle together, and she couldn't do that if she entertained any remaining doubt about his motives or their future.

Not that her motives at the moment were all so lofty or poetic. She was hungry for him, and why should she deny herself that pleasure? Her werewolf was brimming with passion, he smelled delicious, and he deserved to be ridden until neither of them could see straight.

So—sex.

Or as he'd called it, making love.

Eleonore rocked against him, enjoying both the spark of sensation at her clit and the way he hissed and gripped her tighter. Her heart felt too full, like it might burst.

She leaned forward to kiss her way from his eager mouth to his neck, hips moving in waves. Ben's hands traced long sweeps over her back and buttocks, stroking and massaging as he mirrored her movements. He thrust up against her, and she sighed at the feel of that thick, pretty cock rubbing over her. It would feel exquisite inside, stretching her perfectly.

She wanted to taste it first, so she shifted down his body, hair trailing over his chest. He had a lovely penis, thick and ruddy, and when she smoothed his foreskin down, the cap leaked a drop of precum. She lapped it up, swirling her tongue around the crown.

Ben groaned, and she looked up. "You're still wearing your glasses," she pointed out.

"You think I want to miss any details?" he asked, brows rising. His head was pillowed on his left arm while his right hand toyed with her hair.

Eleonore hummed, then tapped his dick against her cheek before turning to press a kiss to the side of it. "I need your help with something."

"Anything."

She twisted her loose hair into a coil, then wound it around and around at the crown of her head. "Hold this, please."

"Fuck." He grabbed the makeshift bun in his right hand, and Eleonore felt a rush of delight at both his firm grip and having prompted him into profanity.

"Good wolf," she said. Then she lowered her head and sucked him into her mouth.

Ben jerked and his hand clenched, eliciting a delicious sting at her scalp. Eleonore hummed on the upstroke, swirling her tongue as much as she was able. She toyed with his testicles with one hand, and with the other she reached up to drag her fingernails lightly over his chest.

She loved the way he was made. Strong in a sturdy way—not a man with a chiseled abdomen that had been built at the gym, but one whose body had been formed through hard work in business and life. A broad, hair-roughened chest; shoulders strong enough to carry other people's burdens in addition to his own.

And an absolute delight of a dick, of course. Eleonore sucked it with appreciation, letting saliva pool in her mouth for extra lubrication. She played with him: fondling his balls before squeezing the base of his shaft, mixing deep sucks with dabs of her tongue. He was going wild, grunting and twitching and muttering broken strings of words.

She paused for breath, jerking him with her hand while she did so. "I'd like to drink from here sometime," she said, tracing the tip of one fang oh so gently over the delicate skin of his shaft.

"Holy shit," he said, hips jerking upward. Another curse word; she was doing well. "That sounds . . ." He cleared his throat. "Way hotter than it has any right to be."

He liked the idea? Eleonore's predatory instincts sharpened. "I wouldn't want to sink my fangs all the way in right now," she purred, following the words with a long, slow lick. "Vampire bites heal quickly, but maybe not as quickly as I would like for the rest of what I have planned." She squeezed him at the base of his cock, which elicited a gasp and an answering clench of his hand in her hair. "But a little scratch . . . that would heal in no time at all."

"Do it," he said instantly, thrusting upward again. Then his eyes widened. "Wait, that's not an order. Please do it, but only if you want to. Please."

Ben remembered his promise even in the throes of passion, which was exactly why she trusted him. Her fangs lengthened at the promise of blood, even if it wouldn't be more than a taste. She grinned, flashing them. "I do want to."

She cocked her head and ran the tip of one fang in a line up his shaft, using incrementally more pressure than she had before. Blood beaded in her wake, a tiny flow she'd need to savor quickly. Still, she took a moment to admire the sight of blood trailing down the side of his cock. Then she opened her mouth over him, took him to the root, and sucked.

"Oh, *fuck*," he shouted. "Oh fuck oh fuck oh fuck oh my *God*." He kept babbling, praise and curses falling from his lips while he thrust into her mouth. Eleonore gloried in the roughness, delighted at having shattered her proper wolf's control. His blood sang on her tongue, rich crimson notes she swallowed eagerly.

He came with a shout, and she drank that down, too, the flavor taking on extra dimensions as it mixed with the remnants of blood in her mouth. Ben shook beneath her, powerful thighs quaking.

Then he let out a trembling groan and relaxed, head hitting the pillow with an audible thump. "Holy shit," he said dazedly as the hand in her hair loosened.

Eleonore finished cleaning him up with her tongue, gently lingering over the cut. Vampire saliva sped healing, and the wound had been so shallow she expected it to vanish in a minute or two.

Ben cleared his throat. "Sorry. I was a bit rough."

"Don't apologize. I loved every second of that." She was buzzing from the psychic energy of his orgasm, and pride swelled in her breast at knowing she was the reason he'd come undone.

"I did, too." He ran a shaking hand over his face. "That was unbelievable, Eleonore."

She sat up, tossing the unraveling coil of hair over her shoulder. "I agree."

His chuckle turned into another groan. "I was not intending to come just yet."

"So? I like when you orgasm."

"Yes, but I want to be up to the task, so to speak."

It took Eleonore a moment to parse the innuendo, and then she smiled. "I'm sure we can find something for you to do until you can manage a second orgasm."

"Damn right we can," Ben growled. He tossed his glasses onto the nightstand, then surged upright, grabbed her waist, and threw her onto her back in a thrilling display of strength.

Eleonore shrieked as she hit the mattress, and then a surprised laugh bubbled out of her. But a moment later Ben buried his face between her thighs, and there was nothing to laugh about there.

"Oh!" Her back arched as she plunged her hands into his hair. He was ravenous, kissing her with open-mouthed passion. His tongue played along her folds, and then he pushed it into her. It didn't slide deep, but the pressure was enough to send a shivering thrill up her spine, particularly when his nose nudged her clit in tandem.

Ben didn't pause seemingly even for breath. He fucked her with his tongue, then replaced it with a questing finger as he licked back up to her clitoris. One finger was joined by two, and Eleonore moaned, holding his head tighter against her.

"You," he said, words rumbling against her, "are *delicious*."

She tipped her head back, staring blindly at the ceiling. This was the passion she'd always known was inside him, the one she'd tasted in his blood that first day. Ben Rosewood was a gentleman, but he *fucked*.

Heat and tension coiled in her belly, and her toes pointed as she strained toward the summit. Perhaps sensing she was close, Ben pumped his fingers, then crooked them while he intensified his attentions to her clitoris.

"Oui!" she gasped.

The orgasm swelled, a tidal wave that broke over her. Heat washed from her core to the tips of her fingers and toes, and she jerked against his face, crying out wordlessly as she rode the spasms.

Then it was her turn to collapse, bones seemingly melted. Her head spun, and her lips were stretched in a giddy smile.

Ben moved to lie next to her, head propped on a fist as he surveyed her flushed face with obvious pride. "Good?" he asked.

Eleonore nodded. Her head felt like it was somewhere up in the branches of the trees, about to float off into the night sky.

Ben stroked a hand down her body, pausing to play with her breasts and circle her navel. He swirled his fingertips in her damp pubic hair, then squeezed her thigh. "I don't suppose you're ready to go again?"

She blinked, surprised. "You can go again already?" Ben was in his prime—if he'd been a whiskey, he would have been top-shelf—but rapid-fire orgasms were normally harder to attain after the intense sexual chaos of youth.

He gestured down to his crotch, where his cock had, indeed, swelled again. The fang mark on his penis was nothing but a faint pink line now, the skin healed over. "I don't think you understand how inspiring eating your pussy is."

Eleonore broke into peals of laughter at the blunt compliment. She felt drunk on the magic they made together. "Engrave that on a trophy for me," she said. Then she pushed herself into a seated position, arms still weak from the orgasm. "I'm ready."

Ben grabbed a condom from the nightstand and rolled it on. "How would you like to do this?" he asked.

He always asked. If her nipples were sensitive, how she liked her clitoris to be touched, how she wanted to have him. Eleonore appreciated it. She surveyed his strong, broad body and decided she liked the view. "I'll be on top."

Ben grinned and flopped onto his back, then patted his thigh. "Then feel free to hop on at your leisure, sweetheart."

This playful, roguish Ben was a new iteration she liked very much. She liked all the versions of him—the serious business owner, the tenderhearted knitter, the considerate breakfast-maker. A complex man, endlessly interesting to explore.

She straddled his lap, then reached between them. She notched him at her entrance, then started bearing down.

Ben sucked in a hissed breath, gripping her hips as she took him in one smooth, wet slide. He filled her just as perfectly as she'd known he would, a stretch that had her lingering to absorb the feel. Then she lifted up and sank down again.

She set a smooth, slow rhythm at first, delighting in the merging and parting of their bodies. There was a poetry to this act, a series of questions asked and answered while their mouths hung open around panting breaths. He looked up at her with such adoration it caused a small, precious pain in her chest.

Had she ever been looked at like that?

No, she had not.

She hoped her own care for him shone in her eyes, that he could see how much he meant to her. How much this act of trust meant.

Soon slow wasn't enough. She rode him more aggressively, nails pressing pink crescents into his chest. He met her motion and elaborated on it, hips surging while he thumbed at her clit. Eleonore tipped her head back until her hair brushed his thighs, abandoning herself to the pleasure.

Then a wicked idea came to her, and she smiled.

Snapping her head back upright, Eleonore pinned Ben's shoulders to the bed and started moving faster and faster until she shifted into vampire warp speed, practically vibrating on top of him.

"Holy—" Ben choked out. One hand flew out to smack the mattress, and the tendons in his neck stood out as he gritted his teeth. "Going to—"

She felt his orgasm in her brain and body, a rush of glittering energy. Delighted, she reached down to rub her clit just as quickly. The buzz of her fingers sent her over the edge, flying into an expanse of pleasure as vast and sparkling as the night sky.

Afterward, she slumped on top of him, resting her head at the crook of his neck. They were both breathing hard.

"That was good, werewolf," she said after a moment.

"Good?" His laugh sounded disbelieving. "Eleonore, you just blew my damn mind. I'm not sure I'll ever recover."

She nuzzled into his shoulder, eyes drifting closed. "That's a shame," she said sleepily. "Because I'd very much like to do that again."

◆ ◆ ◆

ELEONORE WOKE ALL AT ONCE. ONE MINUTE ASLEEP, THE NEXT not, as seamlessly as every other vampire in history.

Unlike most other vampires in history, she woke to a fall of sunlight across her cheek, though the air was cool. Even with the windows shut, the November chill had infiltrated the room.

Under the covers was much warmer, though. She nestled closer to the source of that warmth, who lay naked and breathing deeply, one arm flung over his head.

What a lover her werewolf was. Diligent, detail-oriented, and always giving. But as much as Eleonore loved receiving his attentions, she loved returning them even more. He'd performed feats of heroism last night, making love to her three separate times, and she'd reciprocated his passion just as eagerly.

She traced the strong lines of his face with her eyes, remembering his astonished expression as she'd ridden him in warp speed. She'd felt like a queen. It was only one of many, many things she wanted to do with him.

Not that sex was the only thing she anticipated doing with him. She could envision their lives melding in all sorts of exciting ways—working together, traveling together, learning together. A bright future at Ben's side beckoned, but first she needed to guarantee they *could* have that future.

The first step was breaking the binding spell. The next step would be the witch's severed head so she could never harm another person.

Eleonore sat up, focus shifting and sharpening. Last night had been for passion and play; today was for violence and ensuring her future. Her pulse jumped as her muscles tensed in anticipation of a worthy battle. "Wake up," she said, shaking Ben's shoulder lightly.

Ben groaned. His lashes fluttered. "What time is it?" he asked blearily.

Apparently only one of them was ready for action. "Time to be awake."

Ben fumbled at the nightstand and put on his spectacles, blinking a few times. When he didn't move to get up, Eleonore whipped the covers off him.

He hissed in a breath, curling up on his side like a bug. "Cold!"

"It won't be cold once you're dressed," Eleonore said matter-of-factly. She jumped out of bed herself, shivering as chill air brushed her naked skin. She reached for shower supplies and clean clothes, mind already sprinting the hours ahead to their confrontation with Isobel.

Ben sat up, running his hands through his untidy hair. "Should have brought a razor," he said, rubbing his fingers over the stubble that had started growing in around the neat borders of his beard.

"You look lovely," Eleonore said distractedly as she tested the edges of her knives. "A perfect picture."

He gave her a dry look. "Thank you, but only one of us is the embodiment of perfection here, and it isn't me."

She clacked her fangs. "You're perfect if I say you're perfect." She set aside her thigh holsters and knives, then selected pants with hidden pockets at the ankle to hide two additional small blades. Maybe she should have brought other tools, like a hammer or saw? Torture wasn't something she was practiced in.

"My apologies," Ben said. "I would never doubt your opinion."

"Good," she said, only half hearing him. Maybe she could bludgeon the witch's fingers with a rock . . .

She bit her lip, feeling squeamish at the thought. Eleonore had always appreciated a dramatic threat, but the idea of actually torturing someone, rather than killing them quickly, made her feel ill. But there was no way Isobel would break the binding spell without significant incentive, and if killing her outright might result in Eleonore's death as well . . .

She had been an unwilling monster for years. She could be a monster one more time if it meant ensuring her freedom.

She nodded decisively. "Let's go torture and kill this witch."

THIRTY-FOUR

THE FOREST WAS COLD AND WET, RAIN DRIPPING THROUGH the canopy to ping off trees, rocks, and what leaves remained of the autumn season. Eleonore's thighs burned as she hiked up the slope, stepping over fallen branches. She was no longer in peak physical condition after months of relative rest.

It didn't worry her. Even out of shape she was fast and strong, and she knew how the witch cast her spells. Isobel drew runes in the air, which meant Eleonore would have a warning before being in danger.

Her battle-anticipation of the morning had sharpened into something uglier with every step closer to the witch. The version of Eleonore who had spoken soft words to her lover the previous night had faded, replaced by the seasoned assassin. She felt sick with anticipation and dread, and anger was a burning pain in her chest that grew hotter with each second.

It was strange how the feelings were both familiar and foreign. Hate and defiance were well-worn armor, easy to slip into, but it was startling to realize how quickly she had forgotten the feel of them. Or rather, how quickly she had stopped donning them first thing in the morning.

Ben and his friends and his gentle world had done this to her. She'd softened and put her knives aside, both literally and metaphorically. Last night she'd been glad of it. Now she felt nauseated, wondering if being soft would make her less able to do what needed to be done.

Cold air sawed in her throat, and every sense strained for signs of danger. It felt like time was turning backward. She had walked these woods before: Isobel had cultivated demon allies, and more than one had transported Eleonore out of this forest via portal—first to the demon plane, then to wherever on Earth her targets were located.

A cracking sound made her spin, throwing knife already in hand. Ben froze with his foot on a snapped branch. "Sorry," he said.

He'd been quiet since they'd left their tree-trunk room, both on the drive to the base of this hiking trail and on the first half of the climb. He was clearly thinking about something, and though Eleonore had been tempted to interrogate him, she recognized Ben was more of a prolonged thinker than she was. He marinated in his ideas, for better or worse, and pushing him to articulate them too soon might not be the most effective approach.

The witch's cabin could appear at any moment, though. The time for stewing was over.

"Are you done ruminating yet?" she asked.

"Ruminating? I—" He broke off, then rubbed the back of his neck. "Yeah, I guess I am ruminating. Are you actually going to torture and kill Isobel?"

She blinked. The entire way up this mountain she'd been sharpening her hate so she could put it to action, and he wanted to know if she was actually going to do it? "What kind of question is that?"

Ben looked anxious. Rain splatted on his forehead, and he

flinched before wiping it away with the sleeve of his checkered flannel shirt. "You make a lot of dramatic threats. I wasn't sure if you meant the thing about, you know, intestine knitting."

"I didn't mean that one," she said. He exhaled, looking relieved, so she clarified. "Only because it would be logistically difficult. There are easier things to do with intestines."

"Easier things—Jesus. Are you sure this is a good idea?"

What was this? Eleonore planted her fists on her hips. "What do you mean is it a good idea?" she demanded. "I've never tortured anyone before, but what other choice do we have? The witch stole six hundred years from me. She stole my family from me. I'm not going to let her steal my future, too."

Ben winced. "Sorry. I know. It's just . . . what if you go to jail?" He scuffed at fallen leaves with the toe of his boot. "Maybe we can try talking to her first. Or bribe her or something."

Eleonore scoffed. "Why would I go to jail?"

His eyebrows shot up. "For torturing and murdering someone?"

This time was enjoyable in many ways, but it did not have a good grasp on the laws of blood vengeance. "How would the police find out? We're in the middle of the woods." A suspicion formed, one she didn't like at all. "You wouldn't tell them, would you?" Ben was a genuinely good person, but she hadn't considered that might be a liability.

"No," Ben said, though he didn't sound entirely sure himself. When she narrowed her eyes, he sighed. "Look, I've never been involved in a crime before and I'm not a great liar. Maybe I can turn around and cover my eyes while you do it?"

Had he watched her performances at all? "Killers must be willing to look at what they've done," she said. "It's a serious matter." It was one of the only reasons she'd been able to confront her own face in the mirror sometimes—knowing that no matter what horrible deeds she'd committed, she owned them and was brave enough to let herself suffer for them.

"Wait, I'm not supposed to help torture and kill her, am I?" Panic flashed over Ben's expression. "I don't want to kill anyone. I don't even know how to."

She sighed. "Obviously you are not participating. I am the murder expert. You are my accomplice. But accomplices should also be willing to stand witness to the deed."

Ben shifted from foot to foot. She'd bet anything he was squeezing his toes in those hiking boots, expressing his anxieties with repetitive movements. "You can go to jail for being an accomplice to murder."

Now Eleonore's brows soared. "You can?"

"Yeah, you can." He rubbed a hand over his rain-spotted hair, still fidgeting. "At least, that's what cop TV shows have led me to believe."

Eleonore made a rude noise. "What a ridiculous law." An accomplice was adjacent to a murder; they ought to be adjacent to a prison sentence as well. She considered the issue for a moment. "Well, then you can turn your back and cover your eyes." She still wasn't sure how the police would be alerted, but she didn't want Ben to go to jail either.

"Now I sound like a coward."

Eleonore blew out a frustrated breath. This conversation was not productive. "You don't sound like a coward. You sound like a practical man who doesn't want to be imprisoned." If she'd worn a watch, she would have checked it to see how much time they'd wasted debating jail sentences and who was or was not looking at the murder while it happened.

Ben kicked at a fallen log, and the rich, earthy smell of rot rose into the air. "I'm not just worried about me," he said. "I worry about you. Aren't you tired of violence?"

"In general? Yes. In this case? Not at all." She'd been captured on the battlefield, and now one last act of violence would put an end to this chapter of her life.

"Can we at least try to convince her to lift the spell before you torture her?" he asked. "Maybe we can trick her into doing it."

"If she wants to lift the spell without being tortured, she can be my guest." Eleonore shrugged. "I'm still going to chop her head off after."

"Maybe we could have the cops arrest Isobel instead," Ben suggested. "Force her to spend the rest of her life in prison."

"Mmm." Eleonore gave it brief consideration. As a life witch, imprisonment could last very long. "No."

"Why not?" he asked, looking like he genuinely didn't understand.

She was tempted to shriek in frustration, but she reminded herself Ben was a product of this soft, gentle time where species mingled freely and the police would arrest someone for even being an *accomplice* to murder. He had hot running water and a microwave and a television, and he'd never needed to solve a problem by rearranging someone's insides. "This is who I am," Eleonore said.

Ben shook his head stubbornly. "That isn't all you are. You're also a theatrical performer. A good friend and an incredible lover. Someone who protects vulnerable people like Gigi." His throat bobbed. "People like me."

None of this explained why he was dawdling instead of letting her finish this job. "This is my vengeance," she snapped. "Not yours."

The air seemed colder in the wake of her words. She felt a flash of regret at having spoken to him so harshly, but she could hardly breathe past the desire to be free, and now that they were so close to Isobel, her hate burned hotter than it ever had. It felt like a six-hundred-year scream was trapped in her throat.

Ben's shoulders slumped. "I just want you to be happy and safe. I don't want you to have to kill again." He swallowed. "I don't want to lose you."

"Killing the witch will make me happy and safe." She didn't

like saying Isobel's name out loud—it made her sound like a person and not the formless evil who had stolen Eleonore's free will. She sighed. "One more kill, Ben. That's it. And then I'm done with it forever."

He nodded, gaze still trained on his boots.

Eleonore didn't like seeing him sad or worried, but they didn't have time for this. Isobel probably knew they were coming, whether by scrying or a perimeter alert spell. Every moment they wasted gave her time to prepare a counterattack.

The cold, wary voice in Eleonore's head came back. *Maybe he's stalling for a reason. Maybe he isn't ready to let go of you.*

She could promise Ben she'd stay with him after they were no longer mystically bound, but she knew better than many how little a promise meant. He was an anxious man, unused to being cared for. He was afraid of losing her—he'd admitted it just now.

One foolproof way to never lose her was to keep her chained to his side.

Ben wouldn't do that, she thought, arguing against her own paranoia. She'd decided just last night to trust him fully. They were allies in this fight.

But her gut clenched, and she felt sick.

Eleonore turned and started hiking again. "Come on," she said. "Let's get this over with."

◆ ◆ ◆

A RED DOOR STOOD ALONE BETWEEN TWO TREES. ELEONORE'S heart jumped at the sight of it. She'd walked through that door many times before. "This is it."

Ben looked around with confusion. "Where's the house?"

"Mystically hidden." Eleonore raised her voice. "It's me," she shouted. "Come out, you bloody bitch!"

Nothing happened for a minute. Wind whistled through the treetops, and rain pattered against fallen leaves. Eleonore didn't wipe the drops from her skin—she couldn't afford to lose focus for a single moment. Her knives were comforting weights in her hands.

"Should we knock?" Ben asked.

The door finally creaked open, revealing the shadowed interior of the cabin. Then Isobel stepped out.

Eleonore sucked in a harsh breath. The Witch in the Woods wasn't wearing her cloak, which meant Eleonore could see her plainly for the first time.

Isobel looked more delicate than Eleonore had expected. Her slender body was encased in a burgundy velvet gown belted with a golden chain. She had straight black hair that fell to her waist, eerie midnight eyes, and pointed ears that, together with the ethereal beauty of her face, spoke of fae or elven ancestry.

Eleonore nearly threw a knife straight into the witch's throat, but she restrained herself. "Undo the binding spell or I will torture you horrifically," she ordered.

"Eleonore," Isobel said in her ancient, undefinable accent. "How nice to see you again." Bizarrely, she smiled.

Eleonore's eyebrows shot up. "Is it?"

"I've missed our TV binges. And no one reads me poetry anymore."

The gall of this witch! "That's because you sold me on eBay," Eleonore said. "For ninety-nine cents, might I add. Why did you do that?"

"It was an impulsive and very drunken choice, which I regret." Isobel shrugged, a subtle and graceful movement. "Alas, I thought ninety-nine cents was the required starting price for all listings—I'd assumed bidding would quickly reach one million gold doubloons once people realized what a valuable friend and companion you were."

Merde, the witch looked for all the world like she actually believed what she was saying. Her dark eyes were wide and earnest.

"A friend and companion?" Eleonore asked incredulously. "We were never friends, witch."

Isobel's brow furrowed, and she blinked a few times. "But we've spent so much quality time together."

It was as Eleonore had remembered: Isobel truly, bizarrely did seem to think they were friends. "You imprisoned me for six hundred years," she pointed out. "You made me kill your enemies."

"Destroying enemies can be a lovely bonding experience."

"Only if you destroy them together and everyone involved in the murdering wants to be doing it. You forced me to do it with the binding spell." Belatedly she remembered Ben didn't want to be doing this murdering either, but that was different. She wasn't forcing him to be involved. He could leave at any point.

She resisted the urge to slide him a guilty glance.

"Well, yes," Isobel admitted. "I hadn't had much luck asking people to be my eternal assassin, so I had to improvise." She raised a hand, and Eleonore braced herself for an attack, a hair's breadth from throwing her knife. Instead, the witch examined her fingers, which were long and delicate. "I'm not physically strong. If I hadn't procured protection, I would have been killed long ago."

Eleonore should really get on with the whole torture and murder business, but the angry words she'd bottled up for so many years were forcing their way out. "Maybe you shouldn't have made so many enemies, then." She could see them in her head, a parade of villains who had fallen to her knives or fangs. "There was that warlock whose prized crystal ball you stole, the centaur whose kingdom you tried to usurp, the witch whose hands you removed because you were jealous of her magic . . ." The list went on, but in each case Isobel had angered someone into retaliating, then had them assassinated. Even if they hadn't been good people, Isobel was worse.

"When you live as long as I have, a few enemies are inevitable."

Isobel's gaze drifted to the side, and her eyes lit up. "Ooh, a man! Did you bring me a gift?"

Did she think to steal Ben's life force? Eleonore bared her fangs and let out the nastiest hiss that had ever escaped her lips. "He isn't for you. He's the new owner of the crystal." She shifted to put herself between them, glancing over her shoulder quickly to see how Ben was faring.

Ben looked furious, not fearful. His glare was vicious as he stared at Isobel. "You're a horrible person," he told her.

"Thank you," Isobel replied with a smile.

Eleonore had another grievance to air. "Speaking of the crystal, the cursed thing is plastic now. Didn't I at least deserve quartz?"

"Plastic is resilient." Isobel nodded in Ben's direction. "I assume he brought it with him?"

The crystal was in a bag in Ben's pocket, but they'd agreed not to reveal it until Isobel promised to break the spell. Eleonore didn't know what it would take to get to that point, but she was going to start with ripping off fingernails and get more creative from there.

Leaves crunched as Ben stepped forward to stand at Eleonore's side. She was tempted to place herself in front of him for protection again, but then he spoke. "Free her," he said in a deadly voice that sent a pleasurable shiver down her spine. "Right now." His fists were clenched, and he looked ready to go into battle.

Whatever his prior reservations, he would fight for her. It was what Eleonore needed to know. The suspicious voice in her head quieted, and she exhaled shakily.

She had been right to trust him.

Isobel cocked her head, eyeing Ben in an assessing way that made Eleonore's skin crawl. Hot, possessive anger flared in her chest, and her stomach felt full of knots. "Stay away from him, witch," she snapped.

Isobel took a step forward, and Eleonore flipped the knife in her right hand so she held it by the bladed tip, ready to throw. Her breath sawed in her throat.

"Is *he* your friend now?" Isobel asked. Her voice had taken on a jealous edge. "Who have you killed for him?"

"No one," Ben said. "I don't give Eleonore orders."

"Why not?"

"Because he actually cares about me," Eleonore said. "Unlike you."

Isobel's eyes narrowed on Ben. She raised her hand as if to draw a rune in the air.

Protective fury swept through Eleonore's veins. Without thinking, she shrieked and let the knife fly.

It embedded in Isobel's heart.

Ben gasped and jolted forward. "But the curse—"

Abandoning all plans for a lengthy torture session—they'd moved beyond fingernail-ripping the moment Isobel had turned her attention to Ben—Eleonore bared her fangs. "Break the binding now and I will let you have a quick death. Delay and I will make it hurt."

Either way, they would find out if Isobel's death would result in Eleonore's as well. She couldn't unthrow the knife, though, and she would never feel regret for protecting Ben.

Isobel looked down at the dagger in her chest. Then she gripped it by the hilt and, with a pained grunt, pulled it out. Blood bloomed like a copper-scented flower on her dress, a darker shade against the burgundy, but it stopped far too soon, merely the size of a rose. Her dress ought to be saturated, her heart pumping life out in messy spurts.

"Ouch." Isobel frowned at Eleonore. "That wasn't nice."

Eleonore gaped. The witch was long-lived, but she'd never been immortal in the way that demons or purebred vampires were. She aged like any other person, resetting the clock periodically by magically draining the lives of humans and using their energy to restore her youth. That wound should have been enough to kill her.

Belatedly, she remembered something Astaroth had said: *I tried to regain the immortality she'd stolen.* Eleonore had been in pain and emotional at the time, and she hadn't questioned that odd phrasing. Astaroth was a demon, and Isobel could only harvest the life energy of other mortals.

Except . . .

Astaroth was half human, wasn't he? Someone had told her that, but whether because of his horns or his general demeanor, she'd forgotten.

"Mon Dieu." If Astaroth was half human, he was vulnerable to Isobel's life magic. And if he'd once been immortal thanks to his demon half . . .

Isobel had drained an eternal life and added it to her own. She was now a true immortal.

Isobel was still talking, though Eleonore could barely hear past the ringing in her ears. "I can't believe you stabbed me," the witch said, sounding distressed. "You never stabbed me before. Not that you could have because of the spell, but you wouldn't have anyway. You always said you'd rip my guts out, but that was just your way of joking, right?" Isobel clasped her hands at her bloodstained breast, fixing beseeching eyes on Eleonore. "Right?"

Eleonore was trying to figure out what this development meant for her strategy. Granted, her strategy had been to show up prepared to commit violence and figure it out as she went, but torture didn't work as well when the victim healed instantly.

When Eleonore didn't answer, Isobel's eyes turned watery. "I thought we were closer than that."

"Forced proximity is not friendship," Eleonore said past the lump in her throat.

This wasn't the way the world should be. Enemies ought to be mutual; the rules of engagement ought to be clear.

"I didn't know you hated me so much," Isobel said. "I stopped having you kill people in the sixties—remember? I've made more enemies since then, but I realized you didn't like doing it, so I stopped."

"You realized I didn't like doing it," Eleonore repeated numbly. "You mean all the times over the centuries I cursed your name and said I'd happily eat your heart didn't tip you off?"

She shook her head. "That's how immortals talk to each other. I thought it was all in good fun." She made a face. "Or sometimes in good fun. When you live as long as we do, there are ups and downs in any relationship."

Eleonore was tempted to let her second knife fly. "Break the curse right now," she ordered.

"Didn't you enjoy the *Star Trek*?" Isobel bit her lip. "I was trying to make up for all the killing I had you do."

This was surreal. "Captain Kirk can do many things," Eleonore said, "but that is beyond even his capabilities."

At that, Isobel's tears poured over, trailing in wet streaks down her cheeks. "I'm sorry," she said in a small voice. "I should have apologized long ago."

"You should have freed me long ago." Eleonore hated this feeling in her chest, like a twisting, angry, clawing beast shredding her insides. She hated that the witch was crying, that she could be so deluded as to imagine she'd made up for years of mystical control with a few seasons of *Star Trek*. She hated the confusion and the way this hadn't gone at all to plan.

Isobel was supposed to be screaming and begging while Eleonore carved her up. She was supposed to finally break down and break the spell—right before Eleonore ended her miserable life.

Instead, the witch was immortal—and apparently *liked* Eleonore.

"I'll free you now," Isobel said.

The world seemed to stop. Even the wind lulled, the treetops pausing in their whispers. Eleonore blinked, feeling like she'd been shoved out of a fighting stance and couldn't catch her balance.

Did the witch mean it? She glanced at Ben, who looked as confused and angry and worried as she felt.

Isobel tucked her long hair behind her pointed ears, then raised her left hand palm up. With her right she held the dagger over her pale skin. "It requires a blood sacrifice—I don't know if you remember that part."

As if Eleonore could forget. "Then make a blood sacrifice," she said, still struggling to believe this was real and no torture had been required. She didn't know if the brewing feeling in her chest could be termed hope, laced as it was with fear.

Was Isobel actually *sorry*? And was she insane enough not to realize Eleonore would cut her head off once the spell was broken? *Please, gods, let this be real.*

Isobel hesitated. "I want you to do it," she said, extending the knife toward Eleonore. Her long lashes were wet with tears, and her lips trembled. "If it will make you feel better."

If the witch was going to let this happen, Eleonore wouldn't waste a single moment. Her heart raced, her breath came too fast, and her vision narrowed on the knife. "It *will* make me feel better," she said, taking three steps forward.

This was real. At last, she would be free.

"Eleonore . . ." Ben said.

She snapped her fangs, not looking at him. "Stay put." She didn't want the witch getting anywhere near him.

His footsteps sounded on the wet leaves, but Eleonore couldn't risk looking back at him. "I just think we should take a moment—"

"Don't you dare try to stop me," she said, cutting him off. "I've been waiting for this for six hundred years." An old fear was climbing her throat, edging out the triumph of getting what she wanted at last. Ben could stop her with a single command, but why would he? He'd promised never to do that again.

He'd *promised.*

If he was her clan member in truth, he would never betray her. She focused on Isobel, silently begging Ben to keep his mouth shut. *Don't go back on your word, Ben. Don't prove I was wrong to trust you.*

Isobel still held the dagger out. Her mouth twitched, and her eyes were wet and seemingly fathomless. "Do it, Eleonore."

Eleonore's focus narrowed on her prey. She could smell the witch's blood, and her fangs lengthened. Ben was saying something, but her ears were roaring and she couldn't tell what the words were.

He couldn't stop her. He *wouldn't* stop her.

The wind swirled, sending leaves skating around the clearing. The air felt heavy with anticipation, prickling against her skin. It was finally time. And with Eleonore's speed, it would be over in a blink.

She tensed to sprint forward and grab the knife.

Then Ben shouted again, the words so loud they broke through the haze of bloodlust.

"Eleonore, go back to the car *right now.*"

Eleonore's heart cracked open, and her world ended.

THIRTY-FIVE

ELEONORE WAS GONE.

One moment she'd been tensed to run, eyes fixed on Isobel; the next the air was empty, as if she'd never existed.

Ben barely had a flicker of an eyelid to note the change before a lightning bolt zagged down and struck the leaves where Eleonore had been standing.

He closed his eyes against the painful light, but the afterimage was seared into his retinas. He opened them again, blinking against black spots until the clearing swam into view.

"Oh," Isobel said, looking at the blackened, smoking patch of leaves with a frown.

Ben had never felt such fury. "Yeah, oh," he snarled, marching toward the witch. "I saw what you were doing."

It had been subtle, but the movements were there. Isobel's empty left hand had twitched at her side while she'd waited for Eleonore to take the knife from her right, the fingers twisting in movements that could have been agitation but weren't. At first glance her lips had been trembling, but closer inspection showed something more sinister. She'd been whispering so softly that only supernaturally gifted ears could hear it.

Isobel had been casting a spell, and Eleonore had been so focused on ending her imprisonment she hadn't noticed.

Ben might not have noticed either if he hadn't been paying such close attention. Werewolf senses were sharp. When Isobel had exhaled, seeming to accept her fate, a fragment of a spellword had drifted to Ben on the breeze.

Isobel wiped her teary cheek with the back of her hand, then looked toward the path Ben and Eleonore had taken to her door. "Perhaps that was a hasty choice." Her mouth twisted as she switched her attention to Ben. "Do you think she'll be angry with me?"

Ben was so dumbfounded he stopped in his tracks. Was this witch absolutely out of touch with reality? He'd assumed the tears were an act, but Isobel actually seemed distressed.

"Obviously she'll be angry," he said. "You tried to kill her!"

"I have a necromancer on speed dial," Isobel said, reaching into the pocket of her dress and pulling out a phone. "It would have been fine."

Ben was tempted to throttle her, but his ears picked up another sound in the distance—the firing of a familiar car engine. He swore, then glared at Isobel. "This isn't over," he vowed as he turned to sprint after Eleonore.

"Oh, good," Isobel said.

Ben's heart raced as he ran back down the path. Tree roots tangled at his feet and branches clawed his face, but he didn't slow his frantic pace. Eleonore was already at the car, having moved with vampiric swiftness. He had to catch her so he could explain . . .

But when he reached the parking lot at the base of the slope, it was empty.

Eleonore was gone.

+ ✦ +

"WOW," AVRAM SAID AS HE STEPPED OUT OF HIS CAR AND looked Ben up and down. "That bad, huh?"

Ben had been hiking for hours, heading back up the road toward Griffin's Nest. His eyes felt swollen from crying, and his legs were about to give out. "I have to find her," he said brokenly.

He'd called his cousin as soon as he'd realized Eleonore had stolen his SUV. He'd left the keys in the ignition in case they needed a quick getaway—a horrible choice in retrospect. He would have called Eleonore, too, but she'd left her tablet in Glimmer Falls, and he doubted she would pick up his calls anyway.

Avram grabbed Ben's elbow and steered him toward the car. There was a bulky shape in the passenger seat—Kai, probably, who had been playing poker with Avram in Griffin's Nest at the time of Ben's frantic call. Thank goodness they'd been there rather than in Fable Farms, or Ben would have been walking for even longer.

Unfortunately, he'd now have to explain to both of them what had happened.

How had he been so shortsighted? He'd been desperately worried about the upcoming violence, and with his brain buzzing around all the ways their full-frontal attack might go wrong—torture couldn't be easy to commit, another murder might traumatize Eleonore further, they could both go to prison—he'd failed to think rationally. He would have followed Eleonore into the woods a thousand times, a million, but by *Lycaon*, he ought to have insisted they go in with multiple backup plans.

Instead he'd failed on all fronts. He hadn't supported her the way she needed. He had questioned her methods while offering little that was helpful in exchange. And then he'd committed the ultimate betrayal.

Even if it had saved her life . . . how could she forgive that?

Avram opened the back door of the blue Toyota Camry. Ben

sank into the seat, then groaned when he realized there was some-one else seated on the opposite side.

Lilith, the Mother of All Demons, was glaring at him with arms crossed over her chest. A naked sword rested across her lap. "I was about to win a thousand dollars off these bozos," she complained.

Right. The poker game. "I would say I'm sorry," Ben said as he buckled his seat belt, "but I really don't give a fuck, Lilith."

He'd hit his emotional and mental limit. He was done. Maxed out.

Kai sucked in a breath and twisted to look at Ben with wide eyes, but Ben ignored him. He stared Lilith down, willing her to either shut up or put him out of his misery.

Ben had promised Eleonore he'd never issue an order again, and then he'd broken that promise. She must believe he'd betrayed her at the last second, stealing her vengeance—and her chance at freedom—away from her. She must think him unspeakably cruel.

Nothing Lilith could do to him would compare to the pain he felt right now.

Lilith looked startled at Ben's blunt words. She cocked her head, and her hand hovered over the hilt of the sword.

Ben braced himself, but he didn't back down.

Then Lilith grabbed one of the braids dotting her red hair and started gnawing on it. "That was very nice, puppy," she said around the mouthful of hair. "And here I thought you were the boring one."

Kai exhaled on a soft *whew* and turned to face forward as Avram started the car.

"I don't care what you think," Ben said, slumping back into his seat. "I just lost the love of my life."

"Damn," Avram said, hazel eyes meeting Ben's in the rearview mirror. "Didn't realize it was that serious." When Ben scowled, his cousin held up a hand. "Hey, you didn't exactly talk about the de-tails. Gigi's the only reason I knew you and Eleonore were dating at all."

Kai sniffed a few times. "Why do you smell like ozone?"

Where to begin? His panicked call to Avram had been light on details and heavy on crying. "Evil witch tried to kill Eleonore," he summed up.

Kai whistled and ran a hand through his black hair. "Straight up? How'd that happen?"

Ben sighed. "It's a long story."

Avram adjusted the mirror. "Well, I hate to break it to you, but we've got time."

Once Ben started, the words poured out of him in a flood. He explained how Isobel had treated Eleonore and Eleonore's desire for revenge. How he loved her and wanted to free her, and how he'd chosen to accompany her to finish the mission. How he wanted her to be happy so they could maybe build a life together.

Then he shamefacedly admitted his hesitation regarding Eleonore's violent methods, the bizarre confrontation at the cabin, and how the witch had been casting a spell so subtly Eleonore hadn't noticed it, forcing Ben to violate the one promise she held sacred above all others.

"I violated her free will," he said, eyes welling again. "And I did it right when she thought she was about to gain her freedom."

"I'm amazed she didn't chop your dick off," Lilith said bluntly. "If that had been my vengeance you'd ruined, bits of you would be scattered across three counties."

"Lili," Kai said from the passenger seat, "remember that thing we talked about? It starts with an *e*."

Her forehead furrowed. "Erotic asphyxiation?"

"Jesus Christ," Avram said.

Kai looked over his shoulder. "Empathy, Lili. Empathy."

"Oh. Right." Lilith frowned and a look of concentration came over her face. "I'm supposed to listen to people who are unhappy and not demean or threaten them unless they deserve it."

"Exactly." Kai smiled like he was proud of her. "And in this case, Ben doesn't deserve it. He loves Eleonore and saved her life by issuing that command. She just didn't stick around long enough to hear his explanation."

"I hope she's okay," Ben said sadly, looking out the window. "She was upset, and she's only driven the car a few times before."

"She'll be fine," Avram said. "She's what, six hundred years old?"

"More like thirtysomething with long gaps between birthdays."

"The point is, she's got survival skills. She's probably most at risk of getting a speeding ticket."

Ben winced imagining that interaction. Threatening to tear out a police officer's viscera wouldn't go over well. "She's hours ahead of us." He swallowed, throat feeling thick. "I don't even know where she's going."

"Does she have a cache of weapons in Glimmer Falls?" Lilith asked.

"Yeah, at my place." Her dresser had a drawer of spare knives, and her clothing and PADD were there, too.

Lilith nodded decisively. "Then that's where she's headed. She'll probably lay a trap for you—that's what I would do in her position." She grinned. "It's wolf-hunting season."

Kai cleared his throat.

"Right," Lilith said. "That is an outcome we apparently do not want."

"No, we do not," Kai said. "Ben's a good bloke."

Eleonore could hunt him down if she liked, so long as she gave him a minute to explain himself before doing so. "We're never going to make it there before she does," he said.

"Not in this contraption." Lilith cocked her head, giving him a devilish grin. "But you forget not all of us are constrained by geographical space."

The car was silent for a few moments, air heavy with perplexity. Avram met Ben's eyes in the rearview mirror, then made a face as if to say, "I don't know what that means either."

Then Kai snapped his fingers. "Brilliant, Lili."

"Thank you."

"Uh . . . care to share?" Avram asked.

"Lilith can portal to the demon plane from anywhere," Kai said. "And then she can portal to anywhere on Earth from the demon plane."

A magical shortcut. Hope flickered to life in Ben's chest, a small and fragile flame. "So you could take us back to my house to wait for her?"

"You, yes." She scratched a nail along the armrest. "This vehicle, no. My portals aren't big enough, and I wouldn't be caught dead in it around other demons anyway."

"Thanks a lot," Avram said dryly.

Ben could be home in a few minutes. The thought made him want to collapse with relief. He could make the place ready. Maybe craft a big sign to hang outside his house that would get Eleonore's attention and explain the issue before she packed her weapons and left at warp speed.

It was Saturday, and considering driving time, Eleonore wouldn't arrive back in Glimmer Falls until Sunday. Two days before Election Day, he realized.

"How's Gigi? How's the campaign?" he asked, forcing himself to think about something besides the total disaster in the woods.

Avram made a disgruntled noise as he pulled into the parking lot of a restaurant in Griffin's Nest. "There's an attack ad circulating that implies Gigi worships an ancient chaos entity and is planning to sacrifice children to it, but other than that it's fine."

"It says *what*?" Ben had seen other commercials that implied Gigi was inexperienced, lax on crime, an enemy of capitalism, and unreliable because of the moonshift, but this was a new angle.

"I figure it's a good sign. Cynthia must actually be worried."

Ben pulled out his phone and looked up the latest poll numbers. The mayoral race was neck and neck. He rubbed a dried tear track with the back of his hand and sniffed a few times, then dialed Gigi.

"Hey! How'd the mission go?" Her voice was surprisingly chirpy for someone who had been accused of ritual child sacrifice.

"Don't want to talk about it." Gigi could get the rundown once the election was over—and hopefully once he'd convinced Eleonore to forgive him.

"Damn, that bad? Is everyone okay?"

"Well, no one died." Ben sighed. "I seriously don't want to talk about it."

"Okay," she said slowly. "What do you want to talk about, then?"

"I'll be back in town soon. What's the plan for your next rally?" There was a lot of time to fill between writing his apology all over the house and Eleonore's eventual return, and he needed to keep busy or he'd lose it.

"We're setting up a stage on the green on Sunday," she said. "Music, speeches from the community, face painting, all that jazz. Dr. Salmerón and the Cartographers are doing the opening set and Themmie managed to snag The Pixies (No Not Those Ones) to close it out."

He tried to feel some enthusiasm for her sake. "That's great news." The Pixies (No Not Those Ones) were a local grunge band who were poised to make it big. "What can I help with?"

"Don't suppose you want to make an inspirational speech?"

Ben winced. "Not particularly."

Gigi's exhalation was gusty. "Ugh, no one else wants to either. Well, Astaroth does, but I don't trust him not to say something ridiculous."

"Rani would probably love to say something on behalf of the Glimmer Falls Resiliency Project," Ben suggested. The local nonprofit was dedicated to protecting vulnerable communities and safeguarding Glimmer Falls's future by promoting sustainable development, inclusive policies, and climate action. The nonprofit worked extensively with the Glimmer Falls Environmental Club, where Calladia and Mariel had met Themmie.

"Oh, yeah, she actually did sign up," Gigi said. "I have a few others, but I'm missing a small-business owner to talk about community outreach and buying local and helping the economy thrive and all that, ya know?"

He did, unfortunately, know. Even if Gigi's voice hadn't taken on that wheedling little sister tone, it was obvious what she wanted.

Lilith tapped her fingernails against the armrest, looking impatient. Ben didn't want to irritate his ride home even further—even if she did seem to like him better when he was being rude—so he sighed and accepted his fate. "All right," he said. "I'll make a speech."

Maybe panicking about that would provide a good distraction during the interminable hours spent waiting for Eleonore to return home. *If* she returned home, that was.

If she didn't . . . he had no clue. Would the binding spell compel him to find her? Would she be forced to return to his side eventually?

Gigi squealed, and Ben winced and pulled the phone away from his ear. "Thank you! Mom's going to be thrilled."

"She will be the only one in the audience who feels that way, I'm sure."

Lilith cleared her throat.

"Got to go, Gigi," he said. "See you later. Love you."

"Finally," Lilith said when he hung up. She opened the car door and hopped out, and Ben followed suit.

"Thanks, Avram," Ben said.

His cousin waved a hand through the rolled-down window. "You can pay me back by finally bringing Eleonore to Shabbat dinner."

Ben's heart ached at the thought. He'd been remiss about going to his aunt's Shabbat dinner lately—and not just lately, he realized. It had been . . . shoot, five months since he'd gone?

He missed his family. He missed the comfort and warmth, the food, the laughter. He missed putting work aside for a few hours to enjoy something simple and eternal.

"I will," he said. "If she forgives me."

"If she doesn't, I still expect to see you there." Avram narrowed his eyes at Ben.

Ben winced. "If I am still in possession of my head after she's done with me, yes."

Lilith motioned, and a shimmering, flame-edged oval appeared in the air. She stepped through the portal, then held a hand out and beckoned.

Taking a deep breath, Ben straightened his shoulders and stepped into the demon plane.

◆ ◆ ◆

BEN HAD VISITED THE DEMON PLANE ONCE BEFORE DURING Astaroth's revolt, when the half demon had overthrown his nemesis and pushed the conservative-leaning high council into both embracing demon hybrids and opening the plane's borders to other species. He remembered it as a dismal place filled with ancient stone buildings and hostile gargoyles, with a plum-dark sky lit by the drifting orbs of human souls.

Lilith had opened a portal to the middle of a crowded market square. Vendors hawked wares from their booths—knitted shawls, shimmering daggers, steaming fire wine—while children with small, velvety horns sprinted past, playing a game involving sticks and a wooden hoop. There were no prices listed at the booths, since demons operated on the barter system.

Unlike the last time he'd visited, Ben spotted other species in the crowd: elves and centaurs, humans and pixies, even a griffin perched on a rooftop and lashing their tail as they eyed a bird in the distance. At one end of the square the land tumbled away to a river, and the banks were overflowing with vegetation.

"It looks more alive than I remember," he said. "Did opening the borders do that?"

"Yes." Lilith pointed at a warlock in a top hat who was juggling flaming bowling pins. "Turns out the soul doesn't have to be separated from a human to bring life to the plants and people."

"Are people still making deals?"

Lilith scoffed. "Obviously. As long as humans exist, there will be some willing to do anything for money, power, or love, no matter who they hurt in the process. Even if it's themselves." She drew another portal in the air. "Come on."

Ben would investigate the other changes to the demon plane some other time; right now he needed to focus on winning Eleonore's forgiveness.

Back at his house, Ben raced around, gathering markers, paint, paper, and a spare bedsheet. He started scribbling explanations on the papers, which he would tack up at every entrance. The bedsheet he planned to paint and hang in front of the house, like the sign in that "Welcome Home Cheater" meme, except this one would say WELCOME HOME I'M SO SORRY BUT THE WITCH WAS CASTING A SPELL AND TRYING TO KILL YOU WHICH IS WHY I ISSUED THE ORDER. PLEASE FORGIVE ME AND WE CAN COME UP WITH A PLAN B?

He needed to trim that down a bit.

Lilith eyed the writing with distaste. "This is your grand gesture?"

Ben blinked up at her. ". . . Yes?"

Lilith scoffed. "Men." Then she portaled away.

That was not the most promising reaction, but Ben kept writing, because what other choice did he have?

He just hoped Eleonore actually came home.

THIRTY-SIX

ELEONORE HAMMERED THE STEERING WHEEL WITH HER FIST.
"Le salaud dégénéré!" she spat. "Va te faire foutre, loup-garou." She'd stopped crying hours before, but her voice was still rough from tears.

Her anger, though, burned hot as ever.

The miserable, lying, manipulative, rat fucking bastard. Le traître! There weren't enough words in any language to express her fury. God's righteous ovaries, she wanted to *gut* Ben.

How had she been so stupid? So blind to his true nature?

I don't want to lose you, he'd said. The villain had outright told her his motivations, and for once she'd taken something metaphorically rather than literally.

The ironic part was that he wouldn't have lost her if he'd let her break the spell. She would have chosen to be with him, using her new, unlimited free will to start a life at his side.

She'd *loved* him.

Eleonore screeched and hit the steering wheel again. Some treasures were best known after their loss, and this was one of them. Yes, she'd felt a large, overwhelming feeling for him. Yes, the intensity of it had startled her. But she hadn't put the word to it until it was gone. There was a shelf in her heart where her love for him had rested, and now that it had been stolen like an artifact from a museum, all that was left was the display tag.

Eleonore loves Ben, circa always.

Circa six hours ago, she told herself. A fleeting thing. A century from now when she was once more chained in eternal servitude to the Witch in the Woods, she'd look back at that love with the detachment of viewing a photograph in a textbook.

Except part of her feared that wasn't true at all.

The trees were a green-and-brown blur on either side, the road winding between them aimlessly. An inefficient road, this one, carved to protect the natural curves of the landscape rather than blasting through them. There was probably a speed limit to help inexperienced drivers navigate safely, but Eleonore had excellent reaction time and no use for limitations. Her itinerary had narrowed to a few key objectives.

- First: Retrieve her weaponry, her PADD, and the remainder of her belongings from Ben's house.
- Second: Torch said house.
- Third:
- . . .
- . . .
- . . .

All right, she didn't know the third yet. Wrapping Ben in his entrails like a Christmas tree bedecked in tinsel would have been the obvious choice, but even if the curse had allowed her to hurt him, her mind couldn't jump to that step.

Eleonore was tired of killing. Would never have killed another person after Isobel if she'd been allowed her revenge.

But there was another reason why she couldn't disembowel Ben, she recognized bitterly. It was that stupid love. Not missing from its shelf after all, just smashed with a hammer. Shards of beautiful, delicate feeling.

Eleonore loves Ben, circa now and for a regrettably unforeseeable future.

Lights appeared in her rearview mirror, startling her. Eleonore eyed them, wondering what creature was pursuing her. A dragon of some sort, one that breathed pulses of red-and-blue fire in rapid succession?

A ululating melody started from the beast, obnoxiously shrill. Then the creature drew closer, and Eleonore realized it was a car. A car with something seriously wrong with it, given all the blinking lights and shrieking. Her brows knit together as her eyes darted between the road and the mirror. Was the driver in distress?

Eleonore sighed. Whatever was wrong with it, it was obnoxious. She spotted a wide patch of ground beside the road ahead and pulled aside to let the car pass. To her annoyance, it pulled in behind her. Though it stopped, the lights stayed on, casting red-and-blue flashes against the trees like a spell that had malfunctioned.

Eleonore unclipped her seat belt and stepped out. "What's wrong with your car?" she shouted.

A man in a navy blue outfit exited the car, pointing—was that a *gun?*—at her. "Get back in the vehicle!"

Eleonore eyed the gun with distaste. What a classless weapon. If this man had any courage, he'd fight her with his fists. "If you are looking for assistance, this is a poor way to go about it."

The man squinted at her. "I said, get back in the vehicle!" His voice was less certain now, though.

She spread her arms. "And what will I do there?" she asked, moving from annoyed to downright furious. Not that it was a big step, since she was simmering with rage up to her eyeballs.

"Whatever ails your car will still be a problem, and you will have accomplished nothing but annoying me."

"Whatever ails my—what?"

She gestured at the vehicle. "The curse. Or mechanical malfunction. Whatever is causing that obnoxious flickering."

The man's gun wavered. He cleared his throat. "Um . . . how old are you?"

What a bizarre person. "Biologically or temporally?" Eleonore asked.

"Oh, for fuck's sake." The man pinched the bridge of his nose with his free hand. "Let me guess. Immortal?"

She failed to see how that signified. "Not precisely. A foul witch imprisoned me in a crystal six hundred years ago, yoking my free will to her commands, and—"

"Right," he said, cutting her off. That would have earned him a very mean hiss and perhaps some fangs in his throat if he hadn't lowered the gun. "I'm a police officer."

Eleonore eyed him up and down. She hadn't heard many good things about modern policing. "Are you looking for a criminal? And if so, why are you antagonizing me?"

"Because you were speeding."

"So?"

He looked at her like the answer was obvious. "You were going forty miles an hour above the speed limit."

Apparently she had misunderstood the point of speed limits. "I thought that was a guideline for bad drivers."

"No, it's a law. Which you broke." When Eleonore stared at him, he elaborated. "Which makes you a criminal."

"Putain de bordel de merde," Eleonore exclaimed. "How pathetic is this time? You ought to be wrangling murderous ghouls or saving cities under siege from the forces of darkness. Instead you care that I was *driving too fast*? Do you have any idea how fast I can run?"

The gun came back up at that. Easily alarmed, this police officer. Her respect for the profession diminished further. "I'm giving you leeway because you're an immortal and out of touch—"

"I am not out of touch!" she exclaimed. "I have researched many things on my PADD."

"But," he continued, sounding for all the world like she was being the obnoxious one, "you need to get back in the vehicle. That's the appropriate thing to do at a traffic stop. Then I will approach your window and ask for your driver's license and registration—"

"A license and registration?" she interrupted. "Do you tag drivers like bears to keep track of them?" She'd seen a documentary at Ben's place and had found it concerning that even wild animals were subjected to this time's obsession with surveillance.

"Let me guess," the police officer said flatly. "You don't have a license."

This man was wasting her time and ruining her plan. Even if she only had two steps in said plan, those steps mattered. Her temper reached its limit. "Here's your license," she said, bending her arm at a right angle and slapping her other hand against her bicep. In case he was unfamiliar with the bras d'honneur, she followed it up by extending both middle fingers.

The police officer started approaching. "That's it. You are officially—"

A red-haired blur dropped from the tree overhead, tackling him into the dirt before clubbing him over the head with the butt of a sword. "Unconscious," the demoness Lilith said. She hopped to her feet, dusting off her pants. "Lucifer, I hate police officers."

Eleonore blinked. That was . . . unexpected.

Lilith wore pirate garb with a green sash, and her hair was wild and tangled around her horns. She sheathed her sword, then stepped over the police officer. "I also hate lurking in trees for hours waiting for a certain SUV to pass, so you owe me an apology."

"I—what?" Eleonore asked.

"Come on," Lilith said, drawing a shimmering, flame-edged portal in the air. She stepped through, disappearing into nothing.

Well, what else was she going to do? Mystified but curious, Eleonore followed.

◆ ◆ ◆

THEY EMERGED IN THE DEMON PLANE, AND ELEONORE BARELY had time to take in the crowded streets of a medieval-looking city before Lilith drew another portal and yanked her through.

This time they stood outside Ben's house back on Earth. Eleonore's heart jolted before tumbling into a frantic rhythm. She wasn't prepared to face him yet.

Then reason returned. *Fool*, she told herself. There was no way Ben was here already.

"Look," Lilith said, pointing at the garage door.

A white bedsheet had been duct-taped to it. It was covered in black paint.

THE WITCH WAS CASTING A SPELL. I'M SO SORRY.

Eleonore narrowed her eyes, trying to determine what that was and why Lilith had brought her here. "Who wrote that?"

"Your werewolf did."

She scoffed. "There's no way." She'd left him with no car—he ought to be hiking tragically through the woods for days on end while Eleonore retrieved her weapons, destroyed his house, and embarked on her unknown third step.

"He did write it," Lilith said. "Since a certain beautiful, infinitely wise and far-too-patient demoness portaled him here ahead of you."

"You brought him here?" Eleonore felt illogically betrayed. It wasn't like she even knew the demoness past a few bizarre interactions and one shared crouch behind a newspaper box.

Lilith was studying the bedsheet with hands on hips. "A bit pathetic as grand gestures go, don't you think?"

Eleonore didn't know what Lilith meant by a grand gesture, but she knew bullshit when she saw it. "Does Ben think I'll actually believe that?" she asked, pointing at the sheet and its messy apology. "I was a second away from breaking the curse when he ordered me away. I would have heard the witch chanting or seen her drawing runes."

"I don't think he's a very good liar," Lilith said.

"Exactly. This is a pathetic attempt to excuse his actions."

"Not that," Lilith said, flapping a hand at the sheet. "He was crying all over the car and moaning about your loss for an eternity. I'm pretty sure he meant it."

"The car? What car?" Eleonore wasn't following the demoness's thought process.

"Were you looking at the witch's hands when you were about to break the spell?" Lilith asked, ignoring the question. "*Both* of them?"

"I—" Of course she had been, Eleonore wanted to say. She always paid close attention to her opponents. But when she thought back, all she remembered was the knife in Isobel's right hand and a flood of hate, fear, and triumph.

A frustrated or angry opponent is more likely to make errors.

Eleonore had said that to Gigi about Cynthia Cunnington. It was one of the first lessons a warrior learned—how to use an enemy's emotional state against them.

She'd been myopic in her fury. She had no idea what Isobel's left hand had been up to.

"Merde," Eleonore said.

"Apparently the witch was going to hurt you," Lilith said,

studying her sharp black nails. "But I understand if you still want to chop the wolf into dozens of pieces and scatter them to the ends of the earth."

Eleonore was barely absorbing the demoness's words. She stared at the bedsheet undulating in the wind.

Could it be? Had Isobel been playing a trick on her? She'd always been so strange about Eleonore—seeing her as a friend or a child sometimes, as a tool other times. She was as unpredictable as Lilith or any other immortal who had lived too long to think normally anymore.

Her remorse had seemed so real, and Eleonore had been so desperate to be done with her eternal servitude that she'd accepted Isobel's insanity as the explanation for that remorse. She hadn't paused to think before acting.

Ben was the thinker of the two of them. Ben was the one who paused.

"I didn't hear her recite a spell, though," Eleonore said, feeling like the ground was shifting beneath her. Even if she hadn't seen the witch marking runes with her left hand, she ought to have heard a spell.

"Well, in that case," Lilith said, "off with the wolf's head!" She unsheathed the sword at her back and began marching toward the house.

Alarm spiked. "No, wait!" Eleonore said, speeding to Lilith's side to drag her away from the house. "Let me think."

"Great," Lilith said. "Do it on your time, not mine." She grabbed Eleonore's arm, drew another portal, and yanked her into the demon plane and then back to the side of the road where the SUV remained with its door open and lights on.

"Why are we back here?" Eleonore asked, staggering when Lilith released her. She'd been so close to confronting Ben and hearing the truth from his mouth! "I'm still a day's drive from Glimmer Falls."

"Exactly," Lilith said. "Do you have a phone?"

"No."

The demoness made an annoyed sound. "Here's a map of the area around Fable Farms," she said, drawing in the mud with her sword. "Kai has a spare room you can stay in tonight."

Eleonore blinked at the jagged lines. "Why? You could have left me at Ben's place—"

The demoness drew another portal. "Bye!"

Eleonore stared blankly at the spot where Lilith had just vanished.

What the *hell*?

She swore and slammed her fist into a tree, then regretted it immediately. She shook her hand out, frowning at the broken skin where bark had scraped it. Foolish to damage her dominant hand before a confrontation.

But what kind of confrontation would it be?

Well, she had all of today and much of tomorrow on the road to think about that, and she'd spent far too much of her life acting before thinking. Eleonore trudged to the car, girding herself for some prolonged ruminating.

THIRTY-SEVEN

O N SUNDAY MORNING, BEN WAS ON HIS WAY TO GIGI'S
rally to help set up when Lilith ran in front of his car. He
cursed, slamming on the brakes just in time to avoid running her
over. She stood with her fists on her waist, expression worryingly
determined.

He rolled down his window. "What are you doing?" he asked.

"Resolving this situation in an appropriately dramatic way."
She pointed to the side of the road. "Pull over."

He did, parking at the curb. When he got out, Lilith had a portal open.

Ben groaned. "Another portal? Where is this one going?"

"The demon plane, obviously."

Ben pinched the bridge of his nose. "Yes, but where are we going after that? And why?"

"You're going to make a proper grand gesture."

That . . . was not an answer. "Where's Kai?" Ben asked. He was
used to having his friend as a buffer against Lilith's special brand
of insanity, but he was nowhere to be seen.

"It isn't Kai's grand gesture," Lilith said. "Why would he come?"

"You keep talking about grand gestures." He was familiar with the concept from rom-coms he'd watched with his parents, so it was clear this had something to do with winning Eleonore's forgiveness, but he'd already made a grand gesture. "That's what all the signs are for. So she'll pause before running away and we can have a conversation about what happened."

Lilith stepped closer and jabbed a finger into his chest. "You think talking about the misunderstanding is enough? That woman has been trapped by a curse for six hundred years. All talking does is make that servitude last even longer." She nodded as if he'd agreed with her. "Yes, you have to do something."

"I will," he promised, "but we need to regroup and come up with a new strategy." He and Eleonore would come up with a game plan, refine it until it was foolproof, then execute it.

For some reason Lilith grinned. "Good puppy. That's exactly it."

Then he was being yanked off his feet into the demon plane and, a moment later, into the woods outside Isobel's cabin.

Ben stared at the red door with alarm. "Why am I back here? I don't have any weapons and we need Eleonore—"

In response, Lilith reached into the pocket of her ragged black pirate trousers. She tossed a pair of handcuffs at him, which he fumbled to catch. "I'll pick you up in thirty minutes."

Then she was gone.

Ben looked at the handcuffs with consternation. The message was clear—trap Isobel. He would gladly do that, but how was he supposed to face down an immortal witch with centuries of knowledge and a willingness to kill?

He looked more closely at the steel, feeling slightly relieved at a rune that indicated the cuffs were spelled to prevent magic usage. Trapping a witch or warlock's hands was essential to keeping their powers limited, since physical movement of some kind was required to cast. But how was he going to get close enough to catch her?

The red door creaked open.

"Shit," Ben muttered, heart rate spiking. He shoved the hand-cuffs in his back pocket.

Isobel stepped out. She wore a teal gown this time, and there were shadows under her eyes. "Is Eleonore back?" she asked hope-fully, clasping her hands at her chest.

He needed to think, damn it!

Isobel waited for his answer, eerie midnight eyes fixed on him. The cracked door revealed only the darkness of whatever lay beyond.

Ben had only one choice.

Time to be a werewolf of action.

"I want to talk to you about Eleonore," Ben said, bracing him-self for the most terrifying conversation of his life.

Isobel looked around the clearing. "She's not here?"

"No."

"All right," Isobel said, shoulders drooping. She stepped back from the door. "Come in."

Ben approached the invisible house warily, heart pounding. His palms were sweaty and his head buzzed with everything that could go wrong. Who was Ben to even think about confronting the witch? He didn't have Eleonore's martial skills. Didn't know a thing about Isobel except that she was ruthless, unpredictable, and had a strange fondness for Eleonore that nevertheless allowed for murder attempts.

Was he supposed to club her over the head and drag her back to Glimmer Falls?

The slice of darkness beyond the door beckoned.

Ben ducked his head to fit under the lintel. He had a moment of disorientation as his eyes adjusted to being inside a building where previously one hadn't seemed to exist. The cabin was stone with narrow windows, and the interior was lit by candles and a solitary fire. A cauldron bubbled at the hearth, surrounded by

ornate furniture. At the back of the room a spiraling staircase indicated further rooms above. The only modern touch was a television on the far wall, on which an episode of *Star Trek: The Next
Generation* was playing.

Isobel noticed him looking at the TV. "I always think about
Eleonore when I watch it," she said, taking a seat at a table that
held a crystal ball. She leaned in to peer at the purple orb from an
inch away, then flicked the exterior. "Ugh," she said, sitting back
with a huff. "These things are so vague."

Ben shifted from foot to foot. "What, ah, are you scrying for?
In the crystal ball?"

"Eleonore, of course." She frowned at Ben. "Do you know where
she is?"

"No," he said honestly. "She left me behind."

"As she left me." Isobel sighed heavily, pressing a hand to her
heart. "I know how that hurts."

Ben bristled at that piece of absurdity, temper helping burn
away some of the fear. "You tried to kill her."

"Only temporarily."

"Let me clarify," he said, struggling not to shout. "You tried to
kill her *after* you'd trapped her for six centuries, cursed to do your
bidding."

"We had fun!" Isobel blinked dark eyes up at him. After a long
pause, her lower lip trembled. "Didn't we?" she asked in a smaller
voice.

Ben looked around the dim room, searching for signs of who
this witch was. Who she loved, what she valued. Anything to figure out what was going on in her head and how to manage it.

Dried herbs hung from the ceiling and bookshelves sagged under the weight of hundreds of spell books. An antique writing desk
held a pot of ink and a quill pen. Other than the TV, it was as if
she'd been frozen in time centuries ago.

The desk also held a small picture, he realized. He approached it, then picked up the silver frame, which was tarnished with age. The painting showed a black-cloaked figure with their arm looped around Eleonore's shoulders.

Isobel had commissioned a portrait of herself with her personal assassin. In the portrait Eleonore was grinning, but it didn't resemble her real grin. There was no dimple in the right cheek, no tilt of the lips to bring character to the perfection of her face.

Isobel had wanted Eleonore to look happy in this picture, but she'd never actually seen her smile.

Ben's chest hurt thinking of Eleonore spending so long in misery and anger. Every time she woke from her cursed sleep, the world had changed. Isobel had been her only touchstone, the only constant in a blurred, unhappy life.

Now he wondered if perhaps Eleonore had been Isobel's only touchstone, too.

"She looks so lovely in that, doesn't she?" Isobel asked from the table. "Bring it over."

Ben obeyed, though his brain was turning over possibilities faster than it ever had before. He sat across from Isobel, setting the portrait next to the crystal ball. Then he hid his hands in his lap to disguise the white-knuckled clenching of his fingers. It was taking everything he had to be polite to this monster.

"You care about Eleonore," he said, though it made him sick to say those words.

"I do." Isobel touched a finger to the portrait, tracing her own hooded, concealed form. "I wish this showed my true looks, but Eleonore isn't the only person who promised to memorize my appearance and then, someday, when I least expected it, return and cut my face off." She chuckled. "Eleonore didn't mean it, of course—at least not more than two-thirds of the time. She's always been so delightfully dramatic."

Ben didn't understand how the witch could find amusement in that dynamic. He didn't know how she could find *caring* in it. It was sick, the product of an ancient mind that had taken its own delusions as fact.

But he didn't have to understand the thought process. The point was that Isobel believed it.

"Do you have any friends, Isobel?" he asked. When she pointed at the portrait, he shook his head. "Not counting Eleonore."

Isobel's eyes went distant, and she was silent for long moments. "The warlock Alzapraz and I talk sometimes," she finally said. Then her forehead furrowed. "When was the last time he visited? He'd just come off that Spanish galleon . . ." She shook her head. "It doesn't matter. I'll make more friends now that I'm immortal and don't have to hide to protect myself."

It was as he'd suspected. Isobel was so paranoid, she'd eliminated anyone she feared was an enemy. Or rather, she'd had Eleonore eliminate them. The last time she'd met Alzapraz in person the Spanish navy still used galleons, and her limited encounters with humans had involved murdering them to steal their lives. Eleonore had been her one companion over the centuries, and somehow this twisted woman had convinced herself their dynamic was something other than what it was.

She'd chosen to ignore the fact that Eleonore stayed with Isobel because she was forced to. She'd told herself Eleonore's threats were a fun game they played. She'd decided they were *friends*.

Ben wasn't a man prone to hate, but he hated Isobel with all his heart. She had hurt the woman he loved. For the first time, though, he realized she wasn't an all-powerful, remorseless supervillain. She was cruel, deranged . . . and pathetic.

He would never feel sorry for her. She deserved whatever fate she got, and next time he wouldn't utter a peep if Eleonore decided to behead her.

But now he understood Isobel's weakness.

She was lonely.

"Why did you sell the crystal on eBay?" he asked.

Isobel looked pensive as she stroked Eleonore's cheek in the portrait. "I thought I didn't need it anymore. I'd been immortal for nearly two years at that point, and I'd never felt stronger. I fantasized about striking out on my own, traveling the world and making my enemies tremble at my feet without needing to rely on an assassin." She shook her head. "Also, I had drunk a lot of vodka the night I put that listing up. It was an impulsive choice, one I immediately regretted."

"Do you miss her?" Ben was barely able to keep his voice steady. Even pretending to entertain this woman's delusions was sickening.

Isobel looked at him wordlessly with those dark, fathomless eyes, and he read the answer in them.

Here was his opportunity. Threatening Isobel's life had never been the play—she would protect her existence above all, no matter who she had to destroy. No matter if she thought she cared about that person.

No, Ben needed to offer her something she wasn't used to trading in.

Hope.

"I've grown tired of the responsibility of owning the crystal," he said, praying his mediocre acting skills would be up to this, the most important task of his life. He reached into his pocket for the blue plastic crystal and set it on the table. "You can have it back for five dollars, but we'll need a signed contract."

Isobel's face lit up as she looked at the crystal. "Would you take a gold doubloon?"

Ben had no idea what a doubloon was worth, but he pretended to consider as he slowly pulled the handcuffs out of his back pocket. "Yes," he said. "That would be acceptable."

Isobel was on her feet in an instant, hurrying toward a small box on the fireplace mantel.

Ben didn't let her get that far. He lunged after her, grabbing her arms behind her back so she couldn't cast a spell. It took a few scrabbling, screeching moments to get one of the cuffs snapped around her wrist, but the second was easier.

"Curse your eyes!" she spat. "A hex of boils upon your cock! Release me this instant!"

Ben had never been so happy to be a big, strong man in his life. "No," he said, bending down to hoist her over his shoulder.

He tucked the crystal back into his pocket, then carried Isobel out of the cabin screaming.

Lilith stood in the middle of the clearing, arms crossed. At the sight of the thrashing witch, she smiled wickedly. "I knew you had it in you, wolf." Then she whipped the green sash from her waist and shoved it in Isobel's mouth, muffling her shouts. "Never fuck with redheads."

Ben grinned, feeling a surge of exhilaration. "Let's find Eleonore."

He wasn't sure what would happen next—they'd still need Isobel to break the spell—but a witch in hand was better than one in an invisible cabin in the woods.

"You were right," he told Lilith as she opened a new portal. "This is a much better grand gesture."

THIRTY-EIGHT

—AND THAT'S WHY THE GLIMMER FALLS CHAPTER OF Mages Without Borders is proud to support Gigi Rosewood for mayor!"

Ben clapped along with the rest of the onlookers as the man onstage bowed. A huge crowd had shown up for Gigi's final rally at the village green, and so many of them wore her campaign swag that the gathering resembled a sea of pink. The sun had finally broken through the clouds after a morning of rain, and the atmosphere was that of a carnival, complete with face painters, a catering table, and a hot chocolate vendor.

Ben couldn't appreciate the carnival atmosphere. According to his calculations, Eleonore should be arriving in town in a few hours, and he was beyond nervous. As soon as his speech was over, he'd be running home to pace anxiously and decide how best to present Isobel to her.

Should he buy a card to go with the offering? Hallmark had an extended line of cards for magical towns, but he suspected this situation was too niche even for them.

He rubbed his arms, grateful for his long-sleeved white shirt and wine-red sweater vest. Not only did they hide his nervous sweat, but they also provided some protection against the November chill.

No one else seemed to mind the cold. The makeshift stage on the north end of the green had already seen an hour of speeches, countless chants and cheers, and a performance from Dr. Salmerón and the Cartographers that was about as raucous as folk music could get. Thankfully, only one tree had been accidentally torched by dragon fire during the show, and Mariel had promptly healed it. Gigi was in the middle of it all, introducing speakers and circulating among the crowd. Her own speech would be last, right before the performance by The Pixies (No Not Those Ones).

Ben looked at his watch, wishing he could time travel thirty minutes into the future so his speech would already be over. He might have abducted an evil immortal witch who was currently locked in Calladia's truck with the window cracked—he wasn't about to leave Isobel alone in his house—but his stomach felt worse now than it had during that confrontation.

Werewolf of action, maybe. Werewolf of public speaking? Never.

Rani and Mariel stood near him at the side of the stage, chatting animatedly. Both of them would be speaking as well—Rani on behalf of the Glimmer Falls Resiliency Project and Mariel on behalf of the Glimmer Falls Environmental Club. Though Mariel had admitted public speaking wasn't her favorite thing either, she seemed surprisingly calm about the whole thing.

It probably helped that Oz was lurking at the back of the crowd, ready to wave a bright pink sign that had GO MARIEL! painted on it. Themmie had shaken her wings over the paint to give the letters a glittery sheen. The pixie herself was hovering cross-legged fifteen feet above the crowd, wings a blur as she livestreamed the proceedings. Her Get Out the Vote efforts had resulted in a huge leap in the number of young registered voters. "Local elections matter as much as federal ones," she'd reiterated in multiple posts, and the message seemed to have actually sunk in.

Ben's parents were at the front of the gathering, bedecked in the brightest pink of all. His father had brought bouquets of pink tulips that he flung at anyone whose speech he liked, and Ben's nervousness intensified when he imagined having to dodge floral projectiles.

Lycaon, he didn't want to do this. But Eleonore wasn't back yet, so what else was there to do but support his little sister while he waited?

"Where's Astaroth?" Mariel asked.

Ben winced. Calladia was in the crowd waving a HOWLING FOR CHANGE sign, but Astaroth was posted at the truck, guarding Isobel. Lilith had told him what was happening, and the British demon had been delighted. He'd insisted on helping "facilitate Ben's descent into criminality," though Ben suspected Astaroth's own personal grudge against Isobel was more of a motivating factor. Calladia knew what was going on, since Astaroth hid nothing from her, but she'd agreed to keep quiet for now.

"I, ah, gave Astaroth a task to do," Ben said, rubbing the back of his neck.

Mariel eyed him curiously. "What task? The logistics are already taken care of."

Ben wasn't about to admit in public that he'd kidnapped someone. "Oh, look, Gigi's about to talk."

Ben ignored Mariel's and Rani's suspicious looks as Gigi took the stage to introduce the next speaker. She wore a sparkling blue dress with her pink shoes, and her hair hung loose and curling. "Isn't this great?" she asked into the microphone. The crowd cheered in response. "So many smiling faces and so many people agitating for change. Why, it's—"

A loud voice boomed through the air, making Ben jump in alarm. "Welcome to my final campaign rally, Glimmer Falls!"

What the—

"Oh, no," Mariel said, wincing. "It's Cynthia."

Ben was tall enough to see over the crowd toward the south end of the green, where another stage had manifested out of thin air. Cynthia Cunnington stood atop it, nearly blinding to the eye in a white pantsuit with diamonds glittering at every conceivable place they could glitter. Her golden hair was tied back ruthlessly, smooth as a helmet, and the sharp shoulders of her coat were reminiscent of armor.

She needed no microphone, since magic could amplify her voice. "In two days' time," she said, "the werewolf interloper will be defeated and our community restored to its ideal state of justice, order, and magical traditionalism."

A small crowd was gathering in front of her stage, maybe a tenth the size of Gigi's audience. They waved small Glimmer Falls flags and wore matching white hats that had MAYOR CUNNINGTON! spelled out in rhinestones.

"Well," Gigi said into the microphone. "This is an interesting development. We specifically booked the entire space from the city."

"I *am* the city," Cynthia declared in response.

Ben winced. "This is the loudest argument I've ever heard." Their amplified voices ricocheted off the surrounding buildings.

"Hey, Cynthia," Gigi said. "Want to have a debate somewhere else so the party can keep going? This is harshing the vibe, to put it mildly." Most of the crowd shouted their agreement at the suggestion.

"I don't debate my lessers," Cynthia announced to a smattering of cheers from her supporters.

Calladia showed up at Mariel's side, having pushed her way through the crowd. She grimaced in the way only an estranged child of a publicly misbehaving parent could. "This is so embarrassing," she said, tugging on her ponytail agitatedly. "I don't know how my mom thinks she's going to win votes doing this."

"To be honest, I don't think she understands that anything might not go her way," Mariel said. "She just wants to crush the competition."

"I always say life got better after cutting contact," Calladia said. "And it is better and easier now, don't get me wrong. But then she shows up and does something cruel or obnoxious and I feel hurt and humiliated all over again. Like I need to apologize for her."

It was rare to see Calladia's shoulders slump, but some hurts weren't resolved easily. Ben didn't know what it was like to cut off a family member, but he knew from his own struggles with mental health that growth of any sort wasn't a straight line—there were ups and downs. Sometimes more downs than ups, even if a person was on the right track.

"Oh, honey." Mariel stood on her tiptoes and wrapped her arms around Calladia in a fierce hug. "You don't need to apologize for her."

"You're your own person," Ben agreed. "I promise, no one assumes you're involved in her choices."

Despite the slumped shoulders, Calladia's eyes were dry as she gave a pained smile. She had always been a fighter in more ways than one. "Thanks," she said. "I'll be fine. I'm just pissed on Gigi's behalf."

Gigi looked plenty pissed on her own. Her chin was jutting in a determined way Ben recognized from times she'd been mad at him over the years. One of those times had resulted in Gigi punching him in the testicles with her four-year-old fist, so Ben thought Cynthia should be a bit more concerned. Gigi was a nice person, but all bets were off at a certain point.

"You're not the city," Gigi said, "and I'm not lesser than you. You're a nasty, self-important rich bitch who can't stand being out of the spotlight for a single second."

"Ooh, shit," a nearby pixie said, whipping out his phone.

"We're here in the name of democracy, progress, and opportunity for all members of our community, not just the elite few," Gigi continued. "Not to mention a good fucking time—am I right, everyone?"

Though cheers followed the words, Ben groaned at the obscenity. He wasn't a political strategist, but surely cursing out the existing mayor was a bad move?

"So please take your snooty self somewhere else," Gigi said. "Or book your own space for a rally." She shrugged. "I can't imagine it'll be thrilling, but maybe you can order a few of us peasants around for fun."

The gloves were off, and the crowd was lapping it up. The pink shirt brigade seemed thrilled by Gigi's abandonment of social niceties, shouting their own insults that Cynthia's followers returned. Ben covered his face with his hands, peeking through his fingers at the escalating disaster.

Cynthia looked taken aback at Gigi's hostility. "How vulgar," she said, hand brushing the pearls at her neck. "And no, I will not leave. I'm here to celebrate my imminent victory."

"Okay," Gigi said. She turned to face the green to the left of the stage, where Dr. Salmerón and the Cartographers had been relaxing and eating snacks. "How do you feel about an impromptu second set, Gabriel?"

Gabriel lumbered to his feet, shaking out his green wings. The dragon was sleek, with shimmering crimson scales. "Absolutely," he puffed in a smoky voice, following the pronouncement with a burst of flame that nearly took out the PA system. Gabriel was small as dragons went, but even a small dragon had an outsized presence. "Cooper, the electric mandolin!"

His bandmate grabbed the instrument and started jogging toward the stage. The rest of the band followed, and soon Cynthia's voice was drowned out by the wail of an electric mandolin, some aggressive drumwork from a Norwegian selkie, and the unusual vocal stylizations of a dragon whose roots in Mexican folk music had been flavored by Icelandic death metal. The crowd went wild, dancing and flailing their arms as flames rocketed into the sky.

Ben covered his ears, wincing. He'd never been the type to attend concerts, and that was before he'd hit his thirties and discovered many of the things that had been theoretically fun in his twenties were actually noisy and exhausting, including live music and social gatherings that began after eight p.m. On the plus side, there was no way anyone would hear Cynthia.

Then Ben noticed Gigi marching through the crowd toward Cynthia's camp, fist clenched. Cynthia smirked and caressed the pearls at her neck.

"Oh, no," Ben said. That was a disaster waiting to happen. He started after Gigi, but Mariel grabbed his sleeve. "Ben, wait," she said, pointing toward the street.

He turned . . .

And saw Eleonore standing at the edge of the park.

THIRTY-NINE

ELEONORE WAS UNSURE WHAT WAS OCCURRING AT THE VIL-lage green. She'd expected Gigi's rally, but that didn't explain why Cynthia Cunnington was standing on a separate stage opposite, or why Gigi was approaching her in a threatening manner. It also didn't explain why a small dragon was wailing and smacking an electronic keyboard with its claws.

She pulled over and parked haphazardly, then jumped out of the car. If Gigi was here, Ben probably was, too.

Her eyes found him in the midst of the chaos, as if drawn by a magnet. He stood tall, serious, and sturdy, and her heart stuttered at the sight of him in his sweater vest and khakis.

He truly had tried to save her. She'd thought about it and thought about it on the drive back, pondering Ben's behavior over the past months. Words could lie, but actions spoke silent truths, and everything he'd done—after the initial hiccup of ordering her to put on a stage show—had been to ensure her comfort and happiness. He cared, and he saw the details she didn't.

In the woods he'd seen a danger she hadn't. He'd only broken his word to save her life.

In return, she had stolen his car and abandoned him far from home.

Stars, would he forgive her for that?

Mariel pointed in Eleonore's direction, and Ben turned. The moment he spotted her, Eleonore knew the answer to her question.

Of course he would forgive her. He was the best man she had ever known.

Ben's expression flickered through hope, fear, and guilt. Then he started striding toward her with swoon-worthy determination.

Unfortunately, Eleonore couldn't have the conversation she wanted with Ben while Gigi was bearing down on Cynthia. As much as she would have liked seeing a fistfight, the witch was toying with her pearls like she was about to cast a spell. An intervention was needed, and only one person here was fast enough to stop the confrontation before it started.

Eleonore held up her finger to indicate Ben should wait, then whipped her belt out of its loops and ran at top vampire speed toward Cynthia Cunnington.

"*Melerobbil o*—Oof!" The spell was only half out of Cynthia's mouth when Eleonore tackled her. She hastily bound Cynthia's hands behind her back with the belt, then tore a piece off her own shirt and shoved it in the mayor's mouth as a gag. For good measure, she ripped off the necklace, sending pearls flying and rolling across the stage.

Then, captive subdued, she hoisted the witch over her shoulder and ran away.

Cynthia's kicks were laughably slow compared to how quickly Eleonore was moving. She sprinted down block after block, lamenting the dip in her physical fitness as her thighs burned and the air caught hot and sharp in her lungs. Finally, she chose a random dumpster in an alleyway and tossed Cynthia in.

Not bothering to listen to the muffled shrieks emanating from the bin, Eleonore sped back to the village green.

When she got there, the concert had stopped and everyone was staring at Cynthia's empty stage with open mouths. "Where did she go?" someone asked. Gigi had stopped midstride, blinking in consternation at the place where her opponent had been.

Eleonore hopped onto Cynthia's stage. "Carry on with the rally," she shouted, waving a hand. "The mayor is in the dumpster."

"Wait, literally?" Gigi asked.

"Hi, Eleonore!" Themmie called out from where she was hovering overhead. She was grinning hugely. "My money is on yes, literally."

At that, more cheers erupted, and the dragon started attacking the keyboard again.

Eleonore had waited long enough to talk to Ben. The hours on the road had been interminable and unbearable. Left with nothing but her thoughts, regrets, and a festering resentment for speed limits—which she had continued to violate with enthusiasm—Eleonore had been crawling out of her skin by the time she'd arrived in Glimmer Falls.

She hopped off the stage and sped toward Ben. He was on his way to her as well, and they met in the middle of the crowd. Eleonore was tempted to fling her arms around him, but she wasn't sure if he would welcome her affections yet.

Ben shuffled from foot to foot, eyes wide and jaw working like he was chewing on unspoken words.

"I'm sorry," they blurted in unison, shouting over the noise.

Ben frowned. "Wait, why are you—"

"You don't need to be—" she said.

"I ordered you around and—"

"I left you in the woods and—"

"I should have communicated better—"

"I should have listened—"

The conflicting apologies overlapped, and they both stopped speaking. After a moment, Eleonore ventured to start her speech over again.

"I–"

"So–"

At that, she cracked up. Dear gods, she was tired. She hadn't slept well, tossing and turning as she castigated herself for acting without thinking. Driving was exhausting, too—all that time sitting in a vehicle that operated on a human concept of speed rather than the speed of romantic urgency.

Ben's eyes crinkled with a smile. "Want to go somewhere a bit quieter?"

Eleonore nodded emphatically. "Yes, please."

◆ ◆ ◆

THEY WALKED TOGETHER AWAY FROM THE GREEN. AN AWK-ward but not bad silence had fallen between them, and whenever Eleonore peeked at him she caught him sneaking sideways looks at her, as well.

"How did you get here so fast?" he asked. "I would have been waiting for you at home if I'd known."

It hadn't felt fast, and Eleonore was still unhappy Lilith had forced her to drive all the way back, but she had to admit the time to think had been valuable. Unlike Ben, Eleonore rarely slowed down enough for deep contemplation.

"I drove aggressively," she told him. On that note, she probably ought to confess . . . "I did encounter a police officer, though."

Ben's steps stuttered, and he looked at her with alarm. "Wait, you got pulled over? Did you get a ticket?"

"A ticket? For a show or something?" The officer had been rather dramatic.

"No, a speeding ticket. Something that costs money and possibly requires a court date."

"Oh, nothing like that." Eleonore smiled at him reassuringly. "Don't worry. Lilith knocked him unconscious and I left him at the side of the road. He won't bother us."

Ben did not seem comforted by that news. He gaped at her. "She did *what*? And you did—" He paused, then shook his head sharply. "You know what? That's not important right now. What's important is that you're safe. And even if the cop took my license plate down, that's not the end of the world, right? I'll say I have no idea what happened or who was in the car. Or maybe Calladia can do a memory spell if they do try to arrest either of us for assaulting a police officer." He swallowed hard. "Yes. This will be fine."

Eleonore patted his arm, feeling a rush of affection for her worrier of a werewolf. "It will be. I'm just glad I'm here and we can talk."

"I am, too." He cleared his throat, gesturing toward where a red truck was parked half a block ahead. "I have a gift for you."

Was this customary when lovers made up after a conflict? "But I didn't bring a gift for you. And I haven't even apologized properly yet for—" She broke off midsentence at the sight of Astaroth standing next to the truck with his sword unsheathed and gleaming in the sunlight. "What is he doing here?"

"How do you like being the one ambushed?" the demon asked the truck, poking the window with his sword. "Not so fun on that end, is it?"

Eleonore was wondering if he had gone the way of Lilith and cheerfully lost his mind when movement in the vehicle caught her attention. She gasped at the sight of black hair and a familiar thrashing head.

Eleonore was at the truck in an instant. "What is this?" she asked in amazement.

Astaroth jumped. "Bloody hell, you move quickly."

Isobel was tied up, her mouth stopped with a gag. At the sight of Eleonore, her eyes widened and her movements stilled.

Ben caught up a few moments later. "This is my grand gesture," he said, looking bashful. "An apology for ordering you around and for doubting your methods."

"Oh, Ben. You don't need to apologize. I should have stopped to think about *why* you would have ordered me around." Eleonore pressed a palm to the window, imagining clawing Isobel's eyes out. Isobel blinked in response, long and slow like a cat. "I can't believe the witch is here," she marveled. "How did this happen?"

"Well, Lilith facilitated it—"

"Don't sell yourself so short," Astaroth interrupted. His grin was wickedly delighted as he turned his attention to Eleonore. "Lilith might have teleported him there, but Ben here tricked the witch into trusting him and abducted her all on his own."

Eleonore gasped. "You committed a crime?" she asked Ben. "For me?"

"For you," he confirmed. His blush crept past the edge of his beard. "Because I love you, Eleonore."

"Oh," she said softly. She pressed her palm to her chest as tears welled. What perfect words those were. Three quick syllables, simple to speak but holding a universe of meaning. "Je t'aime," she said in response. "Je t'adore. I love you, too."

Ben's grin spread across his face like a sunrise. He swept Eleonore into a fierce hug, lifting her off her feet. Then he put her back down, cupped her cheeks, and gave her the best kiss of her entire life.

Eleonore kissed him back, putting all her emotions into the movement of her lips. "I love you," she whispered against his mouth. "I'll tell you in every language I know, and then I'll learn how to say it in a dozen more."

"That is the sweetest thing I've ever heard," Ben said before kissing her so deeply he bent her backward over his arm.

Astaroth cleared his throat. "That feels like it ought to be my cue," he said. "Unfortunately, I'm a hopeless voyeur."

Ben brought her upright again, breaking away from her lips to glare at Astaroth. "Clear out, demon."

Astaroth chuckled. "All right, I'll give you some peace. But we still have a witch to dispose of and a curse to break, so you have ten minutes before I bring the group here to finish this off." He sheathed his cane sword, then sauntered off, whistling.

A muffled shriek came from the truck. Eleonore extended her middle finger in that direction, not bothering to look at Isobel. How could she when Ben's eyes were so warm and kind, when he'd told her he loved her? "Let's sit," she said, plopping down on the curb.

Ben followed, long legs sprawling before him. "I guess I should explain what happened."

Eleonore shook her head. "Lilith told me Isobel was casting a spell."

"Damn demoness stealing my thunder," he grumbled.

"Tell me anyway," Eleonore encouraged. She was impatient to get to the part where she apologized, but as she'd learned, there was merit in waiting and listening sometimes. She laced her fingers with his.

"Okay." Ben took a deep breath. "While you were talking to Isobel, I noticed her fingers moving at her side. And you know werewolf hearing is very good, better than most species. I heard her whispering under her breath. She was casting a spell." He shook his head. "I was terrified, Eleonore. I didn't know what she would do to you."

She could see the echo of that fear in his expression. He was always so open-faced and openhearted, his emotions written all over him.

"So I issued a command to get you to safety," he continued. "I'm sorry."

"It's all right," Eleonore said. "I understand, and I believe you." How could she have doubted him in the first place? He'd never been a great liar, but she'd somehow convinced herself otherwise during those moments of instinctive fear and rage. "I wonder what spell she was casting."

Ben winced. "Right after you left, a lightning bolt hit the spot where you were standing. You would have died."

At that, Eleonore whipped her head around to glare at the truck. Isobel's face was pressed to the glass, and Eleonore issued a hiss in that direction. "After all that talk of me being the only person she could watch *Star Trek* with," she said loudly enough for the witch to hear through the glass.

Isobel cringed.

"Weirdly," Ben said, "I think she actually believes all those things she said about you." He went on to quietly explain the details of his confrontation with Isobel, including the fact that she'd had a necromancer on speed dial and how she'd described Eleonore as her only friend.

Disgusted, Eleonore eyed the witch, who was now bumping her forehead against the window in a steady rhythm. It had long been obvious Isobel was time-maddened in the way of many ancient immortals, but while Eleonore had considered her terrifying and unpredictable, she now realized there was a sadder, more predictable truth.

"She's lonely," Eleonore said. "And pathetic."

So lonely she'd imprisoned a person to be her "friend." So pathetic she'd convinced herself she could kill that "friend," resurrect them, and carry on as if nothing had happened.

"It was all I could do not to flip the table when she kept talking about how much she cared about you." Ben shook his head. "That's not love. Nothing she's said or done is how love works."

Eleonore knew that. But for the first time, she felt not just burning, murderous hate toward the witch. She felt disdain . . . and a bitter sort of pity. The enormous, terrifying monster who had shaped her life had ended up being so very small, after all.

"What a miserable life she's led," Eleonore said. "She's commanded and killed and done horrible things to preserve her own eternal life, but what is there to preserve? She has no friends, no family, no love. And she can't face that truth, so she lies to herself." Hundreds, maybe thousands, of years of clinging to something not worth having.

"I have no sympathy for her," Ben said flatly.

"Me neither."

It didn't matter how much an abuser said they loved someone— or even if they truly *believed* they loved that person. An abuser would always consider themselves the hero or heroine of their own story. But their love was a broken facsimile of the real thing, not worth having, and it wasn't worth wasting time feeling sympathy for someone like that.

But recognizing how broken Isobel was, how small and lonely and grasping . . . Well, it was a new view that brought an odd sense of peace with it. Eleonore had been forced to obey this woman's commands for centuries. She'd lived in fear and fury, dreaming of an escape she'd been unable to seize.

Now Eleonore had escaped, and she finally saw Isobel as she was. Not a monster to be feared for eternity, but a miserable thing to be left behind as soon as they could convince her to break the spell. How they would manage that was still to be determined, but now that Eleonore saw Isobel plainly, she knew there would be a way.

Eleonore turned her back on the Witch in the Woods and focused on Ben. Away with her past; ahead with her future. "I'm sorry I left you in the forest without asking any questions," she said. "I was acting on instinct and anger."

Ben rubbed the back of his neck. "I mean, I did promise never to order you around again . . ."

Eleonore shook her head. "It's my turn to explain, please."

He nodded, earnest brown eyes fixed on her.

Eleonore took a deep breath. "When I was young, I trusted my clan. Loved them. We fought beside each other and fed each other and slept side by side, and I never once questioned that people could care for each other without conditions or ulterior motives." She swallowed, growing misty-eyed again. "I forgot what that felt like," she said, voice thickening. "My anger and distrust consumed me for so long, and then there you were: in the same position as Isobel when it came to my life, but wielding that power so differently. Not wielding it at all, actually, once you realized the terms. And deep down, I suppose I couldn't quite believe that was genuine."

It was Ben's turn to squeeze her hand, offering silent support. How wonderful this was. How much she had missed this.

"Even when I started trusting you, I didn't let myself trust all the way. I thought I had when we made love, but then at the cabin . . ." She shook her head. "I instantly assumed the worst. The first test of my trust, and I failed."

"You didn't fail," Ben said. He drew her in gently, then kissed her forehead. "Six hundred years is a long time to build habits."

"Well, I was unconscious for a lot of that—"

"However you define it, it was a long fucking time, Eleonore. If progress was a straight, easy line, we'd all be much less interesting people. This isn't simple, and it won't be simple going forward, and that's okay." He kissed her forehead again. "I'm here no matter what."

She liked him being there. She also liked having his mouth at her forehead and his arm around her, so she nestled in, cuddling close. "The light is most beautiful to those who know the dark," she said, remembering something her father had told her long ago. He'd always pushed himself to the limit of what his vampire body could take, standing at the keep window as the night turned purple and the pink line of dawn stretched across the sky. She'd stood at his side, watching the clouds grow orange and yellow, anticipating that first slice of pure sunlight when the world would be made anew. It had been beautiful, but never as beautiful to her as it had been to him.

Eleonore took a deep breath, filling her lungs with the crisp air of an autumn afternoon in a small town in the United States. She had forgotten the quiet wonder of sunrises and sunsets and the simplicity of closing her eyes and not entertaining a moment of doubt that the people at her side would protect her.

She'd forgotten what it was like to breathe easily.

"I want to start anew with you," she told Ben. "Even if the curse can't be broken right away. I want to love you and trust you and mix our lives however we can."

"I want that, too," Ben murmured against her hair. "But I fully intend on breaking that curse today—especially after I committed a felony for you."

That made Eleonore laugh. She tipped her head up and kissed him, pouring her love and fledgling trust into it. Maybe she would struggle to keep that trust steady over the years to come. She would definitely hiss at him sometimes. But she would put her heart and her effort into loving him as best she could, and even if progress wasn't a straight line, and even if she was never a soft or easy woman to live with, she'd strive to be better each day than she had been the last.

The sound of voices and footsteps approaching made Eleonore reluctantly draw away. Their ten minutes were up, and the Scooby gang had arrived to help with Isobel.

Eleonore stood, then extended a hand to help Ben up. Big and strong as he was, he didn't need it, but he took it anyway, grinning at her. They faced their friend group together—Mariel and Oz, Calladia and Astaroth, Themmie, Rani, Kai, Avram, and the odd combination of Lilith and Mariel's ancestor Alzapraz bringing up the rear.

"Yay!" Mariel said, clapping her hands. "They reconciled!"

"It was the grand gesture that did it," Lilith said confidently. "I expect offerings of gratitude."

Eleonore smiled up at Ben. "It wasn't the grand gesture that did it," she said. "It's Ben. Just as he is and however I can have him."

Astaroth opened his mouth, but Calladia elbowed him in the ribs before he could say something no doubt obnoxious.

"So how do we break the curse?" Mariel asked.

"The person who cast the spell must reverse it," Eleonore said. "Isobel has to cut her palm, and I will cut mine. Then we clasp hands while she speaks whatever the opposite of the binding spell is."

And there was the rub. Isobel wasn't the current owner of the stone, but she still had to agree to free Eleonore from Ben's power. Would she agree under torture? Or as a true immortal, would she wait out the decades until Ben was gone and the crystal—and Eleonore—fell back into her possession?

Eleonore looked over at Isobel again . . . and saw the witch staring back, an unreadable expression in her eyes.

FORTY

As lilith hauled isobel out of the truck none too
gently, Ben grabbed Eleonore's hand again, giving her a look
that promised they were in this together, no matter what.

He felt calmer with her at his side. Centered. The anxious
thoughts that normally circulated in his head like wind-swirled
leaves had settled, and though the situation was a tense one, he
knew they would end up okay so long as they worked as a team.

Eleonore pulled the gag from Isobel's mouth. The witch spit on
the pavement a few times, clearing the saliva that had accumu-
lated. "Hello, Eleonore," she said, giving a weak smile.

Eleonore looked unimpressed. "Are you actually going to lift
the spell this time or do I have to torture you?"

Isobel turned beseeching eyes on Ben. "I thought you were going to sell me the crystal."

"I lied," he said. "You will never, ever get your hands on that
crystal so long as I live."

Isobel frowned. "But I miss her," she said plaintively.

"Seriously?" Themmie asked. "Holy gaslighting gremlins."

Ben made a shushing motion toward his friends. "We've got this."

He wasn't sure how yet, but with Eleonore at his side and his potential for action proven, Ben had less room in his head to entertain catastrophes. He studied the witch with narrowed eyes, considering what might convince her to lift the spell.

Eleonore had her own idea. She pulled a knife out of her thigh holster and licked it in a move Ben was not at all prepared for. "My knife hasn't tasted blood in far too long," she said. "Perhaps today will be the day it drinks its fill."

"Oh, sick," Calladia said from behind them.

Ben concurred. He'd need to ask Eleonore to do that again in private so he could properly appreciate it. However, right now he couldn't shake the feeling there was a less messy method that would yield the same results and not end in a prison sentence.

Isobel's eyes darted as if charting exit routes. "Well, I have a lot of people you can kill," she said hopefully. "Now that I'm immortal we can do it together, if you like."

Eleonore hissed, and Ben nudged her shoulder. "Maybe pause on the torture talk for a second," he whispered. "I'm thinking."

"Better you than me," she muttered back.

Eleonore would always be the action star of the two of them, which was good. While Ben was pleased to know he could be a werewolf of action, that was a lot of pressure and not his natural mode. Instead, he focused on what he did best: overthinking the situation.

Except maybe he didn't need to overthink this one at all.

Lying to Isobel had worked once before, and as the saying went, "If it ain't broke, don't fix it." Except this time, Eleonore would need to be the one putting on the performance.

Ben whispered his idea in her ear. She grimaced initially, but when he finished, she nodded. "You're right," she whispered back.

"It's worth a try." She closed her eyes. "It's just like the theatre. Just like the theatre."

Ben knew she loathed lying. He did, too. But Eleonore was very, very good at acting.

Eleonore took a deep breath. Then her shoulders settled, and she looked at Isobel again. If Ben didn't know Eleonore hated this woman with her entire heart, he would have found the sad look on her face convincing. "Ben says I should tell you the truth," she said. "You know my torture threats weren't serious some of the time, right?"

Isobel nodded. "We were having fun. I know."

There was some uncomfortable shuffling and a few low murmurs from the Scooby gang, but Ben ignored them.

"If we're going to find a way forward, though," Eleonore continued, "I have to tell the truth. No jokes or fun."

"No jokes or fun," Isobel said. "I understand." She looked so pathetically hopeful; she must really believe this could end with them reunited.

Eleonore inclined her head. "Thank you for offering to kill people with me. That always bothered me: that you had me do all those things *for* you. Not *with* you."

"Uh, what?" Themmie asked, but at Ben's sharp look, she snapped her mouth shut.

"My body was weak then," Isobel explained. "You've always been so strong."

"I know. But still, don't you understand how that made me feel? I went from being part of a clan that fought together to fighting with no one by my side." Eleonore shook her head. "We weren't equals. I was under your control, and you *didn't even fight at my side.*"

There was a silent moment while Isobel took this in. She looked so frail with her arms bound behind her back and her black hair

tangled, utterly fixated on the person she'd cared for and hurt beyond reason. A different sort of monster than the ones childhood
fables warned of, and one that needed to be defeated with something other than a sword.

"That's why you hated being an assassin?" Isobel finally asked.
"Because I didn't kill with you?"

"Yes, that's exactly why," Eleonore said, and Ben would nomi-
nate her for an Oscar if he could. "I care for Ben because he's my
partner. My equal. We trust each other—but you made it impossible for me to trust you."

Isobel had begun breathing more rapidly. The expression in
her dark eyes was stark. "You could learn to trust me."

"Not with the spell in place." Eleonore bit her lip. "You know,"
she said after a heavy pause, "you don't have to imprison people to
make them your friends."

And there was the bait, attached to the hook.

You can make her think you could still be friends, Ben had suggested. *You could give her hope.*

Eleonore had taken his suggestions and run with them, mixing
truth and lies into the performance of a lifetime. He couldn't
imagine what it cost for her to confront her abuser like this and
pretend there could still be affection between them.

Isobel looked confused. "But how do you stop them from running away?"

Eleonore shrugged. "You have to trust them." She gestured at
the people arrayed around them. "I haven't imprisoned a single
one of these people, and they're still here to support me. Ben even
kidnapped you without me asking him to."

Isobel's eyes widened. "Really?"

"Really," Eleonore confirmed. "What I'm saying is that we can
still be friends, but not with this curse hanging over me. I need
you to free me."

Ben squeezed his toes in his shoes, silently begging Isobel to take the bait.

The witch hesitated, looking torn. "But we've been through so much together."

"And you'll go through so much more once I'm free," Eleonore said soothingly. "It'll be new and interesting, don't you think?" She was laying it on thick, with only the white-knuckled clench of her hand to indicate how much she absolutely did not mean those kind words.

Isobel paused for what felt like an eternity. And then . . .

"Will you still watch *Star Trek* with me?" she asked.

A muscle in Eleonore's cheek flickered as she clenched her jaw. "Of cour—"

"I'll watch *Star Trek* with you," Lilith interrupted, jostling Isobel. "Janeway is so hot, am I right? Definitely the best captain."

Isobel twitched like she'd forgotten anyone else was there. She looked over her shoulder at the demoness. "Janeway *is* hot," she said. "But Sisko committed war crimes."

Lilith nodded thoughtfully. "Good point. Maybe we can do a rewatch to decide who's the best captain. Or we can duel over it—whoever draws first blood gets to decide. That's what *friends* do, right?"

Complicated emotions flashed over Isobel's face—hope and wariness among them. "I'm immortal now," she said to no one in particular. "I can probably duel."

Lilith grinned and snapped her teeth. "Oh, good. I've been looking for an outlet."

Ben coughed into his fist. Lilith's idea of a fun outlet would probably not be what Isobel was envisioning.

"You can have so many friends," Eleonore said. "But not if you treat them the way you've treated me. So how about lifting the curse so we can both start over?"

Ben held his breath, hoping this was enough. Hoping it would accomplish what threats hadn't.

Isobel bit her lip. "Well . . . all right."

Eleonore swayed at the announcement, and Ben wanted to pump his fist and howl at the sky.

A dusty throat-clearing came from nearby. Alzapraz had hobbled forward. "If you don't mind," he said, "I'd like to observe in case she tries any trickery."

"Alzapraz!" Isobel cried out. "I didn't see you behind that oversized werewolf. It's been far too long."

Alzapraz eyed her. "Has it?"

Lilith released Isobel's cuffs, and Ben braced himself in case the witch tried to run or cast a spell. But Isobel just rubbed her wrists, looking at Eleonore contemplatively. "Does anyone have a knife for the blood sacrifice?"

Eleonore grabbed one from her thigh holster and handed it over. "Here."

Isobel drew a slashing line across her palm, then shook it so blood spattered on the pavement. The wound healed almost immediately, and she had to repeat the cut three times before she'd created a circle large enough for two people to stand in. She stepped into the circle, then gestured for Eleonore to join her.

Eleonore looked up at Ben. "Hopefully she doesn't try to electrocute me this time."

"Alzapraz won't let her," he promised, though he was sweating with nerves. He bent his head and kissed her. "I love you," he whispered against her lips.

"I love you, too."

Then Eleonore stepped into the circle. Her hair began whipping in a sudden wind. Isobel's dress and hair rippled, too, as if a cyclone was spiraling to life within the boundary of blood.

Isobel held out the knife, and Eleonore mirrored the cut on her own palm. Then Isobel reached out her bloody hand. Eleonore hesitated before clasping it.

Isobel began speaking a series of complicated spellwords and drawing runes in the air with her free hand. As she chanted, light rose from the bloody circle, a wall of shimmering blue, white, and gold that obscured the two from view. It was nearly impossible to stay still, but Alzapraz looked unconcerned, so Ben gritted his teeth and waited.

There was a sound like an army's worth of swords clanging, and then came the scent of cold steel and a forest in winter. The light whipped away as if blown by the wind, revealing Isobel and Eleonore, still clasping hands. The blood had burned into the ground, leaving a black, jagged mark on the sidewalk.

Eleonore shuddered and grabbed her chest with her free hand. Ben lurched forward, but Alzapraz made a cautioning motion. "Wait," he said.

This was torture. Ben dug his nails into his palms, sweating and praying to anything that might be listening that Eleonore was okay. That she was free at last.

Isobel let Eleonore go and swayed, looking wan.

"Was that it?" Mariel asked.

Alzapraz smiled and nodded. "That was it."

Eleonore turned to face Ben, and he caught his breath. Her alabaster skin was flushed and glowing with health, and her grin was even brighter. She jumped up and down and clapped her hands. "I'm free!" she said. "Gods, I'm free at last."

He surged toward her, and she met him halfway. They embraced on the sidewalk, arms wrapped tightly around each other, bodies fused as their mouths met in the most perfect kiss this world or any other had seen. He tasted their joy in the salt-wet of relieved tears—his and hers as they wept out the fears of the past to make space for something new.

Eleonore pulled back before Ben was ready. He tried to chase her mouth, but she shook her head, eyes sparkling. "Give me an order."

"Kiss me again," he said.

She did, and his stomach dropped.

Then she laughed. "Not that order. I'm going to do that anyway. Order me to do something strange."

He was tempted to order her to make love to him right here and now, but Eleonore might actually take him up on that, and he would rather keep her all to himself somewhere private. "Eleonore Bettencourt-Devereux," he said, "I order you to do a handstand and sing the ABCs backward."

She wrinkled her nose at him, utterly adorable. "Not a chance."

Ben whooped and punched the air at that. Then he grabbed her again, kissing her and kissing her and kissing her while their friends cheered and provided unnecessary commentary.

He only stopped once their mouths were swollen and slick. He rested his forehead against hers, their breath mingling in the small space between them. "No more orders," he whispered. "Just a question. Eleonore Bettencourt-Devereux, will you stay here in Glimmer Falls with me? Will you be my partner and my love?"

Someday soon he'd ask her another question, but that one required pomp and circumstance and definitely a cake. Weddings were no longer on Ben Rosewood's list of Things To Avoid If At All Possible.

Eleonore ran her fingers through his hair, then settled them at the base of his neck, nails scratching lightly. "I will," she said. "And happily."

EPILOGUE

Two months later

ELEONORE SAT NEXT TO BEN ON THE COUCH, LEGS CURLED under her and head resting on his shoulder. They'd hosted their first backyard barbecue to show off their newly redecorated home. It was no longer a bachelor's minimalistic, peeling-paint den but something brightly colored and cozy, with details that reflected both of them—plants in the windows, a sword collection on the bedroom wall, and bookshelves full of tomes about everything from horticulture to ancient history.

Eleonore sometimes couldn't believe she was free to make a home, but she was. The curse was broken, and she didn't have to worry about the Witch in the Woods ever again. Isobel wasn't gone entirely, but she no longer had power over Eleonore. A mystically enforced restraining order kept her far away, and Eleonore had retained a lawyer to explore other possibilities for legal action.

Had Eleonore yanked out the witch's intestines and knitted a hat from them? No, but strangely, she didn't mind that so much. Her life of violence was over.

It might not be the vengeance she'd imagined, but when Mariel had shared the adage "The best revenge is living well," Eleonore had instantly understood. Isobel didn't *deserve* Eleonore's time or emotion, and Eleonore didn't have room for that hate amid the love filling her life.

That said, it had been gratifying to learn Isobel was suffering a bit. Lilith had gleefully taken on the role of Isobel's new "friend" and was harassing her at every hour. If Isobel was crazy, Lilith was exhibiting the demon equivalent of what Themmie called "hold-my-beer energy." Even if the two of them ended up enjoying *Star Trek* together—when Lilith wasn't popping up in the middle of the night to scare Isobel or brutally beating her in duels—Eleonore wouldn't care. She had better things—and better people—to focus on.

Speaking of those people, their friends—Mariel, Oz, Rani, Themmie, Astaroth, Calladia, and Gigi—were currently sprawled around the room in various states of drunkenness and food coma while a TV newscaster discussed the latest happenings in Glimmer Falls.

"The blaze started at two a.m. Thankfully, a frost fairy contingent was out late drinking at Le Chapeau Magique, and their quick reaction froze City Hall before the flames could spread." The newscaster had a look of barely contained excitement on her face—a clear sign she had more to say on the subject and it was going to be juicy. "In their drunken enthusiasm, however, the fairies also froze the surrounding area—including the arsonist, who was found half a block away, encased in ice with a gasoline can in hand."

"Who cares?" Themmie shouted, waving her alcoholic milkshake. "Get to the good stuff!"

Gigi laughed from where she sat on Ben's other side. "Just wait." She wore the hat Ben had knitted her for Christmas, which was topped by a pink yarn pom-pom.

"To everyone's shock, the arsonist was revealed as none other than former mayor Cynthia Cunnington. She was thawed and taken to the police station, where she drunkenly confessed to lighting the fire."

"Oh, shit!" Themmie shot upright, nearly colliding with the ceiling as her wings thrummed frantically. "Cynthia did it?"

"She sure did," Calladia said. The blond witch was nestled in Astaroth's embrace, the two of them sharing a velvet armchair Eleonore had purchased with some of her performance money. Calladia looked rueful but not overly upset. "Not that I'm necessarily rooting for my mother to go to prison, but honestly, it might do her some good."

"Apparently the former mayor was drinking on the eve of her opponent Gigi Rosewood's inauguration," the newscaster continued. "She doused the grounds of City Hall in gasoline, then lit it with a spell. She also confessed to two other unsolved crimes in Glimmer Falls—the magical assaults on Mayor Gigi Rosewood's campaign rallies."

"Booooo," Gigi called out, cupping her mouth.

"Hello, Captain Obvious," Mariel said. She was leaning against Oz's chest where he stood at the wall, and a few margaritas had turned the witch red-cheeked and giggly. "Who else would have done that?"

"Hear, hear," Rani said, raising her wineglass. "We could have told them that months ago."

The newscaster was practically bouncing up and down in excitement. "Cynthia Cunnington has since sobered up, gotten a lawyer, and denied the allegations, but the damage is done. The only question is what sort of jail time the ex-mayor might face for her crimes. This is Artemis Crumpet, reporting live from the impromptu ice-skating rink outside City Hall."

Eleonore nuzzled Ben's shoulder with her nose. "Remind me never to drink alcohol before committing a crime."

He looked down at her. "How about not committing any crimes?"

She poked him in the abdomen. "Says the man who committed a felony for me." She was giddy and flushed from an evening that had started with drinking Ben's blood and fucking his brains out before the guests arrived and was now wrapping up with several glasses of wine. She felt full, slightly dizzy, and so content she might melt into the couch.

"Thanks, Artemis," the studio anchor said. "Now on to today's big story—the inauguration of Mayor Gigi Rosewood."

"Woohoo!" Gigi said, sloshing the margarita as she waved her arms. Eleonore laughed, wiping stray drops from her cheek. Thank goodness for witches and their cleaning spells.

"Shhhhh," Themmie said, listing to the side before righting herself midair. Eleonore eyed the ceiling fan, wondering if someone should shoo the pixie away from it with a broom. "I wanna hear."

Despite the fears Ben had confided to Eleonore, Gigi cursing at Cynthia Cunnington had given her a boost in the polls, and she'd won the election by a decent margin. The inauguration that morning had been fun, with the entire gang showing up in bright pink shirts and waving flags. Gigi had given a magnificent speech about progress and the bonds of community while Ben and his parents wept all over themselves.

Overall, the future of Glimmer Falls looked bright.

"There was a record turnout for Gigi Rosewood's inauguration outside City Hall," the anchor said. "She enters office with the highest favorability rating of any mayor since the town's founding."

The broadcast cut to a clip of Gigi's speech, and Eleonore grinned as she spied Ben at the edge of the frame, beaming through his tears. She kissed his cheek, then settled back in at his side.

The feature was brief, and Eleonore reached for the remote when the anchor started talking about the unionization of a local coffee shop. "Anyone up for some *Star Trek*?" she asked.

"Hang on," Ben said, snatching the remote from her hand. "I

heard there's an interesting segment coming up about the local arts scene."

Eleonore sat bolt upright. "Wait, that's tonight?"

Mariel and Oz looked at her curiously. "What's tonight?" Mariel asked.

Eleonore pressed a hand to her chest where her heart tapped an excited rhythm. "There was a reporter at my last show. They interviewed me."

"Sick!" Gigi said, bouncing on the couch. "Damn, we should have recorded this newscast."

"Already on it," Ben said. "I'll make DVDs for everyone."

"A *DVD*?" Themmie asked, sounding appalled. "How old do you think I am?"

The rest of the group ignored her, leaning in and watching the screen avidly.

"—Finally, our arts correspondent, Cornelius Crabapple, sat down for an exclusive interview with local theatrical phenomenon Eleonore Bettencourt-Devereux."

The screen switched to a view of Eleonore seated opposite the faun. Cornelius worked for both the *Glimmer Falls Gazette* and the local news station, and he'd been her most regular audience member—aside from Ben, of course.

"Eleonore," the faun said, "I hear you got some good news the other day. Care to share?"

Eleonore's cheeks felt hot. She hadn't told anyone but Ben about this, and she couldn't wait to see her friends' reactions.

How amazing it was that they were *her* friends now, not just Ben's. She hugged them and everything. After six hundred years, she was finally a member of a clan again.

"I am proud to announce a limited artist residency with Seattle's premier experimental theatre company, the Wacky Warlocks," the Eleonore on TV said. "I'm also working with a producer to expand the show, with hopes of eventually bringing it to New York."

The room erupted in a cacophony of noise.

"Whaaaaat?"

"Congratulations!"

"Bitch, that's great!"

"Hecate, I'm so excited!"

"Remember us when you're famous, please."

"I want an autograph!"

Eleonore laughed as the exclamations overlapped one another. "New York is a long way off, if it happens at all," she said, wanting to temper expectations. "This is only the first step to bringing it to a larger stage."

She loved acting. Every week she discovered something new—a new emotion, a new dance move, a new nuance to her own words. Even new interpretations of "Barbie Girl" by Aqua. The play was a living, breathing, horrifically bloody thing, and she was so proud.

She nudged Ben. "Thanks for ordering me to put on a show," she said.

Gigi lightly punched Ben's shoulder. "Yeah, thanks for totally lying about what was going on with Eleonore and then panicking and accidentally creating a theatrical phenomenon."

Ben looked suitably embarrassed as everyone laughed. "You're welcome. I will strive to always be just as anxious and awkward."

"With results like this," Gigi said, "who can complain?"

"Not me," Eleonore whispered, pecking Ben on the cheek again. "You're perfect."

"Not perfect," he whispered back. "Remember this morning when I nearly had a panic attack because I couldn't find my Gigi Rosewood campaign T-shirt?"

He hadn't been able to find it because Eleonore had tossed it behind the headboard during a prior lovemaking session. Oops. She'd found it and soothed her werewolf with a blanket burrito, sitting in his lap and hugging his swaddled form until he'd started breathing deeply again. "You're perfect if I say you're perfect," she said. "I love you just the way you are."

His eyes crinkled behind his glasses. He tapped her nose with his finger. "I love you just the way you are, too."

He would always be anxious and prone to overwork, and he might never love howling and scratching himself on the full moon. She would always be impulsive and too literal, and she might never stop hissing or menacing misbehaving kitchen objects. But their rough edges fit together, and what more could a person want? Eleonore was no longer bound by the curse. She could stay in one place and one time long enough to squeeze all the enjoyment out of it, and she would grow old at Ben's side happily and messily.

"A toast!" Calladia announced, raising her margarita. Astaroth mirrored the movement with his glass of red wine. "To Gigi Rosewood, the kickass new mayor of Glimmer Falls."

"To Eleonore," Gigi said, "the most exciting and unusual theatrical performer this town has ever seen."

"To the Scooby gang," Eleonore said, hoisting her glass, "for being the best, most supportive, strangest bunch of people I've had the fortune to know."

"I have a toast, too," Oz said. He smiled down at Mariel. "To love."

"To love," Ben echoed. "In all its weird and wonderful aspects."

"To love!" the group shouted in unison.

Eleonore could drink to that.

ACKNOWLEDGMENTS

Three books! How is that possible???

As always, I am tremendously grateful to my agent, Jessica Watterson: thank you for being my biggest champion. Thank you to Cindy Hwang, editor extraordinaire, for your enthusiasm and excellent feedback. All my gratitude to the rest of the Penguin Random House team: Jessica Mangicaro, Stephanie Felty, Angela Kim, Elizabeth Vinson, Stacy Edwards, Shana Jones, Tawanna Sullivan, Daniel Brount, Sierra Machado, and everyone else at Berkley who was involved in getting this book to print. For the UK edition, thank you to the wonderful Áine Feeney, Javerya Iqbal, and Jenna Petts, as well as the rest of the Gollancz team.

The covers for this series are gorgeous—I'm beyond grateful to illustrator Jess Miller and art director Katie Anderson for the US version, as well as illustrator Dawn Cooper and senior designer Jessica Hart for the UK version. You knocked it out of the park, and I'm a very lucky author to have my words packaged up so beautifully.

Thank you so much to the booksellers and librarians who have championed this series. I'm especially grateful to Village Books for their support and for coordinating the preorder campaigns. (As well as for a great launch party and some delicious cookies!)

Thank you to Celia Winter for the beta read. Your insights are always incredible, and this book is much better after your feedback. Thank you as well to the Berkletes, the Words Are Hard crew, and the SDLA Sisters for being so encouraging during this long, often stressful writing journey. Thank you also to the Wicked Wallflowers Coven and the Reylos, two other communities who have lifted me up over the years.

My love of theatre is long-standing, and I'm appreciative of everyone who nourished that love and thereby enabled Eleonore in her questionable dramatic choices, with a special thanks to Ms. Buster and Thespian Troupe 879, Musical Theatre Southwest, and the Bellingham Theatre Guild.

I have such a wonderful family. Thank you to my parents for the enthusiastic support and for introducing me to *Star Trek* at a formative age, to Steve and Mahina and the kids for being unending sources of love and interesting conversation, to Cory and Laura for fielding my random text inquiries about Canada, to Sandy for helping me with Spanish, and to the rest of the family for being such funny, informative, and creative people.

I'm lucky not just in my family but in my friends. Thank you to Blaise for advising me on mayoral elections and thus lending a thin veneer of legitimacy to the political subplot (all errors, exaggerations, and 69 jokes are entirely mine). Thanks to Jon and Bronwyn for all the good conversation over the years; I hope you, Rupert, and Wesley enjoyed the meal in Glimmer Falls. Thanks to Brittany for teaching me about plants, to Jeeno and Celia for being my knitting consultants, and to Amy and Caitlin for all the fun we had in high school theatre. A massive thank-you to Sarah Tarkoff— you're brilliant and talented, and I'm lucky to get to collaborate creatively with you. And to Fancy Drunk Lady Book Club—can you believe it's been ten years??? Thanks for all the food, laughter, and excellent book conversations. I'm grateful to more people than I can name here, so I'm sending all my love to everyone who has filled my life with such creativity and happiness.

Finally, thank you to every reader who has picked up a Glimmer Falls book. I hope you found joy in these pages.

*Keep reading for an excerpt
from the first book in a new fantasy
series by Sarah Hawley . . .*

SERVANT
OF EARTH

THE WINTER SOLSTICE CREPT IN COLD, WET, AND HEAVY with dread.

I looked out at the predawn darkness, tracing my finger over the frosted patterns that coated the exterior of the window. A wintry draft slithered through the gap where the wooden frame had warped with age. As the wind surged outside, drops of icy rain smacked against the glass.

Another drop of frigid water splatted on my forehead. I yelped, then scowled up at the roof. This leak was new—I'd already been awoken unpleasantly by the one that had formed directly over my mattress during the night—and it was just one more sign of everything wrong in my life. I wouldn't have the money to replace the thatching for a long time, if ever, so I grabbed a bucket and put it under the leak. Soon I wouldn't need to go to the well for my water anymore.

As I straightened, a glow through the window caught my eye. In the distance, a golden faerie light shivered through the darkness.

Its path was uneven, made more so by the warped glass. As I watched it move, my chest tightened with worry.

The winter solstice wasn't just the shortest day of the year; it was the day the Fae took yet another thing from humans. A faith that yielded no rewards, prayers that met uncaring ears, a legendary history that had decayed into this disappointing reality . . . We gave the faeries our hopes, and for what? Silence and far-off lights that led nowhere.

And now the Fae—or at least our naive belief in them—would steal the lives of four young women.

"You don't deserve any of it," I whispered as I watched the drifting orb.

My mother would have chastised me for the blasphemous words. "Only the luckiest and most worthy humans are chosen to join the Fae," she'd told me fifteen years ago as she unsnarled the tangles in my hair with a wooden comb. It had been another winter solstice morning—a sacrifice year, like this one—and I'd just turned eight. "Those women are favored above all other mortals, and they live out the rest of their lives in splendor in Mistei, the faeries' kingdom under the ground."

There was longing in her voice whenever she'd told me that story. She hadn't been chosen for the Fae during the solstice ritual when she came of age. Life had pushed a different fate on her, and there I was as the result: a ragged child held in her equally threadbare embrace, my father long gone and rain dripping through the roof onto the packed-earth floor of our hut. Still, she'd passed the fables on to me, as if through hearing them maybe I'd one day be granted the blessings life had denied her.

I didn't believe in blessings anymore.

Another drop plinked into the bucket. I made a rude hand gesture at the distant will-o'-the-wisp, then turned my back on it and began my preparations for the day.

The wash basin still held leftover water from the previous

night. I splashed it onto my face, gasping at the shock of cold. Then I scrubbed my teeth and changed my nightdress for a loose shirt and trousers. The day would be a busy one—it was not only a sacrifice year but the first time I'd be eligible—and I didn't want to miss my favorite morning ritual.

The one-room hut was dark, but I knew the layout by heart. I stepped around the small table and two mismatched chairs that served as a sitting area, making my way to the scarred wooden table by the hearth. Bundles of herbs hung overhead, along with a few withered onions. Anya had given me some cheese the last time we'd gone for a walk together, so I cut off a piece and shoved it in my mouth before grabbing my cloak and heading outside.

The rain had thankfully stopped, but the mossy ground was slick and rimed with overnight frost. The snows would come soon, but we were still in the first month of winter with its glittering mornings and spats of icy rain. As I rounded the corner of the hut, the wind grabbed at my messy braid, trying to rip the brown curls loose.

The sky was purpling to the east, the blackness of night slipping away. The wood-and-stone buildings and thatched roofs of Tumbledown stood against the lightening sky like crooked teeth, and smoke began drifting from chimneys as the town woke.

The town wasn't my aim, though. My mornings were dedicated to the bog.

Enterra was curved like an hourglass with a longer and wider lower part, and the bog banded the country like a lady's belt, with Tumbledown its buckle. Just north of my hut, the shrubbed land merged into a vast, glassy wet expanse dotted with low mounds of earth and plant matter. Thick fog sprawled across it, obscuring the far side where the land became faerie territory. Dozens of will-o'-the-wisps drifted through that fog, the floating orbs fading as dawn grew closer.

I watched the lights dim and go out one by one, and a familiar sadness settled alongside my lingering anxiety. On solstice mornings my mother's presence felt especially close. Her faith that she could become one of the Fae's favored ones had never faltered. Supposedly the Fae used to travel across the bog to trade with, seek entertainment from, or rain blessings down on humans—and occasionally abduct those they took a liking to—but now the eerie lights that drifted across the wetlands at night were the only sign they even existed.

Loving the Fae hadn't brought my mother any joy. Yet when she'd died eighteen months back, feverish and agonized, her last words had been for them: "Maybe now they will save me."

They hadn't, of course.

I filled my lungs with icy predawn air, willing my bitterness to wait a few hours. The morning was beautiful, and there were treasures to be found. When pink tinged the eastern sky, the last golden wisp disappeared, and I retrieved my net from a hollow log and wound my way out into the bog.

Most people were too afraid to come here. It was easy to get lost and drown; the ground between pools of water was deceptive, and more often than not what looked like solid earth was actually a pit of mud waiting to suck a traveler down. There were legends, too, of knuckers and other Nasties that lurked in the fens and wet places of the world, eager to rend the flesh of those who misstepped.

I'd spent my entire life at the edge of the bog, though, and I never misstepped—nor had I seen evidence of dragons under the water. The marsh had been my haven for as long as I could remember; a place to be alone and free.

I took familiar twisting paths until a stretch of water blocked any further progress. Then I sat on a tussock of pale winter grass, my feet inches from a patch of clover that hid the edge of a pool, and dipped my net in.

"Fishing" was what my mother had called this odd habit of mine, though I privately thought of it as "collecting." My mother's stories had sparked my interest in the border between humans and the Fae, and the bog's secrets had been so tempting that I'd attached a net to a long wooden pole, determined to see what rested at the bottom.

As it turned out, any number of wonders were hidden in the muck and silt. Smooth skipping stones, carved talismans, even coins tossed in by lovers who braved the treacherous paths to prove their courage and commitment to each other. They wished on coppers, hoping the Fae would bless their union. The Fae didn't care, but I certainly blessed them for it. I'd even found what I thought were faerie artifacts before—pieces of faceted glass or strange twists of bright metal. I'd run my fingers over the objects, thinking about who might have crafted them in the distant past and what their purpose had been. Letting the wonder of my mother's stories slip back into me, if only for a few hours.

Something caught at my net, and I grunted as I jerked it free. The object that came up with the muck was brown and misshapen. "Please don't be something disgusting," I said under my breath as I tipped the blob out onto the grass. Artifacts weren't the only things hidden below; there were occasional bones, too, and in a thick, foul-smelling pool deep in the bog, I'd once found a shriveled hand still covered in leathery skin.

When the bog took, it was greedy.

I wiped away the slimy mud. Not a bone, thankfully. Just a rock. I threw it back in with a plunking splash and fished for more.

I was trying not to think about what awaited later that day, but the memory of that severed hand was making me fret about the solstice sacrifice again. The odds of being selected were minimal, but I wasn't the only one eligible this year—my best friend, Anya, was as well, and she was all I had left in the world. Supposedly the will-o'-the-wisps would lead the chosen women to Mistei, but I'd stopped believing that a long time ago. Probably the first morning I'd fished up a human bone.

I squeezed my eyes shut and focused on my breathing. "This is my place," I said softly. The Fae didn't get to taint everything, and there were still hours left before the ritual.

The rising sun spilled rosy golden light across the landscape, and the fog began to clear. I scooped another stone out of the water and tossed it back. Found a single copper and wiped it dry on my cloak before stuffing it in a pocket. My net didn't pull up anything but thick, slimy mud after that—much of which splattered over my already stained clothes—so I shifted to a different spot and tried again. This time I found a wooden doll the size of my index finger, its face carved with a carefree smile. It had tiny horns that signified it as an Underfae, a type of faerie that was lower in status than the Noble Fae who ruled Mistei.

"Look at you," I whispered, enchanted by the figurine in my palm. This was the sort of treasure I loved most—the kind that made me wonder and imagine. Who had it belonged to, and how had it been lost? It had probably been dropped on accident by an adventurous child from the village, the kind who—like me—had decided to test their mettle on the dangerous paths.

But maybe . . . maybe a Fae child had walked here, instead. Maybe this doll was a thousand years old, a well-preserved remnant of a time when our two species mingled freely and the paths across the bog were clear and well trodden.

I tucked the doll into my pocket before I could start speculating about more tragic reasons it might be here. This was already a more productive morning than most, and I considered ending my collecting expedition on a triumphant note. But the low sun sparked off the water and the world felt free and empty in a rare way, so I slid the pole back into the water. One more try, and then

I would pack up and return to the worries and responsibilities awaiting me.

My net met resistance in the thick mud at the bottom of the pond. When I pulled it free, I could tell I'd caught something substantial. I thought it was a rock at first, but when the net emerged from the water, it contained the most beautiful dagger I'd ever seen.

I gasped, pressing a hand to my mouth. The steel blade and wire-wrapped hilt gleamed in the dawn light, and the pommel was capped with a large crimson jewel. Its shine was unnatural: no mud clung to the weapon, and there wasn't a trace of rust on the blade.

My heart pounded as I pulled it from the net. It was heavy, yet the hilt fit my hand perfectly. Had it belonged to some wealthy lady, or even a faerie? The double-edged blade was wickedly sharp, and the scrollwork on the guard looked ancient and arcane. The bloodred stone capping the pommel was the strangest of all. I hadn't seen many jewels in my life, but the few I had seen had been starbright and faceted. This was a perfectly smooth semicircle, and the dull orb seemed to absorb light rather than reflect it.

I glanced over my shoulder, suddenly afraid that someone had seen me find it, but I was still alone.

This dagger would fetch a fortune. A real fortune, not just the meager coins I earned selling peat and bog trinkets at market. It would be a life-changing amount of money.

For a moment I let myself imagine a future where I was rich and free. I could leave Tumbledown and its small-minded judgments, find a new place to live where I wasn't known as the herbwoman's wild daughter. No more leaking roof, no more nights where my belly echoed with hunger. No more despair as I imagined my life unfolding just like this day after day until I eventually died impoverished and alone the way my mother had. I could become a trader, passing spices and handicrafts between Enterra and other countries, getting to hold and study artifacts that told stories of other legends and other ways of life. Maybe I'd even visit those places someday: cross the western mountains to icy Grimveld and forested Lindwic, then on to other countries I didn't know the names of yet.

Anya could come with me, too—she wouldn't have to marry just to ensure her future. She could take painting lessons, maybe even illuminate manuscripts the way she'd wanted to since she was a girl. We could be new people, unbeholden to anyone or anything but ourselves.

Dreams were nothing but air, though, and real change took more than just hope. Still, my hands trembled as I wrapped the dagger in the folds of my cloak.

I returned to the shore shortly afterwards, unable to focus on anything else.

My hut rose from the mist at the edge of the bog, looking like a boulder with its squat stone walls and inelegant structure. My parents had built the rough house together by hand when they'd first settled here. It wasn't beautiful, but it had stood for over twenty years. Stacks of peat brick—my meager source of income—leaned against the wall, waiting for the next time I could take a full barrow into town.

I paused, considering my options. This dagger was so obviously expensive that I couldn't risk anyone else seeing it. I needed to sell it quickly, and the solstice festival with its crowd of tourists was the perfect time.

I tore a long strip off the bottom of my shirt and wrapped the blade tightly. Then I slid the dagger inside the waistband of my trousers, strapping it to my thigh with the thin leather tie that had secured my braid. My curls sprang free, wild as ever.

There were other things I wanted to sell at market, so I hiked to my secret hiding place: a small cave in a rocky outcropping. The entrance was so short I had to crawl through. Once inside, the space was tall enough to stand in and several body lengths wide.

Every available surface was covered with treasure. Not gold or jewels, of course; if I'd found any, I would have sold them immediately. The objects here were more mundane: simple stone tools, useless household objects, a collection of unusually colored rocks. Each item had been collected from the bog, and each was precious to me. There was the wooden cup that had been one of my first finds. A rusty nail. A chunk of rose quartz. Each object told a story: of the morning when I'd found it, of the people or animals of the unknown past, of the bog and me.

I set the figurine down next to a battered metal cup, then moved to the corner that held things to sell at market. My basket held a rabbit pelt from my last hunt and some faerie fruit I'd harvested the day before. The pebbled blue spheres would fetch a decent price, either from a visiting lady unfamiliar with their bitterness or from the vintner at the top of the hill who would turn it into hallucinatory faerie wine. I grabbed the basket, then headed back towards the entrance.

As I crouched to leave, there was a sharp pain at my right thigh. I yelped. "Damn!"

The dagger must have cut through the bindings. I hurriedly stripped my trousers off, exposed skin pebbling with gooseflesh, then unstrapped the dagger and examined the cut. Luckily, it was superficial: a bleeder, but one that would heal quickly.

The knife edge was clean.

I frowned, inspecting it more closely. Shouldn't there be a trace of blood on the blade? Instead, it shone bright and silver as the moon. I tested the edge gently on my thumb, gasping when it immediately sliced through the skin. My blood slid along the edge of the dagger. Then, as if drawn by some mystical force, it ran *up* from the edge towards a narrow groove in the center of the blade. It sank into the groove like rain into soil.

"How is that possible?" Surely I hadn't seen right. There was no way my blood had just . . . disappeared.

I etched another shallow slice in my thumb, wincing at the sting. Again the blood crawled up from the edge and pooled in the groove before vanishing.

Fae magic. It had to be. What else on this earth could do that? I shivered.

It had been stupid to cut myself, but the blade looked clean and the wounds were already clotting, and I always kept a few lengths of bandage here just in case. I bandaged myself, then wrapped the dagger in the rough white fabric as well, adding far more layers than should have been necessary. I hesitated before tying it to my leg again. It might be impossibly sharp and potentially magical, but showing a dagger this valuable in my poor village would be more dangerous than keeping it strapped against my skin.

A little pain was worth what it would bring me, anyway. Money, possibilities . . . a future.

◆ ◆ ◆

TUMBLEDOWN WAS FULLY AWAKE BY THE TIME I REACHED TOWN with my basket. Smoke curled from chimneys, women swept their doorsteps or clustered at the fences between houses to gossip, and children ran about shrieking solstice blessings at each other. The milkman's cart rattled over the cobblestones, and someone narrowly missed me with a bucket of slops they threw into the gutter.

The street market next to the temple was full of visitors from across the country, men and women who peered at us and our rickety stone and wood homes like they were at a menagerie. Tumbledown was famous for being the closest village to Fae territory, so visitors always seemed surprised to realize we were poor. I found their astonishment amusing. We lived in a miserably wet northern clime next to an impassable bog the Fae never set foot across. Why would we be rich? The tourists who flocked to our faerie festivals made up the majority of our town's economy, though, so we let them gawk all they wanted.

I managed to sell the fruit within the first half hour. Visiting ladies went wild for the stuff, which was rumored to help you see faeries. Tonight they'd look with wonder at the will-o'-the-wisps across the bog, convinced the fruit had done its job, not realizing that the residents of Tumbledown saw those lights every night.

The rabbit pelt was harder to sell. I only found a buyer late that morning, and for a price I wouldn't have taken if I hadn't needed to purchase food. *Hunger is the most efficient way to lower one's standards*, my mother had quipped once, back when she'd still had the energy to make jokes.

Hopefully my standards wouldn't need to stay lowered for much longer. I kept an eye out for a buyer who looked wealthy enough to purchase the dagger, but this sale would need to be handled with care. Plenty of people would accuse me of thievery if they saw me holding a weapon that fine.

The crowd hummed with excitement and trepidation for the selection that would happen at noon, which marked the official start of the solstice celebrations. Even the poorest women I passed had taken the time to wash and press their outfits in honor of the holiday. I spared a glance for my grime-encrusted clothes. I should have changed into something nicer, but what did it matter? After the selection I could go home and change into my one decent dress before the main ceremony that night.

"Kenna!"

I grinned at the familiar voice and turned to see Anya rushing towards me, dimples flashing. She started to hold out her arms, then stopped a few feet away, eyeing my mud-stained clothes.

"No need for hugs," I said. "You'd just get dirty, and you look beautiful today."

Anya always looked beautiful, with her cascading golden-brown hair, creamy skin, and large hazel eyes. She was tall and curvy, the kind of woman people couldn't help gawking at. In comparison, I was short, thin, and usually covered in mud. "A little wild" was what some of the kinder village women called me; "half feral" was more common. Why Anya had taken one look at me when we were children and decided we'd be best friends, I'd never know, but I was eternally grateful.

"I would normally say the same," she said, looking at my stained trousers judgmentally, "but you didn't make even the smallest effort today."

I stifled a laugh. Anya had called me beautiful plenty of times before, but she made no secret of her dismay over my grubby attire. "There's no need to make an effort. Putting on a dress isn't going to make people think any better of me." I raked my fingers through my tangled curls, wincing when I encountered a long strand of grass. I would definitely be the only woman with grass in her hair during the selection.

"I'm less worried about it being a dress and more worried about the mud splatters. Were you in the bog?"

"Yes. Doing some collecting." The bloodstain at my thigh was small and blended in with the dirt, so I wasn't going to mention it and worry her.

She made a face. "I don't know why you like it out there. What if you fall in and drown?"

"I know where I'm going." Up to a point, anyway. Years of rambling hadn't yet shown me a path all the way across. I nodded at her outfit. "Your dress is nice."

A shadow passed over her face. "I didn't exactly have other options. It is pretty, though." The garment under her cloak was thin yellow cotton, best suited for summer, but it was one of the only dresses to survive the fire that had claimed her house and her parents' lives over the summer. She shook her head. "Maybe some rich man will fall madly in love with me today."

The words sounded sad. Anya was an idealist, believing fervently that a love match was possible and would improve her life, but the kind of husband she found out of financial necessity would likely not be worth having in any other sense.

The majority of women in Tumbledown were married by twenty-five, so both of us were nearing the limits of what was considered acceptable. I was unmarried because I was poor, strange, and undesirable—which was fine by me, since the life of a merchant appealed to me more than that of a housewife—but Anya had had no shortage of suitors over the years. She'd been dedicated to her parents, though. Neither had been in good health, and they'd needed strong young hands to help out around the house. Now that they were gone, she was staying with an aunt who had made it clear Anya would not be welcome forever.

We wound through the market together, looking at the stalls while I kept an eye out for anyone wealthy enough to afford the dagger. I didn't mention this quest to Anya, though—she was the dreamer of the two of us, and I didn't want to get her hopes up about the future until the coins were in my hand. The crowd surged, easily five times what we might expect from a normal holiday, and the mood was one of nervous excitement.

Anya kept up a running commentary at my side. She was smiling, as usual, but there was tension in her cheeks, and her anxiety was evident in the speed of her chattering. My own worry lay heavy in my belly, but of the two of us I was more likely to stew in silence. When a horse-drawn cart clipped a vendor stand with a loud crack, Anya jumped.

"Hey," I said, pulling up short next to a booth full of woven textiles. "Are you all right?"

She pressed a hand to her stomach as she leaned back against a wooden post. "I'm nervous about the ritual. The thought of going to Mistei is . . ." She shook her head. "Amazing and terrifying all at once. It's not pious of me to say, but part of me hopes we don't get chosen."

Anya lacked my cynicism. Like my mother, she believed the faerie lights would actually guide women across the bog. Still, even if those legends were true and the chosen women lived out the rest of their days in luxury, anyone would be nervous about leaving behind everything they'd ever known.

Fear thickened in my throat at the thought of Anya heading into the bog at night, trusting her life and safety to a children's story. I knew the hidden paths better than anyone, and even I had never found my way across the bog to Mistei. I shook my head, dismissing the possibility. "We won't be chosen."

"You don't know that."

"There are hundreds of women here," I said, trying to soothe her. All unmarried women in Tumbledown between the ages of twenty and thirty were required to participate, but women came from all over northern Enterra, either because their hearts were full of naive faith or because their families couldn't afford to keep them anymore and were desperate for a magical solution. "The odds are low. And if you do get picked, we can run away before the ritual starts."

Anya looked pensively towards the temple two blocks away. It was taller than any other building in town, formed of glittering gray stone that had supposedly been quarried from Mistei many centuries back. The Elder's acolytes were placing yew branches inside a large copper brazier at the top of the temple steps. "Maybe it would be a good thing to be chosen," she said softly. "Maybe that's the way out."

My entire heart rejected the idea, but I knew why she would say that. Being chosen by the faeries would be a way out of her new poverty, a way out of uncertainty, a way out of this new reality where she needed to marry a man she didn't love in order to have a decent life.

I didn't believe the ritual brought a new start, though, not after the bones I'd found. Maybe the Fae had truly cared about humans once, but no one had even seen a faerie in centuries.

"No," I said fiercely. "There will be another way." One that didn't involve losing her to the bog or to some petty household tyrant who would control what she did and where she went and who she was allowed to befriend. Her parents had allowed her to run wild with a half-feral bog child; a husband wouldn't be so lenient.

Her smile was small, but her eyes had brightened. "If you say so," she said. Anya the dreamer, taking my word that the future would be brighter.

I shoved the fear away. I might not be an idealist, but I was tenacious, and that tended to yield better results anyway. Once the dagger was sold, we'd both have more options.

We walked through the village, and by the way Anya hovered by my side, I knew she wouldn't leave until after the selection happened. Selling the dagger in daylight might be risky anyway—better to wait until tonight, when the village would be drunk and raucous with celebration.

It was a relief, in a way. There was something comforting about carrying a weapon. Women weren't supposed to unless they were hunting. Was this how men felt? Bold and brave, like no one could hurt them?

We passed a group of tavern louts at the edge of the market, the kind with unsteady steps and wandering hands. One of them whistled as he noticed Anya. "Why don't you come over here? I have something to show you." He cupped himself lewdly through his trousers, and his friends laughed.

Anya's cheeks flushed, but she kept her eyes on the ground and walked faster. I stepped between her and the men, baring my teeth.

"Oh ho," one of them said. "The little guard bitch looks feral today."

"I couldn't recognize her through the mud."

"At least she doesn't have to worry today—there's no way the Fae want that scrawny ass."

They burst into uproarious laughter. I scowled and kept moving—I was used to men talking like that—but Anya stopped.

"Shut your mouth," she snapped. Her hands curled into tight fists as they laughed louder.

"It's not worth it." I tugged on her arm, hoping she'd yield. This wasn't a fight worth picking, not when Anya was wearing her yellow dress, when she was nervous about what might happen.

She dug in her heels and kept glaring. This was one of Anya's most frustrating—and endearing—characteristics. She never fought for herself, but she always did on behalf of her loved ones.

Anya yielded to my tugs at last and we walked on, leaving the men laughing behind us. Her cheeks had reached fever brightness. "Pigs," she muttered.

"And what do pigs become?" I asked lightly.

Her lips twitched. "Bacon."

"Exactly."

Anya looked over her shoulder one more time, then faced forward again. "Where to?" she asked. "We have a few minutes before we need to gather at the temple."

I hesitated, eyeing the temple's bell tower. There was a fenced yard behind it filled with small stone markers. "She loved the solstice," I said softly.

Anya understood instantly, as she always had. Her expression softened, and she tucked her arm into mine. "Let's pay our respects."

My mother's grave marker was a crooked flagstone set in an overgrown corner of the yard. Wildflowers would bloom around it in summer, but now it was as unadorned as her life had ended up being. I'd scratched her name into the stone myself, deepening it every few weeks: NEVE SUREN.

I knelt in the dirt, placed my hands in my lap, and closed my eyes. I thought of her curling brown hair, the way her smile had flashed bright and quick as a fish in a sunlit stream. Of her laugh, which she always hid behind her hand, and how at night she tried to cry so I couldn't hear it. She'd smelled like earth and pungent herbs, and her fingertips had always been stained yellow and green from her work.

My jaw clenched as I remembered the way she'd pressed those tonic-stained hands to her breast each night as she begged the Fae for a blessing. "Please let me serve you," she'd whispered. "Let me be worthy."

An icy wind surged through the cemetery, sending dead leaves skittering across the gravestones. "She loved the Fae," I said, eyes still pressed shut. "And they gave her nothing."

Anya's hand came to rest on my shoulder. "They gave her hope," she said softly.

Hope hadn't gotten her much in the end. Maybe Anya was right, though. I found it hard to believe in a better future without the proof of it in my hands, but my mother had always been full of dreams. When she hadn't been dreaming of Mistei, she'd dreamed of love and a marriage that would leave her happy and comfortable. She'd nearly had it once. My father had been clever and charming, with a laugh like a thunderclap and eyes that sparkled with merriment. He was a traveling merchant who had come to Tumbledown for the Beltane festival. One look into her blue eyes and he'd been lost.

Or so she'd said. It was Beltane, after all, a holiday when people's passions ran away with them, and my mother loved her stories.

I was born less than a year later with the odd amber eyes of my father and the wild curls of my mother. I'd been born on a frozen, moonless night, screaming as if I were furious with the world. Perhaps I had every reason to be.

My father hadn't been as wealthy as he'd claimed, and when

his business deals fell through, she'd ended up poor and hungry at the edge of the bog with a man whose charm could never quite make up for the rest of it, and whose patience for having a child and a disappointed wife ran out long before I was old enough to remember him.

I opened my eyes and pressed my fingertips to the cold, rough stone. "Happy solstice, Mama," I whispered. "May your spirit find Mistei."

Bells began to toll in the temple tower, a rapid, melodic cadence that only rang out once every five years.

Anya's anxious eyes met mine. "It's time."

Photo by Mahina Hawley Photography

SARAH HAWLEY lives in the Pacific Northwest, where her hobbies include rambling through the woods and appreciating fictional villains. She has an MA in archaeology and has excavated at an Inca site in Chile, a Bronze Age palace in Turkey, and a medieval abbey in England. When not dreaming up whimsical love stories, she can be found reading, dancing, or cuddling her two cats.

Ready to find
your next great read?

Let us help.

Visit prh.com/nextread

Penguin
Random
House